PENGUIN BOOKS

Chasing the Dead

Tim Weaver was born in 1977. He left school at eighteen and started working in magazine journalism, and has since gone on to develop a successful career writing about films, TV, sport, games and technology. He is married with a young daughter, and lives near Bath. *Chasing the Dead* is his first novel. Find out more about Tim and his writing at www.timweaverbooks.com.

Chasing the Dead

TIM WEAVER

PENGUIN BOOKS

PENGUIN BOOKS

Published by the Penguin Group

Penguin Books Ltd, 80 Strand, London WC2R ORL, England

Penguin Group (USA) Inc., 375 Hudson Street, New York, New York 10014, USA

Penguin Group (Canada), 90 Eglinton Avenue East, Suite 700, Toronto, Ontario,
Canada M4P 2Y3 (a division of Pearson Penguin Canada Inc.)

Penguin Ireland, 25 St Stephen's Green, Dublin 2, Ireland (a division of Penguin Books Ltd)

Penguin Group (Australia), 707 Collins Street, Melbourne, Victoria 3008, Australia
(a division of Pearson Australia Group Pty Ltd)

Penguin Books India Pvt Ltd, 11 Community Centre,
Panchsheel Park, New Delhi – 110 017, India

Penguin Group (NZ) , 67 Apollo Drive, Rosedale, Auckland 0632, New Zealand
(a division of Pearson New Zealand Ltd)

Penguin Books (South Africa) (Pty) Ltd, Block D, Rosebank Office Park,
181 Jan Smuts Avenue, Parktown North, Gauteng 2193, South Africa

Penguin Books Ltd, Registered Offices: 80 Strand, London WC2R ORL, England

www.penguin.com

First published 2010
Reissued in this edition 2013

001

Set in 11.75/14 pt Garamond MT Std
Typeset by Jouve (UK), Milton Keynes
Printed in England by Clays Ltd, St Ives plc

ISBN: 978–1–405–91269–3

www.greenpenguin.co.uk

ALWAYS LEARNING   **PEARSON**

For Sharlé

'And the sea became as the blood of a dead man: and every living soul died in the sea'

Revelation 16:3

PART ONE

I

Sometimes, towards the end, she would wake me by tugging at the cusp of my shirt, her eyes moving like marbles in a jar, her voice begging me to pull her to the surface. I always liked that feeling, despite her suffering, because it meant she'd lasted another day.

Her skin was like canvas in those last months, stretched tight against her bones. She'd lost all her hair as well, except for some bristles around the tops of her ears. But I never cared about that; about any of it. If I'd been given a choice between having Derryn for a day as she was when I'd first met her, or having her for the rest of my life as she was at the end, I would have taken her as she was at the end, without even pausing for thought. Because, in the moments when I thought about a life without her, I could barely even breathe.

She was thirty-two, seven years younger than me, when she first found the lump. Four months later, she collapsed in the supermarket. I'd been a newspaper journalist for eighteen years but, after it happened a second time on the Underground, I resigned, went freelance and refused to travel. It wasn't a hard decision. I didn't want to be on the other side of the world when the third call came through telling me this time she'd fallen and died.

On the day I left the paper, Derryn took me to a plot she'd chosen for herself in a cemetery in north London. She looked at her grave, up at me, and then smiled. I remember that clearly. A smile shot through with so much pain and fear I wanted to break something. I wanted to hit out until all I felt was numb. Instead, I took her hand, brought her into me, and tried to treasure every second of whatever time we had left.

When it became clear the chemotherapy wasn't working, she decided to stop. I cried that day, *really* cried, probably for the first time since I was a kid. But—looking back – she made the right decision. She still had some dignity. Without hospital visits and the time it took her to recover from them, our lives became more spontaneous, and that was an exciting way to live for a while. She read a lot and she sewed, and I did some work on the house, painting walls and fixing rooms. And a month after she stopped her chemo, I started to plough some money into creating a study. As Derryn reminded me, I'd need a place to work.

Except the work never came. There was a little – sympathy commissions mostly – but my refusal to travel turned me into a last resort. I'd become the type of free-lancer I'd always loathed. I didn't want to be that person, was even conscious of it happening. But at the end of every day Derryn became a little more important to me, and I found that difficult to let go.

Then one day I got home and found a letter on the living-room table. It was from one of Derryn's friends.

She was desperate. Her daughter had disappeared, and the police didn't seem to be interested. I was the only person she thought could help. The offer she made was huge – more than I'd deserve from what would amount to a few phone calls – but the whole idea left me with a strange feeling. I needed more money, and had sources inside the Met who would have found her daughter in days. But I wasn't sure I wanted my new life to join up with my old one. I wasn't sure I wanted any of it back.

So I said no. But, when I took the letter through to the back garden, Derryn was gently rocking in her chair with the tiniest hint of a smile on her face.

'What's so funny?'

'You're not sure if you should do it.'

'I'm sure,' I said. 'I'm sure I *shouldn't* do it.'

She nodded.

'Do you think I should do it?'

'It's perfect for you.'

'What, chasing after missing kids?'

'It's *perfect* for you,' she said. 'Take this chance, David.'

And that was how it began.

I pushed the doubt down with the sadness and the anger and found the girl three days later in a bedsit in Walthamstow. Then, more work followed, more missing kids, and I could see the ripples of the career I'd left behind coming back again. Asking questions, making calls, trying to pick up the trail. I'd always liked the investigative parts of journalism, the dirty work, the digging, more than I'd liked the writing. And, after a while, I knew it was the reason I never felt out of my depth working runaways, because the process, the course of the chase, was the same. Most of tracking down missing persons is about caring enough. The police didn't have time to find every kid that left home – and I think sometimes they failed to understand why kids disappeared in the first place. Most of them didn't leave just to prove a point. They left because their lives had taken an uncontrollable turn, and the only way to contend with that was to run. What followed, the traps they fell into afterwards, were the reasons they could never go back.

But despite the hundreds of kids that went missing every day of every year, I'm not sure I ever expected to make a living out of trying to find them. It never felt like a job; not in the way journalism had. And yet, after a while, the money really started coming in. Derryn persuaded me to rent some office space down the road from our home, in an effort to get me out, but also – more than that, I think – to convince me I could make a career out of what I was doing. She called it a long-term plan.

Two months later, she died.

2

When I opened the door to my office, it was cold and there were four envelopes on the floor inside. I tossed the mail on to the desk and opened the blinds. Morning light erupted in, revealing photos of Derryn everywhere. In one, my favourite, we were in a deserted coastal town in Florida, sand sloping away to the sea, jellyfish scattered like cellophane across the beach. In the fading light, she looked beautiful. Her eyes flashed blue and green. Freckles were scattered along her nose and under the curve of her cheekbones. Her blonde hair was bleached by the sun, and her skin had browned all the way up her arms.

I sat down at my desk and pulled the picture towards me.

Next to her, my eyes were dark, my hair darker, stubble lining the ridge of my chin and the areas around my mouth. I towered over her at six-two. In the picture, I was pulling her into me, her head resting against the muscles in my arms and chest, her body fitting in against mine.

Physically, I'm the same now. I work out when I can. I take pride in my appearance. I still want to be attractive. But maybe, temporarily, some of the lustre has rubbed away. And, like the parents of the people I trace, some of the spark in my eyes too.

I turned around in my chair and looked up at them. At the people I traced.

Their faces filled an entire corkboard on the wall behind me. Every space. Every corner. There were no pictures of Derryn behind my desk.

Only pictures of the missing.

After I found the first girl, her mother put up a notice; to start with, on the board in the hospital ward where she worked with Derryn, and then in some shop windows, with my name and number and what I did. I think she felt sorry at the thought of me – somewhere along the line – being on my own. Sometimes, even now, people would call me, asking for my help, telling me they'd seen an advert in the hospital. And I guess I liked the idea of it still being there. Somewhere in that labyrinth of corridors, or burnt yellow by the sun in a shop window. There was a symmetry to it. As if Derryn still somehow lived on in what I did.

I spent most of the day sitting at my desk with the lights off. The telephone rang a couple of times, but I left it, listening to it echo around the office. A year ago, to the day, Derryn had been carried out of our house on a stretcher. She'd died seven hours later. Because of that, I knew I wasn't in the right state of mind to consider taking on any work, so when the clock hit four, I started to pack up.

That was when Mary Towne arrived.

I could hear someone coming up the stairs, slowly taking one step at a time. Eventually the top door clicked and creaked open. She was sitting in the waiting area when I looked through. I'd known Mary for a few years. She used to work in A&E with Derryn. Her life had been fairly tragic as well: her husband suffered from Alzheimer's, and her son had left home six years earlier without telling anyone. He eventually turned up dead.

'Hi, Mary.'

I startled her. She looked up. Her skin was darkened by creases, every one of her fifty years etched into her face. She must have been beautiful once, but her life had been pushed and pulled around and now she wore the heartache like an overcoat. Her small figure had become slightly stooped. The colour had started to drain from her cheeks and her lips. Thick ribbons of grey had begun to emerge from her hairline.

'Hello, David,' she said quietly. 'How are you?'

'Good.' I shook her hand. 'It's been a while.'

'Yes.' She looked down into her lap. 'A year.'

She meant Derryn's funeral.

'How's Malcolm?'

Malcolm was her husband. She glanced at me and shrugged.

'You're a long way from home,' I said.

'I know. I needed to see you.'

'Why?'

'I wanted to discuss something with you.'

I tried to imagine what.

'I couldn't get you on the telephone.'

'No.'

9

'I called a couple of times.'

'It's kind of a . . .' I looked back to my office. To the pictures of Derryn. 'It's kind of a difficult time for me at the moment. Today, in particular.'

She nodded. 'I know it is. I'm sorry about the timing, David. It's just . . . I know you care about what you're doing. This job. I need someone like that. Someone who cares.' She glanced at me again. 'That's why people like you. You understand loss.'

'I'm not sure you ever understand loss.' I looked up, could see the sadness in her face, and wondered where this was going. 'Look, Mary, at the moment I'm not tracing anything – just the lines on my desk.'

She nodded once more. 'You remember what happened to Alex?'

Alex was her son.

'Of course.'

'You remember all the details?'

'Most of them.'

'Would you mind if I went back over them?' she asked.

I paused, looked at her.

'*Please.*'

I nodded. 'Why don't we go through?'

I led her out of the waiting area and back to my desk. She looked around at the photos on the walls, her eyes moving between them.

'Take a seat,' I said, pulling a chair out for her.

She nodded her thanks.

'So, tell me about Alex.'

'You remember that he died in a car crash just over a year ago,' she said quietly, as I sat down opposite her. 'And, uh . . . that he was drunk. He drove a Toyota, like his father used to have, right into the side of a lorry. It was only a small car. It ended up fifty feet from the road, in the middle of a field; burnt to a shell, like him. They had to identify him from dental records.'

I didn't know about the dental records.

She composed herself. 'But you know what the worst bit was? That before he died, he'd just disappeared. We hadn't seen him for five years. After everything we'd done as a family, he just . . . disappeared.'

'I'm sorry,' I said.

'The only thing he left me with was the memory of his body lying on a mortuary slab. I'll never get that image out of my head. I used to open my eyes in the middle of the night and see him standing like that next to my bed.'

Her eyes glistened.

'I'm sorry, Mary,' I said again.

'You met Alex, didn't you?'

She took out a photograph. I hadn't ever met him, only heard about him through Derryn. She handed me the picture. She was in it, her arms around a man in his early twenties. Handsome. Black hair. Green eyes. Probably five-eleven, but built like he might once have been a swimmer. There was a huge smile on his face.

'This is Alex. *Was* Alex. This is the last picture we ever took of him, down in Brighton.' She nodded towards the photograph and smiled. 'That was a couple of days before he left.'

'It's a nice picture.'

'He was gone five years before he died.'

'Yes, you said.'

'In all that time, we never once heard from him.'

'I'm really sorry, Mary,' I said for a third time, feeling like I should say something more.

'I know,' she said quietly. 'That's why you're my only hope.'

I looked at her, intrigued.

'I don't want to sound like a mother who can't get over the fact that her son is dead. Believe me, I know he's dead. I saw what was left of him.' She paused. I thought she might cry, but then she pulled her hair back from her face, and her eyes were darker, more focused. 'Three months ago, I left work late, and when I got to the station I'd missed my train. It was pulling out as I arrived. If I miss my train, the next one doesn't leave for fifty minutes. I've missed it before. When that happens I always walk to a nice coffee place I know close to the station and sit in one of the booths and watch the world go by.' Her eyes narrowed. 'Anyway, I was thinking about some work I had on, some patients I had seen that day, when I . . .' She studied me for a moment. She was deciding whether she could trust me. 'I saw Alex.'

It took a few moments for it to hit me. *She's saying she saw her dead son.*

'I, uh . . . I don't understand.'

'I saw Alex.'

'You *saw* Alex?'

'Yes.'

'What do you mean, you saw him?'

'I mean, I saw him.'

I was shaking my head. 'Wh– *How?*

'He was walking on the other side of the street.'

'It was someone who looked like Alex.'

'No,' she replied softly, controlled, 'it was Alex.'

'But . . . he's dead.'

'I know he's dead.'

'Then how could it possibly be him?'

'It was him, David.'

'How is that *possible*?'

'I know what you're thinking,' she said, 'but I'm not crazy. I don't see my mother or my sister. I swear to you, David, I saw Alex that day. I *saw* him.' She moved forward in her seat. 'I'll pay you up front,' she said quickly. 'It's the only way I can think to persuade you that what I am saying is true. I will pay you money up front. *My* money.'

'Have you reported this?'

'To the *police*?'

'Yes.'

She sat back again. 'Of course not.'

'You should.'

'What's the point?'

'Because that's what you do, Mary.'

'My son is dead, David. You think they'd believe me?'

'Why did you think *I* would believe you?'

She glanced around the room. 'I know some of your pain, David, believe me. My cousin died of cancer. In many ways, the disease takes the whole family with it. You care for someone for so long, you see them like that, you get used to having them like that, and then, when they're suddenly not there, you lose not only them, but what their illness brought to your life. You lose the *routine*.'

She smiled.

'I don't know you as well as I knew Derryn, but I do know this: I took a chance on you believing me, because if, just for a moment, we reversed this situation and *you'd* seen the person *you* loved, I know you'd take a chance on me believing you.'

'Mary . . .'

She looked at me as if she'd half expected that reaction.

'You have to go to the police.'

'Please, David . . .'

'Think about what you're—'

'*Don't insult me like that*,' she said, her voice raised for the first time. 'You can do anything, but don't insult me by telling me to think about what I'm saying. Do you think I've spent the last three months thinking about anything else?'

'This is more than just a few phone calls.'

'I can't go to the police.' She sat forward in her seat again and the fingers of one of her hands clawed at the ends of her raincoat, as if she was trying to prevent something from ending. 'Deep down, you know I can't.'

'But how can he be alive?'

'I don't know.'

'He *can't* be alive, Mary.'

'You can't begin to understand what this is like,' she said quietly.

I nodded. Paused. She was pointing out the difference between having someone you love die, like I had, and having someone you love die then somehow come back. We both understood the moment – and because of that she seemed to gain in confidence.

'It was him.'

'He was a distance away. How could you be sure?'

'I followed him.'

'You *followed* him? Did you speak to him?'

'No.'

'Did you get close to him?'

'I could see the scar on his cheek where he fell playing football at school.'

'Did he seem . . . injured?'

'No. He seemed healthy.'

'What was he doing?'

'He was carrying a backpack over his shoulder. He'd shaved his hair. He always had long hair, like in the photograph I gave you. When I saw him, he'd shaved it off. He looked different, thinner, but it was him.'

'How long did you follow him for?'

'About half a mile. He ended up going into a library off Tottenham Court Road for about fifteen minutes.'

'What was he doing in there?'

'I didn't go in.'

'Why not?'

She stopped. 'I don't know. When I lost sight of him, I started to disbelieve what I had seen.'

'Did he come back out?'

'Yes.'

'Did he see you?'

'No. I followed him to the Underground, and that's where I lost him. You know what it's like. I lost him in the crowds. I just wanted to speak to him, but I lost him.'

'Have you seen him since?'

'No.'

I sat back in my chair. 'You said three months ago?'

She nodded. 'Fifth of September.'

'What about Malcolm?'

'What about him?'

'Have you said anything to him?'

She shook her head. 'What would be the point? He has Alzheimer's. He can't even remember my name.'

I paused, glanced down at the photo of Derryn on my desk. 'Switch positions with me, Mary. Think about how this sounds.'

'I know how it *sounds*,' she replied. 'It sounds impossible. I've been carrying this around with me for *three months*, David. Why do you think I haven't done anything about it until now? People would think I had lost my mind. Look at you: you're the only person I thought might believe me, and you think I'm lying too.'

'I don't think you're ly—'

'Please, David.'

'I *don't* think you're lying, Mary,' I said. *But I think you're confused.*

Anger passed across her eyes, as if she could tell what I was thinking. Then it was gone again, replaced by an acceptance that it had to be this way. She looked down into her lap, and into the handbag perched on the floor next to her. 'The only way I can think to persuade you is by paying you.'

'Mary, this is beyond what I can do.'

'You know people.'

'I know *some* people. I have a few sources from my newspaper days. This is more than that. This is a full-blown investigation.'

Her hand moved to her face.

'Come on, Mary. Can you see what I'm saying?'

She didn't move.

'I'd be wasting your money. Why don't you try a proper investigator?'

She shook her head gently.

'This is what they get paid to do.'

She looked up, tears in her eyes.

'I've got some names here.' I opened the top drawer of my desk and took out a diary I used when I was still at the paper. 'Let me see.' I could hear her sniffing, could see her wiping the tears from her face, but I didn't look up. 'There's a guy I know.'

She held a hand up. 'I'm not interested.'

'But this guy will help y—'

'I'm not explaining this to anyone else.'

'Why not?'

'Can you imagine how many times I've played this conversation over in my head? I don't think I can muster the strength to do it again. And, anyway, what would be the point? If you don't believe me, what makes you think this investigator would?'

'It's his job.'

'He would laugh in my face.'

'He wouldn't laugh in your face, Mary. Not this guy.'

She shook her head. 'The way you looked at me, I can't deal with that again.'

'Mary . . .'

She finally lowered her hand. 'Imagine if it was Derryn.'

'Mary . . .'

'*Imagine*,' she repeated, then, very calmly, got up and left.

3

I was brought up on a farm. My dad used to hunt pheasant and rabbits with an old bolt rifle. On a Sunday morning, when the rest of the village – including my mum – were on their way to church, he used to drag me out to the woods and we'd fire guns.

When I was old enough, we progressed to a replica Beretta he'd got mail order. It only fired pellets, but he used to set up targets in the forest for me: human-sized targets that I had to hit. Ten targets. Ten points for a head shot, five for the body. I got the full one hundred points for the first time on my sixteenth birthday. He celebrated by letting me wear his favourite hunting jacket and taking me to the pub with his friends. The whole village soon got to hear about how his only child was going to be the British army's top marksman one day.

That never happened. I never joined the army. But ten years later I found a jammed Beretta, just like the one he'd let me use, on the streets of Alexandra, a township in Johannesburg. Except this one was real. There was one bullet left in the clip. I found out later the same day that a bullet, maybe even from the gun I'd found, had ended the life of a photographer I'd shared an office with for two years. He'd dragged himself a third of a mile along a street, gunfire crackling around him, people leaping over his body – and died in the middle of the road.

At the house I rented later that night, I removed the bullet from the gun, and have kept it with me ever since. As a reminder of my dad, and our Sunday mornings in the forest. As a reminder of the photographer who left this world, alone, in the middle of a dust-blown street. But mostly, as a reminder of the way life can be taken away, and of the distance you might be prepared to crawl in order to cling on to it.

It had just gone nine in the evening when I called Mary and told her I'd take the case. She started crying. I listened to her for a few minutes, her tears broken up by the sound of her thanking me, and then I told her I'd drive out to her house the next morning.

When I put the phone down, I looked along the hallway, into the bowels of my house, and beyond into the darkness of our bedroom, untouched since Derryn died. Her books still sat below the windowsill, the covers creased, the pages folded at the edges where she couldn't find a bookmark. Her spider plant was perched above it, its long, thin arms fingering the tops of the novels on the highest shelf.

Since she's been gone I haven't spent a single night in there. I go in to shower, I go in to water her plant, but I sleep in the living room on the sofa, and always with the TV on. Its sounds comfort me. The people, the programmes, the familiarity of it – they help fill some of the space Derryn used to occupy.

4

I got to Mary's house, a cavernous mock-Tudor cottage an hour west of London, just before ten the next morning. It was picture-perfect suburbia, right at the end of a tree-lined cul-de-sac: shuttered windows, a wide teak-coloured front porch and flower baskets swinging gently in the breeze. I walked up to the door and rang the bell.

A few moments later, it opened a sliver and Mary's face appeared. Recollection in her eyes. She pulled the door back and behind her I could see her husband, facing me, on the stairs.

'Hello, David.'

'Hi, Mary.'

She moved back, and I stepped past her. Her husband didn't move. He was looking down at a playing card, turning it over in his hands. Face up. Face down.

'Would you like some coffee or tea?'

'Coffee. Thanks.'

She nodded. 'Malcolm, this is David.'

Malcolm didn't move.

'Malcolm.'

Nothing.

'*Malcolm.*'

He flinched, as if a jolt of electricity had passed

through him, and he looked up. Not to see who had called him but to see what the noise was. He didn't recognize his name.

'Malcolm, come here,' Mary said, waving him towards her.

Malcolm got up, and shuffled across to us. He was drawn and tired, stripped of life. His black hair was starting to grey. The skin around his face sagged. He was probably only a few years older than Mary, but it looked like more. He had the build of a rugby player; maybe once he'd been a powerful man. But now his life was ebbing away, and his weight was going with it.

'This man's name is David.'

I reached out and had to pull his hand out from his side to shake it. He looked like he wasn't sure what I was doing to him.

When I let go, his hand dropped away, and he made his way towards the television, moving as if he was dosed up. I followed him and sat down, expecting Mary to follow. Instead, she headed for the kitchen and disappeared inside. I glanced at Malcolm Towne. He was staring at the television, the colours blinking in his face.

'You like television?' I asked him.

He looked at me with a strange expression, like the question had registered but he didn't know how to answer it. Then he turned back to the screen. A couple of seconds later, he chuckled to himself, almost guiltily. I could see his lips moving as he watched.

Mary returned, holding a tray.

'Sorry it took so long. There's some sugar there, and some milk.' She picked up a muffin, placed it on to a side plate and handed it to her husband. 'Eat this, Malc,' she said, making an eating gesture. He took the plate from her, laid it in his lap and looked at it. 'I wasn't sure how you took it,' she said to me.

'That's fine.'

'There's blueberry muffins, and a couple of rasp-berry ones too. Have whichever you like. Malcolm prefers the raspberry ones, don't you, Malc?'

I looked at him. He was staring blankly at his plate. *You can't remember what muffin you prefer when you can't remember your own name.* Mary glanced at me, as if she knew what I was thinking. But she didn't seem to care.

'When did Malcolm first show signs of Alzheimer's?'

She shrugged. 'It started becoming bad about two or three years ago, but I guess we probably noticed something was wrong about the time Alex disap-peared. Back then it was just forgetting little bits and pieces, like you or I would forget things, except they wouldn't come back to him. They just went. Then it became bigger things, like names and events, and eventually he started forgetting me and he started forgetting Alex.'

'Were Alex and Malcolm close?'

'Oh, yes. Always.'

I nodded, broke off a piece of blueberry muffin.

'Well, I'm going to need a couple of things from you,' I said. 'First up, any photos you can lay your hands on. A good selection. Then I'll need addresses for his friends, his work, his girlfriend if he had one.' I nodded my head towards the stairs. 'I'd also like to have a look around his room if you don't mind. I think that would be helpful.'

I felt Malcolm Towne staring at me. When I turned, his head was bowed slightly, his eyes dark and half hidden beneath the ridge of his brow. A blob of saliva was escaping from the corner of his mouth.

'Stop staring, Malc,' Mary said.

He turned back towards the TV.

'Was Alex living away from home when he disappeared?'

She nodded. 'Yes. But he'd come back here for a holiday for a few weeks before he left.'

'Where was he living?'

'Bristol. He'd gone to university there.'

'And after university?'

'He got a job down there, as a data clerk.'

I nodded. 'What, like computer programming?'

'Not exactly,' she replied quietly. The disappointment showed in her eyes.

'What's up?'

She shrugged. 'I asked him to come back home after he graduated. The job he had there was terrible. They used to dump files on his desk all day, and he'd input all the data, the same thing every single day. Plus the pay was awful. He deserved a better job than that.'

'But he didn't want to come back?'

'He was qualified to degree level. He had a first in

English. He could have walked into a top job in London, on five times the salary. If he had moved back here, he'd have paid less rent and it would have been a better springboard for finding work. He could have devoted his days to filling out application forms and going for interviews at companies that deserved him.'

'But he didn't want to come back?' I asked again.

'No. He wanted to stay there.'

'Why?'

'He'd built a life for himself in Bristol, I suppose.'

'What about after he disappeared – you never spoke to him?'

'No.'

'Not even by telephone?'

'Never,' Mary reaffirmed, quieter this time.

I made her run over her story again. Where she saw Alex. When. How long she followed him for. What he looked like. What he was wearing and, finally, where she lost him. It didn't leave me a lot to go on.

'So, Alex disappeared for five years, and then died in a car crash –' I glanced at my pad '– just over a year ago, right?'

'Right.'

'Where did he crash the car?'

'Just outside Bristol, up towards the motorway.'

'What happened with the car?'

'How do you mean?'

'No personal items were retrieved from it?'

'It was just a shell.'

I moved on. 'Did Alex have a bank account?'

'Yes.'

'Did he withdraw any money before he left?'

'Half of his trust fund.'

'Which was how much?'

'Five thousand pounds.'

'That's it?'

'That's it.'

'Did you check his statements?'

'Regularly – but it was pointless. He left his card behind when he went, and he never applied for a replacement as far as I know.'

'Did he have a girlfriend?'

'Yes.'

'Down in Bristol?'

Mary nodded.

'Is she still there?'

'No,' Mary said. 'Her parents live in north London. After Alex disappeared, Kathy moved back there.'

'Have you spoken to her at all?'

'Not since the funeral.'

'You never spoke to her after that?'

'He was dead. We had nothing to talk about.'

I paused. Let her gather herself again.

'So, did he meet Kathy at university?'

'No. They met at a party Alex went to in London. When he went to uni, she followed him down there.'

'What did she do?'

'She worked as a waitress in one of the restaurants close to the campus.'

I took down her address. I'd have to invent a plausible

story if I was about to start cold-calling. Alex had been dead for over a year.

As if reading my mind, Mary said, 'What are you going to tell her?'

'The same as I'll tell everyone. That you've asked me to try and put a timetable together of your son's last movements. There's some truth in that, anyway. You would like to know.'

She nodded. 'I would, yes.'

Mary got up and went to a drawer in the living room. She pulled it open and took out a letter-sized envelope with an elastic band around it. She looked at it for a moment, then pushed the drawer shut and returned, laying the envelope down in front of me on the table.

'I hope you can see now that this isn't a joke,' she said, and opened a corner of it so I could see the money inside.

I laid my hand over the envelope and pulled it towards me, watching Mary as she followed the cash across the table.

'Why do you think Alex only took half of the money with him?'

She looked up from the envelope and for a moment seemed unsure of the commitment she'd just made. Perhaps now the baton had been passed on, she'd had a moment of clarity about everything she'd asked me to do – and everything she believed she'd seen.

I repeated the question. 'Why only half?'

'I've no idea. Maybe that was all he could get out at once. Or maybe he just needed enough to give him a start somewhere.' She looked around the room and quietly sighed. 'I don't really understand a lot of what Alex did. He had a good life.'

'Do you think he became bored of it?'

She shrugged and bowed her head.

I watched her for a moment, and realized there were two mysteries: why Mary believed she had seen Alex walking around more than a year after he'd died; and why Alex had left everything behind in the first place.

His room was small. There were music posters on the walls. His A Level textbooks on the shelves. A TV in the corner, dust on the screen, and a VCR next to it with old tapes perched on top. I went through them. Alex had had a soft spot for action movies.

'He was a big film buff.'

I turned. Mary was standing in the doorway.

'Yeah, I can see. He had good taste.'

'You think?'

'Are you kidding?' I picked up a copy of *Die Hard* and held it up. 'I was a teenager in the eighties. This is my *Citizen Kane*.'

She smiled. 'Maybe you two would have got on.'

'We would have *definitely* got on. I must have watched this about fifty times in the last year. It's the best anti-depressant on the market.'

She smiled again, then looked around the room, stopping on a photograph of Alex close by. Her eyes dulled a little, the smile slipping from her face.

'It's hard seeing everything left like this.'

I nodded. 'I know it is.'

'Do you feel the same way?'

'Yes,' I said. 'Exactly the same.'

She nodded at me, almost a *thank you*, as if it was a relief to know she wasn't alone. I looked towards the corner of the room, where two wardrobes were positioned against the far wall.

'What's in those?'

'Just some of the clothes he left behind.'

'Can I look?'

'Of course.'

I walked across and opened them up. There wasn't much hanging up, but there were some old shirts and a musty suit. I pushed them along the runner, and on the floor I could see a photograph album and more books.

'These are Alex's?'

'Yes.'

I opened up the album and some photographs spilled out. I scooped them up off the floor. The top one was of Alex and a girl who must have been his girlfriend.

'Is this Kathy?'

Mary nodded. I set the picture aside and looked through the rest. Alex and Mary. Mary and Malcolm. I held up a photograph of Malcolm and Alex at a caravan park somewhere. It was hot. Both of them were stripped down to just their shorts, sitting next to a smoking barbecue with bottles of beer.

'You said they were close.'

'Yes.'

'You don't think Malcolm would remember anything?'

'You can try, but I think you'd be wasting your time. You've seen how he is.' She glanced back over her shoulder, and then stepped further into the room. 'There were times when I felt a bit left out, I suppose. Sometimes I would get home and the two of them would be talking, and when I entered the room they'd stop.'

'When was that?'

'For a while before Alex disappeared, I guess.'

'*Right* before he disappeared?'

She screwed up her face. 'Maybe. It was a long time ago. All I know is, the two of them, most of the time, were attached at the hip.'

I looked around the room again, my eyes falling upon a photo of Malcolm and Alex. The one person who knew Alex the best was the one person I had no hope of getting anything from.

5

I left Mary's just after midday. Once I hit the motorway, the traffic started to build; three lanes of slowly moving cars feeding back into the centre of the city. What should have been an eighty-minute drive to Kathy's family home in Finsbury Park turned into a mammoth two-hour expedition through London gridlock. I stopped once, to get something to eat, and then chewed on a sandwich as I inched through Hammersmith, following the curve of the Thames. By the time I had finally parked up, it was just after two.

I locked the car and moved up the drive. It was a yellow-bricked semi-detached, with a courtyard full of fir trees and a small patch of grass at the front. A Mercedes and a Micra were parked outside, and the garage was open. It was rammed with junk – some of it in boxes, some just on the floor – and shelves full of machinery parts and tools. There was no one inside. As I turned back to the house, a curtain twitched at the front window.

'Can I help you?'

I spun around. A middle-aged man with a garden sprayer attached to his back was standing at the side of the house, where an entrance ran parallel to the garage.

'Mr Simmons?'

'Who's asking?'

'My name's David Raker. Is Kathy in today, sir?'

He eyed me suspiciously. 'Why?'

'I'd like to speak with her.'

'Why?'

'Is she in today, sir?'

'First you tell me why you're here.'

'I was hoping to speak to her about Alex Towne.'

A flash of recognition in his eyes. 'What's he got to do with anything?'

'That's what I was hoping to ask Kathy.'

Behind me I heard the door opening. A girl in her late twenties stepped out on to the porch. Kathy. Her hair was short now, dyed blonde, but a little maturity had made her prettier. She held out her hand and smiled.

'I'm Kathy,' she said.

'Nice to meet you Kathy. I'm David.' I glanced around at her father, whose gaze was fixed on me. Water tumbled out of the hose on to the toes of his boots.

'What are you, an investigator or something?' she asked.

'Kind of. Well, not really.'

She frowned, but seemed intrigued.

'Where's Kathy fit into all this?' her father said.

I glanced at him. Then back to Kathy. 'I'm doing some work for Mary Towne. It's to do with Alex. Can I speak with you?' She looked unsure. 'Here,' I said, removing my driving licence and handing it to her. 'Unofficial investigators have to make do with one of these.'

She smiled, took a look, then handed it back. 'Do you want to go inside?'

'That would be great.'

I followed her into the house, leaving her father standing outside with his garden sprayer. Inside, we moved through a hallway decorated with floral wallpaper and black-and-white photographs, and into an adjoining kitchen.

'Do you want a drink?'

'Water would be fine.'

It was a huge open area with polished mahogany floors and granite worktops. The central unit doubled up as a table, chairs sitting underneath. Kathy filled a glass with bottled mineral water then moved across and set it down.

'Sorry to turn up unannounced like this.'

She was facing away from me slightly. Her skin shone in the light coming from outside, her hair tucked behind her ears. 'It's just a surprise to hear his name again after all this time.'

I nodded. 'I think Mary feels like she needs some closure on his disappearance. She wants to know where he went for those five years.'

Kathy nodded. 'I can understand that.'

We pulled a couple of chairs out and sat down. I placed my notepad between us, so she could see I was ready to start.

'So, you and Alex met at a party?'

She smiled. 'A friend of a friend was having a house-warming.'

'You liked him from the beginning?'

She nodded. 'Yeah, we really clicked.'

'Which was why you ended up following him to Bristol?'

'I applied for a job there. It was supposed to be a marketing position. Alex had already got his place at university, and I wanted to be close to him. It made sense.'

'What happened?'

'It wasn't marketing. It was cold-calling; selling central heating. I gave it a week. In the interview, the MD told me I could earn in commission what my friends earned in a year. I never stuck around long enough to find out.'

'So, you started waitressing?'

'Yes.'

'What did the two of you use to do together?'

'We used to go away a lot. Alex loved the sea.'

'You used to go to the coast?'

She nodded.

'How often?'

'Most weekends. Some weeks too. After uni, Alex got a job in an insurance company. He had a kind of love-hate thing with it. Some Monday mornings he wouldn't want to go in. So we bought an old VW Camper van and took off when we wanted.'

'Did his parents know about him skipping work?'

'No.'

'I didn't think so,' I said, smiling. 'What about your job?'

'They were pretty good to me there. They let me come and go as I pleased – they sometimes even let me choose my own hours. So, if we disappeared for a couple of days, when I got back I worked for a couple of days to make up for it. The pay was terrible, but it was useful.'

She drifted off for a moment. I waited for her to come back.

'What did you think of Alex's dad?'

She shrugged. 'He was always very pleasant to me.'

'Did Alex ever tell you what they talked about?'

'Not really. Not what they talked about. More where they went and what they did. I'm sure if there was anything worth knowing, he'd have told me.'

I nodded.

'Alex didn't contact you in the five years before he died?'

'No.' A pause. 'At first, I just used to wait by the phone, from the moment I got home until three or four o'clock in the morning, begging, praying for him to call. But he never did.'

I looked at my notes. 'When was the last time you spoke to him?'

'The night before he left. We'd arranged to take the Camper down to Cornwall. He had some time owed to him at work, so he'd been back to his parents' for a couple of weeks to use up some holiday. When I called him, his mum said he had gone out and hadn't come home. She said she wasn't worried, but that he hadn't phoned and he always tended to.'

'Was he depressed about work at the time?'

'No,' she said, seeming to consider it. 'I don't think so.'

I changed direction. 'Did you have any favourite places you used to visit?'

She looked down into her hands, hesitating. I could tell they'd had a favourite spot, and that it had meant everything to her.

'There was one place,' she said eventually. 'A place down towards the tip of Cornwall, a village right on the sea called Carcondrock.'

'You used to stay there?'

'We used to take the Camper there a lot.'

'Did you go back after he disappeared?'

Another pause, longer this time. Eventually she looked up at me. It was obvious she had – and it had hurt a lot.

'There was a place right on the beach,' she said softly. 'A cove. I went back about three months after he disappeared. I didn't really know what to expect. I guess in my heart of hearts I knew he wouldn't be there, but we loved that spot and never told a soul about it. Not a single person. So it seemed like the most obvious place to look.'

'You two were the only ones who knew about it?'

'Only myself and Alex. And now you, I guess.' She looked at me, her eyes half-closed, as if she had something else to add. When it didn't come, I got up to go.

'Wait a second,' she said, placing a hand on my arm, then blushing slightly as she took it away again.

I looked at her. 'Was there something else?'

Kathy nodded. 'The cove . . . If you go right to the back of it, there's a rock shaped like an arrowhead, pointing up to the sky. It's got a black cross painted on it. If you find it, dig a little way beneath and you'll find a box I left there for Alex. Inside are some old letters and photographs – and a birthday card. That was the last time I ever heard from him.'

'The birthday card?'

'Yes.'

'Did he give you the card before he went back to his parents for those two weeks?'

'No. He sent it from their place. By the time it got to me, he'd already disappeared.'

'I'll take a look,' I said.

'I don't know what you'll find,' she replied, looking down into her lap. 'But the last time we saw each other he said something strange to me: that we should use the hole by the rock to store messages, if we ever got separated.'

'Separated? What did he mean by that?'

'I don't know. I mean, I asked him, but he never really explained. He just said that, if it ever came to it, that was our spot. The place I should look first.'

'So, did he ever store anything in there for you? Any messages?'

She shook her head.

'You checked regularly?'

'I haven't been down for a couple of years. But for a time I used to go back there and dig up that box, praying there would be something in there from him.'

'But there wasn't?'

She didn't say anything. She didn't need to.

6

The sky was starting to lose some of its colour by the time I left Kathy's. I opened the car door, tossed my notepad on to the back seat and then looked at my watch. Three-thirty. I still had something to do before heading home. Something I hadn't had the strength to do the day before.

I got in the car, fired up the engine and headed off.

On the drive over, I stopped at a florist and bought a bunch of roses and some white carnations, and then spent the next twenty minutes in traffic. When I finally got to the gates of Hayden Cemetery, the sun had almost fallen from the sky. In the car park, lights were flickering into life. The place was deserted. No other cars. No people. No sound. It wasn't too far from Holloway Road, sandwiched between Highbury and Canonbury, but it was supernaturally quiet, as if the dead had taken the sound down with them. I turned the engine off and sat for a moment, feeling the heat escape from the car. Then I put on my coat and got out.

The entrance was big and beautiful – a huge black iron arch, intricately woven with the name *Hayden* – and, as I passed through, I could see leaves had been pushed to either side of the path, pressed into mounds and stained by the rust from a shovel. I had a flicker of déjà vu. There and gone again. I'd been in this same position, treading the same ground, a year and a half before. Except, that time, Derryn had been with me.

The Rest, where she was buried, was a separate area. Tall trees surrounded it on all sides and dividing walls had been built within it, with four or five headstones in each section. As I got to the grave, I saw the flowers I'd put down a month before. They were dead. Dried petals clung to the gravestone, and the stems had turned to mush. I knelt down and brushed the old flowers away. Then I placed the new ones at the foot of the grave, the thorns from the stems catching in the folds of my palm.

'Sorry I didn't come yesterday,' I said quietly. The wind picked up for a moment, and carried my words away. 'I thought about you a lot, though.'

Some leaves fell from the sky, on to the grave. When I looked up, a bird was hopping along a branch on one of the trees. The branch swayed gently, bobbing under its weight, and then – seconds later – the bird was gone, swooping downwards and ranging up left; up into the freedom beyond.

I was coming down the path and through the entrance to the car park when I saw someone walking away from my car. His clothes were dark and stained, and his shoes were untied, the laces snaking off behind him. He looked homeless. As I got closer, he flicked a look at me. His face was obscured beneath a hood, but I could see a pair of eyes glint, and realized there was surprise in them – as if he hadn't expected to see me back so soon.

Suddenly, he broke into a run.

I speeded up, and saw that the back window on the left-hand side of my car had been smashed, the door swinging open. Glass lay next to my tyre, and my notepad, coat and a road map were on the gravel next to it.

'Hey!' I shouted, running now, trying to cut him off before he got to the entrance. He glanced at me again, panicking. 'What the hell are you doing?'

The edges of his hood billowed out as he picked up speed, and I caught a glimpse of his face. Dirty and thin. A beard growing from his neck up to the top of his cheekbones. He looked like a drug addict: all bone and no fat.

'Hey!' I shouted again, but he was ahead of me now, fading into the darkness at the entrance to the cemetery.

I sprinted after him, out on to the main road, but by the time I got there he was about sixty yards away, pounding down the pavement on the other side of the street. He looked back once to make sure I wasn't following, but didn't drop his pace. And then he disappeared around the corner.

I jogged back to the cemetery and gave the car a quick once-over. It was an old BMW 3 series I'd had for years. No CD player. No satellite navigation. Nothing worth stealing.

The glove compartment was open, most of its contents thrown all over the front seats. The car's handbook had been opened and left; a bag of sweets had been ripped apart. He must have been looking for money. And now he'd just cost me a new window.

7

I woke at three in the morning to the sound of Brian Eno's 'An Ending (Ascent)' playing quietly on the stereo, the TV on mute. I sat forward and listened for a while. Derryn used to tell me my music taste was terrible, and that my entire film collection was one big guilty pleasure. She was probably right about the music. I considered 'An Ending' as close to socially acceptable as I was ever likely to get; a song I loved that even she thought was wonderful.

In the area I'd been brought up in, you either spent your days in the record shop, or in the cinema. I'd chosen the cinema, mostly because my parents were always late with new technology; we were pretty much the last family in town to get a CD player. We didn't have a VCR for years either, which was why I spent most nights, growing up, watching films at an old art deco cinema called the Palladium in the next town.

Her music collection still stood in the corner of the room, packed in a cardboard box. I'd been through it about three weeks after she died, when it had struck me that the one thing music had over movies was its amazing way of pinpointing memories. 'An Ending' had been our late-night song, the one we'd play just before bed when Derryn was weeks away from dying.

When all she wanted was for the pain to end. And then, when it finally did, it was the song that was played inside the church at her funeral.

When the song finished, I got up and walked through to the kitchen.

Out of the side window, I could see into next-door's house. A light was on in the study, the blinds partially open. Liz, my neighbour, was leaning over a laptop, typing. She clocked my movement through the corner of her eye, looked up, squinted, and then broke into a smile. *What are you doing up?* she mouthed.

I rubbed my eyes. *Can't sleep.*

She scrunched up her face in an *aw* expression.

Liz was a 42-year-old lawyer, who'd moved in a few weeks after Derryn had died. She'd married young, had a child, then got divorced a year later. Her daughter was in the second year of university at Warwick. I liked Liz. She was fun and flirty, and, while cautious of my situation, had always made her feelings clear. Some days I needed that. I didn't want to be a widower who wore it. I didn't want all the sorrow and the anger and the loss to stick to my skin. And the truth was, especially physically, Liz was easy to like: slender curves, shoulder-length chocolate hair, dark, mischievous eyes; and a smattering of natural colour in her cheeks.

She got up from the desk and looked at her watch, pretending to double-take when she saw the time. A couple of seconds later, she picked up a coffee cup and held it up to the window. *You want one?* She rubbed her stomach. *It's good.*

I smiled again, rocked my head from side to side to show I was tempted and then pointed to my own watch. *Got to be up early.*

She rolled her eyes. *Poor excuse.*

I looked at her and something moved inside me. A tiny flutter of excitement. The feeling that, if I wanted something from her, the experience of being close to someone again, she would do it. In her eyes, I could see she was waiting for me to break free from what was keeping me back.

But, just as there were days when I still needed to feel wanted, there were others when I didn't feel ready to step outside the bubble. I wanted to remain inside. Protected by the warmth and familiarity of how I felt about Derryn. Most of the time, even now, I was caught between the two. Wanting to move on, curious about letting myself go, but wary of the aftermath. Of what would happen the next morning when I woke up next to someone, and it wasn't the person I'd loved, every day, for fourteen years.

8

After getting the car window repaired early the next morning, I followed up Mary's library lead and immediately hit a dead end. Even if Alex had gone there on the day Mary had followed him, it wasn't for books. She'd told me it was about six o'clock when he'd got to the library, but their computers had no record of anyone borrowing anything during the fifteen minutes he was inside. Once I was back at the office, I called the company he'd worked for in Bristol. It was just as fruitless: like talking to a room full of people who didn't speak the same language as you. His boss remembered him, but not well. A couple of colleagues could only give me a vague description of what sort of person he was.

Next, I called the friends he'd lived with. Mary had told me she'd kept in contact with one of the them, John, for a while after Alex's disappearance and that, as far as she knew, they still lived in the same place. She was right. There were three of them. John was working when I called. The second, Simon, was long gone. The third, Jeff, was home, but seemed as perplexed by what had happened to Alex as everyone else.

'So, how can I reach the other two guys?' I asked him.

'Well, I can give you John's work address,' he said. 'But, I doubt you'll be finding Simon anywhere.'

'How come?'

'He kind of . . . disappeared.'

'Disappeared?'

'He had some problems.'

'What kind of problems?'

A pause. 'Drugs mostly.'

'Did he leave around the same time as Alex?'

'No. A while after.'

'Do you think he might have followed him?'

'I doubt it,' he said. 'Alex didn't get on with Simon at the end. None of us did. Simon was a different guy in those last few months. He . . . well, he kind of hit out at Kath when he was high one night. And Alex never forgave him for that.'

I put the phone down, and turned in my chair. On the corkboard behind me, in among the pictures of the missing, was a hand-drawn map of a beach.

My options were narrowing already.

Winter suddenly came to life as I crossed into Cornwall five hours later, the colours of late autumn replaced by a pale patchwork quilt of fields and towns. About forty miles from Carcondrock, I stopped at a café and had a late lunch. Through the windows, turning gently in the early afternoon breeze, I could see the wind turbines at Delabole.

Carcondrock itself was a quaint stretch of road with shops on both sides, and houses in the hills beyond. It was framed by the Atlantic and the smudged outline of the Scilly Isles. The beach ran parallel to the high street, while the main road wormed out of the village and upwards along the edges of a rising cliff. The higher the road, the bigger the houses – and the better the views. Below, against the cliff walls, the beach eventually faded out, replaced by sandy coves, dotted like pearls on a necklace along the line of the sea.

I found a car park between the beach and the village, and then headed to the biggest shop – a grocery store – armed with a picture of Alex. No one knew him. At the end of the high street, where the road followed the rising cliff face, there was an old wooden shack. Beyond that, a pub and a pretty church, its walls teeming with vines. Everything had an old-world feel to it: walls greying and aged; windows uneven beneath slate roofs. It was obvious why Kathy and Alex had loved it. Miles of lonely beach. The roar of the sea. The houses like flecks of chalk among the scrub of the hillside.

I got out the map Kathy had drawn for me of the hidden cove, and walked a little way on the road as it gently rose upwards along the cliff. Halfway up, leaning over the edge, I found it. Two hundred feet below me was a perfect semi-circle of sandy beach, surrounded on three sides by high walls of rock and on the fourth by the ocean. Waves foamed at the shore.

The only way I was going to get to it was by boat.

*

The wooden shack turned out to be the place to hire boats. It was starting to get dark by the time I reached it, and the old man who ran it was closing up. Behind him, attached to a jetty, four boats bobbed on the water.

'Am I too late?'

He turned and looked at me. 'Eh?'

'I need to hire a boat for an hour.'

'It's dark,' he said.

'Almost dark.'

He shook his head. 'It's *dark*.'

I looked him up and down. Red and green checked shirt; mauve suspenders holding a pair of giant blue trousers up; yellow mud-caked boots; unruly white beard. He looked like the bastard love child of Captain Birdseye and Ronald McDonald.

'How much?' I asked him.

'How much what?'

'How much for an hour?'

'Are you *deaf*?'

'Sorry, I didn't catch that.'

He paused, his eyes narrowing. 'Are you takin' the piss out of me, sonny?'

'Look,' I said. 'I'll double whatever the going rate is. I just need one of those boats for an hour. And a torch if you've got one. I'll have everything back here by seven.'

He pursed his lips, thinking about it, then turned around and opened up the shack.

It took about twenty minutes to row around to the cove. I moored on the sand and dragged the boat up, away from the tide. The cove was small, probably twenty feet across, and the cliff walls towered above me. I flicked on the torch and swept it from left to right. At the back of the cove, in the torchlight beam, I could see a pile of loosened rocks and boulders. Some had fallen. Others had been washed up. As I stepped closer, I could see the arrow-shaped stone Kathy had talked about. It had tilted, but still faced upwards. At the bottom was a tiny mark – a cross – in black paint. I knelt down, clamped the torch between my teeth and started digging.

The box was buried about a foot under the surface. Its bottom sitting in water, its sides speckled with rust. Kathy had wrapped its contents in thick opaque plastic. I picked at it with my fingers but couldn't break the seal, so removed my pocket knife and sliced it open. The contents were dry. I reached in and pulled out a stack of photographs and, around them, a letter. The birthday card was inside. A rubber band kept everything together.

I placed the torch in my lap and flicked through the photographs using the cone of light. Some of the photos were of the two of them, some just of Kathy, others only Alex. In one of the photographs, I noticed Kathy had her hair short. I guessed it had been taken by someone other than Alex, some time after he'd disappeared. I flipped it over and on the back she'd written: *After you left, I cut my hair* . . . On closer inspection, I could see all the photographs had comments on the back.

I picked up the torch and turned my attention back to the letter. It was dated 8 January, no year, and still smelt faintly of perfume.

I've no idea why you left, Kathy had written. *Nothing you ever said to me led me to believe that one day you'd drop everything and walk away. So, if you came back now, I'd cherish you as I always did. I'd love you like I always did. But, somewhere, there would be a doubt that wasn't there before, a nagging feeling that, if I got too close to you, if I showed you too much affection, you'd get up one morning and walk away.*

I don't want to feel like a mistake again.

I looked at my watch. It was almost six-thirty. In the distance, thunder rumbled across the sky. I folded the letter up, placed everything inside the box and took it with me as I rowed back around to the village.

9

I drove out of Carcondrock and found a place to stay about three miles further down a snaking coastal road. It was a beautiful greystone building overlooking the ocean and the scattered remnants of old tin mines. After a shower, I headed out for some dinner and eventually found a pub that served hot food and cold beer. I took the box with me and sat at a table in the corner, away from everyone else. There was a choice of three meals: steak and kidney pie, steak and ale pie or steak pie. Luckily, I wasn't vegetarian. While I waited for the food, I opened the box, removed the contents and spread them out.

I picked up the birthday card first. The last contact Kathy ever had with Alex. She'd kept it in pristine condition. It was still in its original envelope, opened along the top with a knife or a letter opener to avoid damaging it. I took it out.

The card itself looked home-made, without being amateurish: a detailed drawing of a bear was in the centre, a bunch of roses in its hands. Above that was a raised rectangle with HAPPY BIRTHDAY! embossed on it, and a foil sticker of a balloon. I flipped it over. In the centre, in gold pen, it said: *Made by Angela Routledge.* I opened it up. Inside were just seven words: *Happy Birthday, Kath. I love you . . . Alex.*

I closed the card and studied the envelope. Something caught my attention. On the inside, under the lip, was an address label: *Sold @ St John the Baptist, 215 Grover Place, London.* I wrote down the address and turned to the photographs.

There was a definite timeline. It began with pictures of Kathy and Alex when they'd first started going out, and ended with two individual portraits of each of them, both older and more mature, at a different stage of their lives. I sat the two portraits side by side. The one of Kathy was a regular 6x4, but Alex's was a Polaroid. When I turned them over, I noticed something else: they had different handwriting on them.

'Mind if I sit here?'

I looked up.

One of the locals was staring down at me, a hand pressed against the back of the chair at the table next to me. The subdued light darkened his face. Shadows filled his eye sockets, thick black lines forming across his forehead. He was well built, probably in his late forties.

I looked around the pub. There were tables and chairs free everywhere. He followed my eyes, out into the room, but didn't make a move to leave. When he turned back to me, he stole a glance at a couple of the photographs. I collected them up, along with the letter and the card, and placed them back into the box.

'Sure,' I said, gesturing to the table. 'Take a seat.'

He nodded his thanks and sat down, placing his beer down in front of him. A couple of minutes later, the landlady brought my meal over. As I started picking at it, I realized all I could smell was his aftershave. It was so strong it buried the smell of my food completely.

'You here on business?' he asked.

'Kind of.'

'Sounds mysterious.'

I shrugged. 'Not really.'

'So, where does she live?'

I looked at him, confused.

'Your bit on the side.' He laughed, finding it funnier than he had any right to.

I smiled politely, but didn't bother answering, hoping that the less I talked, the quicker he'd leave.

'Just messing with you,' he said, running a finger down the side of his glass. As his sleeve rode up his arm, I could see a tattoo – an inscription – the letters smudged by age. 'Boring place to have to come for work.'

'I can think of worse.'

'Maybe in summer,' he said. 'But in winter, this place is like a mausoleum. You take the tourists out of here and all you're left with are a few empty fudge shops. Want to hear my theory?' He paused, but only briefly. 'If you put a bullet in the head of every Cornishman in the county, no one would even notice until the fucking caravan parks failed to open.' He laughed again, putting a hand to his mouth as if trying to suppress his amusement.

I pretended to check my phone for messages. 'Nice theory,' I said, staring at my empty inbox. When I was finished, he was still looking at me.

'So, what do you do?' he asked.

'I'm a salesman.'

He rocked his head from side to side, as if to say he didn't think I was the type. 'My friend's a salesman too.'

'Yeah?'

'Yeah.' He nodded. 'A different kind. He sells ideas to people.'

I smiled. 'You mean he works for Ikea?'

He didn't respond. An uncomfortable silence settled between us. I couldn't believe he hadn't taken the hint yet. He cupped his pint glass between his hands, rolling it backwards and forwards, watching the liquid slosh around inside.

'I bet you're thinking, "How do you sell ideas to people?" – right?'

Not really.

He looked up at me. 'Right?'

'I guess.'

'It's pretty simple, the way he tells it. You take something – then you try to apply it to people. You know, give them something they really *need.*'

'Still sounds like he might work for Ikea.'

He didn't reply, but his eyes lingered on me, as if I'd just made a terrible error. *There's something about you,* I thought. *Something I don't like.* He took a few mouthfuls of beer, and this time I could make out some of the tattoo – '*And see him that was possessed*' – and a red mark, running close to his hairline, all the way down around his ears and along the curve of his chin.

'Got hit with a rifle butt in Afghanistan.'

'Sorry?'

He looked up. 'The mark on my face. Fucking towelhead jammed his rifle butt into my jaw.'

'You were a soldier?'

'Do I look the salesman type?'

I shrugged. 'What does a salesman look like?'

'What do any of us really look like?' His eyes flashed for a moment, catching some of the light from a fire behind us. He broke into a smile, as if everything was a big mystery. 'Being a soldier, that teaches you a lot about life.'

'Yeah?'

'Teaches you a lot about death too.'

I tried to look pissed off, and started cutting away at some of the pie's pastry – but the whole time I could feel him watching me. When I looked up again, his eyes moved quickly from me to the food then back up.

'You not hungry?'

'Looks better than it tastes,' I said.

'You should eat,' he replied, sinking what was left in the glass. 'You never know when you might need the strength.'

He placed the beer glass down and turned to me, his eyes disappearing into shadow again. They were impenetrable now; like staring into one of the abandoned mine shafts along the coast.

'Where you from?'

'London.'

'Ah, that explains it.' He flicked his head back. 'The home of the salesman.'

'Is it?'

'You telling me it isn't? Millions of people whose only reason for being anywhere *near* that hole is so they can live on the top floor of a skyscraper and try to convince people poorer than them to live beyond their means? That's a city of salesmen, believe me. Take a step back from the rat race, my friend – see what's going on. No one's there to help you.'

'Thanks for the advice.'

'You jest,' he said. His eyes locked on to mine. 'But I'm being serious. Who's going to be there for you in that city when you wake up with a knife in your back?'

I could hardly make him out now, he'd sunk so far back into the darkness. But I wasn't liking what I was hearing. I looked away and focused on my food.

'Do you want to be left alone?'

He had a smile on his face now, but it didn't go deep. Below the surface, I caught a glimpse of what I'd seen before.

A second of absolute darkness.

'It's up to you.'

He continued smiling. The smell of aftershave drifted across to me again. 'I'll leave you alone. I'm sure you'd rather be earning commission than listening to me, right?'

I didn't say anything.

'Nice meeting you, anyway,' he said, standing. 'Maybe we'll see you again.'

'Maybe.'

'I think so,' he said, cryptically.

Then I watched him leave, walking past the locals and out through a door on the far side of the pub, where the evening swallowed him up.

10

That night, I had difficulty sleeping. It had been a long time since I'd slept in a bed. A longer time since I'd been away from the house overnight.

I left the curtains slightly ajar and the window open. Just after one, I finally fell asleep, curled up in a ball at the bottom of the bed. In the dead of night, maybe an hour later, I stirred long enough to feel a faint breeze against my skin. And then a noise outside. Rotting autumn leaves caught beneath someone's feet. I lay there, too tired to move, and started to drift away again. Then the noise came a second time.

I flipped the duvet back, got up and walked to the window. The night was pitch black. In the distance, along the coastal road, were tiny blocks of light from the next village. Otherwise, it was difficult to make anything out, particularly close to the house.

The wind came again. I could hear leaves being blown across the ground, and waves crashing against the rocky coast – but not the noise that had woken me. I waited for a moment, then headed back to bed.

I got up early and sat at a table with beautiful views across the Atlantic. Tin mines rose up in front of me like brick arms reaching for the clouds. Over breakfast,

I spread the contents of the box out in front of me again, and studied the Polaroid of Alex. He was too close to the camera; some of his features weren't completely defined. His hair was shorter. There were dark areas around the side of his face where stubble was coming through. Behind him, there was a block of light that looked like a window, but it was difficult to see what was through it. Part of a building maybe, or a roof.

I turned it over.

Written on the back was: *You were never a mistake.*

I decided to call Kathy.

She answered after a couple of rings.

'Kathy, it's David Raker.'

'Oh, hi.'

'Sorry it's so early.'

'No problem,' she said. 'I was getting ready for work.'

'I've got the box here.' I turned the Polaroid over and looked at Alex again. 'Do you remember what photos you put inside?'

'Um . . . I don't know – I think there's a couple of us at a barbecue . . .'

'Do you remember the one of Alex on his own?'

'Uh . . .' A pause. 'I'm trying to think . . .'

You were never a mistake.

'Tell you what, I'm going to take a picture of it and send it to you, okay?'

'Okay.'

'I'll send two photos – one of the front and one of the back. Take a look at them when they come through and call me right back.'

I hung up, took a picture of the front of the photograph, then flipped it over and took a shot of the back. I sent them to Kathy's phone.

While I waited, I looked around. The owner was filling a giant cereal bowl with cornflakes. Outside, in the distance, a fishing trawler chugged into view, waves gliding out from its bow as it followed the coastline.

A couple of minutes later, my phone went.

Silence.

'Kathy?'

Gradually, fading in, the sound of sobbing.

'Kathy?'

A long pause. And then I could hear her crying again.

'Kathy – that's Alex's handwriting, isn't it?'

She sniffed. 'Yes.'

'Did you take that photograph?'

'No.'

'Any idea who did?'

More crying. Longer, deeper gasps of air.

'No.'

I looked at the Polaroid again. Turned it over. Traced the handwriting with a finger. Then I picked up the letter Kathy had written Alex.

But, somewhere, there would be a doubt that wasn't there before, a nagging feeling that, if I got too close to you, if I showed you too much affection, you'd get up one morning and walk away.

I don't want to feel like a mistake again.

'Do you know where Alex is in this picture?'

'No.' She started to sob again, a long, drawn-out sound that sent static crackling down the line. 'No,' she said again – and then hung up.

I placed my phone down.

So, Alex had used the box after all.

I I

Alex died on a country road between Bristol's northern edge and the motorway. I felt I should go there, but first I wanted to see his friend John. Jeff had given me a work address for him the previous day. When I called enquiries to get a telephone number, it turned out to be a police station south-west of Bristol city centre.

John was a police officer.

By the time I got there, it was lunchtime and had been raining: water still ran from guttering, and drains had filled with old crisp packets and beer cans. The street was deserted, except for some kids further down, their cigarettes dying in the cool of the day. I parked on the road and headed into the station.

It was quiet. There was a sergeant behind a sliding glass panel, framed by a huge map of the area. Dots were marked at intervals in a ring around the centre of the city.

The sergeant slid the glass across. 'Can I help you?'

'I'm here to see John Cary.'

He nodded. 'Can I ask what it's about?'

'I want to speak to him about Alex Towne.'

It didn't mean anything to him. He slid the glass panel back and disappeared out of sight. I sat down next to the front entrance. Outside, huge dark clouds rolled across the sky. Somewhere in the distance was the snow they'd been promising, moving down from Russia, ready to cover every can, needle and blood-stain that had ever been left on the streets.

Something clunked. At the far side of the waiting room a huge man emerged from a code-locked door. He was chiselled but not attractive. His Mediterranean skin was spoiled by acne scarring that ran the lengths of both cheeks. I walked across to him.

'My name's David Raker.'

He nodded.

'I'm looking into the disappearance of Alex Towne.'

He nodded again.

'Alex's mum came to me.'

'She told you he's dead, right?' he said, eyeing me.

'Right. I was hoping I might be able to ask you a couple of questions.'

He glanced at his watch, then looked at me, as if intrigued to see what I might come up with. 'Yeah, okay. Let's go for a drive.'

We drove north to where Alex had died. It was a pictur-esque spot: rolling grassland punctuated by narrow roads, all within sight of the city. Cary parked up and then led me away from the car, across to a field sloping away from the road. I looked down. A sliver of police tape still fluttered in a tree nearby. Apart from that, there was no sign that a car had once come off the road here.

'Were you on duty when he died?' I asked.

He shook his head.

'So, you went to see him at the morgue?'

'Yeah, once he'd been ID'd. It took a week and a half to get confirmation on the dental records.'

'You actually saw his body?'

'What was left of it. His hands, his feet, his face – they were all just bone. Some of his organs were still intact, but the rest of him . . .' Cary looked out at the fields. 'They reckon the tank must have ruptured when the car hit the field. It was why the fire consumed everything so quickly.' He glanced at me, sadness in his eyes. 'You know how hard you have to hit something in order to rupture a petrol tank?'

I shook my head.

'That car looked like it had been through a crusher. The whole thing was folded in on itself. Old model like that: no airbag, no side impact bars . . .' He paused again. 'I just hope it was quick.'

We stood silent for a moment. His eyes drifted to the space where the car must have landed, and then – eventually – back to me.

'He'd been drinking,' I said. 'Is that right?'

He nodded. 'Toxicology put him at four times over the legal limit.'

'Did you see the autopsy report?'

'Yeah.'

'It was definitely him?'

He looked at me like I was from another planet. 'What do you think?'

I paused for a moment.

'What are the chances of me getting hold of some of the paperwork?'

A little air escaped from between his lips, as if he couldn't believe I'd had the balls or stupidity to ask. 'Low.'

'What about unofficially?'

'Still low. I go into the system, it gets logged. I print something out, it gets logged. And why would I anyway? You're about as qualified to be running around, chasing down leads, as Coco the fucking clown.'

He shook his head, astonished into silence. I didn't say anything more, just nodded to show that I took his point, but didn't necessarily agree.

'Strange he should end up dying so close to home.'

Cary looked at me. 'What do you mean by that?'

'I mean, he disappears – *completely disappears* – for all that time . . . I would have expected him to have turned up somewhere further afield. Instead he dies on your doorstep. Maybe he even stayed nearby the whole time he was gone.'

'He didn't stay around here.'

'But he died around here.'

'He was on his way through to somewhere.'

'What makes you say that?'

'If he'd been staying around here, I would've known about it. Sooner or later, someone somewhere would've seen him. It would've got back to me.'

I nodded – but didn't agree. Cary was just one man in a local area of thirty or forty square miles. If you wanted to, you could easily disappear in that kind of space and never be found.

'So, where do you think he went?'

Cary frowned. 'Didn't I just answer that?'

'You said not around here – so where?'

He shook his head and then shrugged.

'Do you think there was any connection with your other friend's disappearance?'

'Simon?'

'Yeah. Simon –' I glanced at my notepad '– Mitchell.'

'I doubt it.'

'How come?'

'Jeff tell you about him?'

'He said he had a drug problem.'

He nodded.

'He said he hit out at Kathy.'

He nodded again. 'That night, we were all there. Simon didn't know what the fuck he was doing, but when he tried to hit her, he crossed the line. Especially in Alex's mind. That night was when we realized he had a serious problem. But by then he was too far gone. He promised to stop, but that was why eventually he left. He couldn't stop. I don't think he could face us any more – the way we used to look at him. Even after Alex left, things were never the same. So one day he just packed his bags and was gone. We only ever heard from him once after that.'

'When?'

'A long time after Alex disappeared. In fact, probably after he died. Simon had been in London all that time, in and out of whatever place would put a roof over his head.'

'You tell him Alex was dead?'

'Yeah. Didn't register with him. He sounded strung

out. Just kept going on about this guy he'd met who was going to help him.'

'Did he say who the guy was?'

'No. Just said he'd met him on the streets and they'd got talking. Sounded like this guy was trying to straighten him out.'

'Do you think Simon followed Alex?'

His expression told me that it was the least likely thing he could imagine happening.

'You've no idea where Simon lives these days?'

'London.'

'That narrows it down to about seven million people.'

Cary shrugged. 'Playing detective ain't easy.'

'You ever tried to find him?'

'I tried once. Didn't get far. The one thing Simon and Alex *did* have in common was that neither of them wanted to be found.'

Cary raised his eyes to the skies. The first spots of rain were starting to fall. He pulled his jacket close to his body and zipped it up. Rain spattered off the shoulders, making a sound like pebbles caught in a tide.

We walked back to the car, and got in.

'I did some asking around at the beginning,' he said as we drove off, the field sliding away behind us. 'I think you'll struggle to find anyone who can give you a reason for Alex's disappearance. It wasn't like him to just leave everything behind. Not unless something was seriously wrong. That wasn't how he was programmed.'

We drove the rest of the way in silence.

*

Cary had changed his mind by the time we got back to the station. I sat in an office full of paperwork and desks, most of them unmanned, while he used a computer close by to access Alex's case file. At the other end of the room, there were four detectives with their backs to us. Two of them were on the phone. He glanced around at them, then to the door, then hit 'Print'.

'I'm willing to take a risk with this,' he said. 'But if anyone finds out I've given these to you, I'll be taking early retirement.'

'I understand.'

'I hope you do.'

He got up and went to the printer, then came back with a stack of paper and slid it into a Manila folder he already had open on the desk. I took the file, keeping it low and in front of my body. He sat down at his desk again, looked around, then removed an unmarked DVD from his top drawer.

'You might want to take a look at that too,' he said, tossing it across the desk.

'What is it?'

'A video one of the fire crew shot of the crash site.'

I took the DVD and slipped it into the file, then held up the printouts. 'Is there anything in here?'

He shrugged. 'What do you think?'

'You reckon it's open and shut?'

He frowned. 'Alex was drink-driving. Of course it's open and shut.'

I nodded, and scanned the first page of the printout. When I looked up, he was staring at me, eyes narrowed.

'Let me tell you something,' he said, leaning across the desk. 'The night of the crash, and for about three months after, I was balls-deep in a double murder. A woman and her daughter, both raped, both strangled, left in a field in the pissing rain for five days before anyone found them. Which case do you think my DCI wanted done first: those two women? Or some fucking drunk who couldn't even keep to his own side of the road?'

I nodded. 'I wasn't passing judge—'

'And since then? Take a drive down the street. I've got guys out there on PCP who think they're the fucking Terminator. I've got seventeen-year-old kids from the council estates with knives the size of your arm.' He paused, looked at me. 'So, no, I haven't spent a lot of time with that file over the last year. I put in my fair share of time when he first went missing, and I got the support of some of the people in here. But as soon as he put his car through the side of a lorry, it became a zero priority case. And you know what? It's even less than that now.'

I nodded again then decided to move the conversation on.

I removed the Polaroid of Alex I'd taken from the box. Cary eyed me, wondering what I was looking at. I put the picture down on the desk in front him. He glanced at it, then sat forward.

'Is that Alex?'

'I think so.'

Cary picked up the picture, holding it in front of him. 'Who took this?'

70

'I don't know.'

He went quiet again. 'Where did you get it?'

'It was in among Kathy's stuff.'

'She took it?'

'No.'

'So, how did it get there?'

'I'm not sure.'

He looked like he didn't believe me.

'All I know is what I found. I've no idea how it got there – but I can take a guess.'

'So take a guess.'

'Alex put it there.'

'After he disappeared?'

I nodded.

'Why?'

'They had an arrangement.'

He frowned. 'An arrangement?'

'A spot they liked going to together. A place where they used to hide personal stuff.'

He looked at me for a moment, his eyes narrowing a little. Then his expression changed. He opened up the top drawer of his desk and started shuffling around inside. He brought out a notebook, in tatters, the cover falling off, the pages missing their edges. He laid it down, opened it up and studied it. Words, diagrams and reconstructions of crime scenes were crammed into every space. He flicked through it, got halfway, then looked up.

'You might want to write this down,' he said.

I took out my notepad.

'Like I said, I did some asking around when Alex first went missing. Called a few people. I asked his mum for his card numbers, and his bank details. Basically, anything he could draw on I wanted to know about. It was the best lead we'd have.'

'But he didn't take his card with him.'

'He didn't take his *debit* card, no.'

He looked at his notebook. At the top of the page, written in black and circled in red, was a number.

'He left his debit card behind, but he took his credit card with him,' Cary said, prodding the number with his finger. 'It was valid for another five years after he went missing, so I figured it was worth keeping an eye on. I arranged with Mary and the bank to have all his credit card statements redirected to me. And they kept coming, and coming, and coming, and every time the statements arrived on my desk, I'd open them up and they'd be blank.'

'He never used the card – not even once?'

Cary shook his head. 'Every month there'd be nothing in them. I spent four and a half years looking through his statements, and four years and a half years putting them straight in the bin.'

He ran a finger along the number in the notebook.

'Then, about six months before he died...' He paused, glanced at me. 'The statements stopped coming.'

'Because the card had expired?'

'No. The card had about six months left to run.'

'So, why'd they stop?'

'I called the bank to find out. They wouldn't release any information initially, so I kind of . . . *pretended* it was part of an investigation. They accessed the account for me and said the statements were still being sent out, and would only stop once the card had expired.'

'But it hadn't expired.'

'No. The obvious assumption was that the last statement got lost in the post, so I asked them to send out a duplicate. The guy said he'd put it in the post overnight.' He paused, sat back. 'But that never arrived either.'

'How come?'

'I called the bank again, told them the duplicate hadn't turned up, and they asked me to confirm my address. So, I gave it to them—'

'But it wasn't the address they had.'

He looked at me, nodded. 'Right. Four and a half years after he disappears, and suddenly he changes his address.'

'Alex changed it?'

He shrugged. 'I spoke to the bank a third time, pushed the whole investigation angle, and they made the new statements available to me. Same as always – the card remained unused. But it wasn't registered to Alex any more. It was registered as a business account.'

'A business account?'

'The Calvary Project.'

'That was the name of the business?'

'Who the fuck knows? I had their name and address from the bank and I still couldn't find any trace of them. There's no Inland Revenue records, no website, no public listing anywhere – nothing. You want my opinion, it's vapour.'

'You mean some sort of front?'

He shrugged again. I looked at him, trying to figure out why he wasn't more determined to dig deeper. He pushed the notebook towards me and leaned over his desk, jabbing a finger at the number.

'Treat yourself,' he said.

'That's part of the credit card number?'

'No. That's the telephone number for the Calvary Project.'

It was a landline, but there was no area code in front, which was why I hadn't worked out what it was.

'You tried calling it?'

'About a hundred thousand times.'

'No answer?'

He shook his head.

'Where's the street address?'

'London.'

'You went up there?'

'No.'

'Why not?'

'Have you been listening to *anything* I've been saying? The whole case is a lockdown. The card's expired, and a year ago I spent three hours picking up bits of Alex's skull from a fucking field.'

'Did you tell Mary?'

'About what?'

'About what you'd found.'

'No. What's the point?'

'Don't you think she has a right to know?'

'A right to know *what* exactly?' he said. 'That she should take a long, hard look at another dead end? Forget it. I didn't tell her anything because nothing leads anywhere. The case – if it even *was* a case – is over. It's done.'

Suddenly it came to me. I saw why the case had never been taken further: Cary didn't want to expose himself to new, corrupting information about Alex. He loved his friend. He was disappointed by the way he'd died. He didn't want to taint any more of his memories of him.

Yet I could see something else too. Just a flicker. A part Cary had always tried to bury. A part desperate for answers.

'So, where in London is it based?'

'Some place in Brixton. I gave the details to a guy I know who works for the Met and he pissed himself laughing. Apparently the only businesses being run out of there are from suitcases full of crack.'

Cary laid a thick hand across the notebook and pulled it back towards him, dropping it into his top drawer. When he looked up, his eyes narrowed again as if he'd seen something in my face.

'What?' he said.

'I've got one more question.'

He didn't move.

'Well, more of a favour, to be honest.'

'That file not enough for you?'

'Basically, I was hoping you might be able to give me some . . . *technical* help.'

'What the hell does that mean?'

I held up the picture. 'With the photograph.'

'What about it?'

'It must have been taken by someone Alex met after he disappeared, and the picture's a Polaroid, which means that person probably handled it as it was develop—'

'No.'

He'd second-guessed me.

'I just need it checked for prints.'

'Just need it? *Just* need it? You realize what you're asking me to do? Get forensics involved, log it into the system, start a paper trail. What do you think would happen if people find out I've been pushing personal work through?'

'I know it's diff—'

'I'm *fucked*, that's what.'

'Okay.'

'No way. Forget it.'

'I felt I should ask.'

'No way,' he said again.

But I could see the conflict in his face. The embers of Alex's memory hadn't died out yet. Something still burnt in him. And I still had a shot at getting the picture looked at.

12

As I travelled east, I could see sunlight up ahead, breaking through the clouds. But by the time I got to Mary's, it was gone. Evening was moving in.

After she answered the door, I followed her through to the kitchen and then down a steep flight of stairs into the basement. It was huge, much bigger than I'd expected, but it was a mess as well: boxes stacked ceiling-high like pillars in a foyer; pieces of wood and metal perched against the walls; an electrical box, covered in thick, opaque cobwebs.

'I come down here sometimes,' she said. 'It's quiet.'

I nodded that I understood.

'Sorry about the mess.'

I smiled at her. 'You want to see a mess, you should come to my place.'

Then, from upstairs: 'Where am I?'

We looked at each other. It was Malcolm. Mary turned towards the stairs, then back to me. 'I'm really sorry. I'll be back in a few minutes.'

After she was gone, I looked around the basement. On the other side, half-hidden behind boxes, was an old writing desk, an open photo album on it. Dusty. Worn. I walked over and turned some of the pages. A young Alex playing in the snow, paddling in the sea, eating ice cream on a pier. Later on, some of the pictures had fallen out, leaving only white blocks on faded yellow pages.

Right at the back was a photograph of Alex, Malcolm and Mary, and someone else. The guy was in his thirties, good-looking, smiling from ear to ear. He had one arm on Alex's shoulder and one around Malcolm. Mary was out to the side of the shot, detached from the group. Most of the time you couldn't read much into pictures: people put on smiles, put arms around those next to them, posed even if they didn't want to. Pictures could paper over even the most significant of cracks. But this one said everything: Mary was the odd one out.

Quietly, she came down the stairs.

I turned to her and held up the photo. 'Who's this guy?'

'Wow,' she said, coming across the basement towards me. 'I haven't seen him in a while. I thought we'd managed to burn all the photographs of him.' But she was smiling. She studied it for a while. 'Al. *Uncle* Al. He was a friend of Malc's.'

'But not a friend of yours?'

She shrugged. 'I think the feeling was mutual, to be honest. Al was a wealthy guy. We weren't. He bought his way into their affection, and the only way I could counter that was by staying close to them. He wasn't so keen to spend money on me.'

'He wasn't Alex's real uncle?'

'No. Malcolm used to work for him.'

'So, is he still around?

'No. He died in a car accident.' She paused. 'Just like Alex.'

I put the photo back into the album. 'Did Alex ever go to church?'

'Church?' She frowned, as if the question had taken her by surprise. 'Not at the end, no. But when he was younger he used to come to our church in town. He was part of the youth group there. He made some good friends.'

'Anyone he kept in regular contact with?'

'He was friendly with one guy there . . .' She stopped. 'I'm trying to remember his name. He used to lead worship, take the occasional service, that kind of thing. He went travelling for a while, and never came back to us. I think Alex still kept in touch with him though.' She stopped a second time. 'Gosh, I *must* be getting old.'

'It's probably worth following up, so if you remember him, drop me a line.' I thought of the birthday card. 'What about the name Angela Routledge – does that ring any bells?'

She thought about it, but it obviously didn't. I hadn't expected it to get me far. Angela Routledge was probably just an old woman raising funds for the church.

'Well, I better be go–'

'Mat,' she said. 'With one tee.'

I turned to look at her. 'Sorry?'

'I knew I'd remember it eventually.' She smiled. 'Alex's friend from the church. His name was Mat.'

79

13

Before I went to sleep, I opened the case file containing the printouts Cary had given me and took out the DVD. I sat down, dropped it into the disc tray and pressed 'Play'.

Taken with a hand-held video camera, the recording was shaky and disorientating to start with, but became steadier. The film began with some shots of the fields surrounding the crash site and the area the car had landed in. There was a dark, scarred trail left on the field. The grass was scorched. Something from the car – perhaps the exhaust box – was embedded in the mud. I was hoping whoever had taken the film might zoom in, but they didn't.

Instead it cut to where the car had come off the road. There was petrol left on the tarmac. Smashed glass. The light wasn't particularly good, and when I glanced at the timecode in the corner, I could see why. 17.42. Evening.

The film cut to the car itself.

The roof had collapsed. One door had come off, and the boot had disappeared, pushed into the back of the car. The engine was up inside the dashboard on the right-hand side. As the camera panned from left to right, I could see bits of windscreen glinting in the grass. The grille at the front of the Toyota had been tossed free and lay in front of the car, alongside shards of coloured plastic from the headlights. The film cut in closer and – with the aid of a light attachment – revealed the inside of the car. Everything was black, melted, burnt.

The film cut to a spot about twenty feet away. Scattered in the grass was debris that had been thrown free of the car: a burnt mobile phone; a shoe; a wallet, the tan leather charred. The wallet was open. Some of the contents had spilled out. Part of a blackened and melted driver's licence, Alex's face on it, sat in the grass.

Then the film finished.

I ejected the DVD and spread some of the paperwork out in front of me. The investigators were fairly certain the crash had been caused by Alex's being drunk. There were some fuzzy photographs on one of the printouts, including a shot of the tyre marks on the road, and one of the lorry Alex's car had hit. The lorry driver had escaped with only minor cuts and bruises. In his statement he said another car had overtaken Alex's and then, about ten seconds later, the Toyota had drifted across to the wrong side of the road. A third photograph showed the Toyota from head on. The right side had sustained more damage than the left. It explained why, in the film, the engine seemed further back inside the car on the right. I skimmed through the crime scene analysis, and found a technician's diagram of the crash trajectory.

I moved on to the post-mortem. Like Cary had said, the age of the Toyota meant there was no airbag, and no real impact protection. The damage was severe: teeth had been found in Alex's stomach and what was left of his throat, torn from the gum when his face hit the steering wheel. I read on a little further and then, towards the back, found two pages missing. Cary must have forgotten to pick them up when he'd printed them out. I made a note to ask him about it the next time we spoke.

A couple more pictures were loose in the Manila folder, showing Alex's body. It was a horrific sight. His hands had been burnt down to the skeleton; his feet and lower legs too. His face, from the brow down to his jaw, was also just bone, and there was a huge crack in his skull, all the way down one side of his cheek, where his face had hit the wheel on impact. I turned back to the file. It got worse the more I read. His body had been pulverized: bones smashed, skin burnt away. Everything broken beyond repair. It was obvious from the damage sustained that he had died before the car caught fire.

Except, according to Mary, he hadn't died at all.

The Corner of the Room

The first thing he could hear was the wind, distantly at first, and then louder as he became more aware of it. He opened his eyes. The room was spinning gently, the walls bending as he moved his head across the pillow.

Am I dead?

He groaned and rolled on to his side. Slowly, everything started to shift back into focus: the right angles of the walls; the dusty shaft of moonlight; the lightbulb moving gently in the breeze coming through the top window.

It was cold. He sat up and pulled a blanket around him. It brushed against the floor, sending dirt and dust scattering into the darkness. When he moved again, the mattress pinged beneath him. A sharp pain coursed through his chest. He placed a hand against his ribs and pressed with his fingers. Beneath his T-shirt, he could feel bandages, running from his breastplate down to his waist.

He breathed in.

Click.

A noise from the far corner of the room. A pillar poked out from the wall, a cupboard beside that. Everywhere else was dark.

'Hello?'

His voice sounded quiet and childlike. Scared. He cleared his throat. It felt like fingers were tearing at his windpipe.

And now he could smell something too.

He felt a pulse in his chest, like a bubble bursting. The first scent of nausea rose in his throat. He covered his mouth, and moved back across the bed, trying to get away from the smell. Opposite him, lit by a square of moonlight, he spotted a metal bucket. The rim was speckled with puke. Next to that was a bottle of disinfectant. But it wasn't that he could smell.

It was something else.

Click.

The noise again. He peered into the darkness in the corner of the room. Nothing. No sound, no sign of movement. Shifting position again, he moved right up against the wall, where the two corners joined, and brought his knees up to his chest. His heart squeezed beneath his ribs. His chest tightened.

'Who's there?'

He pulled the blanket tighter around him, and sat there in silence. Staring into the darkness until, finally, sleep took him.

*

He's standing outside a church, peering in through a window. Mat is sitting at a desk, a Bible open in his lap. Across the other side of the room, a door is ajar. He looks from Mat to the door, and feels like he wants to be there. Standing in that doorway.

And then, suddenly, he is.

He places a hand on the door and pushes at it. Slowly, it creaks open. Mat turns in his chair, an arm resting on the back, intrigued to see who has entered.

Then his face drops.

'Dear God,' he says gently. He gets to his feet, stumbling, his eyes wide, his mouth open. He looks like he's seen a ghost. 'I thought . . . Where have you been?'

'Hiding.'

Mat stops. Frowns. 'Why?'

'I've done something . . . really bad.'

He opened his eyes. A blinding circular light was above him. He tried to cover his face, but when he went to move his hands, they caught on something. Suddenly he felt the binds on his arms, digging into the skin, securing him to the chair beneath.

He turned his head.

Beyond the light, the room was dark, but immediately beside him he could make out a medical gurney, metal instruments on top. Next to that was a heart monitor. Behind, obscured by the darkness, was a silhouette, watching him from the shadows.

'What's going on?' he said.

The silhouette didn't reply. Didn't even move.

He could see further down his body now. His wrists were locked in place on the arms of a dentist's chair. He wriggled his fingers, then tried to move his hands again. The binds stretched and tightened.

'What's going on?'

He tried moving his legs. Nothing. Tried again. Still nothing. In his head, it felt like they were thrashing around. But, further up his body – where he still had feeling – he knew they weren't moving. They were paralysed.

He looked to the silhouette again.

'Why can't I feel my legs?'

Still no reply.

He felt tears well in his eyes.

'*What are you doing to me?*'

A hand touched his stomach. He started, and turned his head the other way. Standing next to him was a huge man – tall and powerful, dressed in black. He had a white apron on, and a surgical face mask. He lowered it.

'Hello,' he said.

'What's going on?'

'You're standing on a precipice. Did you know that?'

'*What?*'

'You're standing on the edge of opportunity, and you *will* know it, though. You will come to know opportunity in the coming days, to understand the sacrifice we've made for you. But first we need to take care of some things.'

'Please, I don't know wha–'

'I'll see you on the other side.'

The tall man pulled his mask back over his chin and stepped back from the dentist's chair, into the darkness.

A woman came forward in his place, dressed in a white coat and wearing a surgical mask, a blue medical cap tied around her dark hair. A bloodstained apron squeezed her short, plump frame. She leaned into him. There were blood spatters on the mask too.

'Please . . .'

The woman placed a hand over his eyes, over his face. Then she slid something into his mouth. A huge, metal object – like a clamp. It clicked. He tried to speak, tried to scream, but the clamp had locked his mouth open. All he could do was gurgle.

He watched her.

Please.

From somewhere, a quiet metallic buzz. His eyes flicked left and right, trying to see where the noise was coming from. It got louder.

What are you doing? he tried to say, but it was just another gurgle. He swallowed. Watched her. Saw her fiddling with something, and listened as the buzz got louder. Then, from her side, she brought up a dental drill, its point spinning.

He looked from her to the drill.

Oh God, no.

And then he blacked out.

He woke. Everything was quiet. It was the middle of the night, when the shadows in the room were at their deepest and thickest. And it was cold. *Freezing* cold. He pulled the blanket right up to his neck and turned on his pillow, facing the ceiling.

His mouth throbbed.

He ran a tongue along his gums, where his teeth had once been. All that was there now were tiny threads of flesh, spilling out of the cavities. They'd taken them without asking, like they were taking everything else.

Click.

The noise again. The same noise, every night, all night, coming from the corner of the room. He slowly sat up, and looked into the darkness.

He'd got up and examined the corner of the room in the daylight, when the sun poured in from the top window. There was nothing there. Just the cupboard and the space behind it, a narrow two- or three-foot gap. In the dead of the night, when the silence was oppressive, it was easy to see things and hear things that weren't there. Darkness messed with you like that. But he'd seen it for himself: there was nothing there.

Click.

He continued looking into the shadows – facing them down. Then, pulling the blanket around him, he got to his feet and took a step towards the corner of the room.

He stopped.

Out of the darkness and into the moonlight came a cockroach, its legs pattering against the floor, its body clicking as it moved. He watched it come to the bed then turn slightly, heading deeper into the room towards the door they always kept closed. It stopped for a moment, half-under the door, its antennae twitching, its legs shaking beneath it. And then it disappeared into the light on the other side.

A cockroach.

He smiled, slumped back on to the bed. Breathed a sigh of relief. Deep down, he knew no one could be watching him from the corner of the room. Not for all this time. Not all night. No one would do that, would even *want* to do that. The mind could play tricks on you. It could make you doubt yourself; it bent reality and reason and, at your weakest, you started to question what you knew to be true.

It had only ever been a cockroach.

He brought his arms out from under the blanket and wiped the sweat from his face. Wind came in through the top window. He lay there, letting the cool air fall against his skin. And, as he closed his eyes, he could – very distantly – hear the sea.

'Cockroach.'

His eyes flicked open.

What the fuck was that?

'I see you, cockroach.'

He scrambled back across the bed, towards the wall. Brought his knees up to his chest. From the darkness came a second cockroach, forming out of the shadows, following the path of the first one. It started to arc left, towards the light on the other side of the door.

'Don't run, cockroach.'

A hand came out of the night and smashed down on top of the insect. Its shell exploded under the force of the blow, clear blood spraying out either side. Then the fingers twitched and moved, turning over to show the remains of the cockroach, flattened and in pieces, coated on the skin of the hand.

Slowly, the hand started to become an arm, and the arm a body, until a man emerged from the gloom, a plastic mask on his face.

It was the mask of a devil.

A smell came with the man as he looked up from the depths of the night, blinking inside the eyeholes. The mouth slit was wide and long, moulded into a permanent leer, and inside it the man smiled, his tongue emerging from between his lips.

'Oh God.' A trembling voice from the bed.

The man in the mask moved his tongue along the hard edges of the mouth slit. It was big and bloated, red and glistening, like a corpse floating in a black ocean.

And, at the very tip, it was cut unevenly down the middle.

The devil had a forked tongue.

From the bed, he felt his heart stop, his chest shrink, his body give way beneath him.

The man in the mask blinked again, inhaled through two tiny pinpricks in the mask's nose, and slowly rose to his feet.

'I wonder what you taste like . . . *cockroach.*'

PART TWO

14

The address that Cary had given me for the Calvary Project was a block of flats called Eagle Heights, about a quarter of a mile east of Brixton Road. On the way over, my phone started ringing, but by the time I'd scooped it up off the back seat I'd missed the call. I slotted the phone in the hands-free and went to my voice messages. It was Cary.

'Uh, I've thought about . . .' He paused, sounding different now: less officious than the last time we'd talked. 'Just give me a call when you get the chance. I'm in this morning until ten, and then after lunch I'm here until four.'

I looked at the clock: 8.43. I tried calling him, but the sergeant said he wasn't around. Stuck in traffic ten minutes later, I tried again, and the same desk sergeant said he still wasn't around. I left a message just as Eagle Heights emerged from behind a bank of oak trees.

It was featureless and grey. The concrete walls were marked all the way down, as if the building was rotting from the inside. It was twenty-five storeys high, and flanked by two even bigger blocks of flats on the other side of a ringed fence. At the front entrance, there was a board with Eagle Heights written on it. Someone had spray-painted *Welcome to hell* underneath.

I parked my BMW next to a battered Golf, its wheels up on blocks and its windows smashed in. Across from me, a bunch of kids who were supposed to be in school were kicking a ball about on a patch of muddy grass. I got out of the car, removed my phone and my pocket knife, and headed for the entrance.

Inside, there were mailboxes on my left, most with nothing in. I checked the slot for number 227: empty. To my right, stairs wound up and around. As I started to climb, a huge metal cage came into view, an air-conditioning unit inside. The higher I climbed, the worse the place started to smell.

The door to the second floor hung off its hinges and the glass had cracked. I pulled it open. Background noise came through from the flats: the buzz of a TV, a woman shouting, the dull thud of a baseline. There were fifteen doors on either side, all painted the same shade of muddy brown. Flat 227 was right at the end.

I knocked twice and waited.

A council notice was nailed to the door. It was almost four years old, and warned people not to enter due to health and safety violations. Some of the sticker had peeled away and the bits that remained were faded.

I knocked again, harder this time.

Further down the corridor, two flats along on the opposite side, I heard the sound of a door opening. Someone peered through the crack, their eyes darting backwards and forwards.

'Who you lookin' for?'

It was a man's voice.

'The guy who lives here,' I said. 'You know him?'

'Nah.'

'You seen him around?'

'What are you, a copper?'

'No.'

'Social services?'

'No.'

I knocked again on the door.

'You ain't gonna find nothin', mate.'

'How come?'

'There ain't no one there.'

I looked at him. 'Since when?'

'Since for ever.'

'No one lives here?'

'Nope.'

'You sure?'

'Am I *sure*? You *can* read English, can't you?'

'Only if the words aren't more than three letters.' I glanced at the council notice. 'So, the council cleared out the last tenants?'

'*Last* tenants? I been in this shithole twenty years. Ain't no one lived in that flat since the floor gave in. Hole the size of Tower Bridge in there.' He opened the door a little more. It was a white guy. Unshaven. Old. 'No one gives a shit about us here, so ain't no one been round to fix it. Must've been five years since it went.'

'No one's lived here for five years?'

'Nope.' He paused. 'Sometimes the council come

round. Inspecting it, I s'pose. But no one's lived in there for a long time.'

I started along the corridor towards him. As I got closer he pushed the door shut. I passed his flat, walked out to the landing area, and stood away from the door, out of sight. Then I waited. A couple of minutes passed. Once he was definitely back in his hole, I moved into the corridor and returned to the flat, taking my pocket knife out on the way.

Slipping the blade into the crack between door and frame, I gently started to jemmy it open. The door was damp and warped. There was a curve about two-thirds of the way up. As I worked the blade, I felt some give. I removed some broken slivers of wood and started opening up a hole. Through it some of the interior was brightened by the light from the corridor. Inside it was stark. No carpets. No furniture. No paint on the walls.

More wood started to break, and the further down the door frame I got, the easier it came away. I tried the handle. The door moved in the frame. I glanced along the corridor, then gently used my shoulder to apply some pressure. Sliding the blade back in, this time at the lock, I wriggled it around and pressed again at the door. The wood was incredibly soft, bending against my weight. Finally, it clicked open.

I stepped inside and closed the door behind me.

There were no curtains at the windows, only rect-angular sheets of black plastic. Small blocks of light escaped around the edges and on to opposite walls. A kitchen counter was to my left. The room smelt damp but not unpleasant, and the floorboards were dirty. Some were broken. The old man had been wrong, though. There were small holes in the floor, but they didn't go through to the room below. They went to a concrete support. Some of the floorboards differed in colour to the rest of the flooring and looked as if they had been replaced recently.

I hunted for a light switch and found one a little way along the wall. When I flicked it on, nothing happened. I walked across to the windows, flipped the blade and slashed through the plastic. Morning poured into the room in thick cubes of dust-filled light.

The flat was like a skeleton: every piece of furniture had been removed. There were Coke bottles and empty crisp packets on the kitchen counter. In a small rubbish bin there was an apple core and two sweet wrappers. I picked up one of the crisp packets and turned it over. The expiry date was six months away.

The flat had definitely been used recently.

I looked around. Pinned to the wall was a newspaper cutting, curled at the edges. BOY, 10, FOUND FLOATING IN THE THAMES. Parts of the story had been underlined in red pen. I stepped in closer: 13 April 2002. It was nearly eight years old.

I walked to the bedrooms. Both were empty, dust on the floorboards and paint blistering on the walls. The windows had also been covered in black plastic sheeting. The third door led to the bathroom. The bath was filthy, mould climbing up the sides and around the taps, spreading like a disease across the enamel. Tiles were cracked and missing, and bits of tile were in the bath. The sink was cleaner, though, and there was a bar of soap on it, tiny bubbles on its surface. It had been lathered recently.

Back in the kitchen, I checked through the cupboards. Two saucepans. A frying pan. Both had been washed. In another drawer I found washing-up liquid. Cornflakes. Matches. Cutlery. Orange juice. In the smallest drawer, right at the bottom, was a notepad. Nothing written on it. I took it anyway.

I ran my fingers along the underside of the units, then climbed on to them and looked on top of the cupboards. They hadn't been cleaned since they'd been put in. The dirt was an inch thick.

The flat was obviously used as a base of some sort; a hiding place. Maybe Alex had even hidden here for a time. No one would live here. Not in conditions like this. There weren't enough provisions and utensils for anyone to stay full-time. But as a place to disappear, it was ideal. The old man thought it was the council he'd heard – but it wasn't them.

I glanced at the slashed plastic sheeting and the jemmied lock, and realized they'd know someone had been here. But it was too late to worry about that now. Whoever owned this place wasn't making contact with the neighbours and it was unlikely they were paying rent or rates. Any break-in was going to go unreported.

Then, suddenly, a telephone started ringing.

I stood completely still in the middle of the room, trying to figure out if it was coming from inside the flat.

When I realized it was, I followed the sound through to the bedrooms.

I checked the first one over. Nothing.

In the second, the noise got louder. At the bottom of one of the walls was a phone jack, a small wire running up and out of it, disappearing behind one of the black sheets. I stabbed my knife into it and tore away the plastic. On the windowsill was a cordless phone with a digital display, sitting in a recharging cradle.

The ringing stopped.

I picked up the phone and looked at the display. LAST CALL: NUMBER WITHHELD. In the options menu, there were no names in the address book. Nothing on the 'recent calls' list. No messages on the voicemail. I punched in my own mobile number, and pressed 'Call'. A couple of seconds later, my phone started buzzing. On the display: PRIVATE. *So, the landline's withheld as well.* I deleted my number from the 'recent calls' list, and placed their phone back in the cradle. The fact that there was nothing on it – no history, no record of anything – meant either it was brand new, or they wiped it clean after every use.

It was time to go.

I went to the windows in the living room, trying to see if there was any way to reconnect the sheeting. There wasn't.

Then I caught sight of something else: two floors down, a man was standing next to my car, a mobile phone in his hands. The handset was flipped open, as if he'd just been using it.

The caller.

He leaned forward, cupped his hands to the glass and peered through the window into the front seat. He didn't move for a long time. Then he straightened up, took in the full length of the car and looked up towards the flat. I stepped back from the window. Waited. Checked my watch thirty seconds later. When I looked again, he was gone.

I made sure I still had the notepad I'd pocketed earlier, and moved to the door, opening it a fraction. I peered through the gap.

The man was already inside the doors at the end of the corridor.

Shit – he's coming to the flat.

I pushed the door gently shut and backed up against the wall, just to the side of the hinge. Gripping the knife, I listened for his footsteps. Then the door started opening.

Hesitation.

It opened further, but not the whole way. Through the slit between door and frame, I could see his face. He had a thick scar running towards the corner of his lips, which seemed to extend his mouth. He took another step forward. All I could see now was the back of his head. Another inch forward. His foot came into view at the bottom of the door.

'Vee?' he said quietly.

He took a step back.

'Vee?'

Another step.

It was so quiet in the flat now, I was sure he could hear me breathing.

He backed up another step and, before I realized what was happening, a thin sliver of face was filling the gap between door and frame – and his eyes were moving from the knife in my hand, up to my face.

Suddenly, we were eye to eye either side of the door.

A heartbeat later, he ran.

When I got out into the corridor, the doors at the end were already swinging open and he was out of them. I sprinted after him, taking the stairs two at a time, adjusting the knife so the tip of the handle faced down and the blade pointed towards my elbow. When I got to the bottom, he was looking back over his shoulder, heading out across the grass to where a length of metal fencing separated the buildings from the road. He looked younger than me, twenty-two or twenty-three. I'd run a lot since Derryn had died, pounding out the frustration and the anger, but at his age he would be naturally fitter. It was unlikely I could catch him on a straight run.

Then the chase swung in my favour.

The kids I'd spotted earlier had moved their game of football further up, closer to the flats. As he looked around again, one of the kids ran across in front of him. The two of them collided. The kid went spinning, almost pirouetting on the spot, before collapsing to the floor. The man tried to avoid him, but failed, falling over him, his body hitting the floor hard. For a couple of seconds, he was dazed. He scrambled on to all fours, on to his feet, then his shoes slipped in the mud.

He went down again.

As I came at him, he jabbed a boot up into my stomach. I staggered backwards, losing my footing, but managed to cling on to his coat. I pulled him towards me. He jabbed at me again with a foot, catching the side of my face. The impact stunned me for a moment. I dropped the knife. Blinked. Tried to re-focus. He looked between me, the knife and the fencing. The tiny delay worked in my favour: I grasped the front of his coat and landed a punch in the side of his head.

He pushed back and grabbed my arm, trying to snap it. Wriggling free, I pumped a fist at his face, and missed. Then did it again. He rolled to the left, my fist slapping against the ground, then used my weight transfer to push me off. When I swivelled to face him again, he was already on his feet, caked in mud.

'Stop!' I shouted.

But he didn't stop. By the time I was on my feet again, he had made it to the metal fence, then dropped to his knees and quickly crawled through a gap. As he stood up, safe on the other side, he pulled up the hood on his jacket so I couldn't see his face properly, and jogged away.

I got to the fencing and pressed against it. He was halfway along a narrow alleyway that led from the opposite side of the road, moving more slowly now to prevent himself from losing his footing again. Puddles were scattered around him, reflecting the sky. I watched him all the way to the end. When he got there, he stopped and looked back at me.

Then he disappeared for good.

On my way back to the car, about twenty feet from where the kids were playing football, I spotted something: a mobile phone. Mud was caked to it, the display face down, wet grass matted to the casing. I knelt, picked it up and wiped it clean. As soon as I unlocked the keypad, it erupted into life. I hit 'Answer'.

On the phone: silence. Then the sound of cars in the background.

'You're gonna wish you hadn't picked that up,' a voice said.

I paused. Stood. I could see my knife about six feet across the grass from me. I walked over and scooped it up, then glanced towards the fence, back to the flats and out to the main road again.

I was being watched.

'Did you hear me?'

'Who are you?'

'*Did* you hear me?'

'Yeah, I heard you,' I replied, and looked around again. 'Who does the flat belong to?'

'You just made a big mistake.'

'Yeah, well, I've made them before.'

'Not like this.' The line crackled and hissed. '*Listen to me:* you get back in your car and you drive back to wherever the fuck it is you're from, and you forget about everything you've found. You don't ever come out of your hole again. Is that clear?'

I took the phone away from my ear and looked at the display. Another withheld number. 'Who does the flat belong to?'

'Is that clear?'

'What's the Calvary Project?'

'Is that *clear*?'

'Where's Alex Towne?'

'You're not listening to me, *David*.'

I stopped. 'How do you know my name?'

'One chance.'

'How the fuck do you know my name?'

'This is your one chance.'

Then the line went dead.

15

The restaurant overlooked Hyde Park. At the windows were a series of booths, dressed up like an American diner, with mini jukeboxes on the tables playing Elvis on rotation. Above me on the wall was a clock showing 10.40, Mickey Mouse's arms pointing to the ten and the eight. Three booths along were a French couple and, beyond them, a group of kids eating toast and jam. Apart from that, the place was empty.

On the table in front of me, I had the pad I'd taken from the apartment and the mobile phone I'd picked up off the grass outside. Just like the phone in the flat, there were no contact numbers in the address book, nothing on the 'recent calls' list and no saved messages. Maybe they'd never used it. Or maybe they really did wipe it clean after every use.

A waitress came over carrying my breakfast. An omelet, some toast and lots of coffee. She set it down and wandered off again. I loved coffee, sometimes even lived off it. It was probably as close as I got to an addiction. Food didn't appeal to me in the same way as it had once, mainly because eating on your own wasn't fun, but also because I'd become lazy during marriage. Derryn had been an incredible cook, and it had been safer, and tastier, for us both if she made the meals. Since she'd been gone, I tried to have a good breakfast and then usually didn't worry too much about lunch. Maybe a sandwich from a packet, or a salad in a tub. Always a coffee. In the evenings, I ate small and late, usually in front of the news or watching something on DVD.

I filled my mug and, while I waited for the food to cool, started going through the phone again. Dropping it had been a mistake, but a mistake they could probably live with. There was nothing on it that would lead back to them. No incriminating evidence. No numbers. Nothing traceable. But whatever their connection to Alex, they were still warning me off something. Perhaps I was close, perhaps I wasn't, but it was clear I'd made some inroads.

I pulled the pad towards me.

When I'd been inside the flat, the light from the windows had been shining across the surface of the paper. It had highlighted the scars and grooves left from notes that had been made on previous sheets. I asked the waitress for a pencil and gently rubbed the tip of it across the pad. Slowly, words started to emerge. In the top right: *Must phone Vee*. In the middle, lighter and less defined, a series of names: *Paul. Stephen. Zack*. Towards the bottom, barely even legible until I held it right up to the window, was a telephone number.

I picked up my phone and dialled it.

Eventually, someone answered. 'Angel's, Soho.'

I waited, could hear people talking in the background.

'Is this Angel's *pub*?'

'Yeah.'

I waited some more, then hung up.

I gave directory enquiries the number, and they told me the address that was listed for it. It was a pub on the edge of Chinatown. But I knew that even before I'd made the call. During my apprenticeship, I was paired with an old guy called Jacob, an experienced reporter who covered the City. Angel's was his local at the time. He stopped going a couple of years later, after retiring to the Norfolk countryside.

But I didn't.

I continued going right the way up until Derryn got ill.

My car was on the other side of the park. I entered at Hyde Park Corner and headed towards the Serpentine. Everything was quiet. The trees were skeletal and bare; the water in the lake dark and still. The only movement on its surface were two model boats, gliding and drifting, their sails catching the wind. I carried on walking, taken in by the smell and sounds of the place; of the grass covered by a blanket of fallen leaves; of the oaks and elms stripped bare as winter approached.

Kids ran across in front of me, their muddy footprints a reminder of where they'd been and how often. Their parents watched from the side: chatting, laughing, their breath drifting away. It made me ache with loneliness. I remembered the times Derryn and I had talked about wanting a family, about what it would be like to hold our baby for the first time, or walk, hand in hand, with our son or daughter to school. We'd been trying for fifteen months when she got cancer, and – after that – we never got to try again.

Sometimes I remembered the sense of finality as I watched her coffin being lowered into the ground. The feeling that there was no doubt any more; she was gone and she wasn't coming back. I knew, deep down, there was no way Alex could have died in that car crash and still be alive, in the same way I knew there was no way Derryn could be. Yet, when I looked in Mary's eyes, I only saw conviction there, so lucid, as if she had no doubt in what she was telling me. And I knew a small part of me wanted her to be right. I *wanted* Alex to be alive, however impossible it seemed. And the need to find out was driving me on, and, at least temporarily, helping me forget the loneliness.

After days of heavy skies and biting winds, snow finally started falling as I got back to the car. I climbed in, put the heaters on full blast and started scrolling through the numbers on my mobile. When I got to the one I wanted, I hit 'Call'.

'Citizens Advice Bureau.'

I smiled. 'Oh, come *on*.'

'Who's that?' the voice said.

'Citizens *Advice*?'

'*David?*'

'Yeah. How you doing, Spike?'

'Man, it's been *ages*.'

We chatted for a while, catching up. Spike lived in Camden Town and was the dictionary definition of illegal: a Russian hacker on an expired student visa running a cash-only information service out of his flat. During my days on the newspaper, when I still cared about naming and shaming politicians, I used him a lot.

'So, what can I do you for you, man?'

He spoke that form of American-influenced English that a lot of Europeans used, picked up by watching hours of music videos and TV shows.

'I need you to fire up the super computer.'

'Course I can. What you got?'

'A mobile phone – I want to find out who it belongs to. It's got no numbers on it, no address book. If I gave you the serial number and the SIM, could you find out where the phone was bought – maybe who it's registered to?'

'Yeah, no problem. You'll have to give me a couple of hours, though.'

'Sure.'

I gave him all the details and then my phone number.

'Oh, and my fee's gone up a bit,' he said.

'Whatever it takes, Spike.'

I hung up – and, within seconds, the phone was buzzing again. I looked down at the display. JOHN CARY. I'd forgotten to chase him up again.

'John,' I said, answering. 'Sorry I didn't get back to you.'

No response.

'I left a couple of messages.'

'I can't talk for long,' he replied.

'Okay.'

'You still want that photograph looked at?'

'Definitely.'

'Send it to me *at home*. I know a couple of people at the Forensic Science Service, and one of them owes me a favour from a while back. I can ask him to take a look at it.'

'Are you sure?'

'No.' The line drifted. 'But make the most of it.'

'Look, I really appreci–'

'I'm probably making the biggest mistake of my life.'

I didn't know how to respond to that, so I said nothing. But I knew my instincts had been right: what had happened to Alex still ate at him, and a part of him longed for closure.

I killed the call and watched the snow slide down the windscreen, my thoughts turning back to Angel's. The last time I'd ever been inside, the winter had been the same as this one: long and cold, stretching from the beginning of November all the way through to the end of February. Two different times, both connected – like a small part of my past was now merging with the present.

16

Angel's was a thin building, west of Charing Cross Road. Snow was already piling up against the door when I arrived. Next to it, barred like a cell, was a small window. I peered inside. It was dark; a square of white light at the back was all I could make out. Above me were a pair of neon angel's wings, and next to the doorway a sign that said it wasn't open until midday. I looked at my watch. 11.40.

'You're early.'

I turned. 'Woah! Where did you come from?'

A woman was standing behind me, looking me up and down. She was in her mid-forties, pale and boyish, her blonde hair from a bottle, her eyes grey and small. I smiled at her, but she just shook her head. She glanced from the door of the pub to the sky, then pulled her long, fake fur coat tighter around her.

'Come back in twenty minutes.' She started unlocking the door.

'I'm not here to drink.'

She turned to me, disgusted. 'You wanna strip joint, you've come to the wrong place.'

'I'm not here for that either.'

She pushed the door open and stepped into the open doorway. 'You wanna chat?'

'Kind of.'

'This ain't the Samaritans.' She went to push the door closed, but I shoved a foot in next to it and took a step up to the doorway. She didn't look surprised – as if it happened a lot.

'There ain't no money here.'

Her accent was strong. East End.

'Don't worry,' I said. 'I'm not here to rob you.'

She stared at me, then rolled her eyes. 'The Old Bill. Shit, this must be my lucky day.'

'I'm not a police officer either.'

She tossed her coat inside, across one of the tables near the door. 'What do you want?'

'Can I come in?'

'No.'

I rubbed my hands together. 'We'll just freeze to death out here, then.'

She glanced up and down the street as snow settled around us, then looked at me and rolled her eyes. 'Whatever,' she said, sighing, and gestured for me to follow her in.

It had hardly changed since the last time I'd been in. They'd replaced the wallpaper – but nothing else. The room was long and narrow, with a five-pointed cove at the back big enough for a couple of tables, and a jukebox wired up to the far wall.

'So, what's going down, Magnum?' she said.

I turned back to her. She was smiling at her joke. I removed my pad and a pen and set it down on the bar, sliding in at one of the stools. 'What's your name?'

'What's it to you?'

I got out my driver's licence and held it up to her. 'My name's David Raker. I used to be a journalist.'

She frowned, leaned in towards the licence. 'Journalist?'

'Used to be.'

She glanced at me. 'Jade.'

'That's your name?'

'Yeah.'

'Pretty name.'

'Whatever.'

'You're not used to compliments?'

'From good-looking boys like you?' She shook her head. 'No. Last time I had a man tell me my name was pretty, he was twenty stone and had a comb-over that went all the way to his chin.'

I smiled. 'That's my weekend look.'

She went to smile and then it disappeared again, as if she'd reined it back in. She looked me up and down a second time, but didn't say anything.

'So, how long you on for today?' I asked her.

'Till seven.'

'Looking forward to it.'

'Like a hole in the head.'

I fiddled with my notepad. It was a new page. Blank. She walked behind the bar, and leaned across it, staring down at the pad.

'Looks like an interesting story.'

'Could be, yeah.'

'So, what's a journalist want in this shithole?'

I turned on the stool. 'At least this shithole's got new wallpaper since the last time I came in.'

'That a fact?'

'How long you been here?'

'I don't know – six months maybe.'

I noticed a couple of photos on the wall behind me. I got down off the stool and wandered over. One was a picture of a woman I recognized. She was surrounded by a bunch of regulars on New Year's Eve, three years ago. Her name was Evelyn. She worked behind the bar back when I used to come in with Jacob. I'd got to know her pretty well – well enough to tell her a little of my life, and for her to really mean she was sorry when I told her Derryn had cancer.

'Evelyn still around?'

'No.'

I turned back to her. 'When did she leave?'

A flicker of something. 'Dunno.'

I studied her. 'You don't know when she left?'

'It was before my time.'

I walked back to the bar and sat down on the stool again. She didn't look or sound convinced by what she was saying, but I couldn't see a reason for her to lie.

I moved on.

'I'm trying to find someone who might have had a connection with this place. If I show you a picture of him, maybe you could tell me if you've seen him in here or not.'

She nodded. I took out a picture Mary had given

me of Alex and handed it to her. She squinted at it, as if she was a little short-sighted.

'What's his name?' she asked.

'Alex Towne.'

Her eyes flicked to me across the top of the photo. 'You know him?'

She took a moment more, then handed the photo back to me. 'No.'

'You sure?'

'Course I'm sure.'

In my top pocket I had a list of names, taken from the pad in the apartment at Eagle Heights. I unfolded it.

'You got any regulars with names like these?'

I'd rewritten the names on a separate piece of paper, one under the other. She read down the list and shrugged. 'Probably.'

'You do or you don't?'

'How the fuck am I supposed to know?' she said. 'This ain't exactly the Ritz, I know, but this place gets busy. Lotta people comin' and goin'.'

I took the list back. 'I'll take that as a no.'

'For someone who's not a copper, you ask a lot of questions, Magnum.'

'Just interested,' I said, and looked around the pub again.

Something didn't feel right about what Jade had said. Either she knew when Evelyn left or she didn't. And there was something else too. Her eyes had moved when I'd first handed her the picture of Alex, and her skin had flushed. I'd read books back when I first started getting big interviews on the paper, about kinesics and how to interpret body language. Pupil dilation, skin flushing and changes in muscle tone were all unconscious responses to lying.

I turned back to her. She looked suspicious now, unsure about what I was doing. Maybe it was a natural suspicion, built up from her hours working in here. Or maybe she really was lying to me, and was starting to think I'd seen through it.

Suddenly, the door to the pub opened. We both looked round as a couple of old men came in talking. One of them laughed and glanced towards the bar.

'Morning, Jade. Are we too early?'

She looked at me, then back to them.

'No, Harry.'

They shuffled up to the bar. One of them slid in at a stool and started fiddling in his pockets for change; the other stood next to him and eyed up the beers on tap. When they were finished, they both glanced at the photograph of Alex, and then at me.

'Morning,' Harry said.

I nodded at both of them, then turned to Jade. 'Is Alex Towne alive?'

For a second I thought I saw something in her face, before she moved to the back of the bar and picked up two empty pint glasses.

'Jade?'

The two men looked between us.

She started filling one of the glasses, pulling on the pump and looking straight at me – as if proving she had nothing to hide. When she was done with the first beer, she duplicated the movement for the second.

'You okay, Jade?' Harry said.

She nodded.

The old men looked between us again, trying to figure out if I was bothering her. They probably already knew what I'd found out in the ten minutes I'd been talking to her: Jade couldn't be pushed around, and wouldn't be intimidated – at least not while she was inside the safety of the pub.

I scooped up the notepad and the photo and left. But that wasn't the end of it. I'd be back at seven when she came off her shift – and this time she wouldn't see me coming.

17

St John the Baptist church was in Redbridge, a depressing pocket of London close to the North Circular. Ugly, fading tower blocks cast shadows across the streets; melting snow ran from holes in the flyover; black exhaust fumes disappeared into the sky. As I parked the car, half-hidden behind an Indian takeaway, the church's triangular roof rose out of the grey.

Despite the setting, it was an attractive, modern building: all cream walls and exposed beams. A huge crucifix hung above the door, beautifully carved from wood. Christ looked down from the centre of the cross, a glimmer of hope in his face.

The main doors were locked, so I walked around to the back. A door marked OFFICE was partly open. Through the gap, I could see an empty room, with a series of desks and a bookcase at the back. I glanced along the side of the church. Further down was a small annexe. The door to that was open too.

I headed for it.

The structure was about fifteen feet by twenty feet; really just a glorified shed. There were no windows, and its exterior hadn't been treated properly, so the wood was still a raw orange colour. Inside it was sparse: a couple of posters, a desk, a power lead for a laptop that wasn't there, a pad, some pens. There was a bookshelf, high up behind the desk, stacked with Bibles, biographies and reference material.

'Morning.'

A voice from behind me.

It was a young guy, a silver laptop under his arm, dressed in a casual shirt and a pair of jeans. Early thirties, blond shoulder-length hair, parted in the centre, and the eyes to match: big, bright, alive. He smiled as he stepped forward.

'Morning,' I said. 'I'm looking for the minister here.'

'Well, it must be your lucky day,' he replied. He took another step towards me and held out his hand. We shook. 'Reverend Michael Tilton.'

'David Raker.'

'Nice to meet you. You're not a Bible salesman, are you?'

I smiled. 'No. Don't worry – you're safe.'

'Ah good!' he said, and stepped past me into the annexe. 'Sorry about the mess in here. I've got a youth pastor starting in a few weeks and I'm trying to get things in shape before he arrives. Except, at the moment, it's just a dumping ground for all my stuff.'

He set the laptop down then slid a small heater out from under his desk and turned the dial all the way up to ten. He closed the door.

'Pretty humble surroundings, huh?'

There was only one chair, but a couple of removal crates were lying in the corner. He dragged the crates across towards me.

'And sorry about the seat too. You're our first visitor in here.'

I sat down. 'This place looks new.'

'Yeah, it is,' he said. 'We finished it in October. It's a temporary home for my youth pastor while we raise some money to build an extension on the church.'

He sat down at his desk and glanced at his laptop. On-screen, I could see a password prompt.

'Well, I won't take up too much of your day, Reverend Tilton,' I said, and got out the photograph of Alex.

'Call me Michael, please.'

I nodded, placing the picture down on the desk in front of him. 'I'm looking into the disappearance of someone who might have visited you here at one time.'

'Okay. This is him?'

'His name was Alex Towne.'

Michael picked up the photograph and studied it. 'I'm trying to think,' he said. 'I'm sure I haven't seen him around – not in the last couple of months, anyway.'

'It won't have been in the last few months.'

'Oh?'

'Here's the real killer: it would be more like six years ago.'

Michael looked up to see if I was being serious. 'Really?'

'Unfortunately, yes.'

He looked at the photograph again. 'How old is he?'

'He'd be about twenty-eight now.'

'So, would he have been part of our Twenties group?'

'I'm not sure he came to this church regularly. It could have been just once, it could have been a few times. He had some connection with your church – but I haven't been able to figure out what yet.'

He gritted his teeth. 'I remember most of the youth quite clearly – I used to be the youth pastor here myself – but . . .'

As he continued looking at it, I took out the birthday card.

'This is the connection,' I said, flipping it over so he could see the sticker on the back. 'It was a card he bought here, and it says it was made by a woman called Angela Routledge. Is she still around?'

His expression dropped. 'Angela died a couple of years ago.'

'Anyone else who might remember selling these cards?'

Michael thought about it – but not for long.

'Angela ran the card stall on her own. She did it all on her own. Got the materials, made the cards, did everything herself. She was an extraordinary woman. She raised a lot of money for us. It's because of people like her that we have blessings like this.'

He meant the annexe.

'Wait a minute,' he said, picking up the photograph again. 'Can I borrow this photograph for a couple of minutes?'

'Sure.'

'I used to draft in a friend of mine for the youth

meetings. Let me go and call him and see if he remembers your guy.'

'You can borrow my phone if you like.'

'No, it's fine. I left my mobile inside, and I should probably lock up the church if I'm going to be out here.' He pointed at the picture. 'What did you say his name was?'

'Alex Towne.'

He nodded. 'I won't be long.'

He stepped past me and headed towards the church.

I sat for a while on the edge of the crates, looking out through the door. Snow slid down the roof of the main church and spilled out over the drainpipe.

My phone started ringing.

'David Raker.'

'David, it's Spike.'

'Spike – what you got for me?'

I could hear him using a keyboard. 'Okay, so the mobile phone was bought in a place called Mobile Network, three weeks ago. It's on an industrial estate in Bow. I'm guessing it's some kind of wholesaler, working out of a warehouse.'

'Okay.'

'You got a pen?'

I looked around. There was one on Michael's desk.

'Yeah – shoot.'

'The phone's registered to a Gary Hooper.'

'Hooper?'

'Yeah.'

I wrote *Gary Hooper* on the back of my hand.

'I don't know whether that's any help.'

'That's great.'

'I've got a statement here too.'

'Perfect.'

'Looks like the phone's hardly been used. There have only been three calls on it in the past three weeks. Do you want me to read the numbers out?'

'Yeah.'

He read them out, and I wrote them under *Gary Hooper*.

The first two numbers I didn't recognize. The third I definitely did. It was the number for Angel's.

'Spike, you're the magic man. I'll get you the money later.'

'You got it.'

I killed the call, and immediately tried the numbers I didn't recognize.

On the first, an answerphone kicked in after three rings. 'Hi, this is Gerald. Leave a message and I'll get back to you.' I hung up and wrote the name *Gerald* down.

As I was putting in the second number, Michael returned. He placed his phone down on the desk and turned to me. His expression said everything.

'Sorry,' he said, handing me the photograph of Alex. 'My friend doesn't know him either. It's hard to describe how your guy looks over the phone, but I could probably list every member of our youth group over the past seven years, and Alex . . . well, he isn't one of them. I'm really sorry. I hope I haven't spoiled your day.'

'No, don't worry. I appreciate your efforts.'

I glanced down at his phone. On the display it said: LAST CALL: LAZARUS — LANDLINE. He smiled at me again, then scooped up the phone.

'Is there anything else?'

'No, that's fine,' I replied. I shook his hand and stepped out into the snow. 'Thanks for your help.' And then I headed back to the car, letting the cold bite at my skin.

The traffic was terrible as I made my way back into the centre of London. The deeper I got into the city, the slower things became, until finally everything ground to a halt. I watched the snow continue to fall, settling in thick mounds on chimneys and street lights, road signs and rooftops.

Nothing moved but the weather.

After a while, I popped my phone in the hands-free cradle and punched in the second number. It clicked and connected, but no one picked up. I left it for about a minute and, when it was obvious no one was home, reached over to end the call.

Then someone answered.

A voice I recognized.

'St John the Baptist.'

It was Michael Tilton.

18

I posted the Polaroid of Alex to Cary, and then made my way back towards Soho. By the time I was parked, it was almost seven o'clock – and the end of Jade's shift. After buying myself a coffee I found a spot in the shadows, across the street from Angel's. I didn't want to scare her, but if she saw me straight away, she'd probably disappear back inside. That was her safety net.

Laughter sounded nearby.

A couple, dressed in business suits, stumbled into a nearby restaurant. Opposite, a group of teenaged girls giggled and stopped outside the pub. They looked at each other. One played with her hair; another adjusted her skirt. Then they all reached into their bags for fake ID.

From inside, probably fresh on the evening shift, came one of the barmen, emptying an ice bucket into the gutter. I backed up, further into the shadows. He registered the movement and glanced across the street, eyes narrowing, head tilting. He lingered for a second more, as if trying to satisfy his curiosity, before disappearing back inside.

The street quietened. More snow started to fall.

I sipped at the coffee.

The lull was disturbed by a group of women, out on a hen night, moving along the street. Behind them, a man followed close by, his boots dragging in the slush. Some of the women looked over their shoulders at him – a look that suggested that if they'd been on their own, somewhere less populated, they might have been worried. He dropped back a little as they passed the front of Angel's, his face disappearing into his coat, but then, when he was past the entrance, he speeded up once more. Some of the girls at the back of the group flicked a look at him again; one of them – fired up with alcohol – turned and asked, 'What's your fuckin' problem?' But the argument fizzled out when she saw his attention was no longer focused on them or where they were headed. He was looking across the street.

Right at me.

Our eyes locked for a split second and he seemed to hesitate. But then he tagged on to the group again, breaking into a jog and eventually passing them. When he was clear, he looked up ahead to where the road split.

Something stirred in me. A memory.

By the time he started disappearing west, parallel to Chinatown, it had come to me: *the guy who broke into my car at the cemetery.*

He looked back, saw I was still watching him, and quickened his pace. I tossed the coffee aside and followed. He turned right at the end of the street, then started moving through the crowds working their way down towards Shaftesbury Avenue. It was packed. Shops were still open. Restaurants were luring people in. A queue from a theatre curved out and along the pavement towards me.

He glanced back again, bumped into someone and then upped his pace, disappearing into a crowd of tourists. I headed after him, to where the group – gathering around a tour guide – were blocking the pavement. He emerged the other side and crossed the street.

Then he broke into a run.

Forcing my way through the crowd, I could see him barging through another group of tourists further down. One of them stumbled as he pushed past. Her husband called after him. But when he looked back, it wasn't to apologize. It was to see how close I was.

I tried to move faster, put my head down for a second, and lost him. He'd gone behind a theatre queue. I crossed the street. There was a back alley close to the queue, black and narrow. Steam hissed out of a vent high up on one of the walls. As I got closer, he burst out from a knot of people about halfway down, glanced at me once, then disappeared into the alley.

The darkness sucked him up.

When I got to the mouth of the alley, I could only hear the echo of footsteps at first. Then he emerged from the shadows, partially lit by a window above. I started down the alley after him. He was a long way ahead of me, almost on to the next street. He stopped when he got there. Looked back. And then disappeared out of sight.

By the time I'd got to the end, he was gone. I stood for a moment, looking both ways. There were crowds on both sides of the street, and cars passing along it. And there were shadows everywhere, doorways to disappear in, tiny vessels of lanes and alleys. Slices of night that would hide him for as long as he needed.

I looked at my watch. Ten minutes past seven.

A thought hit me. Maybe this was the point: they were luring me away from Angel's so I couldn't get at Jade. Tricking me. Manipulating me. Maybe the barman had glimpsed me in the shadows out front after all, and gone in and raised the alarm.

But then I stopped dead.

About a quarter of a mile down on my left, Jade was crossing the road. She looked both ways, a cigarette glowing between her fingers, and moved off in the opposite direction. I hesitated, suddenly unsure it was her.

But it was.

It was Jade.

I followed her, keeping to the other side of the street, moving in and out of the pools of light cast by the street lamps. When I drew level with the alley she'd emerged from, I looked along it and saw a big green door, partially open. Above it were a pair of neon angel's wings. She'd left through the rear entrance – which meant they knew I was waiting.

So why lead me back to where Jade would come out of?

Because it's a trap.

I hesitated.

What if it was? What if the first guy had led me here and now Jade had been told to lead me somewhere else? What if that phone call outside Eagle Heights *had* been my one chance to walk away? The one chance I hadn't taken.

She disappeared from sight at the end of the road.

I stood there, frozen to the spot, uncertainty pumping through my veins. Something flooded my chest, a sense that I'd been here before, in the first few weeks after Derryn's death: standing on the edge of a precipice, watching the ground crumble beneath my feet.

But then I saw my reflection in a nearby shop window and realized how much direction this case had brought to my life, the energy it had returned to me. And I understood that if I wanted to carry on moving forward, this was something I had to do. A step I had to take.

So, I went after her.

When I got to the end of the road, I saw Jade about forty yards along a street to the right. She was crossing the road and heading for a thin sliver of back street, partially lit. There was a restaurant on the corner, its front decorated in tinsel and Christmas trees. Otherwise it was another London back alley full of exit doors and second-floor windows.

I caught up quickly, and then slowed as I got closer to her.

'Jade?'

She stopped and turned. She couldn't see me to start with, then I moved out of the dark and under the light of a Christmas tree.

Her face dropped. She sunk her hands into the pockets of her fur coat: a reflex action. She felt threatened by me. Maybe she hadn't actually been leading me anywhere.

I held up a hand. 'I'm not going to hurt you.'

She didn't reply. Her eyes darted left and right.

'I just want to talk to you.'

She nodded, slowly.

'Were you leading me somewhere?'

Her face creased a little. A frown. 'I was tryin' to get *away* from you.'

'Why?'

''Cos you're trouble.'

'You knew I was coming?'

She nodded. 'One of the guys saw you out front.'

The barman. I'd been right.

'What was the point of the decoy?'

She frowned again.

'The scruffy guy,' I said.

Her expression didn't change.

'The guy who led me to you. What was the point of that?'

She shrugged and looked away. But when she turned back, her expression had changed to a kind of relief, as if she'd just reached the biggest decision of her life.

'What d'you want with me?'

'I just want to talk.'

She shrugged again, and nodded. 'Then we talk.'

Her eyes got darker as we walked; harder to read. I tried to figure out whether she was scared, or confident, or both, but I gave up as we got to the car. Men were probably drawn to her suddenly and easily – but left just as quickly when they realized she'd never let them in.

'Is this what you drive?' she asked, looking at the BMW.

'This is it.'

'I thought you'd have something better.'

'I'm not *really* Magnum, Jade.'

She glanced inside, then back at me, as if anticipating the question to come.

'So, what's going on?' I said.

'Can't we go somewhere?'

'Where do you want to go?'

'I'm hungry.'

'Okay.'

We got into the car, and I started it up.

'What's on the menu?'

'Cheeseburgers.'

'Where?'

She smiled. 'If you're paying, there's a place I know.'

19

We headed east, past the shells of old stadiums and storage yards. Everything was dark, almost decaying, as if the city were slowly dying. Tightly packed housing estates emerged from the night, lonely and deserted, windows dark, street lamps flickering on and off.

'Where are we going?'

'It's near,' she said, staring out of the window.

I looked at the clock. 8.34.

'Will they still be serving?'

She didn't say anything.

'Jade?'

She glanced at me, then shifted in her seat. 'You lost someone, Magnum?'

'Huh?'

'You lost someone?'

'What do you mean?'

Her eyes caught the light again, her expression perfectly still. 'You're sad.'

I didn't reply. Didn't want to. But I needed her – more than she needed me. She had turned away from me now, her face reflected in the glass.

'I lost my wife.'

'How?'

'She got cancer.'

She nodded. 'What was her name?'

'Derryn.'

She nodded again, looking out of the window. 'What was she like?'

'She was my wife,' I said. 'I thought she was amazing.'

We drove for about half a mile more, then she told me to take a left. Out of the dark came huge blocks of flats, wrapped in the night.

'What do you miss most?'

'About Derryn?'

She nodded.

I thought about it. 'I miss talking to her.'

The restaurant, Strawberry's, was an old carriage set inside a series of railway arches. A blue neon sign that said HOT FOOD buzzed above a serving hatch. We got out of the car and Jade led me to one of the tables out front. There were seven of them. Each one had a heater attached, their orange glow lighting the yard in front of the carriage. There was a couple on the table furthest away from us. Apart from that it was empty.

'Didn't realize we were going à la carte,' I said.

Jade ignored me and sat down. She reached into the pockets of her coat, trying to find her cigarettes, and laid the contents out on the table: keys, a wallet, an ATM statement, some cash, a photo which she placed face down. It had writing on the back: *this is the reason we do it*. She found her cigarettes, removed one and popped it between her lips.

'Get the burger with everythin' on,' she said.

I nodded. 'This a favourite haunt of yours?'

'In a previous life,' she said. 'I used to come with my mum and dad. They loved places like this. Places with personality.' She turned and pointed at the carriage. 'They used to have a guy called Stevie runnin' it back when it was called Rafferty's. He liked my mum and dad. Always cooked somethin' special for them.'

'Your parents still around?'

A pause. Then she shook her head.

The heater was pumping out plenty of warmth. Jade removed her coat, lit her cigarette and looked at me. 'So, what's your story, Magnum?'

'I'm not a PI, Jade.'

She smirked. 'But you *want* to be one.'

'Do I?'

'You're actin' like one.'

A woman emerged from the carriage wearing a retro waitress's uniform, a name badge that said *Strawberry's* and a face that could turn a man to stone.

'What can I get you?' she barked.

'Two burgers with everythin' on,' Jade replied. 'I'll have a beer. Magnum?'

I looked at the waitress. 'A big coffee. Black.'

The waitress disappeared again. Jade and I stared at each other. Light from the heater glinted in her eyes, making her seem mischievous. Then she started to put the things she'd laid out on the table back into her pockets.

'That your mum and dad?' I asked her.

She followed my finger. I was pointing at the photo.

She picked it up and turned it over. It was a picture of a young kid, perhaps five or six. The photograph was old, discoloured. The boy was running across a patch of grass, kicking a football about. To the left of him was a wire fence. To the right, almost out of picture, a block of flats and a sign.

Eagle Heights.

'I know that place,' I said.

She didn't say anything, hardly even moved.

'Who's the boy?'

She glanced at the picture. '"This is the reason we do it",' she said.

'What does that mean?'

She smiled. 'I'd tell you if I knew. But I don't. I don't know what that means. But I know what the boy represents.'

'What's that?'

'Making a difference.'

'Making a difference?'

'What's that sayin'? Uh . . .' She took a drag on her cigarette and stared off into the night, blowing a flute of smoke out into the chill of the evening. 'The end justifies the means.'

'Okay.'

'That's what this is.'

'You've lost me, Jade.'

She nodded, as if she hadn't expected me to keep up, then pulled the photo back across the table towards her. 'You ever had to keep somethin' secret?'

'Sure.'

'I don't mean no birthday present.'

'Neither do I.'

'So, what secret have you had to keep?'

'I worked in Israel, in South Africa, in Iraq.'

'So?'

'I saw things in those places I'll never forget.'

'What sorta things?'

I thought of Derryn, of keeping my work away from her. The things I saw. The bodies I stepped over.

'What sorta things?' she repeated.

'Things I could never bring home to my wife.'

The waitress returned with our drinks.

'Come on, Magnum. You're gonna have to try harder than that.'

'I'm not playing this game with you.'

'It's not a game, it's a trade.'

'I'm not trading with you.'

'Why not?'

'We didn't come here to trade. That wasn't the agreement.'

'I don't remember makin' no agreement.'

She put the cigarette between her lips and took a drag.

'I shouldn't really be smokin' these,' she said. 'But I guess we all have our demons.' She pressed a thumb against her lips, knowing and playful, and then a small smile escaped. 'You follow this little project of yours any further, you're gonna have to face down a few demons of your own.'

'What are you talking about?'

'I'm talkin' about what you're gonna find if you get to the end . . .' She turned her beer bottle around. 'I guess mostly I'm talkin' about the fact that, if you're not strong in this life, you fail. And I'm about to fail, Magnum – 'cause I'm tired.'

'Of what?'

'Runnin'. Lyin'. Startin' again.'

'What do you mean, starting again?'

'I mean, you won't find anythin' at Angel's now. Everyone associated with it as of now will be gone. You askin' questions, that just makes it harder for you. You go back, it'll be new people. It'll have all changed.'

'Why?'

'Why d'you think?'

I paused. 'The bar's a front.'

She clicked her fingers and smiled.

'For what?'

'It helps us do what we *really* want to do. It makes money for us. It pays our way.'

'You own it?'

'Not me.'

'Who?'

She picked up the statement from the table and opened it, placing it down in front of me. The bank account belonged to Angel's. There were two pages of listings, but about halfway down was a direct debit payment: CALVARY PRO. 5000.00.

The Calvary Project.

Every month, Angel's was paying five grand to a company the Inland Revenue didn't know existed.

'There's a paper trail half a mile long,' she said, pre-empting the question I was about to ask. 'You'd be wandering in the dark, lost like a puppy dog, trying to find out *anything* about that company.'

The waitress arrived with our meals. Jade didn't waste any time, biting down on the burger, juice bubbling beneath the bun.

'So, where will everyone from the pub go?' I asked her.

'The others . . . I don't know. I don't make those decisions.'

'What about you?'

She paused. 'I'm not going back. I can't now.'

'Why?'

'I'm sittin' here with you – why d'you think?'

'So, where are you going to go?'

She shrugged.

I thought of the numbers Spike had got me.

'Who makes the decisions, then? This Gerald guy?'

She started laughing, almost choking on her food. '*Gerald?*'

'Yeah.'

'No. Not Gerald.'

'Who's he?'

'Gerald doesn't even know we exist. Gerald's just a crook, living in some shithole in Camberwell. I just go to him for . . .' She paused. 'Identity changes.'

'Fake ID.'

She winked. 'You're good, Magnum.'

She took another bite of her burger.

'For you?'

'For all of us.'

'Who's us?'

She smiled. 'You could be a good copper. You ask the right questions. But you realize the whole reason we're sittin' here now isn't because you're good, but because we made mistakes. Droppin' that mobile phone like that, that was a stupid, careless thing to do. Thing is, Jason didn't expect you to turn up like that. He got jumpy.'

'So, who's Gary Hooper?'

'He's no one.'

'The phone your guy Jason dropped is registered to Gary Hooper.'

'My phone's registered to Matilda Wilkins. That don't make me her.'

'So, who is he?'

'I told you – he ain't no one. He's a ghost. You'll be chasin' your tail all fuckin' day with that one. It's just a name. Just another lie.' I watched her push some fries around her plate. 'I hate to disappoint you, Magnum, but what you have here –' she gestured to herself '– is a foot soldier, not a general.'

'Who's Vee?'

'Vee?'

'Jason – he asked for Vee. What's that short for? Veronica?'

She looked at me and suddenly became serious. 'I'm gonna tell you what I know,' she started quietly. 'I'm gonna tell you what I know because I'm tired of runnin'. I'm tired of havin' to start again when people like you start puttin' their fuckin' beaks where they don't belong. I'm tired of lyin' to protect somethin' I don't . . .' She stopped. Her eyes narrowed. 'Look, first, forget Gerald – he don't know nothin'. Forget Vee too. That's just a stage name. And forget the Calvary Project. That won't lead nowhere but more made-up shit.'

'What does it do?'

'What do you think it does?'

'I don't think it does anything. You just pass money through it.'

'It's a means of protection.'

'So you can launder money.'

'*Launder* money?' She smiled. 'This ain't the mafia.'

'So the Calvary Project only exists in name?'

She opened a wallet and took out a credit card. 'All our money comes and goes through it. All our cards are registered to it. It buys our food and our clothes.'

'So none of the purchases can be traced back to you.'

'Right.' She turned the card over. Company Barclaycard. MISS MATILDA WILKINS was printed at the bottom. 'Jade ain't bought a pair of shoes in years.'

'This Michael guy, at the church – what's he got to do with it?'

'I don't know much about that.'

'So, tell me what you *do* know.'

'The church is where he recruits people.'

'Michael?'

140

She nodded.

'What do you mean, "recruits"?'

'Helps them to start again. Sells 'em an idea.'

Selling ideas.

Suddenly, from the darkness of my memory, a face stepped out: the guy with the tattoo in Cornwall. *My friend's a salesman,* he'd said. *Sells ideas to people.* I looked at Jade. She was picking at her food.

'Who's the guy with the tattoo on his arm?'

She shot me a look – a sudden, jerking movement like she'd just been punched. Her eyes widened, her face lost colour. She was trying to work out how I'd made the connection.

'Walk away from that,' she said quietly.

'From what?'

'From him.'

'Who is he?'

She paused, ran her tongue around her mouth, then jabbed a finger at the photograph of the boy. 'He'll protect what that represents above all else. He will go to the ends of the earth to do it. If you can get what you need and get the fuck out without him seeing, then you should do that. Because the only other way to stop him would be to bring the whole thing down.'

'Bring it down?'

'The house of cards.'

'You mean your organization?'

She nodded. 'But I think it might be too late for that.'

'Why?'

'They know who you are. They warned you off once. That's what they do. They give you a chance. But you coming to the bar this morning, going to the church like you did . . . They only give you one warning.'

'So what happens next?'

'What happens next?' She paused, looked at me, and we both understood the silence. My heart dropped. *You know what happens next, Magnum.*

'Why?'

'Why d'you think?'

'Alex?'

She took a sip of beer, didn't answer.

'*Jade?*'

I could hear myself getting impatient. She was still protecting the cause. Still dancing around my questions, even while she was telling me she wanted out. A part of her wanted to break free. But another part of her was so deeply attached to her life, she felt scared about letting go. And she was terrified about the consequences.

'Why help me?' I said.

'Because this whole thing's outta control.' She looked at me. Brushed food away from her mouth. 'We've been careless.'

'Who's we?'

She didn't reply.

'Jade?'

'We. Us.' She paused. '*Him.*'

'Who?'

She glanced at the photograph of the boy, still out on the table.

'The boy?' I asked her.

'No,' she said quietly. 'His father.'

'The man with the tattoo?'

She was teetering. Unsure whether to commit.

'Jade?'

'No, not the man with the tattoo.'

'Who then?'

'The boy's father . . .' She stopped, looked at me. Something glistened in her eyes. 'I think, in some ways, he's even worse.'

'Who's the boy's father?'

'You've pissed him off.'

'Who is he, Jade?'

'You've *really* pissed him off. But maybe it's happening for a reason. I'm not sure I believe in him any more, in what he's fighting for and the way he's fighting it.' She stopped, a sadness in her eyes, then looked up at the sky. 'And I'm not sure He does either.'

I followed her gaze.

'*He?* What is this – some sort of mission from *God*?'

She didn't reply, but I could tell I'd hit on something. She picked up the statement and the photograph.

'Jade?'

She pushed her plate aside. 'I need to pee.'

And then she was gone, weaving between the tables. She passed the serving hatch, scooped up what looked like a napkin, and headed towards a toilet block next to the carriage. She looked back once, then walked around to the door and out of sight.

I gave it eight minutes. The thought that Jade might try to escape crossed my mind the instant she left the table. I slid out and headed to the toilet block.

It was a dumping ground at the back – drinks cans, carrier bags, a shopping trolley, needles. Beyond, the railway arches continued, gradually melting into the night. I could see one of the windows was open, and there was a crack in it, top to bottom. I looked at it more closely. In the middle of the crack, about three-quarters of the way up, something had been smeared across it, on the inside of the glass.

'Jade?'

The door to the women's toilet was open, swinging in the wind coming in off the arches. Inside, the light was on, and I could see blood spatters on one of the walls closest to the door.

I stepped inside.

Jade was slumped against one of the cubicle doors, her head tilted sideways. Her fingers were wrapped around the steak knife that had come with her burger, the blade streaked in blood. The cuts in her wrists were deep and long, and her lifeblood was still chugging out of them, on to her hands, her clothes, the floor.

I backed away, watching a fresh trail of blood carve down one of the cubicle doors, then turned and looked out towards the arches. They were big mouths of darkness that sucked the noise out of the night.

And in them I saw something that made me pause: that Jade would rather kill herself than face the consequences of walking away from her organization. Rather die than stand in front of the people she worked for.

The breeze picked up again, and – faintly – I heard a noise, like paper flapping. I looked down at her body. Beneath one of her hands, half-hidden by her balled fingers, was a piece of card. I leaned over, took it from her grasp and pocketed it.

Then I got out my phone and called the police.

20

The police arrived at Strawberry's ten minutes after I called. There were two of them: Jones and Hilton. Jones was about sixty-five, while Hilton was much younger, nervous, reeking of inexperience. It might even have been his first night on the job. He held up pretty well when Jones beckoned him to the toilet block, both of them kneeling down to look at Jade's pale body.

They drove me to a station in Dagenham. Taking my statement didn't last long. It was obvious Jones didn't believe I'd killed her. Witnesses at the restaurant backed up my account of what had happened. When he asked me why we were there I told him the truth, or a version of it. I knew her, wanted to talk to her and she'd agreed as long as I drove her to her favourite restaurant.

'You get what you wanted?' he said.

'I don't know. Maybe.'

Jones shook his head. 'Hope she paid for the petrol.'

I got the feeling he was so close to retirement he could smell it. Any case that wanted to stick around wasn't going to be one of his. That suited me fine. If he'd been a couple of years younger, I might have got a rougher ride. He told me they'd have to keep my

BMW for a while, as well as my clothes, and that they'd want to speak to me again once the coroner had looked at the body.

'That might be a couple of days,' Jones said, 'but I wouldn't bank on it. More likely you won't be hearing anything from us until the new year.'

After that, he showed me the door.

Liz arrived about forty minutes later. She was the only person I knew who would be up at one in the morning. Perhaps the only person I could turn to in an emergency now. After Derryn died, people stuck close to me for a while. Cooked things, offered advice, sat with me in the still of the house. I had no family left, so I relied on colleagues from my newspaper days, on friends of my parents, on people Derryn had known. Most of them were very good to me – but most of them eventually grew tired of babysitting the sad man. At the end of it all, Liz was the only one left. And the irony was she never even got to meet Derryn.

On the phone I told her where she could find the spare key, and asked her to get some clothes for me. Jones lent me a pair of police-issue trousers and a training top while I waited. When she arrived, she handed me a pair of jeans, a T-shirt and a coat and I changed in an empty locker room at the back of the station. She waited next to the front desk, dressed in tracksuit trousers and a zip-up training top.

'You okay?' she asked when I finally emerged again.

I nodded. 'I'm fine. Let's get out of here.'

We walked to her Mercedes, parked around the corner from the station. Inside she turned the heaters on full blast and handed me a takeaway coffee from a cardboard carton. Steam rose out of a small hole in the plastic covering.

'I popped into the petrol station on the way over. Thought you might want an energy injection. Black, no sugar.' She paused. 'Just how you like it.'

I smiled. 'Thanks.'

She pulled out, and we drove for a while.

'I appreciate this, Liz.'

She nodded. 'You going to tell me what happened?'

I glanced at her. She looked back. She had a dusting of make-up on. Maybe she hadn't taken it off after work. Or maybe she'd just put it on before she came out. Either way, she looked really good. And, as her perfume filled the car, I felt a momentary connection to her. A buzz. I looked away, out into the night, and tried to imagine where the feeling had come from. It had been a long day. A traumatic one. Perhaps it was just the relief of going home. Or perhaps, for a second, I realized how alone I was again.

'David?'

I turned back to her. 'Things got a bit messy today.'

'With a case?'

I nodded.

'Are you in trouble?'

'No.'

'Are you sure?'

We stopped at some traffic lights. Red light filled the front of the car, and was reflected in her eyes as she looked at me. In front of us was the glow of London City airport.

'David?'

'I'm fine,' I said. 'Honestly.'

Her eyes moved across my face. 'Because if you're in trouble, I can help you.'

'I know.'

'I'm a lawyer. It's my job. I can *help* you, David.'

There was a brief pause. Something passed between us; something unspoken. And then the feeling came again. An ache in the pit of my stomach.

'Whatever you need,' she said quietly.

I nodded again.

'You don't have to do everything on your own.'

You don't have to be lonely.

I looked at her. She leaned into me a little, her perfume coming with it. The fingers of her hand brushed against my leg. *Whatever you need.* Her eyes were dark and serious.

'I can help you,' she said, almost a whisper.

She leaned in even closer. My heart shifted in my chest, like an animal waking from hibernation. I moved towards her.

'I need . . .'

I thought of Derryn, of her grave. *It's too soon.* Liz was so close to me I could feel her breath on my face.

'What?' she said. 'Tell me what you need.'

The lights changed. I looked at them, then back to her. The roads were empty. Behind us there was nothing but dark, cavernous warehouses. Her eyes were still fixed on me.

'I just . . .'

She studied me – and something changed. She nodded slowly. Then she moved away, slipped the car into first and took off.

'Liz, I just–'

'I know.'

'It's not that I–'

'I know,' she repeated, and glanced at me. One of her eyes glistened. 'You don't need to explain, David. I understand.'

I looked at her, my eyes wandering down her body. *You don't have to be lonely.* Her breasts. Her waist. Her legs. When I looked up again, she was staring at me.

It's too soon.

'I don't know what I think,' I said quietly.

She nodded. 'I understand.'

'Some days . . .' I paused. She turned to me again, her face partially lit in the glow from the streets. 'Some days it's what I want.'

She nodded again.

'But some days . . .'

'I'm not going anywhere,' she said gently, and her fingers touched my leg again. 'I can help you, David.'

'I know.'

'When you're ready, I can help you.'

*

When I got home, I took out the card Jade had left for me. Blood was spattered across it, her finger-prints marking the corners. It was headed with the Strawberry's logo. I thought she'd taken a napkin, but she'd picked up one of the restaurant's business cards instead.

Inside the *b* of the restaurant's name was a burger; the lines of the *t* were fries. And in the middle, in shaky handwriting, was '*Jade O'Connell, 1 March, Mile End*'.

21

I fell asleep at three-thirty and woke again at four. The TV was on mute. An empty coffee mug sat on the floor next to the sofa, the remote control resting on top of it. I turned off the TV, picked up the mug and took it through to the kitchen.

That was when I noticed the security light was on.

I stepped up to the kitchen window and looked out into the night. Footsteps led all the way up to the house, one after another in the snow. Then up to the porch, and around to the side of the house.

None of them were mine.

I put the mug down on the counter and walked back through the house to the bedroom. The curtains weren't quite drawn. Outside, I could see a trail of footprints right in front of the windows, running parallel to the house, and U-turning at the end and coming back on themselves.

Then: a noise.

Somewhere inside the house.

Swivelling, I looked across the darkness of the bedroom. All I could hear now was snow dripping from the gutters. I edged towards the bedroom door and along the hallway.

Click.

The same noise for a second time.

Is that the door?

I tried to remember what the front door sounded like when I opened and closed it, tried to remember *anything* about *any* of the noises the house made. But as I looked along the hallway and waited for the sound to come again, all I could hear was silence.

Maybe it's an animal.

Liz had a cat. It set the light off all the time.

Click.

The noise again.

And this time something moved: the handle of the front door.

For a split second, it felt like the soles of my feet were glued to every fibre of the carpet. Then, as I fixed my gaze on the handle, it moved again: slowly, quietly, tilting downwards until it couldn't go any further. The door started to come away from the frame. If I'd been asleep, I wouldn't have heard a thing.

The door opened all the way. The security light leaked a square of yellow light across the hallway, but nothing else: no movement, no shadows, no sounds.

Then a man stepped into the house.

He was dressed head to toe in black, looking into the darkness of the living room, his back turned towards me. On the top of his head was a mask. He pulled it down over his face, felt around in his belt for something – and then turned and looked down the hallway towards me. I stepped back into the bedroom, my back against the wall.

Oh, shit.

In the light I could see he'd had a gun, silencer attached. And on his face was a plastic Hallowe'en mask. Eyeless. Mouthless. Unmoving. Staring down the hallway and looking for me in the darkness had been the devil.

I turned back to the bedroom.

Two stand-alone wardrobes, full of clothes and shoes. A bookcase. A dresser. The door into the ensuite. No hiding places. No weapons to hand. Nothing to fight back with.

Click.

A noise from the hallway.

He's coming.

The door into the bedroom swung back into a tiny cove, about two feet deep, cut into the wall. It was my only option. I slid behind it, pulling the door as far back towards me as it would go. I could only see in two directions now: right, through the narrow gap between the door and the frame; and left, to the far edge of the bed and the dresser. I looked left.

As I turned, the sound seemed immense; every noise amplifying in my ears, every beat of my heart, every blink of my eyes. I expected to be able to hear the man as he approached, hear *something*, but the house was silent now. No footsteps. No creaks.

In the mirror on the dresser, I could make out all of the bedroom. The bedside cabinets. Derryn's books. Her plant. The bath, basin, shower. The door, and beyond it into the blackness of the hallway.

Nothing moved.

Nothing made a sound.

But then, suddenly, he was there.

A flash of red plastic skin. The toes of his boots, dark but polished, shining in the glow from the security light. More of the mask emerged from the hallway, as if it were consuming the darkness. The man stopped, scanned the room, his body turning. But he made no sound at all, even as he stepped further in.

I didn't move. Didn't breathe. I couldn't risk any noise. I had nothing to compete with a gun, and only one way to protect myself: make him believe I wasn't home.

Another step.

He brought the gun up slightly, his finger wriggling at the trigger gently. It sounded like he was breathing in. Sniffing. Like a dog trying to pick up a trail. He glanced towards the dresser, into the mirror, seeming to look right at me. And then he moved. Past the bathroom. Along the edge of the bed.

I could smell something then. A horrible, degraded odour, like decaying compost, trailing the man as he moved. I swallowed, felt like I had to, just to try to get the smell out of my throat and nose. But the stench didn't go away. It was coming off him like flakes of skin. I swallowed again, and again, and again, but couldn't get rid of it.

The man in the mask bent slightly and scanned under the bed, then came up again and leaned forward to look at Derryn's bedside cabinet. I heard the gentle slide of drawers opening and closing, then another noise: a picture frame being picked up. When he turned around, his hands were down at his side again – one holding the gun, one empty – and the picture frame was gone. A photograph of Derryn and me on our last holiday together.

It took everything I had not to make a sound. Whoever was behind the mask had just crawled beneath my skin. Violated me. My wife. Our memories. A bubble of anger worked its way up through my chest, then fear cut across it as the man approached, the gun slightly raised in front of him. Faster, more determined, as if he suddenly realized where I was.

He stopped again in the doorway. Turned back. Scanned the bedroom a second time. Then he breathed in through the mask; a long, deep intake of air. As he breathed out, I could smell him again. His decay. His stink. I held my breath, desperate not to swallow. Desperate not to make a noise.

Eventually, he turned for the final time and headed out, across the hallway, into the spare bedroom. In the mirror, I watched the night swallow up his entire body – except for the mask. In the darkness, the red of the plastic never disappeared.

He scanned the room, the mask moving with him, left to right; one long, snake-like movement. When he was done, he did the same thing again, replicating the action exactly. Then, finally, he turned and stepped back into the half-light of the hallway, pausing, and looking across towards me. I stood motionless, soundless, staring through the gap between the door and the frame, right into the darkness of the mask's eyeholes.

Then, finally, he left.

The Programme

He was sitting on the edge of the bed, looking across at the door out of the room. It was open. Beyond was a living area, stripped of almost all decor. The only furniture he could see was a table in the middle, and a single chair pushed under it.

It was a trick. Had to be.

He tried to work out how long they'd kept him, how long he'd been waking in the middle of the night and staring into the corner of the bedroom. Two or three weeks. Maybe a month. Maybe more. And during that time the door had never been open.

But now it was.

He leaned forwards a little. He could make out more of the living area now: a second door to the right of the table, closed. A bookcase, empty, next to that. On top of the bookcase was a book. It had gold lettering on it, a Post-It note attached to the front.

He got to his feet, dropped the blanket on to the bed and slowly shuffled to the bedroom door. Stopped. Now he could see what the book was.

A Bible.

Hesitating, he took another couple of steps forward, into the living area. The floorboards were cold against his bare feet.

'Hello there.'

He turned and, through the corner of his eye, saw a man standing next to the door to the bedroom. Leaning against the wall, dressed entirely in black. Tall, broad, well built.

'How are you feeling?'

I recognize you, he thought, looking across at the tall man, trying to find the tail of the memory. But it wouldn't come to him. Memories were starting to swim away, disappearing every day – and they weren't coming back again.

'Have you lost your voice?' the tall man said, and stepped away from the door. 'My name is Andrew, by the way.'

'Where am I?' he said, his words indistinct as they passed through his toothless gums.

Andrew nodded. 'Ah, so you *do* speak.'

'Where am I?'

'You're safe.'

'Safe?' He looked around him. 'From who?'

'We will get to that.'

'I want to get to it now.'

Andrew paused. Something flared in his eyes, and then it passed again.

'You remember what you did?'

He tried to think. Tried to grasp at another memory. 'I, uh . . .'

'You made a mess of your life, *that's* what you did,' Andrew said, his voice harder now. 'You had nowhere else to go, no one to turn to. So you turned to us.'

'I turned to Mat.'

Andrew smirked. 'No, you didn't.'

'I did.'

'No, you didn't. Mat doesn't exist.'

'What?' He frowned. 'I want to see Mat.'

'Are you *deaf*?'

He looked around the room, towards the door. 'Wha– where is he?'

'I told you,' Andrew said. 'He doesn–'

'I want to know where he is!'

In the blink of an eye, Andrew was on him, clamping a huge hand on to his throat. He leaned in so they were almost touching noses, and squeezed with his fingers. 'You have to earn the right to speak. So, don't *ever* speak to me like that.'

Andrew shoved him away, and – as he stepped back – a memory came to him: pinned down on the dentist's chair, looking up at a tall man in a surgical mask.

Andrew.

'You . . .' he said quietly, touching his gums with his fingers.

'Don't say anything you're going to regret.'

'You took out my teeth.'

Andrew looked at him.

'You took out my teeth,' he said again.

'We saved your life.'

'You took out my *teeth*.'

'*We saved your life*,' Andrew spat. He took a big step forward again, his hands opening and closing. 'I'm willing to help you here, but I can just as easily feed you to the darkness.'

The darkness.

He swallowed. Looked at Andrew.

He meant the devil.

'Is that what you want?'

'No,' he replied, holding up a hand.

Andrew paused, steel showing in his face. 'I don't care about your teeth. There are things going on here more important than your *vanity*. Soon you will come to understand the situation you are in – and the situation you were pulled out of.'

He stared blankly at Andrew.

'I don't expect you to understand. That's why I've left something there for you to read.' Andrew nodded at the Bible. 'I suggest you study the passages I've highlighted. Process them. Because you'd better start to appreciate that you're standing in the middle of this room with your heart still beating in your chest.'

Andrew stepped closer to him.

'But if you cross us, we will kill you.'

And then he left.

*

He's in an apartment, two floors up. There's no furniture, and holes in the floor. He's sitting at a window, facing Mat. He feels scared.

'What am I going to do?'

'I have friends who can help you,' Mat says. 'They run a place for people like you.'

'I don't want to run any more.'

'You won't have to. These people – they will help you. They will help you to start again. The police will never find you.'

'But I don't know who I can trust.'

'You can trust me.'

'I thought I could trust my own family.'

'You can count on me, I promise you that. These people will help you to disappear, and then they will help you to forget.'

'I want to forget, Mat.'

Mat shifts closer, places a hand on his shoulder. 'I know you do. But do me a favour. Don't call me Mat from now on.'

'I don't understand.'

'My friends, the people who are going to help you, I'm not Mat to them. Mat is dead now.' He pauses, looks different for a moment. 'You can call me Michael.'

When he woke, Andrew was sitting at the bottom of the bed. He brought his knees up to his chest, glanced at Andrew, and then looked out through the top window. Early morning. Or maybe late afternoon. He wasn't sure any more.

'Have you read the book I gave you?' Andrew said.

The book. The book. The *book*. He tried to find the memory, a spark that would lead him to the book, but it wouldn't come.

'I can't remember,' he said quietly.

'It was a Bible,' Andrew replied, ignoring him. 'The book was a Bible. You remember I gave you a copy of the Bible, right?'

'No.'

Andrew paused, studied him. 'That's a shame,' he said eventually. 'We've been treating you differently from the others, you know that?'

'The others?'

'Your programme is different.'

'I don't understand.'

'Your room, the food we give you, the way we've been with you – it's not our normal way of working. I don't think you realize how lucky you are.' Andrew's eyes shifted left and right, suspicion in them. 'But I worry about you, you know that? I worry that you think the best way to get better is to fight us.'

He didn't say anything.

'Am I right?'

He shook his head.

'Normally, that doesn't concern me. On our regular programme, we have ways of dealing with problems. But with you here, among this luxury, it's more difficult.'

Andrew looked at him.

'Do you want to fight us?'

He shook his head again.

'Good,' Andrew said, standing. 'Because you *don't* want to fight us. But if I see that look in your face again, I'll put you on the same programme as everyone else.'

Andrew moved across the room and placed a hand on the door.

'And, believe me, you don't want to be on that programme.'

He lifted his head. He was sitting in the corner of a different room, pitch black. He couldn't remember how he'd got here. Didn't know how long he'd been out. His arm was raised to head height and locked to something. Knotted maybe, or clamped. It pinched his skin when he moved, and pin and needles prickled in his muscles.

Where the hell am I?

He could see a thin shaft of moonlight bleeding in through a window further down the wall. And as his eyes started to adjust to the darkness, other shapes emerged: a door, on the far side, closed most of the way; and a white shape, like a sheet, diagonally across from him. There was a breeze coming in from somewhere, and the sheet was moving, billowing up as the wind passed through.

Something specked against his skin. He turned. The wall beside him was wet, almost glistening. There was a liquid on it, dribbling down. He brushed it with his hand. Water. It was running down the walls, all the way along the room.

Next to him, at his eyeline, was a square metal plate, bolts in all four corners, with an iron ring coming out of it. Water was on that too – and something else as well. Darker. It smelt of rust. Maybe copper.

Oh shit, it's blood.

He tried to move his arm away from the wall – but something glinted and rattled. He felt handcuffs pinching his skin. One loop was attached to the ring, the other clamped around his left wrist. He couldn't move. Couldn't escape. Couldn't even get to his feet without being pulled back down again.

He glanced towards the door.

The sheet had moved now. Edged a little closer to him, parallel to the wall. This time, he could make out something beneath the sheet: a shape.

'Hello?'

The shape twitched.

'Hello?'

It twitched again. The sheet slid a little, falling towards the floor. And from beneath the white cotton, a face looked out at him.

A girl. Maybe only eighteen.

'Hello?' he said again.

She was thin. Her mouth flat and narrow. Her skin pale. In the darkness of the room, she looked like a ghost.

'Where are we?'

She looked towards the door – a slow, gradual, prolonged movement – and then back to him. But she said nothing.

'Are you okay?'

No reply. Her head tilted forward a little, as if she was having trouble holding it up. He tried edging away from the wall, as far across the room as he could go.

'Are you okay?'

And then he felt something soaking through his trousers. He looked down at the floor. A pool of vomit was under one of his legs. He backed up, away from it, and slipped. The handcuffs yanked at him as they locked in place, and pain shot through the top of his arm, like his shoulder had popped out of joint.

'Keep quiet.'

He looked across at the girl.

She was staring at him now, her eyes light like her skin, her hair matted and dirty. The sheet had fallen away. Beneath, she was only wearing a bra, some panties and a pair of socks.

'Are you okay?' he asked.

She didn't reply.

'Can you hear me?'

She twitched, as if someone had jabbed her with the point of a knife, then turned to look out through to the landing again. She stared into the darkness beyond.

'What's your name?'

She finally turned back to face him 'Keep quiet.'

'What's going on? Where are we?'

She shook her head.

'What's your name?'

She paused. Looked at him. 'Rose.'

He edged away from the wall again, careful not to stand in the puke this time. The smell in the room was starting to get to him.

'Listen to me, Rose. I'm going to get us out of here – but you're going to have to help me. You're going to have to tell me some things.'

She stared out through the doorway. Her spine was dotted down the middle of her back; and there was a bruise, big and black, on her left side, just next to her bra strap.

She said something, but he didn't pick it up.

'What did you say?'

She pulled the sheet around her again, and faced him. Her arm was also handcuffed to the wall. He noticed there were more rings running the length of the walls on both sides of the room. Equal distances apart.

Then he spotted something else.

A sharp piece of tile, maybe from a bathroom wall, or a roof, about four feet in front of him. It was shaped like a triangle. Jagged on one side. He moved as far away from the wall as he could get, the hand-cuffs locking in place again, and swept a leg across the floor.

'What are you *doing*?' Rose whispered.

He tried to get to the tile again. His boot made better contact this time, and the tile turned over, the noise amplified inside the stillness of the room.

'Stop it,' she said. 'He will hear you.'

He looked at her. 'Who?'

'The man.' She glanced out through the door. 'The man in the mask. The devil.'

I wonder what you taste like, cockroach.

A shiver passed through him.

'Who is he?' he whispered.

She shrugged. 'A friend of the tall man.'

The tall man. The tall man. He fished for the memory, but it wouldn't come. He stared at her blankly.

'Andrew,' she said quietly.

Andrew.

Then the memory formed. The man dressed all in black. The tall man. The one who had been there when they'd taken his teeth.

He looked at Rose. 'I can't . . .'

'Remember anything?'

He paused, a part of him scared to admit it. 'Yes.'

'Yeah, well, that's what they do,' she said. 'That's how they make you forget about what you've done. You want my advice?' She glanced at the doorway again, then at him once more. 'Hang on to what you can, because once it's gone, it ain't coming back.'

'What do you mean?'

'I mean, eventually, you'll forget everything.'

'Forget everything?'

'Everything you've done.'

'What do I need to forget?'

'I don't know,' she said. 'What *do* you need to forget?'

She watched him for a moment, as if trying to figure out the answer for herself, then turned her attention back to the doorway. The sheet had slipped again. Against her pale skin, the bruise on her back looked dark, like spilt ink. He imagined it was painful too. Right down to the bone.

'Did the man in the mask give you that bruise?'

Rose looked down at herself and brought her free hand around to her back, running her fingers across the surface of her skin.

'Yes.'

'Why?'

'I tried to run.'

'Run from what?'

'What do you think? This place. The programme.'

'The programme?'

A creak outside the room.

'Rose?'

She put a finger to her lips and studied the darkness beyond the door. 'Seriously, you need to be quiet,' she said eventually. 'He likes to surprise you. He likes to watch. Give him an excuse and he will hurt you.' She paused, felt for her bruise again. 'The people who help run this place, I've watched them. Most of them still believe in something. They still seem to have rules. But the devil . . . I don't know *what* the fuck he believes in.' Rose stared at him. 'He will hurt you,' she said quietly. 'And he will hurt me. That's what he does for them.' She paused, blinked. 'Sometimes I think he might actually *be* the devil.'

Click.

They both looked towards the corner of the room. Into the darkness. The one corner where no light reached.

Then out of the night came a cockroach.

Its body clicked as it scurried across the floorboards. The girl's eyes fixed on the insect, and, as they did, her mouth dropped open. She started to sob, moving back against the wall, her handcuffs rattling above her.

169

'You going to save her, *cockroach*?'

A voice from the blackness of the night.

He shuffled across the floor on his backside, moving in as tight to the wall as he could. Water soaked through to his back. And even from across the other side of the room, he could smell the man in the mask now: an awful, decaying stench. Like a dead animal.

From the corner of the room, a sliver of a horn emerged, sprouting from the top of a red mask.

'What are you going to do, cockroach?' the voice continued, fleshy and guttural. 'Break free and take her with you?' Laughter, the sound muffled by the mask. 'Andrew kept telling me you had to be treated differently. But I never saw it that way. You're a mistake. You don't fit in here. You complicate things, go against everything we've built. And you're holding on to the miserable fucking existence you once called a life, with no intention of letting go. If anything, we should be treating you *worse*.'

More of the mask emerged from the darkness: an eye hole.

'I *never* agreed with Andrew when he said you weren't to go on the programme. I went along with it, but I lobbied hard to have you brought back down to earth. All the way back down.'

A second eye hole. Half the mask was visible now.

'And now I win. Deep down, Andrew knows there can't be one rule for you and one for everyone else. No one deserves special favours. That's not what this place is about. You accept what we offer you – or you fight us. And you've been fighting us since the first day we brought you here. Maybe you haven't tried to run like that skinny little *bitch* over there. But it's been in your head. In your eyes. I've seen it. You *want* to fight us. And you know something?'

A long pause. Then, suddenly, the devil came out of the darkness, the smell with him, leaning in over the man handcuffed to the walls of the room.

'I *love* it when you fight.'

He looked at the devil and tried to speak. But the words refused to rise through his throat. Breath hardly passed between his lips.

'So, you're on the real programme now, you filthy piece of *shit*. No more luxury. No more favours. And I hope you fight. I *really* hope you fight.' Slowly, his tongue emerged from his lips, sliding along the ridge of the mouth slit, one end to the other. 'Because I really, *really* want the chance *to cut you up*.'

Deep underground, in the bowels of their compound, was another place. The biggest room they had. It was split into two and divided by a set of double doors.

The largest part of the room was once used as an industrial fridge, but there was nothing in it now. It sat empty, its strip lights buzzing, its walls stained brown and red with rust, its floor dotted with tears and blood.

Next to it, on the other side of the double doors, was a second, smaller room. When they came for him at dawn four days later, unexpectedly, violently, that was where they took him. They dragged him to a solitary chair in the middle of the room and made him face what awaited.

The final part of the programme.

PART THREE

22

The sun had been up for two hours and I was still behind the door. On the ground, knees up to my chest. A thin shaft of light escaped between the curtains in the bedroom and shone across the bed, flashing in the dresser mirror. Outside, next door, I could hear Liz talking.

I looked at my watch. 9.44. I'd been in the same position for over six hours.

My eyes snapped open. I'd fallen asleep.

My mobile was ringing in the living room.

I got to my feet, bathed in sweat, and pushed at the bedroom door, edging around it to the hallway. Quietly, I moved through the house, checking every room. Every hiding place. The front door had been locked again. The only evidence the devil had ever existed was a tiny piece of dirt on the carpet immediately inside the door.

The phone was on the living-room table.

I looked at the display. ETHAN CARTER. Ethan had been in South Africa with me during the elections, and was now the political editor at *The Times*. I'd phoned him when I got in from the police station the night before, and left a message for him, giving him the name Jade O'Connell, the date of 1 March and the keyword 'Mile End'. I asked him to look into the information, and to give me a call back.

The call ended. I waited for a couple of minutes, checking the house over a second time, and then went to my voicemail. He'd left a message.

'Davey – I emailed you what I could find. Enjoy.'

The computer was in the spare bedroom. There was a message waiting from Ethan, with three attachments. The first was a copy of a *Times* front page. It was dated 2 March 2004. At the bottom was a story about a shooting at a bar in Mile End. Three dead, five injured. I read a little way, then opened up the other two attachments. One was a second-page story, dated 3 March, a column headed by a photograph of the bar with a caption beneath that read: *The scene of the shooting*. The third, dated 6 March, was smaller, a 'News in Brief' piece, with no picture. Each of the attachments had been blown up big.

I went back to the first attachment.

THREE DEAD IN EAST END SHOOTOUT

Three people were killed and five injured during a shootout at a bar in Mile End, London, yesterday.

Police couldn't confirm the names of the dead but did say they believed all three victims were members of the Brasovs, a violent splinter group previously affiliated to notorious Romanian gang, Cernoziom.

Witnesses reported hearing gunshots go off inside the Lamb, a pub on Bow Road, as well as shouting and screaming, before two gunmen exited the building, eventually escaping in a white van. Police said they were interviewing witnesses, and are appealing for anyone who saw anything to come forward.

I closed the attachment and opened up the second one.

MILE END VICTIMS NAMED

The three members of the Brasov gang, killed on Friday at a pub on Bow Road in Mile End, London, have been named.

Drakan Mihilovich, 42, his brother Saska Mihilovich, 35, and Susan Grant, 22, were all murdered when two gunmen walked into a pub on Bow Road and opened fire on them.

The Mihilovich brothers are widely thought to be responsible for the recent murder of Adriana Drovov, wife of George Drovov, a leading member of Brasov rivals, Cernoziom. The third victim, Susan Grant, was reported to be Saska's girlfriend.

Four others were injured during the shooting. Two are described as being in a critical condition.

I looked at Ethan's email. *Don't worry – she's in the third story.*

MILE END VICTIM FOUND DEAD

In a bizarre twist, one of the victims of what police are dubbing 'The Mile End Murders' has been found brutally murdered in her hospital bed.

Jade O'Connell, 31, thought

to be an innocent victim of a violent gang war in the Tower Hamlets area, was discovered by nurses yesterday, only hours after doctors had given her the all clear. Police said the victim's head and hands had both been removed.

'This is one of the most sickening crimes I've ever seen,' Detective Chief Inspector Jamie Hart, the officer leading the hunt for the killer, said yesterday. Ms O'Connell had no surviving relatives.

Jade was dead.

Looks like she's a goner, Ethan had written. *I remember that story. I was doing a piece on Cernoziom at the time. Vicious bastards. They never found out who killed her, but everyone knew it was Cernoziom. Had to be. She must have seen one of their faces. What a way to go.*

I thought about Alex, about the parallels between him and Jade. They knew each other. Maybe not well, but she'd heard of him. And now there was a further link too: they were both supposed to be dead.

I let the water run down my body. I'd been in the shower for thirty minutes, hardly blinking. When I closed my eyes, all I could see was the devil coming down the hallway to kill me.

I knew I was standing on the edge of the darkness now. If I stepped back, I'd step away from the case and from what I'd found so far. Whatever was behind me would be left there. But I still wouldn't step away from *them.* They'd offered me the chance to walk and I hadn't taken it. Maybe I'd thought they were bluffing. Or maybe the reason I had carried on was because everything Mary had said to me that first time – and everything I'd felt since – was connected to how I felt about Derryn. Deep down, perhaps I'd hoped my own answers would be waiting for me when I found out what had happened to Alex.

The good things are worth fighting for.

She'd told me that once, when she'd first been diagnosed. And now I knew, like then, the only way forward was into the darkness in front of me.

Whatever happened, there was no going back.

23

I called Spike and got him to source an address for Gerald – Jade's fake ID contact – based on the number I had for him. It took thirty seconds for him to find out that Gerald lived on the third floor of a dilapidated four-storey townhouse in Camberwell. The police still had my BMW, so I hired a rental car and headed south of the river.

It took an hour to travel eleven miles. When I got to Camberwell, I managed to find a space straight away, right opposite the building. I turned off the engine. The road was like one long concrete storm cloud: narrow, grey-bricked terrace housing; oily sediment cascading from collapsed guttering; dark, blistered paint on the doors and windowsills. There was a big pile of bin liners right outside Gerald's building, torn apart by animals, the contents spilling on to the pavement and across the dirty, stained snow.

After a couple of minutes I spotted a woman walking towards the house, digging around in her handbag for keys. I got out and crossed the road, catching the door just as it was about to close behind her. I let the woman disappear into the belly of the building, and then stepped inside and pushed the door shut. It smelt old, musty, as if its hallways hadn't ever been cleaned.

To my left were the stairs. I headed up, and found Gerald's flat halfway along the third floor.

I knocked a couple of times, and waited.

'What?'

A voice from inside the flat.

'Gerald?'

'What?'

'I need to speak to you.'

'Who are you?'

'My name's David. I'm a friend of Jade's.'

'Who's Jade?'

'I think you know who Jade is.'

He didn't reply immediately. 'I'm havin' breakfast here.'

I looked at my watch. It was two-thirty. 'Well, you can eat while we talk.'

A thud. His feet hit the floor on the other side of the door. He was looking through the spyhole at me. I looked back, into the eye of it.

'Come on, it'll be fun,' I said. 'We can talk about the forgery business.'

He whipped the door open on the chain. 'Keep your fuckin' voice down.'

He was pale and fat, about forty, his brown hair disappearing fast. He looked like he hadn't seen daylight since he was a teenager.

'You going to open up?'

'What d'you want?'

'I need to talk to you.'

'About what?'

'About some IDs.'

He looked me up and down. 'I don't know what you're talkin' about.'

I sighed. 'Come on, Gerald. You can save the act.'

He eyed me again, then closed the door. I listened to the chain fall from its runner and swing against the door. When he opened up again he waved me in.

The flat was a mess. Clothes were strewn across the back of chairs and sofas; packets of crisps and burger cartons dumped on the floor. Curtains had been pulled most of the way across the only window I could see, leaving a sliver of a view across the street. On one wall was a painting. On the others were shelves full of books and equipment. Towards the back of the room was a guillotine, rolls of laminate and a pile of large silver tins containing different coloured inks.

'Nice place,' I said.

'Yeah, a real penthouse.'

He picked up a couple of sweaters and a pair of trousers and tossed them through the door to the bedroom.

'I need something.' I reached into my pocket and took out a roll of banknotes. 'There's a hundred here. All I want from you is some help. It's as simple as that.'

'Help?'

'A few names.'

He raised an eyebrow. 'What are you, the Old Bill?'

'No.'

'My snitchin' days are over, pal.'

'I'm not a cop. I'm a friend of Jade's.'

'You're a friend of Jade's, huh?'

'That's right.'

'Bollocks you are.'

'Listen—'

'No, *you* listen. This conversation is over.'

I nodded. 'Okay. What would it take?'

'Take?'

'For you to lose your newly developed conscience.'

I looked at him. He was going to ask for more money. I couldn't go back – not now – even though I only had a hundred on me. But this was the way to play him. At the end of the day, as Jade had told me, Gerald was just a crook.

He shrugged. 'Gimme five hundred and we'll talk.'

'*Five?*'

'You wanna talk, we talk big.'

'Okay,' I said. 'But you give me everything I ask for.'

He nodded. As I stepped towards him, for the first time I could feel the kitchen knife at the back of my trousers. There for emergencies.

'So, you know Jade?' I asked him.

'I know a lotta people.'

'We're not dancing any more, Gerald.'

He looked at me. 'Yeah, I know her.'

'You provided her and her friends with IDs. I want to know who you spoke to, who came here. Specifically, if you're sending IDs out, I need to know where they're going. You tell me that and you get this.'

He looked at the hundred, then at my pockets, where I presumed he thought the rest of the money was.

'Okay,' he said eventually.

'First: did you deal only with Jade?'

'Mostly her.'

'What does "mostly" mean?'

'Her, yeah.'

'She came to pick up IDs for herself?'

'No,' he mumbled. 'Some others too.'

'Speak up.'

'Some others too.'

'Who else's?'

'I don't know. She never told me. I don't work for her, or whatever the fuck she's a part of. I work for *myself*. I'm independent. She just gave me the pictures and the names and addresses and I made them.'

'Are they the same people every time?'

'Yeah, mostly.'

'The same people are getting different IDs every time?'

'That's what I said.'

'You keep a record of the names and addresses they give you?'

He laughed. 'Oh, yeah. I keep a record of *all* of them, so when the pigs raid me I can make it easy for them. Of course I don't keep a list of fuckin' names.'

'Did Jade ever tell you who she worked for?'

'No.'

'She ever mention a guy called Alex?'

'How the fuck am I supposed to remember? I've

met a lot of people doing this, and most of them don't come in here trying to make nice.'

'How many IDs did Jade pick up?'

'In four *years*?'

'You've been doing this for her for four years?'

'Yeah.'

'How many?'

'Fifty. Maybe more.'

'When does she come round?'

'Whenever she needs something.'

'She doesn't have particular days?'

'No.'

'When was the last time she came around?'

'I dunno. Week ago maybe.'

I paused, nodded. 'Okay. You doing IDs for them at the moment?'

'Yeah.'

'For when?'

'Friday.'

'Day after tomorrow?'

'That's Friday, as far as I know,' he said, smirking.

I could feel the knife against my back again.

'Is Jade supposed to be picking them up?'

'Not any more.'

'You know why?'

He looked at me, shrugged. 'No. Someone just called this morning.'

'And said what?'

'That I'd have a new contact. Some guy called Michael.'

I nodded. 'They tell you why Jade wasn't coming?'

'No. Just that she wouldn't be my contact any more.'

'How many IDs are you doing for this new guy?'

'Four or five.'

I fished around in my pocket for the photo of Alex and held it up. 'You recognize him?'

'I can't see.'

'So, take a closer look.'

He shuffled forward and squinted at the photograph. 'No.'

'His isn't one of the IDs you're doing?'

'No.'

'You ever done an ID for him?'

'Dunno.'

'Be more specific.'

'I dunno. Don't remember if I have or haven't.'

'You better not be lying to me, Gerald.'

'I ain't lyin'.'

He looked like he was telling the truth. He was staring straight at me, barely flinching as he spoke.

'How long does it take you to make up these IDs?'

'Depends.'

'On what?'

'On what it is. If it's a driver's licence, I can do it in a coupla hours. A passport takes longer. You gotta get the marks right, everything in the right place.'

'They ever ask for passports?'

'No.'

'Do you get anything else for them?'

He shrugged.

'What?'

He flicked a look at me. 'Guns.'

I paused. Studied him. 'You ever post their stuff instead of them coming here?'

'I can't tell you where I send them – it changes every time.'

'I don't believe you.'

'I don't give a shit *what* you believe.'

I took a step forward and pocketed the money. He looked me up and down, then held up both his hands, nodding towards the pocket with the money in it.

'Okay, okay,' he said. 'This new guy wants to use a drop-off. A deposit box. He said he'd be leaving his place at 6 p.m., so he needs them to be there by then.'

'Where's the deposit box?'

He got up and walked through to the bedroom. While he was in there, I reached around to the back of my trousers and repositioned the knife so I could get at it more easily.

I waited.

He came back out, a piece of paper in his hands, and held it out to me. I took it without taking my eyes off him, and slid it into my back pocket.

'You'd better not be messing me around, Gerald.'

'It's all there.'

'It'd better be. If I find you've dicked me around, I'll be back.'

'Okay, Arnold Schwarzenegger. Gimme my money.'

I held up the banknotes for him to see, then tossed

them at him. We both watched them scatter across the floor.

'What the *fuck* is this?'

'Your money.'

'This ain't five hundred notes.'

'You said you'd help me. If I get anything from your information, I'll send you the rest. If I don't, you just made a hundred quid for doing nothing.'

'You little *prick*.'

I yanked out the knife and held it up as he came at me. The tip of the blade stopped an inch from one of his eyes. Along the serrated edge, I could see a strip of his face, his eyes wide, bulging, surprised. My heart was racing, thrashing around inside my chest, but the knife was hardly moving.

'You just made a hundred quid,' I said.

Gerald held up both hands and backed away. He'd probably had knives at his throat before. Guns too. It was the kind of business he was in. He probably thought it was the kind of business I was in as well. I edged around to my left, towards the door, and wrapped my fingers around the handle.

'Thanks for your help,' I said, and slipped out.

I drove north-east across London, crossing the Thames, and parked half a mile from the church in Redbridge. Then I waited. Evening started to move across the sky at about four-thirty. It worked its way in from the horizon, sucking up the light until all I could see were the stars. I put the heaters on full blast and felt the warm air against my body. Ever since I'd watched the man in the mask come into my home, I couldn't warm up. Couldn't shake the unease that came with staring into the darkness and not knowing what was staring back.

I knew I was doing the only thing I could now. There was no returning to the places I once felt safe. They knew where I lived. And they would know where I worked now too.

They knew everything about me.

This was all I had left.

24

At ten-thirty, I stepped out of the shadows and made my way around to the back of the church. The building was alarmed. I could see a box high up next to the statue of Christ, winking on and off – but there was no alarm on the annexe. They wouldn't have had the chance to wire it up yet.

There were two locks requiring two different keys, but the wooden door meant that this was only token security. I slid my pocket knife in through the gap between door and frame and started prising at the opening. Some of the door split straight away. I could see the dial box for the keys. More of the door broke off, coming away in cable-thin strips. I kicked them out of the way, and took a quick look around, then started levering some more.

My hands got numb quickly. It was freezing cold; colder than at any point in the past few days. I jemmied the door some more, digging in deeper and deeper each time, fighting the cold as much as the wood. Then, finally, a whole panel came loose in my hands. I threw it to one side and it landed in the snow with a dull thud.

I waved a hand inside the annexe and waited. Ten seconds passed. No alarm. I reached in, flipped the lock on the handle and pulled what was left of the door open.

It was dark inside, but I'd brought a penlight. I went for the desk first. There were three drawers, all locked. I put the penlight between my teeth and dug the knife into the top drawer. It sprang open without too much effort. Inside were a couple of pens, some envelopes and a church newsletter. The second drawer was empty. In the third were four slide files, all empty.

Next to the door were the crates Michael hadn't unpacked.

I stopped for a moment. Listened. I knew the weather would help me: snow would crunch under foot, so I'd be able to hear any approach. In fact, the night was so still now, the noise would probably carry all the way up from the main road.

Turning back to the first crate, I flipped the top on it. It was a mess, crammed with books, magazines, and folders full of notes and photos. I looked through the photos. Michael was in all of them: with his mum and dad; with what could have been a girlfriend or a sister; with some friends at a twenty-first birthday party. One was taken at a service, him high up in the pulpit, one hand on a Bible.

Below that, half sliding out of an envelope, was another picture.

A boy running around on a patch of grass, chasing a football. Jade had the same one. I flipped it over. Written on the back was exactly the same message: 'this is the reason we do it.'

Chucking the photos back in on top of the books, I pulled the crate off the one below. It landed on the floor with a bang. Inside the second was more of the same. Then, at the edge, I noticed a small address book with *Contact numbers* written on it.

Inside, names were listed alphabetically, every page full of addresses. Most were local – Redbridge, Aldersbrook, Leytonstone, Woodford, Clayhall – but others were further afield, in Manchester and Birmingham. I flicked through the book, stopping briefly under each letter to see whether I recognized any names. I didn't.

Until I got to Z.

Right at the back of the book I found a name I knew: Zack. I got out my notepad and flipped back through the pages to the names I'd collected from the flat in Brixton: *Paul, Stephen, Zack.*

The listing for him didn't have a surname, but it did have an address in Bristol – and something else.

A line leading to a second name: Alex.

25

It took three hours to get to Bristol. By the time I came off the motorway, it was two o'clock in the morning. I needed rest desperately. I drove for a while, heading deeper and deeper into the deserted city, until I found a dark spot next to a railway yard. I backed in, under a bridge, and kept the heat on for an hour. Then, eventually, I turned off the engine, climbed on to the back seat and fell asleep.

I woke suddenly. It was light – almost midday. Fresh snow had fallen, settling beyond the bridge and all around the car. I was freezing cold, disorientated for a moment, as if I'd been pulled too quickly from my sleep. Maybe this was the way it was going to be now: every sleep bookended by the feeling I was being watched.

I got back into the front seat, fired up the engine and moved on.

The address was for a house in St Philips. It was an ugly area and an ugly street, bordered by a wasteland of broken concrete and an imposing Victorian factory building. I did a circuit in the car, up to the main road, back around and then down past the house. The curtains were drawn, and there was no sign of life.

I parked within view of the house and waited, low in my seat, looking out along the road. After a couple of minutes a bus wheezed to a stop at the end of the street. An old couple got off. Behind them a mother and her two children, huddled together, their jackets zipped up to their chins. They veered left, into the side road about halfway down, but the old couple continued along the street towards me. When they passed the car, they looked in, eyeing me suspiciously.

Ten minutes passed.

Another bus pulled up, and then a third. More people got off, all disappearing into houses on the street, or passing the car and moving on somewhere else. When it got quiet again, I fired up the engine and turned up the heaters.

About thirty minutes later, an Astra entered the street from behind me. I watched it approach in the rear-view mirror and then brake, reversing into the space in front of me. It bumped up on to the pavement and then off again, stopping about a foot from the front of my hire car. A woman moved around inside, the hood up on her jacket. She glanced in her rear-view mirror, picked something up, then got out.

Wind carved up the road. Some tendrils of hair that had escaped from her hood whipped around her face. She pushed the door shut with her backside, trying to juggle a shopping bag and her keys. On the key-ring I could see a silver crucifix, dangling down, brushing against the side of the door as she turned the lock.

She headed up the street. Her hood ballooned out as the wind came again. It was stronger this time and she momentarily lost her balance. Her foot drifted from the pavement to the road and the shopping bag suddenly hit the floor, fruit scattering everywhere. She stopped, looked along the street, then bent down and started picking it up. When the wind came a third time, she put a hand flat to the floor to balance herself and her hood blew back. A tangled mop of black hair.

She glanced in my direction. Stopped. Looked away.

I watched her start to pick up the fruit again, quicker this time. Suddenly, she looked nervous, grabbing hold of an apple only to drop it, then doing the same thing a second time. Another apple rolled all the way across the street, then another.

Then, strangely, she straightened and started walking away, leaving the fruit rolling around in the gutter. She didn't care about it any more, barely had hold of the shopping bag, and was trying to sort through her keys with her spare hand as she walked. More fruit escaped from the bag, tumbling into the road. She didn't look back. She just carried on, finally stopping when she got to her house.

It was the house I'd been watching.

She put the bag down and started going through the keys properly, one after the other, flipping them until she found the right one. Then she looked in my direction once more. Her head didn't move. Just her eyes.

She was looking right at me.

And then it hit me.

Her hair was a different colour, longer and more unruly. Her face was pale and serious. Older. Weathered. And her nose looked different: it was more tapered, thinned out. Before, when I'd seen her working in Angel's, it had been wider, less shapely. But it was definitely her.

It was Evelyn.

I got out of the car, set the alarm and started towards her. As I got closer, her movements became frantic. She couldn't unlock the door. From behind me I heard a voice, distant at first, then louder. I looked back and saw a black guy coming towards me, shouting, 'Oi! You can't park here!' I ignored him. When I turned back, Evelyn had opened the door. She left the shopping bag where it was, on the step, and ran inside.

'Evelyn!' I called as I got to the door. It was on a slow spring, creaking as it swung back. I stepped inside the house. 'Evelyn?'

It was warm. A floorboard creaked to my right. She was disappearing upstairs. I went after her, taking two steps at a time, and heard a series of creaks on the landing, then more movement. At the top, there were three doors. One of them was closed. I knocked on it.

'Evelyn?'

No response.

'Evelyn?'

I placed a hand on the door.

'Evelyn – it's me, David.' No response. 'David – from Angel's.'

The sound of a window sliding along its runners.

I opened the door in time to see her leaning half out of the window, one foot on the bedroom floor. She looked at me once, then swung her leg over the windowsill and disappeared. I ran over to the window. A flat corrugated-iron roof stretched for ten feet below, a narrow alleyway below that running parallel to the street I'd parked on.

I watched her on the roof, taking small steps, careful not to lose her footing on the ice. When she got to the end, she looked back, hesitated, then jumped down. I could see the pain in her face as she landed, but she didn't make any noise. Instead she got to her feet, kicking up gravel, and ran.

I headed downstairs. The front door was now closed. The house reminded me of the flat in Brixton: the walls were plain, probably painted once, and there was no carpet on the floor, only the original boards. Along the hall I could see a kitchen, some bay windows and another closed door. No furniture in any of them except for the kitchen units and a microwave. I stepped out on to the front porch.

Then from inside the house: 'Uuhhh . . .'

A voice.

I stopped. Listened.

Nothing.

I went back down the hallway, into the kitchen. The house smelt of something. It became stronger the deeper into it I got.

There were two doors off the kitchen. The first led to a small patch of back garden, strewn with weeds and rubble. The other led into a living room. No furniture, no TV, just a few books scattered across the floor and a blanket in the corner. There was one window, the curtains pulled, and a small archway leading to an adjacent room. From where I was standing, I could see through the archway to the edge of a sofa. Small wooden arms, big leather cushions.

And, poking out, resting on one of the arms, a head.

I edged forward. The head. The chest. An arm locked in place, hanging off the side of the sofa, the knuckles brushing the floorboards. Inches from the fingers was a needle. It had rolled away, out of reach. Some of the liquid had escaped, pooling on the floorboards next to an ashtray over-run with cigarettes. It was a man. A boy, really. His trousers were wet, a dark patch crawling from his groin down the inside of one leg. And at the end of the sofa was a bucket.

It was full of vomit.

The stench was immense. Totally overpowering. I turned away, covering my face with my sleeve.

He couldn't have been older than eighteen, but his arms were dotted with track marks. His veins were puffy and enlarged, clearly visible through the skin. He was as white as the snow outside, his eyes half-closed, dull yellow marks smeared below his eyelashes like badly applied make-up. I couldn't get any closer. The smell was absolutely horrible.

Then a door opening and closing somewhere.

I looked up.

The door into the kitchen was still open. The one closer to me, leading back out to the hallway, was closed. On the other side of the hallway door, I heard footsteps. A shadow passed below the door, footsteps moving along the hall. I looked down at the kid sprawled on the sofa, and saw something else: a glass vial, empty, the film at its neck punctured by a needle. On the side it said KETAMINE.

A sound from the kitchen.

I went to the hallway door and slowly opened it. I waited. I could hear someone moving around in the kitchen. Drawers opening. To my right, the front door was still closed, but now there was snow on the mat in front of it. To my left I could see the black guy who had shouted after me in the street. He was probably in his early thirties, no taller than five-ten, but wide: muscles moved beneath the skin of his neck and shoulders, and a vein wormed its way out from the corner of one eye, up on to his shaved head. He was looking out through the kitchen door at the garden.

I looked back at the kid. His eyes were closed, but his mouth was open. His tongue came out, slapping against his lips like it was too big for his mouth. His gums were bleeding. Then, as his tongue moved again, I saw something else: *he had no teeth*.

They were all gone.

He coughed, a sound muffled by saliva and vomit, but loud enough to carry through the house. In the kitchen, the man turned around and looked along the hallway at me.

And he smiled.

I went for the front door, but as I got there it opened in at me. Evelyn stepped in, her cheeks flushed, anger streaked across her face. A split second later, she brought her hand up from her side. She was holding a gun. The barrel drifted across my face and I instinctively stumbled back, my hands coming up to protect me. The muzzle flashed, and plaster and dust spat out of the wall above me and to my left. Then another shot, louder this time.

I held up both hands.

'Evelyn, wait a minute . . .'

She walked towards me, the gun out in front of her. It was new, in beautiful condition. A gun that had probably never been fired until today.

She stopped about two feet from me. She was going to shoot me in the head. The gun was level with one of my eyes, held incredibly still. Her fingers were pressed so tightly against the grip, perspiration was running out from under her hand.

'What are you doing, David?'

I didn't speak. I had a horrible feeling she would fire as soon as I did, even though she'd asked me in a gentle, almost admiring way. Even though I'd known her before Derryn died, talked with her and laughed with her.

'What are you doing?' she said again.

There was the smell of gunfire in the air now, burnt and nauseating. A smell that reminded me of driving through the townships before the sun was up. Behind me, I could hear the man coming along the hallway. I didn't move. Any movement might be enough of an excuse for her to pull the trigger.

'You should have left us alone,' she said.

She moved towards me. My body tensed and I lowered my head, angling it away from the gun. She was behind me now, and the next thing I felt was the gun at the back of my neck.

'Do you hear me, David? *You should have left us alone.*'

'I don't want you, Evelyn. I don't want this.'

She didn't say anything.

I turned slightly and could see her standing behind the black guy. He had the gun now, pointed right at me.

'I don't want either of you. I just want Alex.'

'Alex doesn't–'

'That's enough, Vee,' the man said.

He stepped forward. Swapped the gun from one hand to another. Turned it. And – before I'd even had a chance to react – smashed it into my face.

I blacked out.

26

I opened my eyes. The first thing I saw was a red brick building. It was the factory I had seen earlier. It stood empty and derelict: its windows smashed, its walls decorated in graffiti, its doors torn from their hinges. In front of me was a vast expanse of concrete, weeds crawling through the cracks, snow in patches.

They'd gagged me. When I moved, I could feel my hands had been bound, and I'd lost most of the sensation in my feet. I had my jeans, T-shirt and zip-up top on, but my coat had been removed, and they'd taken my shoes and socks. I was sitting barefoot, my soles flat to the ground. The cold was making my bones ache. There were just a few tinges of daylight still staining the sky. Night was creeping in.

I listened. I could make out cars passing on a distant road somewhere, but little else. There were two squares of old walls, half demolished, about forty feet to the side of me, the skeletons of outhouses that had once stood on the site but were now long forgotten.

That was the point. No one came here.

No one would find me.

I thought I heard movement, the sound of birds flapping their wings. I saw something arc up to my left and around. Then there were footsteps, the noise of rubble being kicked across concrete, and the crunch of snow. Someone was approaching out of sight. I tried to move, but my whole body throbbed. I could feel bruising around my jaw and at the back of my head. When I tried to turn, pain shot all the way up from my mouth to my eye. It felt like blood was running down my face.

A bitter wind came then, cutting in across the open ground, and suddenly, with it, the smell of something. Something warm and saccharine, like boiled sweets. When the wind died down again, I could feel someone's breath, right at my ear. I tried not to move, tried to maintain my composure, but having someone so close sent a shiver through me. It seemed to amuse them: whoever it was backed away after that, as if they'd secured a little victory.

I thought about shouting for help, about making as much noise as I could. But I didn't have any cards to play. Out here, away from the road, no one would hear me. And even if I did somehow shake off the binds and make a break for it, I wouldn't know which direction to run in. I'd be running into the darkness as if I was blindfolded.

More wind. Louder and colder this time.

'Evelyn?'

The gag muffled my voice. I cleared my throat and could feel my muscles tighten. More pain throbbed in my head, and when it passed I felt dizzy and nauseous. I tried to say her name for a second time, but the word got stuck. And as I searched for it, trying to pull it out through my teeth, I felt someone breathing against my ear again. Only this time I could also feel lips – skin brushing skin, only briefly, but long enough.

Footsteps in the snow, moving away.

I started to turn my head, despite the pain, needing to see who was behind me. But as I did, I felt a hand grab me under the chin and a thumb press in against my cheek.

'Don't do that again.'

A man.

He let go of my face and pushed my head forward so my chin touched my chest. He held it there. Between my legs I could see blood dripping down from my face, into the snow.

'Stay like that,' he said. 'And close your eyes.'

I could taste blood on my tongue. He'd pressed so hard my teeth had cut the inside of my mouth. I spat it into the snow, and watched it spread out in tiny lines.

Behind me, the man cleared his throat. Then more footsteps in the snow, crunching, fading away and coming back again. He'd been to collect something. I moved my head, discomfort forcing me to raise it slightly. I felt his hand spread across the back of my skull and a gun slide past my ear and in under my chin.

'What did I say to you?'

'I can't hold it there,' I said through the gag.

'Move again and I'll put a bullet through your brain.' He shoved the gun in harder against my throat. 'Now stay like that and keep your eyes closed.'

I realized in the silence that followed that I vaguely recognized his voice. My first thought was the man with the tattoo. But it wasn't him. I knew I'd remember his voice if I heard it again. *Who then?* My thoughts drifted quickly. I was struggling to concentrate. The cold and the fear were starting to catch up with me.

He pressed the gun in harder against the side of my face, then – just as suddenly – took it away again. I stayed still, looking down between my legs, thinking it might be a trap. Instead, he reached around and pulled the gag away from my mouth.

'Make any noise louder than a whisper and my people will be picking bits of your face up off the floor for a week.'

My people. He was in charge.

He tossed the gag past me, and it landed in the snow. I could smell his breath again. 'Now, I'm going to ask you some questions and you're going to tell me the truth. Hold *anything* back, and I will rip out your throat.'

He was close to my ear again.

'First, what the *fuck* are you doing here?'

'Alex,' I said quietly.

'Oh, I *see*.' A short, aggressive burst of laughter. 'I'm sure during your cosy little chat with Jade, she must have warned you off this . . . I'm not sure *what* you would call it, really. A quest, perhaps.'

He'd spat out the word *quest* and I could feel his saliva on the side of my face, slowly running down my cheek.

I shrugged.

'What's that supposed to mean?'

I didn't say anything. Didn't reply.

'*Huh?*' he said. He was closer now.

I didn't reply a second time, just looked down between my legs. To my blood in the snow. To my feet, gradually turning blue.

'You going to answer me, David?'

I let the silence hang.

He didn't wait long. As I was trying to formulate a plan, he hit me across the back of the head with the butt of the gun. And the white of the snow became the black of unconsciousness.

When I came to, I was somewhere else. It was dark. I could hear the wind but couldn't feel it. I looked around me. High up, to my left, was a window. Moonlight shone through. I turned my head slightly to the right and, behind me, through the corner of my eye, I could see a doorway. I was inside the factory I had been facing earlier.

It took time for my eyes to adjust to the gloom. When they did, I could see someone sitting with their back to me, on a stairwell towards the end of the room. He was smoking a cigarette. It glowed orange rhythmically. I knew it was a man: broad shoulders, hair closely cropped, a big white hand resting on the step.

'Are you hard of hearing, David?' he said.

I remained still.

'*Answer me.*'

'No,' I replied. I sounded groggy. My lower half was absolutely numb from the cold and the back of my head felt like it was on fire.

'Good.'

He nodded to himself, took a last drag on the cigarette and flicked it out to the side. It died in the night. He came down the stairwell, his shoes clunking against the metal, and disappeared in the darkness. I could hear him moving, but couldn't see him. His footsteps became muffled.

I tried to think again where I'd heard the voice before. He spoke differently to the others. More control. More authority.

'Are you in charge?' I said.

No reply.

Then, suddenly, he was behind me.

'What did Jade say to you?'

'Nothing.'

He sighed. 'Don't lie to me.'

'I'm not.'

He stopped. All I could hear was my own breathing. Then, slowly, from my side, the gun snaked into view.

'These hurt,' he said, and shoved it hard up under my chin. My muscles twitched. 'You'd better start dancing with me, David, or I guarantee I'll be putting you in the ground next to your wife.'

They knew all about me. They knew my name. They knew about Derryn. There had been a hole in the case and now my life was pouring out of it into someone's open arms.

'Jade told me I was in danger.'

'Well, she was right. Do you know why?'

'I can guess.'

'So take a guess.'

'Alex.'

'*Please*. You think this is all to do with him?'

I shrugged.

'*Don't* shrug at me.'

'I don't know.'

A pause. 'I'm guessing that little mess at the church was yours.'

I didn't answer; didn't want to admit I'd been through Michael's stuff.

'Breaking and entering is a crime,' he said.

'What the fuck do you call *this*?'

The man laughed. 'Difference is, you don't know who I am. I know who you are. I know all about you.'

He pressed the gun in against my cheek, and I could feel the outline of the muzzle.

'Was the address for the church in that box?'

I paused. *The box*. He knew about the box.

'*David*.'

'Yes.'

'Where?'

'On the back of a birthday card.'

'What else was in there?'

I thought of the picture I'd given to Cary. 'Nothing. Just photos.'

'Just photos?'

I nodded.

'Don't lie to me.'

'I'm not.'

His hand dropped away, the gun with it.

'Okay, let me tell you something. The reason you're here and not sitting with your feet up by the fire at home is because you're standing on the outside of a circle, and you've caught a glimpse of what's on the inside.' The smell of boiled sweets again. 'Unfortunately for you, once you've caught a glimpse of the inside, you can't just walk away again – which is why you're freezing to death in the middle of this fucking hole.'

I was starting to drift in and out of consciousness.

'I know about you, David,' he continued. 'I know about your background, where you come from, what you do. It's my job to know all that, because it's my job to ensure people like you don't fuck up what I've built. And you know what? Reading about you made me wonder: this quest of yours, is it about the kid – or is it about your wife?'

I looked up, turned, and he held up a hand. Grabbed the side of my face. Forced it back down, further this time, until my head was almost between my knees.

I felt blood rise in my throat.

'You're a big man, David,' he said, 'but her death makes you easy to control. When people die, it hurts. It sucks you dry. You feel so hollow inside, you wonder if you're ever going to be normal again. But when people die, you've got to let them go, because they're not coming back. They're *gone*. Your wife, the kid you're trying to find, they're gone.'

'If he was gone, I wouldn't be here,' I said.

He yanked my head towards him and moved in next to my ear, his lips brushing against the side of my face. 'You *want* to die, David – is that it?'

I felt his fingers wriggle at either side of my head, like he was trying to get a better grip before he reached round and put the gun in my mouth. Then – lightning fast – he punched me in the side of the face – so hard it was like being hit by a freight train. I tipped sideways, the chair going with me, hitting the ground head first.

Darkness.

I opened my eyes. My head was being pressed down between my legs. All I could see were my feet, flat against the floor, my toes in a puddle of melted snow. His hand was around the back of my neck, his fingers locked in place behind my ear. A trickle of blood broke free from my hairline. It ran down across my forehead and into my eye.

'What else do you know?' he said.

I twitched, tried to shake the blood away from my eye, but his hand pressed harder against my head. Forced me down even further between my knees.

'What else?' he said again.

'You recruit people.'

'Is that what Jade told you?'

I nodded.

'What do you mean, "recruit"?'

'I don't know.'

'Are you lying to me again, David?'

'No.'

'Okay. What else?'

'Some of you are supposed to be dead.' I paused, tasting the blood in my mouth. He pushed down on my neck again – he wanted me to continue. 'You've got a flat registered to a company that doesn't exist, and a pub you're using as a way to make money. A front. Full of your people, who rotate when questions start getting asked. When a hole starts to appear, you shift them somewhere else and the hole closes up.'

'What else?'

'That's all I know.'

'Bullshit. What else?'

I stopped, tried to think. That was pretty much it. When he'd told me I was on the outside of the circle looking in, he was right. I'd caught a glimpse of something on the inside; I knew something wasn't right, that something was up – that Alex *could* actually be alive. But I didn't know how and I didn't know why.

'What *else*?' He forced my head down again, and something clicked. A bone in my neck. I felt a shooting pain arrow along my spine, up into my skull.

He thought I knew more, and – as I tried to form a plan – I realized I could play on that. Maybe it would be the only way out. Pretend I knew more than I did and he'd have to find out what. See how far I'd dug my way in.

'You think whatever you're doing is a mission from God.'

He released his grip ever so slightly, and leaned in closer to my ear.

'What did you say?'

'You think it's a mission from God.'

'I *think*?'

I felt him shift his weight. He was pinning me down with one hand and reaching for something else.

'You know, David, I'm not a fan of politics. All it's ended up teaching me is that power corrupts. You give weak men absolute power and you only breed more weakness.'

Prickles of fear rippled across my skin. My heart felt like it was swelling up. He'd given up asking me questions. We'd got to the end of the line.

'Wait,' I said.

'But something sticks in my mind. Something Josef Stalin once said. I don't admire the man – I just happen to agree with his sentiments.'

'Wait a minute, I haven't told you everything I–'

'Do you know what he said, David? He said: "Death solves all problems – no man, no problem."'

I heard a beep and then a ringing sound. He was using a phone.

'Zack, it's me. You can take him now.' A pause. Silence. 'And make sure you bury him where no one will find him.'

27

I came to as they pulled me out of a car. It was still dark and freezing cold – probably three or four in the morning. I was dressed only in my jeans and T-shirt. No top. No coat. No shoes.

Someone pushed me against the car and turned me around. It was the black guy from the house in Bristol. He had a knife in his hands. He stabbed it down through the duct tape they'd used to bind my wrists, and pulled my hands apart. I looked around me. We were on a country lane, muddy and black, trees looming overhead on both sides. It was quiet. We must have been miles from the nearest main road.

Behind me, the passenger door opened and closed, and from my left came a second man: Jason, the man I'd chased at the apartment in Eagle Heights. He moved around to the front of the car, a gun in one hand, a torch in the other, and zipped his coat up to his chin. He looked at me. A half-smile broke out on his face, as if he'd figured out what I was thinking: *They're going to kill me, and no one's ever going to find my body.*

'You don't have to do this,' I said to them.

Jason pulled me away from the car and along the path. I shuffled forward, pain in my legs, staring ahead into the darkness. When I looked at the ground in front of the trees, full of dead leaves and disturbed earth, an image came back to me of Derryn standing next to her grave, looking down into the darkness herself.

I'd always wanted to be close to her when it happened; to be thinking of her at the end. I'd thought about my own mortality a lot since she'd died, and I wasn't scared of facing it down. But here, a hundred miles from the pictures I had of her, the memories, the reminders of what she once was to me, I realized – as she must have done – that all I would feel at the end was pain.

Suddenly, we veered off the path, into the woodland on the right-hand side. Jason's hand tightened around my arm as the ground gently started to rise, sloping upwards through snow-covered undergrowth. I looked back over my shoulder at him.

'Why do you have to do this?'

'Shut the fuck up.'

Behind him the guy from the house was scanning the woodland. His torch was sweeping from side to side, illuminating a dense clutch of trees to his right.

'Jason,' he said from behind me. 'Wait a sec.'

Jason told me to stop, and then looked back at his partner. Further up the slope, deeper into the forest, moonlight carved down through irregular gaps in the canopy, forming pale tubes of light. Where it couldn't penetrate the foliage, the woods were black as oil. Between my toes I could feel grass, and hard, uneven ground – the sort of ground you could break an ankle running across.

I looked back.

Jason was closer to the other guy now, whispering. It was incredibly still; so still their voices carried across the night: 'You know what he told us. Take him to the usual spot. Come on, Zack, you know how it plays out.'

The black guy was Zack.

'This is a better spot,' Zack said.

'It's right on the fucking road.'

'Look how dense it is there.'

'Who gives a shit?' Jason said, his voice rising. Then he quietened again as Zack stared at him in silence. Zack was the senior partner. Jason nodded his apology and leaned in closer. 'All I'm saying is, I don't really wanna piss him off. He told us to take him up to the top and do it there. That's where we put the others.'

The others. There were more like me. More that had got too close. My heart tightened and a feeling of dread snaked along my back and down my legs: the anticipation of being put in the ground, of lying there in the freezing cold praying the end would come. I turned to face the darkness in front of me.

Run.

My face burnt, even in the cold.

You have to run.

I looked up the slope, then back to them.

They were still talking. Jason was gripping the gun tightly, his finger moving at the trigger. Zack glanced at me, his eyes narrowing, as if he sensed I might be on the cusp of doing something stupid.

Run.

215

I scanned the woodland in front of me again. They knew the terrain. They knew the path. They'd know where to force me to go, and where to head me off. But then I thought of the alternative: the two of them leading me through a maze of trees to a dumping ground full of skeletons. Making me beg for my life. Putting a bullet in my chest.

Watching me die in the snow.

Do it now.

I looked back once more – right into Zack's eyes.

And then I made a break for it.

I almost fell before I'd started, my toes grazing a tree stump. But then I was away, pushing through the darkness, heading for a pool of light about twenty yards up the slope.

'Hey!' Zack's voice. It echoed after me, suppressed by the canopy of the trees, bouncing off the bark. Then I heard him say, 'I'll take the road.'

Something punctured the underside of my foot – a stone, maybe even a sliver of glass – but I didn't stop. I tried to make my strides as long as possible, tried to swallow up as much ground as I could. Huge trees lurched out of the night and knocked me off balance. I arced further right, deeper into the forest. Then I finally stole a look behind me: Jason was about forty feet further down – concentrating on where his feet were landing – but he looked up, once. Our eyes met. He lifted the gun and lost his footing, adjusting himself almost instantly. He was quick and fit. Used to running. I knew that from before. He was probably closing on me already.

I passed through one pool of light, and headed for the next. As I did, I tried to up the pace, every bone in my body aching, every nerve prickling, and saw that the foliage thickened about twenty feet ahead. It got dense quickly, most of it hidden from the moonlight. It would make for a difficult chase. I headed for it, ducking down. Thorny branches scratched my skin, and snow flecked against my face. Darkness set in around me. I moved through the foliage as fast as I could. Beyond the noise of the branches cracking and splintering against me, I expected to hear Jason follow me – but there was no other sound. He was no longer chasing me. He'd gone a different route.

I stopped and dropped to the floor.

All I could hear was blood being pumped around my body, a thumping baseline so loud it felt like it was echoing through the forest.

Something cracked to my right, as I faced up the hill. I turned, narrowed my eyes, willing myself to see into the darkness. They'd both had torches – but they'd both switched them off. There was no light close to me now, and I realized, in some ways, that was worse: they knew this area. They knew the hiding places, the holes. They could be right on top of me and I wouldn't even see them.

I reached down, slowly, and felt around for something to use as a weapon. The ground was covered in a layer of snow, hard and crystallized, and all I could feel were thick tangles of thorn bushes. In the silence, I started to notice the pain in my feet: it felt like there were deep cuts on the balls and arches of my left foot, and I'd bruised the ankle on my right. I felt blood slowly trickle down from my hairline again, but I didn't wipe it away this time. Because, over to my right, I saw a flash of colour: pale blue, the colour of Jason's jacket, catching in the moonlight close to where he was standing.

My heart was punching against my skin so hard – so *fast* – it felt like it was about to explode. Another flash of pale blue. Moving up the slope, but maintaining the same distance from me. No sound came with it – not even the faintest crunch of snow. He was lithe and quick, every foot landing where it was supposed to. More blood broke free of my hairline; this time it ran down the centre of my forehead, over the bridge of my nose and down to the corner of my mouth.

Then I made him out against the night.

He was about ten feet to my right, up the slope from me, coming around the edges of the thorns. The jacket had been a bad idea. If he'd taken it off, he could have been standing next to me and I wouldn't have even seen him. But, instead, the jacket was reflecting back what little light there was. He turned where he was, then swung back round in my direction, the gun out in front of him, and stared straight at me. I gazed back, looking at him, frozen to the spot. But then his head swivelled to face further up the slope, and he took a step up.

I could wait him out, wait for him to pass and move further up into the forest. Then I could make a break for it, back in the direction of the bottom road. But there was another problem: Zack. I had no idea where he was. He said he was going to take the road, so presumably it wrapped around the forest, and came back again at the top in a rough semi-circle. But I didn't know how close the road was. It could be a way off. Perhaps if I waited for Jason to disappear up the slope, and then ran, Zack would be even further behind me. Or maybe the road was nearby above me and, when I got up to run, they'd both be standing side by side and put a bullet in my back.

Either way you don't know where the fuck you are.

Whether Zack was close or not, I'd still be running blind. The best I could hope for would be to get back to the car and head down the road the way we'd come in. Eventually it would lead somewhere.

I turned as quietly and slowly as I could and saw Jason continuing to climb. He was about fifteen feet up, at a diagonal from me, but slowly coming back around in my direction. He stopped. Looked down the slope again. Then something flashed – a blue light – and I saw him take a mobile phone out. He had it on silent. He looked at the screen, then back towards my spot. They were communicating by text now. I glanced back in the other direction. Had Zack spotted me? Was he telling Jason where I was?

Jason's eyes were fixed on my position now, the gun in one hand, the phone in the other. I held my breath as he took a step closer. Then another. Coming down the slope towards my position.

He can see me.

He stopped, dropped the phone back into his pocket, and put both hands on the gun.

He can really see me.

He edged even closer, padding across the forest floor, until he was about three feet from me, looking across the tangle of bushes I was hiding in. The gun drifted across my face.

He gazed across the top of my head, his eyes fixed on something beyond, and then raised a hand and pointed at himself. He was signalling.

Zack.

Jason was in front of me, up the slope.

Zack was behind, below.

Surrounded.

Jason scanned the forest, left, right, into the darkness of what was around him. He didn't move, just stood there, listening to the sounds: the movement of the leaves, the creaking of the earth, the faint *drip, drip, drip* of water. A thought came back to me then of my dad, standing in the middle of the woods close to the farm, doing exactly the same thing. Dad had been an amateur tracker. He listened to the noises, took in the smells, knew what footprint belonged to what animal. But Jason was the real thing: confident enough to separate the sounds of nature from the sounds of what had encroached upon it. He knew I was close by. I couldn't have got clear of him in the time available to me. He knew that. Now it was just a question of pinpointing my position.

A waiting game.

The smallest of noises. I turned an inch. From the darkness behind me, side-lit by a pale shaft of moon-light further down, came Zack. He looked up at Jason, Jason at him. Jason placed a finger against his lips. I watched them: they were communicating with only the barest minimum of movements. Zack nodded up the slope; Jason shook his head. They looked back down the slope, over my head. Jason made a circle motion with his hand: *He's in this area somewhere.* He'd seen me go into the undergrowth and hadn't seen me come back out. The undergrowth was thick and wild, but I hadn't lost them. I wouldn't lose them now. They were sure I was here – and they'd only leave again with my body.

Do something.

Slowly – so slowly it was hardly even a movement – I guided my hand to the ground and felt around again, my palm flat to the floor. Immediately around me there was nothing: just soft mud and hard snow. Zack took a step forward. I reached further out into the undergrowth, and my fingers brushed something. Rocks. There was a pile of them but only a couple felt big enough. One was larger than the other. I picked it up and brought it into me, then did the same with the second. My sleeve brushed against a branch, but the sound didn't carry and neither of them regis-tered it.

I wrapped my hand around the smaller one.

Steadied myself.

Waited.

Waited.

Then, slowly, I opened up my body and threw the stone as hard and as far as I could to my left. It hit the forest floor with a thud, snow spitting up, brambles crackling.

The two of them spun around. Zack was quicker off the mark, moving forward, and around the thorns, towards the noise, gun primed. Jason seemed more reticent – as if he knew it might be a trick – but followed at a distance, walking rather than running. I gripped the thicker stone, and moved on to my haunches. The hardest, sharpest end poked out the top of my hands. Jason was about six feet away from me now, the gun still at his side. In his face I could see he hadn't been fooled by the diversion at all.

Do it now.

I squeezed the stone and sprang at him. He half-turned towards me, his eyes widening as I jabbed the stone's point into the top of his head. It made a hollow, splitting sound, like a punctured watermelon. His blood speckled against my face, his eyes rolled up into his head, and then he fell forward, hitting the ground almost silently.

I dropped to my knees next to him. There was blood all over his jacket. When I leaned in a little closer, I realized he wasn't breathing.

I'd killed him.

A shot rang out and a puff of bark flew from a tree about a foot to my left. I fell flat to the floor and tried to pick Zack out against the darkness. Next to me,

Jason's gun was lying on a patch of snow. I scooped it up and peered at it. I didn't recognize the make. Didn't have time to check it was loaded. I just gripped it and started to run.

I headed right, around the thorns, and down towards the road, parallel to the way we'd climbed. A second shot rang out, shattering the silence. I kept running. A tree loomed out of the dark and I grazed my arm against the bark, my body swerving too late to avoid it. An ache shot up through my muscles, into my shoulder. I pushed it down with the rest of the pain, and carried on running.

A third shot, then a fourth. A fifth narrowly missed me, hitting a tree as I passed it. My lungs felt like they were squeezing shut. I knew I was losing ground. I knew I was slowing down. I couldn't keep this pace up – my feet were torn to shreds and there was still no sign of the road. I wasn't even sure I was heading in the right direction.

Then I fell.

My left foot clipped the grasping arm of a tree root. I tumbled head first, hitting the ground hard. Collapsed on to my front and cried out in pain. It felt like I had broken my arm.

Looking up, I could see Zack, about twenty feet away to my left. He hadn't spotted me yet, but he'd heard me and he was heading in my direction. I looked around. The gun was wedged against the bottom of an oak tree, its gnarled bark closed around the weapon. I scrambled to my feet and reached for the gun, pulling it out. When I turned, Zack was lurching towards me, his own gun out in front of him.

I fired twice.

He jolted sideways. The first bullet went through his shoulder, the second hit him in the chest – then he stumbled, his feet giving way, and hit the ground. His gun tumbled away from him, making a metallic clang as it bounced across the frozen mud.

When my eyes snapped back to him, Zack was looking at me, blood oozing out of his chest. In his eyes I could see an acceptance. That sooner or later, whatever he was involved in was going to catch up with him. He blinked once, twice, and then his eyes started to lose some of their shine. He didn't blink again.

Zack had the car keys in his pocket. I took them out and headed back down to the road. The sky was starting to lighten a little, turning from black into grey, and grey into green. By the time I found my way back to their car, the green had finally become blue.

As I got in, I realized it was a week since Mary had first entered my office.

I was still barefoot. I looked in the mirror and saw I had a thin, deep gash right on the hairline where Zack had clocked me with the gun at the house. My face was bruised and battered, streaked purple and blue, and one of my eyes had started to close. My shoulder wasn't broken, nor was my arm, but they both hurt right down to the bone. And I could see a knuckle imprint, close to one of my ears, where the man in charge – the man with the saccharine breath – had punched me in the side of the face.

I sat still for a moment and composed myself. Studied my reflection.

Who are you?

I wasn't the same man who had worked that first missing persons case. I wasn't even the same man who had woken up the day before. I'd killed twice. I knew that changed me; a part of me knew it changed everything. Suddenly, I was capable of ending a life; of looking into another man's eyes and, for a split second, losing enough control to pull the trigger. Somewhere buried beneath the surface I'd discovered a man I knew nothing of.

A man who knew nothing of order.

I wondered, for a moment, what Derryn would have made of what I'd done. Would she still have trusted me? Would she still have wanted to lie next to me in our bed? Would she have been able to feel a change in me, a sudden barrier between us, as if there were two men now – the one she had always known, and the one she didn't recognize.

I started up the car and turned on the heaters.

As air pumped into my face, I realized the thing she'd probably have been most scared of was that I felt so little for what I'd done. I'd killed, but I wasn't a killer. I'd done what I'd needed to do in order to come out of those woods alive. I didn't want to have to do it again, but I knew, in some part of me, if I had to, I would. They'd come for me, and when they did, I'd pull the trigger again. Maybe that made me less than the man Derryn would have wanted me to be. But this wasn't about missing people any more.

This was about survival.

I looked at the clock. 7.49. They all thought I was dead now, so I had to use that. We must have been gone a couple of hours, and burying a body would take another couple on top of that. That gave me two, three hours tops before they realized Zack and Jason weren't coming back.

28

The place where I was supposed to have died wasn't on the map they had in the car. But when I finally pulled up at the main road, four miles down a winding gravel path, I saw we were about twenty miles from Bristol, in the middle of the Mendips.

In the glove compartment there was a phone, empty like the last one of theirs I'd found. No names in it. No recent calls. I sat there for a moment, deciding what to do next, then used the phone to dial into my answerphone at home. I had one message. It was John Cary. He'd rung the previous day, at five o'clock in the evening.

'I've got something for you,' he said. 'Call me.' He left a number. There was a pen in one of the side pockets on the door. I took it out and scrawled his number on the back of my hand, then called him. He answered after two rings.

'John, it's David Raker.'

'I've been trying to get hold of you,' he said. He sounded annoyed. 'You ever answer your phone?'

'I've been . . .' I paused.

Should I tell him?

The truth was, I could use some help. I could use some protection too. But I'd just left two dead bodies lying in woodland four miles behind me. And if I told him that, I had to tell him everything else, and face whatever consequences came with it. And I wasn't ready to give this case – or myself – up. Not yet.

'I've been busy,' I said finally.

'Yeah, well, that makes two of us. Let me transfer you.' I waited. Two clicks and he was back on, whispering this time. 'I got your stuff back from the lab. If you get anything out of this, that's great. You take it as far as you want. But whatever you choose to do with it, I don't want to be kept informed. Understood?'

I paused. A bizarre start.

'Understood?' he said again.

'Understood.'

'Okay,' he continued, 'so the lab lightened the Polaroid. Alex is in the middle of the shot, in what looks like the front bedroom of a house. The whole background is a little out of focus, but there's clearly a window behind him, and on the other side of that, some kind of veranda. To me, it looks like the type of thing you'd get on the front of a farmhouse.'

'Anything else visible through the window?'

'Just grass and sky.'

'No recognizable landmarks?'

'No. It's taken from a weird angle. Kind of shot from below. Alex is looking down. The window, and the veranda, they're both on a slant because of the angle. You on email there?'

'Uh, I'm not at home.'

'I can email you a copy.'

228

'Okay. Email it to my Yahoo.' I gave him my address.

'You asked about prints before,' he said.

'Right.'

There was a hesitant pause. 'There's two sets of prints.'

'Okay.'

'You know a Stephen Myzwik?'

'Is that a Stephen with a ph?'

'Yeah.'

Something sparked. The name was on the pad I took from Eagle Heights.

Paul. Stephen. Zack.

'Maybe.'

'Stephen Myzwik, aka Stephen Milton. Thirty-two years of age, born in Poland, moved to London, served ten years for stabbing a sixty-year-old man with a piece of glass. After that, he violated the terms of his parole, and, under the alias of Stephen Michaels, used a fraudulent credit card to rent a vehicle in Liverpool.'

I could hear him turning pages. He'd obviously printed them out from HOLMES – the police database where all serious cases were logged – like he'd done for me a couple of days before.

'Wait a minute . . .'

'What?'

'There's stuff missing here.'

I thought of something.

'There were pages missing in Alex's file as well.'

'What do you mean?'

'I was going to ask you about them.'

'What was missing?'

'A couple of pages. Some of the forensic stuff. The pathologist's report.'

More pages being turned.

'Where the fuck have they gone?'

'Has someone deleted them?'

'Deleted information from the *computer*?' A long silence came down the line. I could hear him flicking through the file, faster this time. Then he stopped. 'This file's fucked.'

Something had got to him. Something more than just pages missing from a file.

'Do you want me to call you back?'

'No,' he said. 'I haven't got time for this shit. I'll look into it later. Let's just get it over and done with.' He started on the file again. Pages turned. 'He's dead, anyway.'

'Who, Myzwik?'

'Yeah.'

Somehow another dead body wasn't all that surprising. First Alex, then Jade, now Myzwik: all of them dead – or supposed to be.

'How'd he die?'

'Looks like his body was dumped in a reservoir near here.'

'Near Bristol?'

'Yeah. Divers dredged him up about two months later. He must have made some dangerous friends.'

'How come?'

'His head had been stoved in with a baseball bat, and both his hands were found on the other side of the reservoir.'

'They'd been chopped off?'

'With a bandsaw.'

Just like Jade.

I heard Cary flicking through more pages.

'You said there were a second set of fingerprints?'

'Yeah. They're Alex's.'

'That's not such a surprise, is it?'

'Depends,' he replied. 'We took Alex's prints off some of the stuff he left behind when he went missing. I did that – set up the missing persons file myself.'

'Okay.'

'Have you got any idea why Alex disappeared?'

'I haven't managed to find that out yet, no.'

A long drawn-out pause.

'The prints we pulled off the photograph match some pulled off the wheel of a silver Mondeo used in a hit-and-run six years ago.' More paper being leafed through. 'Witnesses recall seeing a white male about Alex's age having a big fucking barney in the parking lot of a strip joint called Sinderella's in Harrow. I quote: "At eleven twenty-two p.m. on 9 November it is alleged the suspect drove the silver Mondeo—"'

'Wait a minute. Ninth of November?'

'Yeah.'

'That's the day before Alex disappeared.'

'Correct. "Suspect struck the victim – Leyton Alan Green, 54, from Fulham – as he was coming out of the bar, causing critical internal injuries. The victim died a short time later. Witnesses recall seeing a silver Mondeo with a Hertz sticker on the bumper depart the scene shortly after." The silver Mondeo was recovered in a long-term parking lot at Dover, five months later, on 12 April.'

We both stopped to take the information in.

'Alex *killed* someone?'

'Looks that way.'

'This Green guy – has he got a record?'

'No. He's clean.'

'And the car was a rental?'

'Yeah.'

'What did Hertz say?'

'Not a lot. Alex used fake ID. Registered under the name Leyton Alan Green.'

'Cute.'

'Yeah. You could say that.'

'You believe it?'

'What do *you* think?'

I paused and tried to take it in. Things were changing fast.

'Can I get a copy of those files?'

He didn't reply straight away.

Then, quietly, he said: 'I sent them to you yesterday.'

29

It took me three hours to get home. I parked at the end of my street and sat and watched the house. A biting wind pressed at the windows. Snowflakes blew across the street. Without the engine on, and the heaters off, the car cooled down almost instantly, and slowly my body started to react: adrenalin passing out of my system, cold crawling back in. I still had no coat, no shoes, no socks. I reached down to the ignition, my hands shaking now, my teeth chattering. Every cut in my face and feet, every bruise on my body, ached. I turned the key. The heaters kicked back in, the noise of the engine with it. And, finally, as I slowly started to warm up, my body began to settle.

Leaning in against one of the heaters, I looked down the street again, towards my house. The road had always been quiet, so I was hoping anything out of place would stick out a mile. But I also knew from the night before that they weren't just barmen and youth pastors – they were trackers and marksmen. And they were killers. They could fade in and out, and they could disappear. The advantage was still with them.

I looked at the clock. 11.27. They were probably starting to realize Zack and Jason weren't coming back. The likelihood that they were already here, watching the house, waiting for me to arrive, was remote. However, I wasn't about to take any chances. I needed basic provisions. I needed a shower. I needed to patch myself up. I needed shoes and extra clothes. But, most of all, I needed to be sure I was alone.

I got out of the car, locked it and crossed the road towards the house. I looked up and down the street. No one sitting in cars. No one watching the house. They'd removed everything from my pockets the previous day, including my keys, so I headed around the back of the house and took the spare key out of one of the dead hanging baskets next to the rear door.

Inside, the house was cold. I approached each room carefully, just in case, but there was no one inside and nothing had been touched. The files Cary had sent the day before were on the floor, under the letterbox, handwritten but otherwise anonymous.

I showered and briefly caught sight of myself in the mirror.

There were cuts all over my face, bruises creeping down my throat and across the muscles at the top of my chest. My body was toned, but now it was marked as well. A reminder of how badly they wanted me dead.

I dug out the warmest clothes I could lay my hands on: a pair of dark jeans; a long-sleeve thermal training top I used for jogging; a T-shirt; a black zip-up top; and a black overcoat Derryn had bought me one Christmas. I packed some extra clothes into a holdall, and grabbed an old laptop I never used from the cupboard in the second bedroom. It had been a work computer but no one had ever asked for it back. There was a spare mobile in the bedside table with some credit left on it, and my credit card. I took both, grabbed a knife from the kitchen, along with the files, a photograph of Derryn, and bandages and plasters to make running repairs to myself once I got somewhere safe. Then I locked up and left.

At the bottom of the garden, I looked back up the drive and glimpsed Liz moving around in her front room. In the windows of the house, I could see my reflection.

A man on the run.

A wound crawled out from my hairline. My face was bruised. I looked gaunt and tired. I wondered whether I'd allow myself to sleep again until this was over. It could be days, weeks, months. It could be never. Maybe the next time I closed my eyes would be with one of their bullets in my chest.

I turned and started towards Zack's car again.

Then stopped.

There was someone leaning in against the passenger window, the hood up on his coat, cupping his hands against the glass. I backed up and crouched down behind one of the garden walls. He glanced along the street towards the house, didn't see me, and moved around the front of the car to the driver's side. He tried the door. When he stepped away from the car a second time, I caught a glimpse of his face and recognized him straight away: the man who had broken into my car at the cemetery; the man I'd followed outside Angel's. He was scruffy and unkempt, and looked thinner in the daylight – and that immediately concerned me. This was the type of trap they liked to lay: making you believe they were one thing, weaker than you, and then turning everything on its head.

He looked back at the house and fixed his gaze on the front. I could see his eyes narrowing, as if he knew something was up. It was like he'd studied the street before my arrival – had seen which cars were where, and who they belonged to – and now saw a piece of the puzzle that didn't fit.

He patted the front of his jacket. *Has he got a gun?* I unzipped the holdall and took out the knife. It wouldn't be much of a fight, unless he got close without seeing me. But it was better than surrendering. If there was one thing I'd learned over the past couple of days, it was that there was no point in surrendering. They'd kill you anyway, whether you gave them what they wanted or not. Fighting back didn't give me much of a chance – but it did at least give me something.

I gripped the knife as hard as I could, adrenalin pumping my heart faster. But then the man took another look at the car, spun on his heel and headed the other way. I watched him go, reaching the end of the road. He looked back once and disappeared around the corner.

I stayed put. It was a trap. Had to be. He knew the car belonged to them, and if it was parked in my street, he knew I was home. He could have gone to make a call. He might not want to come at me alone. He could have heard by now what I'd done to the others. Either way, I had to make my move.

I got to my feet and headed across the street, flipping the locks on the car with the remote and sliding in and starting it up in one swift motion. I looked in my rear-view mirror, put my foot to the floor and drove away. When I got to the bottom of the road, I checked my mirrors again. There was no sign of him – at least for the moment.

30

There was a Starbucks about three miles north. I left the car in a multi-storey a mile down the road. If I was driving one of their vehicles, it made it easier to find me. I'd noticed a satellite tracking sticker on the front windscreen. If they were smart – which they were – they'd call the tracking company and locate the car.

I chose a sofa at the rear of the coffeehouse with the least amount of lighting above it, and sat with my back to the wall. I used their wi-fi connection to log into my Yahoo. In my inbox there was an email from Cary. The subject line was *Pic*. Underneath, he had written: *This doesn't exist on the server any more – if you want another copy, tough. It's gone.*

I dragged the attachment to the desktop and opened it up. It had been blown up big. At its default size I could make out the side of Alex's face and some window in the background. I took it down in size.

The photograph was much lighter. Alex's face was more defined. I could make out the scar on his right cheek, the one he'd got playing football as a kid, and could see his hair properly now. It wasn't shaved, as it had been when Mary saw him, but it was cut so close his scalp reflected light coming in through the window. Cary was right. It was taken at an odd angle. It looked like Alex might be on the bed while the photographer – maybe Myzwik – was on the floor.

I looked at the view through the window.

Beyond the veranda, beneath the endlessly blue sky, just a tiny speck in the corner of the photograph, was another patch of blue. A different shade. I moved closer to the screen and zoomed in.

Sea.

The room overlooked the sea.

Then I noticed something else. I resized the picture, and zoomed in on the window pane on the left-hand side. There was a reflection in the glass: veranda railings looking out over a hillside covered in heather; a sign nailed to a railing, reading backwards in the reflection. I flipped the photo to reverse the picture, and the writing read the right way.

LAZARUS.

A couple of days before I'd seen the same name on Michael's mobile phone.

I got a second coffee and called Terry Dooley, one of my old contacts at the Met, to tell him the car I'd hired the day before – still in Bristol – had been stolen.

'You don't call me for months and then you call me up to tell me your hire car's been stolen?' Dooley said. It sounded like he was having lunch. 'Fuck do I care?'

'I can't get down to your hole in the ground to report it. So, I need you to fill in the paperwork for me.'

He laughed. 'Do I look like your secretary?'

'Only when you've got your lipstick on.'

He said something through a mouthful of food. Then: 'Davey boy, you and me used to have an understanding. You scratched my back by leaking a few case details as and when I needed you to, and I scratched yours and got you what you needed on whatever investigation tickled your fancy. Now?' He paused. Continued eating. 'Now you ain't got *anything* I want.'

'You still owe me.'

'I don't owe you shit.'

'I'll email you the details, you fill out the form for me and liaise with the rental company, and I'll carry on pretending I don't know where Carlton Lane is.'

He stopped eating.

Carlton Lane was where Terry Dooley and three of his detectives were one night about four years before I left the paper. There was a house at the end, hidden from the street by trees, that doubled up as a brothel. One of Dooley's detectives ended up having too much to drink and punched a girl in the face when she told him he was getting a bit rough. She got revenge the next day by leaking enough details to the newspaper to protect her income and the brothel while landing Dooley and his friends in serious trouble. Luckily for Dooley – and his marriage – the call came through to my phone.

'You gonna use that on me for the rest of my days?' he said.

'Only when I need something. So you'll do it?'

He sighed. 'Yeah, whatever.'

'Good man, Dools.'

'Just send over your fucking shit, Raker.'

And then he hung up.

I emailed him all the information he'd need to complete the paperwork, then called the car rental company to fill them in, and request a replacement car. They said I'd have to pay an excess on the stolen vehicle, but because I'd taken out premium insurance cover when I'd hired it, the amount would be minimal. Next, I called Vodafone. I told them my phone had been in the car when it was stolen and asked them to redirect all incoming calls to the new phone. They set it up there and then.

After that, I put the two files Cary had sent on the table in front of me.

The first was Myzwik's. It detailed his record before and after prison, right up until his body was discovered in the reservoir. There was a black-and-white photograph of him from his last arrest. The file confirmed that Myzwik's body was brought ashore by police divers after part of his coat had been spotted floating on the surface of the water. They'd found his credit cards in a wallet on the other side of the reservoir. Forensics had worked on the recovered hands, but a definitive fingerprint match couldn't be made, owing to the amount of time the body had been underwater.

Then something hit me.

I reached down into the holdall, took out Alex's file, and flicked to the odontologist's findings. Teeth had been found in Alex's stomach and windpipe.

Although the intensity of the fire had shrunk some of them, a fairly precise approximation of his jaw had been reconstructed. This had allowed for eventual identification. At the bottom, before the two pages that were missing, I found what I was looking for: only two teeth had been left in his skull, both loose, both less damaged by the fire. Both had traces of bonding glue – used to secure braces – and an etching agent, which prepares the enamel for sealant. This was consistent with orthodontic work Alex had had as a child, which was why I'd skim-read it the first time round. But now I noticed a pattern: like Alex, Myzwik's identity had been confirmed using dental records; and, like Alex, he had been found with bonding glue on one of his teeth.

But not just on the enamel.

In both files, in both pathology reports, traces of the same bonding glue had been found on the *root* of the tooth as well.

Oh, shit.

Parts of the odontologists' findings were missing from both files; but wherever they'd gone, and who-ever had deleted them, they hadn't got rid of enough. Because I knew what I was looking at now.

Myzwik couldn't be fingerprinted because the longer the body was in water, the less accurate the technique became; without a face, no one could ID him either. And as Alex's body was more skeleton than flesh, burnt black from a two-thousand-degree fire, dental records were all anyone had to go on.

Except, like Myzwik, Alex's teeth weren't his.

And neither was his body.

The second file was much thinner than the first.

Leyton Green owned two electronics stores in Harrow, and a third in Wembley. The night he died, he'd been driving a dark blue Isuzu Trooper. It was new, bought the week before from a dealership in Hackney. The police had done some background checks on the vehicle, toying with the idea of the murder being related to the purchase of the jeep. But, like everything else in the case, it was a dead end.

The report detailed the night Green was hit by the silver Mondeo. Eyewitness accounts were thin on the ground. A couple of people identified the Mondeo. No one could identify who was driving it.

Towards the back were some photographs. The biggest was of the murder scene. Green's body was under a white sheet, only the sole of his shoe poking out. Blood had stained the sheet. Little circles of chalk were dotted around the body, ringing pieces of the Mondeo. The next pictures confirmed this: shots of pieces of the bumper, and even a chunk of the bonnet. He must have been hit hard. Close-ups of his face followed, bloodied and battered. One of his left hip, black with blood and misshapen, where the Mondeo had struck him.

I was about to return the printouts to the holdall when right at the back, close to a description of the strip bar, I found another photo. Staring up at me, dressed in a black suit, his hair parted, a familiar smile creeping across his face, was Leyton Alan Green.

The same man I'd seen in a photograph in Mary's basement.

Leyton Alan Green was Alex's Uncle Al.

31

Gerald opened the door a fraction. Recognition sparked in his eyes and he pulled it all the way back. 'What the fuck d'you want?' he said, glancing over his shoulder to where the guillotine sat in the centre of the room, pieces of card and cellophane strewn on the floor around it. Half-finished IDs lay on top of empty cartons of food.

'I need to speak to you.'

'You did all your talkin' last time.'

'I want to buy something from you.'

He smirked. 'You must be outta your fuckin' mind.'

I reached into my pocket. He backed up half a step, as if I might be taking out a gun. Instead, it was my wallet. I opened it up. There was over £800 in it.

He glanced at the money, then back at me. 'You shouldn't be walkin' around with that.'

'I know.'

'So, what do you want?'

I closed the wallet.

'I want a gun.'

Michael left the church at six o'clock. The night was cold, steam hissing out of vents, warm air rising out of the ground as the Underground rumbled through the earth. I waited for him in a darkened doorway outside the Tube. As he approached I zipped up my top and followed him inside. He went through the turnstiles and down the steps to the platform. A train was already in the station when I got there.

I had a ski hat on. I pulled it down as far as it would go over my face then stepped on to the train a couple of doors down. He sat and removed a book from a thick slipcase that probably had his laptop in as well.

With a jolt, the train took off. Michael looked up, then around at the other passengers. I turned away, staring down into my lap, conscious of him seeing my reflection in the windows. After a while, I flicked a look at him and could see he was sitting with his legs crossed, the book held up in front of him.

After we changed at Liverpool Street, I glanced at the scrap of paper Gerald had given me the first time I'd been to see him – written at the top was the address where he'd been told to drop the IDs: *Box #14, Store 'N' Pay, Paddington*. I'd found it in the Yellow Pages and called them from Starbucks. It was a storage facility; a thousand lockers. People paid a daily or monthly rate for a unit and got a swipe card that gained access to the building any time they wanted. The lockers weren't huge, but big enough to store holdalls and briefcases, coats and suits. They'd certainly be big enough for what Michael was going to pick up.

When we got to Paddington, commuters filed out; a tidal wave heading for the exit. Michael went with them. I waited until the last minute then bundled out after him.

The escalators were rammed. I could see him halfway up, his face still buried in his book. I followed him, taking two steps at a time all the way to the top. On the other side of the turnstiles he headed for the mainline trains, then moved through the crowds and out into the night.

He headed south-east. We were moving in the direction of Hyde Park, slivers of residential streets running like capillaries either side of us. I maintained a distance from him, following from the other pavement where it was darker and safer. I could see the park up ahead as he veered right into a narrow road with cars parked on either side and a shop front at one end. A sign hanging above the door said STORE 'N' PAY. I stopped as he climbed the steps up to the front. He slid a swipe card through an electronic lock and pushed the door open.

Store 'N' Pay had a big window at the front, a blue neon SECURE LOCKERS sign buzzing at the top. There was an unmanned front desk and a series of red lockers behind it. Michael stepped past another man, who was standing in front of an open locker, and up to Box 14. It was on the left of the window. He put his laptop case down, punched in a combination number and pulled open the locker. Inside was a small brown envelope.

As Michael looked through the envelope, the other man finished up and started coming towards the main door. I quickly crossed the street and headed up the steps, catching the door as he left. He glanced at me, then did a double take when he laid eyes on what they'd done to my face, turning round and looking again as he moved off down the street. Five cars down, he passed my new rental vehicle. Before getting the Tube out to Redbridge, I'd parked it there.

I'd need the car close by – for when we left.

I stepped inside and pulled the door shut. Michael was standing with his back to me, the locker open, still checking the contents of the envelope. After a few seconds, he pushed the locker shut, picked up his laptop and turned around.

He locked eyes on me.

'David,' he said. He looked shocked, his mouth dropping a little, the colour draining from his face. But, quickly, he regained control of himself. 'I've got to admit, I didn't think we'd see you again.'

'Well, even the Church doesn't get it right all the time.'

'No,' he said, smiling. 'We certainly don't.'

'Where's Alex?'

He acknowledged the name, but only with a slight nod of the head.

'Do you need me to speak up?'

'No, I heard you. Why do you want to know?'

'Where is he?'

'Why do you want to know?'

'I'm not going to ask you again.'

'I'll tell you what,' he said, 'why don't we trade? You tell me why this is so important to you, and I'll tell you where Alex is.'

I didn't reply this time. He was trying to redirect the conversation.

Trying to force me into another trap.

'Oh, don't worry, I'm not going to turn this into a confessional.' He paused, smiled again. 'Our Catholic friends seem to find forgiveness in the blink of an eye. A couple of Hail Marys and you're away. I believe you should have to work a little harder at redemption.'

'I don't give a shit about anything you believe. Where is he?'

His eyes narrowed. 'You're making big problems for yourself here, David.'

'You tried to kill me.'

He shrugged.

'You *tried* to *kill* me.'

'That was nothing to do with me.'

'Oh, of *course*,' I said, nodding at the envelope in his hands. 'You've got no idea what goes on outside the walls of your church.'

'A name means nothing, David.'

'You saying you came all this way for nothing?'

He shook his head. 'I don't understand what drives you. I mean, *why*? Why come this far? This has nothing to do with you. You could have turned away at any time. But you didn't and now . . . now you're going to get torn apart. *Why*? Is it the money?'

I didn't reply.

'I don't believe it's the money. You've probably earned enough already. Are you a completist, David – is that it? You want to finish what you started. I respect that. I'm the same. I like to finish what I start. I don't let anything get in the way of what I want.'

I could see where this was going: the same place it had gone before. *This quest of yours, is it about the kid – or is it about your wife?* They'd hit on something, and now they were going back to it again. Derryn mattered to me. She was the chink in my armour.

'Did you think there was any hope for your wife, even at the end?'

'Shut the fuck up.'

'There's always hope, right? If there wasn't, you wouldn't be here.'

'Are you *deaf*?'

'Death's not something you can fight. It's not a *tangible* thing. It's an undefeatable enemy, an unfair battle, an adversary you can't see coming.' The corners of his mouth turned down: a sad expression, but only skin deep. 'I know how you feel. I know about the fear of death, David – and the fear of what comes after. I know that you were scared for her.'

I looked at him.

'Weren't you scared for her, David? A man of no religion, of no beliefs, weren't you scared about what came next for the person you loved?'

He could see he had got to me.

'Wouldn't you like to find out?'

He took a step closer.

'That's why you're still interested in this, isn't it? That's why you're here.'

Another step.

'You want to find out where she went. *Why* she had to go.'

Another step, bigger this time.

'As hard as it is to hear, only God knows when and why our time comes to an end, David. And when He sees some of the people we have in our world, some of these young people getting out of their depth, walking a tightrope between life and death, deciding for *themselves* how close they want to brush with the afterlife, He is disappointed. I'm sure of that. Because you and I, we don't decide when our time is up. That's not our job.'

He paused, and started to reach out for me.

'That's the job of God. And the job of the people he choos–'

I slapped the envelope away, out of his hands. As he watched it go, the IDs spilling across the floor, I reached around to the back of my trousers and brought out the gun. He rocked on his feet, staggering a little, holding up both hands.

'David, wait a min–'

I grabbed his shirt, pushed him around the front desk, and down on to the floor behind. We were shielded from the street. Hidden from passers-by.

'I like what you're saying,' I said, shoving the gun under his chin. 'And I want to believe you. I want to believe my wife is somewhere better than here. But all I see when I look at you is a fucking snake. You say one thing while you think another. And whatever good you *think* you're doing, the truth is you're wrapped up in this as much as the rest of them. You're the *same* as them. And nothing you've said to me tonight can wipe that away.'

I cocked the gun. Pressed it in harder.

'So, now you're coming with me.'

32

There were a series of empty warehouses about seven miles east where I used to meet sources during my paper days. I parked outside one, marched around the front of the car and pulled Michael out of the passenger seat and in through a broken, rusting door.

Inside there was no lighting. It had all been smashed, the glass from the bulbs and strip lights lying on the floor. I tied Michael's hands behind his back with some duct tape I'd brought with me, and then kicked his legs out from under him. He hit the ground with a thud, crying out in pain. I rolled him over until he was positioned in a block of moonlight shining in from a window high up on the wall.

Then I put the gun to his head.

He looked at me. There was something in his face. He looked like a man standing on the edge. A man terrified of going over. But not of me, and not of the gun.

'What are you scared of?' I said.

'I'm not scared of anything, David.'

'What are you *scared* of?'

He blinked.

'Are you scared of dying?'

'No,' he said quietly. 'I'm not scared of dying.'

'So, what are you scared of?'

He blinked again. 'What difference does it make?'

'I want to know what you're scared of. I want to know why everyone's too frightened to tell me where you've put Alex. *So* . . . what are you scared of?'

His mouth flattened. A kind of half-smile.

'You want to know what I'm scared of? I'm scared of my time running out before I've done all I need to do. I want to *help* people. But we've done things, and I've had knowledge of things, that I fear I might not be forgiven for. And the project . . . I still believe in its aims, because I still believe it's a mission from God. A gift. But we've done things we shouldn't have done. And we have people who have drifted from the course we set. So, the thought of my time ending now is what scares me. Because when I die I want to *deserve* to be where I am. And if you kill me now, I won't deserve anything.'

'You're full of shit, you know that?'

He didn't reply. Just looked at me.

'You *know* that?'

'I don't care whether you believe me or not,' he said, looking up at me. 'It's the truth. But it's probably too late for me already – and it's certainly too late for you.'

'It's not too late.'

'*It's too late, David.* You've messed everything up. If you'd walked away when we'd asked you to, the storm would have passed by now. I could get back to the reason I signed up in the first place, and you could be looking at a life that extended further than a couple of days. Instead, you've turned this into a war. A war you can't win. And I can't do anything for the people we're helping until the war is over, and you've been stopped. And if I can't do anything for them, I can't do anything for myself.'

I pushed the gun in harder against his face.

'*Listen* to me: you want your shot at redemption, is that it?'

He just stared at me, silent.

'You tell me what I need to know and maybe I'll do it for you. Maybe I'll turn this thing around and this whole . . . whatever the fuck it is you're protecting, maybe it'll start again. Better than it was before. But I can't do that until one of you gives me what I need. I see the same look in you as I saw in Jade: you're scared about what will happen when you open the door, but you won't do anything about it. Well, this time *I'm* going to do something about it.'

I forced the gun in hard a second time.

'And you're going to tell me who's waiting.'

33

It was almost eleven by the time we got to Michael's apartment. It was on the corner of a new development that overlooked the Thames in Greenwich. We stopped at the entrance, a tall, narrow foyer with a glass-domed roof, which was connected to the main building by a corridor on the other side.

'What do you want me to do?' he said.

'What do you think?'

He dug around in his pockets and took out his keys. I looked both ways, just to make sure we were alone. The apartment building was eight storeys high, and stretched for about fifty metres in both directions. Thin, conical lights ran the length of a path that snaked in from the main road. Tiny rock gardens had been constructed either side of the foyer doors, WREN GREEN spelt out in red flowers. The building looked less than a year old.

Michael pulled open the entrance doors. On the wall, immediately inside, was a floorplan and a picture of the top-floor roof garden. The garden was smart: stone flagging, interspersed with squares of pebbles, and a covered area where cream awnings stretched across sets of wooden benches.

'Who pays your rent?' I asked him.

'I do.'

'Bullshit. You work in Redbridge, not Canary Wharf.'

He didn't reply.

He unlocked the doors into the corridor, and I followed him along to a set of lifts. Doors to our right and left led through to the ground-floor apartments. He called one of the elevators, then turned to me. I was carrying his slipcase over my shoulder and his mobile phone in my hand. The phone had been empty, just like the others, and the laptop, during my brief look at it, needed a six-digit password to get beyond the loading screen.

We rode the elevator up.

When we got to the apartment door, he took out his keys again.

'This is ridiculous, Da—'

'Just open the door.'

He unlocked it and we stepped inside.

The apartment was warm. He'd left the heating on. A decent-sized living area bled into an open-plan kitchen, a door leading from it into a bathroom and another into his bedroom. I locked the door and told him to sit in the corner of the room with the lights off. There was enough street light coming in from outside. He did as I asked, his hands no longer tied.

I set the slipcase down and unzipped it. I took out his book and dropped it on the floor, then removed his laptop.

'Where's the lead for this?' I said.

'At work.'

'I don't believe you. Where is it?'

'At work.'

I took out the gun, moved across the living room and thumped the butt into the side of his head. He jerked sideways, falling off his seat, and rolled on to his back, looking up at me.

'*Shit*,' he said, clutching his face.

'I'm not playing,' I said. 'Where's the lead?'

He glanced at me, shocked, blood pushing through the skin at the side of his head – then nodded at the TV. There was a power lead snaking out from behind a flatscreen. I took the laptop over to it and plugged it in. It loaded for thirty seconds before stopping at a password screen.

'What's your password?' I asked him.

'Eleven, forty-one, forty-four.'

I put in the code and the password prompt disappeared.

'What's the significance?' I said.

'Of what?'

'The numbers.'

He didn't reply. I turned and looked at him. He was still nursing the side of his head. He looked woozy. I placed the gun down on the glass table next to me with a clunk. Through the corner of my eye, I saw him looking between me and the gun.

The desktop appeared, loaded with folders. There were four on the right of the screen – Monthly Budgets, Twenties Group, December Sermons and December Scripture – and a further two on the left, Pictures and

Contacts. I clicked on Contacts. A second password prompt came up. I tapped in the same code. This time the prompt box juddered and told me I'd put in the wrong password.

'What's the password for the folders?' I asked him, trying Monthly Budgets. It opened immediately, and was full of Excel spreadsheets. The others all opened too. I looked across at Michael. 'What's the password for the Contacts folder?'

He just stared at me.

'You want me to hurt you again?'

He stared at me. Unmoved.

'What's the password for the Contacts folder?'

'Go to the folder marked Pictures.'

'Give me the password for the Contacts folder.'

'Humour me.'

'Have you been listening to anything I've been saying?'

'*Please*,' he said quietly.

My eyes lingered on him, then I double-clicked on the Pictures folder. There were a series of files, about thirty, with filenames like 'thelastsupper.jpg' and 'jesusandpeter_water.jpg'. I opened a couple up. They were paintings of biblical scenes: the virgin birth; Jesus being tempted by the devil; the parable of the two sons; Jesus on the cross.

'Open "widow-underscore-nain",' he said.

'I haven't got time for a sermon.'

'It might answer a few questions for you.'

I looked for the file and found the name halfway

down the list. It was a painting of Jesus standing over an open coffin, a widow beside him. A man was sitting up in the coffin.

'Do you know what the significance of the numbers eleven, forty-one, forty-four are?'

I glanced at him. The expression in his face worried me. He looked like he'd worked out a plan in his head. A way to get back at me. A way to force my hand.

'Come on, David. We both know why you're here, why you didn't turn around and walk the other way the moment you started to feel like you'd waded too deep into the swamp.'

'What the fuck are you talking about?'

'You know what that painting is of? It's the raising of a man in Nain. Jesus and his disciples visited there after leaving Capernaum, and came across a funeral procession. When Jesus saw the widow weeping for her dead son, he felt compassion for her. He understood her torment, *experienced* it, almost as if he'd experienced the loss of the boy himself. And he felt so much compassion for the widow that he raised her son from the dead. He *raised* him from the *dead.*'

'What's the password for the Contacts folder?'

'There are three accounts of Jesus bringing someone back to life in the Gospels. The young man in Nain, which is in Luke; the daughter of Jairus, which is in all of them except John; and, of course –'

'What's the password for the Contac–'

'– the raising of Lazarus.'

I looked at him and he smiled a little.

'Some scholars argue that the story of the young man in Nain and the raising of Lazarus are, in fact, one and the same. If that were the case, that would reduce the number of resurrections down to two, Jesus's own notwithstanding.'

I thought of the photograph of Alex. 'What's Lazarus?'

'Two resurrections.'

'What's Lazarus?'

'I guess, in a way, that's what you've been looking for.' I picked up the gun.

'*What's Lazarus?*'

'Two resurrections, right? Alex – and your wife.'

I shot across the living room, rage boiling in me, and wrapped a hand around his throat. He looked up at me, his face reddening as I started to shut off the air to his brain. I pushed the gun into his mouth.

'Mention her again.'

He blinked once. I stared into his eyes, knowing I was on the cusp of losing control, but knowing even more that what he had said was right. That I'd got this far, waded this deep into the swamp, because some-where, deep down, I wanted to find Derryn like Mary had found Alex. This wasn't just a disappearance to me. This was something more.

He blinked again.

This time his expression changed. He was backing down. I released the pressure on his throat, and he breathed; a long drawn-out grasp for air.

'Don't *ever* mention her again.'

He held up both hands.

'Now tell me what Lazarus is.'

'Eleven, forty-one, forty-four,' he said, slightly hoarse.

'No more riddles.'

'John, chapter eleven, verse forty-one to forty-four. The raising of Lazarus. When we recruit people, when we help them, that's what we promise them.'

'To raise them from the dead?'

'To give them a new life. A new start.'

'Is that what you did to Alex?'

'We helped him.'

'Is that what you did to him?'

'We *helped* him, David.'

'You've got a fucked-up idea of help, you know that?'

He laughed. 'The one thing we've been is consistent. We've never drifted from the course we set, whatever the challenges. You . . .' He looked me up and down, as if I'd just crawled out of the sewer. 'You're running around pretending you're some sort of – *what?* – vigilante.'

'No, I'm not a vigilante.' I paused, looked at him. 'You think I wanted any of this? I didn't want this. But the moment your friends walked me into the middle of nowhere to bury me, everything changed. So, I *will* hurt you, Michael. If it's you or me, I will hurt you.'

He nodded. 'But you're not a cold-blooded killer, David.'

'What's the password for the Contacts folder?'

'You're not a killer.'

'What's the password?'

He smiled. Said nothing.

I cocked the gun. 'What's the password?'

'You're not a killer, *David*.'

I placed the gun against the outside of his thigh.

And pulled the trigger.

The noise was immense: a huge, tearing sound that shattered the silence into millions of pieces. Michael cried out in agony – a tortured wail – and scrabbled around at his leg, clutching the wound as blood oozed out between his fingers.

'*Fuck!*' he shouted, both hands on his leg now, one pressed against the lip of the wound, the other trying to stem the flow of blood. He looked up at me.

Now he was scared.

I sat down at the laptop.

'What's the password for the Contacts folder?'

He looked up, as if he couldn't believe I was still asking.

'I've seen a lot of gunshot wounds,' I said to him. 'During my time abroad, I saw a man get shot in the chest and still survive. The outside of the thigh is probably one of the best places to get shot – lots of fat, no major organs nearby. So, unless it's gone all the way through to the femoral artery, you won't die. But you'll *definitely* die from the next one, because I'll put it in the middle of your fucking head.'

Michael transferred hands. Both were covered in blood.

'I'm sick of running from you people. Of being led around in circles while you tell me you're doing good. Maybe you're right. Maybe I'm *not* a cold-blooded killer. But I've killed, and I'll do it again, because I know I'm too far into the darkness not to. So, I'm going to ask you again and for the final time: what's the password for the Contacts folder?'

He looked, gawping, hesitated. Then: 'Two, five, one, five.'

I put the code into the password prompt and the Contacts folder opened up. Inside was a Word document. I double-clicked on it. At the top of the document was an address: *Stevenshire Farm, Old Tay, nr Lochlanark, Scotland.* Beneath that were two other names: *Building 1 (Bethany)* and *Building 2 (Lazarus).* And beneath that was a further line: the numbers *2-5-15,* followed by a URL.

'Go to the farm,' Michael said, his voice starting to fade a little.

I clicked on the URL and the web browser booted up. Within seconds another painting started to load. A man was knelt in front of Jesus, his face lifted to the sky. He was tormented. Eyes like fires. A mouth like the opening of a tomb.

'What's two, five, one, five?'

'The second Gospel, Mark; the fifth chapter; the fifteenth verse. "And they come to Jesus, and see him that was possessed with the devil . . ."'

And see him that was possessed.

Then it hit me like a sledgehammer.

The man in Cornwall. The same inscription had been tattooed on to his arm.

'I tried to help you, David. I tried to tell you to turn around and walk away. But you didn't want to listen.

You wanted to wade across the swamp to the darkness beyond. You wanted to see what was on the other side. Well, now you get to find out.'

'Who is he?'

Michael didn't reply.

'Is he in charge?'

'No, not in charge.' Michael looked at me. 'We got him in at the start, just for one thing. His . . . *experience* helped us. But then we started needing him more and more, and slowly he became more powerful. Manoeuvred himself. And, after that, he started bringing his own . . . ideas.' He stopped, shook his head. 'So, no, he's not in charge. But he might be out of control.'

'So stop him.'

Michael said nothing.

'*Stop* him.'

'He can't be stopped, David. The God that I know, the God that has your wife, isn't the same as the God he works for.'

I frowned at him. 'What the fuck are you talking about?'

'"And they come to Jesus, and see him that was possessed with the devil, and had the legion, sitting, and clothed, and in his right mind: and they were afraid."'

'Speak in English.'

'His name's Legion . . .' Michael said, and glanced towards the laptop, and the painting open on it. '"Because many devils were entered into him."'

*

I wrapped duct tape around his wrists and ankles until the roll was finished and then bundled him into the corner of the room, tying him to one of the radiators.

'I'll phone for an ambulance,' I said.

'So you're *not* a killer after all?' Michael said. 'No – don't phone for an ambulance. We don't like to involve the authorities unless necessary. I think you can probably understand why. If I don't check in every six hours, someone will come for me. It's a routine we have. A form of protection against people like you. Until then, I'm sure I'll be fine.'

He studied me while I collected up my things.

'You know, I never felt any animosity towards you, David. I was always fascinated by you. By the determination you have.'

I didn't say anything.

He looked down at the wound in his leg. 'But they will hurt you now.'

'I've already been hurt.'

He shook his head. 'Not by him.'

He watched me with a look I recognized. I'd seen it before in war zones; in the little pieces of hell I'd walked through and written about. It was the look people had when they were in the middle of a street reduced to rubble, cradling someone they loved in their arms.

It was the look people had when they were gazing into the face of a dead man.

Legion

Legion came out of the darkness and clamped a hand on to the man's face. The man shifted in the chair, trying to wriggle free, but every effort to lean away from the hard plastic of the mask saw the devil move in closer, eyes darting, breath crackling through the tiny nose holes. The man's wrists and ankles were bound to the chair; the chair was bolted to the floor. Legion's fingers dug deeper into his skin. Then, slowly, he turned the man's head, forcing him to look directly at the mask.

'Do you know where you are?'

The man shook his head.

'You're at the gateway to your next life.'

Legion smiled inside the plastic mouth slit and then pushed his tongue out between his lips. The two ends emerged, wriggling like fat worms breaking the surface of the earth.

'Oh, God.'

Legion stopped. Stared at him. 'So, do you believe in God?'

'Please . . .'

'*Do* you?'

'I don't kn—'

'Do you *believe* in *God*?'

He felt alarm move through his chest again. He closed his eyes, trying to prevent himself having to look at the mask. Then, something Rose had said came back to him: '*Sometimes I think he might actually* be *the devil.*'

He kept his eyes shut and tried to force his arms up, hoping the duct tape might tear. But the harder he tried, the harder Legion pressed his nails into his face. When he stopped trying to fight, the pressure released. He felt blood run down his cheeks, a residue on his skin where Legion's hand had been. He wanted to touch his face, wanted to wipe himself clean, but he couldn't move.

Finally, he opened his eyes.

In front of him, Legion placed a hand on the mask and lifted it, up past his chin, his nose, his eyes, until it was on top of his head. His real face was angular and taut, his skin pale, his eyes dark, blood vessels running like a road map across the top of his cheekbones where the skin, bizarrely, appeared almost translucent. He looked in his late forties, but he moved with the purpose and efficiency of someone much younger.

'I never joined because I believed what they did,' Legion said, his fingers touching a scar running along his hairline and down to the ridge of his chin. 'The people here, they believe this is some higher purpose. A calling. A mission from an understanding God.' Legion moved in closer, putting a finger playfully to his lips. But then he smiled again and there was nothing playful in it; only darkness and menace. '*Sssshhhhhh*, don't tell anyone, but I just saw this as an opportunity. They needed me to do some dirty work for them. And after I left the army, I needed some-where to stay.'

He pulled the sleeve up on his right arm.

'That doesn't mean I'm not a believer. I just don't believe in the same God as them. Most of them here, they believe in a God that forgives; a God that will bend to whatever mistakes we make, and sanction a second chance. I don't. I suppose you could say I'm more of an Old Testament kind of guy.'

He turned his arm so the tattoo was more visible. It was bluey-black, smudged by age, and ran along the centre in two lines, from his wrist to the bend in his arm.

And they were afraid.

He touched a finger to the last four words of the tattoo.

'I've seen the wrath of God. I've watched people being blown to pieces. I've seen men bleeding out of their eyes. I've seen floods and earthquakes. I've seen *destruction*. And you know what? We *should* be afraid. *You* should be afraid.' He paused, pulling the sleeve of his shirt back down. 'Because God doesn't forgive. He doesn't believe in second chances. He punishes. He tears apart. He consumes. And the question I always ask myself when I see Andrew and Michael and all the others preaching about the power of redemption is: if God doesn't care about *me*, why the fuck should I care about you?'

Legion stepped aside.

Beyond him, a double door opened up into the next room. It was semi-dark, but the dull glow from a strip light showed what awaited.

'No,' the man said. 'No, please.'

'*This*,' Legion said, waving an arm towards the next room, 'is my contribution to this place. *This* is the gateway to your new life.'

In his ears all he could hear was his heart crashing against his ribcage, battering against the walls of his chest. When he tried to swallow, he realized his throat was closing up. Sweat had soaked through to his clothes. Saliva was running down his face. He looked at Legion, then ahead again, into the room where they were going to take him. At the device standing in the middle.

And then he gagged.

His throat forced up whatever he had left, and he leaned forward and let it fall from his lips. It hit the ground and spread, filling the cracks in the concrete; spreading like a disease across the floor. He was breathing heavily now. Struggling to take in air. The panic, the crushing sense of what was in store, felt like it was closing down his body, one organ at a time. His veins were pumping out blood, but nothing was coming back in.

Finally, he summoned the strength to look up again. Legion was gone.

He glanced left and right. Around him nothing moved. Nothing made a sound. There was no sign of the devil. He swallowed. Tears started filling his eyes.

'Do you know who Lucifer was?'

A voice, right behind his ear, fierce and violent, like shattered glass.

He whimpered.

A pause. 'Are you *crying*?'

He tried to hold the tears back. But then he looked at the device in the other room, a massive, harrowing shape in the darkness, and imagined himself being dragged across the floor towards it. Quietly, he tried to beg for his life again, but as he went to speak, his words got lost. And then he felt a wet patch move out from his groin, along the inside of his leg.

'Oh dear,' Legion mocked. 'Someone's made a mess.'

In the corner of his eye, he saw Legion loom out of the darkness, about six feet away. The mask was in place again, eyes blinking in the eye holes, tongue moving in the mouth slit.

'In Ezekiel,' Legion said, his voice crawling with power, 'it says, "Thou art the anointed cherub that covereth; and I have set thee so." It's talking about Lucifer here. It's talking about the origins of Satan. "Thou wast upon the holy mountain of God; thou hast walked up and down in the midst of the stones of fire. Thou wast perfect in thy ways from the day

that thou wast created, till iniquity was found in thee."'
Legion paused. 'Do you know what that means?'

He shook his head.

'It means Lucifer had everything he could possibly want. He had God's ear. But even that wasn't enough for him. So, God cast him out of heaven.'

The devil glanced to his left, to the room with the device.

'Do you think a God that cast out one of his own angels can hear you when you beg? *Do* you? He doesn't hear anything you say. *Nothing.* God wants you to be scared of him, *cockroach.* And he wants you to be scared of *me.*' Legion leaned into him. 'Because *I* am the real Lucifer. *I* am God's right-hand man. *I* am His messenger.'

'*Please*,' he sobbed.

Legion stepped away, his fingers like a nest of snakes, opening and closing. 'And His wrath moves through *me.*'

His skin crawled – the feeling moving up his arms and across his chest – as he stared at the devil. Trying to make eye contact. Trying to look inside the mask, and seek out whatever goodness Legion had left. But as the man in the mask came at him, darkness swirling around him like a cloak, he realized something terrifying: there *was* no good in him.

PART FOUR

34

Lochlanark was a small town halfway between Oban and Lochgilphead. It looked out over the islands of Scarba, Luing and Shuna, to the Firth of Lorn, and to the misty, grey Atlantic beyond. It took seven hours to drive up from London, and I stopped only twice the whole way. Once to fill up the car, and once to call in at a petrol station to make sure I was on the right track. They told me Old Tay was a one-street village about seven miles north, right on the edge of the sea.

When I got there, I found five cottages and a sloping village green that dropped all the way down to the ocean. Inland, there were woods. The rising peaks of Beinn Dubh were beyond, streaked black and green, small streams of snow in every fold.

And right at the end of the village was the entrance to the farm.

I parked in a frozen field, about a hundred yards from the entrance. The sun clawed its way up past the mountains behind me just before eight o'clock, and an hour later no one had come and no one had gone. The place – the farm, its surroundings – were deserted; as quiet and still as if the bomb had dropped.

Wire-mesh fencing circled the property and the main gate was locked. A CCTV camera was positioned to see who came and went. Next to it was a keypad. Using binoculars, I could pick out two main buildings. One, the smallest, was close to the road, about twenty yards from the entrance. A path, footprints frozen in the mud, led down an incline and around to the back of it. There was another CCTV camera on the front, pointing up towards the gated entrance to the farm.

The second building, the farmhouse, was large enough to incorporate at least five bedrooms, and was much further down an uneven gravel track. Its windows were blacked out. The walls were peeling. If snow hadn't been brushed into neat piles either side of the front door, it would have looked as if it had never been lived in. A third CCTV camera was bolted to the roof, pointed towards the front door.

The approach to the second, bigger building was untidy. Old, disused barns littered the path, full of frozen hay bales and rusting chunks of machinery. Beyond the farmhouse was the sea, crashing on to sand scattered with sheets of ice. Every time a wave reached for the shore, it pushed the smell of the place towards me on the back of a bitter Arctic wind.

I leaned over and flipped the glove compartment. Inside was a pair of wire cutters. I'd go in through the fence at the furthest end to the property, where the CCTV cameras weren't trained, and then head into the first, smaller building.

From there, I'd figure out my next move.

I removed the wire cutters, checked them over, and

looked back into the glove compartment. It was empty now, except for a box of .22 bullets.

And the gun.

It was a fully loaded Beretta 92. The same series as the fake one Dad had got mail order. The same series as the one I'd found in a South African war zone, and from which I'd taken the bullet I always kept on me.

I undid my black jacket and took out the bullet from the inside pocket. Let it roll around in my hands. I remembered that day in the township: the gunfire; the fear; the sun melting the tarmac beneath our feet. Then I remembered my dad shadowing me, moving behind me as I headed into the forest. As a kid, I'd fired the Beretta to please him. Never with any passion, any commitment, any intention of taking it beyond the boundaries of the woodland we'd hunted in. Now I held a real one in my hands.

I'd fired a gun two days before and taken a life. And I still felt nothing for Zack. Nothing for Jason either, as he lay there with his brains leaking out of his head, his blood spattered across my clothes and my skin. A realization, a flutter maybe, but nothing more. It was why I couldn't call the police. The reason I had to do this alone.

I'd killed twice already.

And I'd have to do it again.

35

The smaller building had an old cottage-style look to it: pale red windowsills and frames; trays of dead flowers; a nameplate next to the door that said BETHANY. I came in diagonally from the hole I cut in the fence, using the empty barns as cover. There was a second door at the back, blistered and old. I slid the gun into my belt, and pushed at it. The door shuddered and slowly creaked open.

Immediately inside was a kitchen. The sink was missing taps and parts of its plumbing. Some of the cupboards had been dismantled. A table had been chopped into pieces and left in the centre of the room. Off the kitchen were two doors: one to a pantry, the second to a living room without any furniture. A door in the living room led to the stairs.

I headed up.

There were three doors on the landing but no carpet. The first was for a bedroom. An 'A' was carved into the door. Inside, about halfway along, a square chimney flue ran from floor to ceiling, coming out of the wall about three feet. At the windows, there were no curtains, just sheets. They moved in the breeze as I stepped up to the door. No beds. No cupboards. Water trails ran down one of the walls, coming from holes in the ceiling.

I looked into the second bedroom, a 'B' in the centre of its door. This one was different. It was bigger, and the crumbling stone walls had thick cast-iron rings nailed into them, spaced out at intervals of three or four feet. From each of the rings, a set of handcuffs hung down. I moved forward, into the room. It was about twenty feet long and smelt repellent. Exposed wooden floorboards, scarred and dirty, ran the length of it, and there were four windows, all covered by sheets. I turned and looked down at one of the rings closest to me, half-hidden behind the door. Above it, someone had gouged out a message: *help me*. I leaned in closer. In the grooves of the letters were pieces of fingernail.

I backed out, and turned to face the third door.

The bathroom.

It had most of its fixtures, and a basin, toilet and bath. The bath was filthy – full of hair and broken pieces of tile – but the basin was clean, used recently, droplets of water next to the plughole. There was a mirror on the wall above. I moved to it. The bruises on my cheeks, and at the side of my head, had faded a little. But my eye was still full of blood. I leaned into the mirror to take a closer look.

Then, behind me, I spotted something.

The bath panelling didn't fit properly. I knelt down and pushed. It popped and wobbled, then regained its shape. I pushed again. This time the corners of the panel came away. The edges were slightly serrated, all the way around, like they'd been cut using a saw.

I pulled the panelling out, fed a couple of fingers in through the gap and pulled at it. It came away completely.

Inside the bath, stacked around the half-oval shape of the tub, were hundreds of glass vials. They climbed as tall and as wide as the bath allowed, dark brown, opaque and identically labelled. Instructions for use were printed at the bottom of each vial in barely visible type, underneath the message *Caution: for veterinary use only*. At the top, printed in thick black lettering: KETAMINE.

I reached in and took one out.

Snap.

A noise from outside. Stones scattering.

I went to the window of the bathroom. Someone was approaching. A woman. She was young, probably nineteen or twenty. Dark brown hair in a ponytail. Pale, creamy skin. Tight denims, a red top and a white and pink ski jacket. On her feet was a pair of chunky, fur-lined boots. She crunched along in the snow, kicking loose pieces of gravel into the fields.

I didn't have time to get out – didn't even have time to get down to the pantry – so I put the bath panel back and moved into Room B, the room with the rings. Behind the door, I took out the Beretta and flipped the safety off. My hands were clammy despite the cold.

Then I remembered the extra bullets.

Still in the car, buried in the glove compartment.

Shit.

Footsteps sounded at the staircase. I had a narrow view between the door and the frame. Enough to see the woman get to the top of the stairs, move across the landing and into the bathroom.

I heard the squeak of the bath panel being removed. Vials clinking together. Then she started humming to herself. I moved out from behind the door, took a big stride from the door of the bedroom to the door of the bathroom and placed the gun at the back of her head.

'Don't move.'

She jolted, as if a current had just cut her in two. Her eyes swivelled into the corners of her skull. She looked back over her shoulder at me without moving.

'Get up.'

She stood slowly, three vials clasped in one hand, her other outstretched to tell me she wasn't going to be any trouble.

'What's your name?'

'Sarah,' she said quietly.

'Okay, Sarah. Now tell me: what the fuck is going on here?'

She didn't reply, so I lowered the gun and grabbed her by the back of the neck. The sudden movement made her drop the vials. They smashed against the bathroom floor. She winced, as if I was about to hit her, and did so again when I turned her around and pushed her into Room B. I forced her downwards, so she was almost doubled over. Her face was right in front of the *help me* message.

'Can you read that?'

She nodded. Her breathing was short and sharp. Scared.

'Good. So you speak English. Someone carved that message in the wall and left half their fingernails in there. You can see their fingernails, can't you?'

She nodded again.

'Speak up, I can't hear you.'

'Yes.'

'Good. You any idea how painful that is? You any idea how desperate someone has to be to carve a message in a wall with their own *fingernails*?'

She didn't move.

'Sarah?'

'Yes.'

'Yes what?'

'Yes, I know.'

'Good. Which is why you're going to start answering some questions for me. Because if you don't, you're going to scratch a new message in the door next to it, with your fingernails. Got it?'

She nodded.

I pulled her up and guided her out of the room. I couldn't stand the smell any longer.

On the landing, I forced her to kneel down facing one of the walls. For a moment, I caught a glimpse of myself in the bathroom mirror, and didn't like the person I was seeing. But things had changed now. *I* had changed. There was no going back to the man I'd been before. Not now. They'd made certain of that.

'I don't want to hurt you,' I said. She was kneeling down, one of her hands on the wall in front of her. 'But I *will* hurt you if you don't give me what I want.'

I paused, let her take it in. She nodded.

'Okay. First. What is the room with the rings used for?'

A little hesitation, then: 'Acclimatization.'

'What the hell does that mean?'

'We bring them here to dry them out.'

'Dry them out?'

'Yes.'

'What are they – *drug* addicts?'

She nodded again.

'We're not doing sign language any more. Yes or no?'

'Some, yes.'

'Some, but not all?'

'Not all. But most.'

'You're running a drug programme?'

'Kind of.'

'You are or you aren't?'

'We are. But it's not . . .'

'Not what?'

'Not like a normal programme.'

I glanced into the room with the rings. Saw the handcuffs, the blood spatters. Smelt the decay and the sickness.

'No kidding,' I said. 'So, what is it then?'

'It's a way to help people forget.'

'Forget what?'

'The things they've seen, and the things they've done.'

'Like what?'

She paused, finally dropped her hand away from the wall, and turned her head slightly so she could look at me.

'I'm not sure you'd understand.'

'I guess we'll see.'

Another pause. She turned back to the wall.

'They've all suffered traumas,' she said.

'Like what?'

'Life-affecting traumas.'

'Specifics,' I said.

She turned her head again, and this time her eyes fixed on mine. They moved across my face, flashing. In her expression, I could see the fear I'd glimpsed after I'd surprised her. But now, somehow, it looked less convincing . . . as if she might be playing me. As if all of this – the scared little girl, the soft voice – might be how she turned the game on its head.

'Life-affecting traumas like what?' I said.

She smiled a little, sadly. 'Like Derryn.'

I grabbed her by the neck and pressed her head into the wall. A puff of plaster spat out at her face, forcing her to close her eyes. She coughed.

I leaned into her ear.

'Don't try to get inside my head. Don't mention her name. Don't ever try to use her as a way to get at me. I hear you say her name again, I'll fucking kill you.'

She nodded.

I released the pressure on her neck and she opened her eyes again.

'Keep your eyes closed.'

She frowned, as if she didn't understand.

'Keep your eyes *closed*.'

She shut them.

'Specifics,' I repeated. 'Give me specifi—'

'Sarah?'

A man's voice at the front of the house. The crunch of snow underfoot. It sounded like he was coming around towards the back door. I leaned in close to her.

'Don't make a sound, got it?'

Those eyes snapped open again and she looked at me. She wasn't beautiful, but her face had a hypnotic quality. It lured you in, and forced you to lose precious seconds.

'Sarah?'

He was inside the house. I covered her mouth and hauled her to her feet, then slowly backed up, with her in front of me, into Room A.

'Sarah?'

A creak on the stairs.

I pushed her into the centre of the room, and moved back, behind the door. She looked at me and saw what I was telling her: *don't do anything stupid*.

'Sarah?'

She faced the door. 'I'm up here.'

I looked through the gap in the door, to the stairs. A head appeared, but slowly, as if he knew something was up.

'You okay?' he said.

'Yeah, fine.'

'What are you doing?'

Eastern European accent.

He stopped short of the top of the stairs and looked around. I could see snatches of his face between the bars on the staircase. His eyes were darting between the doors.

'Just getting the supplies.'

He took another step.

'What's taking so long?'

She paused. Looked at me.

I could see the man's face now. It was Stephen Myzwik. Older than in the mugshots, but leaner and more focused. He had a hand placed at the back of his trousers as he stepped up on to the landing. Reaching for a gun.

'It's warm in here.'

I shot a look at Sarah. *What the hell are you talking about?* She just stared back at me. Didn't move. Didn't say anything else. When I glanced back in Myzwik's direction, I could see his gun was up in front of him, aimed in the direction of the bedrooms. His eyes flicked left to the smashed vials on the bathroom floor as he moved across the landing almost silently.

'Where?'

'Room A,' she said.

They were speaking in code.

I gripped the gun, and watched as Myzwik moved to the door, then stopped. He looked in at Sarah. And without her saying anything, he seemed to immediately know where I was.

I ducked as he fired twice through the door.

The noise shattered the silence, piercing the walls of the building and cracking across the fields outside. Wood splintered above me as bullets passed through the door. A shower of plaster rained down into my hair and face.

I kicked the door closed. It slammed shut, rattling in its frame. Sarah glanced at me, then at the door, trying to work out if she could get there before I got to her. But she didn't move for it. Instead, she turned, her hands up again, backing away. I raised the gun and pointed it at her, then darted across the room, grabbed her by the arm and brought her into me.

'Myzwik!' I shouted through the door.

Nothing. No noise from outside.

'I've got her and I'll k–'

A mobile phone started ringing on the other side of the door. It was Myzwik's. Slowly, the door handle started turning. I squeezed Sarah in closer to me, one arm locked around her neck, the other out over her shoulder, aiming the gun at the door.

It opened.

Myzwik stood with his gun down by his side and his mobile phone at his ear. His eyes were pale, almost the colour of his skin, and he was growing a beard – jet black – which gave him an odd, alien appearance. A face cut through with light and dark. He didn't take his eyes off me, even as his mobile phone started up again.

He answered it.

I could hear the faint murmur of someone else on the line, but it was impossible to make out words. Myzwik just listened, staring at me. It was an obvious play: him standing in the doorway, blocking my exit, telling me he didn't believe I would shoot him. In front of me, Sarah could probably feel my heart thumping against her spine. Maybe I fell short of the man I needed to be. Because the man I needed to be was the one who aimed his gun at Myzwik and put a bullet in his skull before things spiralled even further out of control.

Myzwik nodded at the voice. 'Yes, he has her.'

'Put the phone down,' I said.

He didn't. The voice continued, a constant barrage of instructions.

'Are you sure?' he said.

'Put the phone *down*.'

This time I spat the words at him with venom, and in Myzwik's face I saw a flitter of surprise. As if he hadn't expected it, even from a man determined enough to come right into their nest.

Finally, the voice stopped.

Myzwik flipped the phone shut.

'What do you want, David?'

'I want to know what the fuck's going on here.'

'Why?'

'No. You've had your turn asking questions. Now it's my turn.'

'Turn? We don't take turns.'

'Wrong. You'll answer my questions – and you know

why? Because I will kill her if you don't. If it's kill or be killed, you better believe I will do it.'

Myzwik glanced at Sarah for the first time, and then back at me. Something was up. A movement in his eyes betrayed him. For a moment, I swore I saw some sadness in his face.

Then he shot Sarah in the chest.

The bullet entered high up, just above her left breast. She jerked back, her blood spitting into my face, and then fell away. In an automatic response, I tried to prevent her hitting the floor, tried to yank her back up towards me, but she folded completely. The transfer of weight was too much and too fast for me to cling on to. I laid her down. When I looked up, Myzwik was almost on top of me, his gun aimed at my head.

'*What the fuck are you doing?*'

'Get up,' he said.

I glanced at Sarah. She was at my feet, clutching her chest, blood pumping out between her fingers. In her eyes some of the light had already disappeared.

'She's going to die.'

'Get to your feet or you're next.'

I stood. Sarah's eyes followed mine, but then she seemed to lose focus and her gaze drifted off. I wiped some of her blood from my face.

'She'll die here, Stephen,' I said, trying to reason with him, using his first name as a way to get at his humanity.

But it didn't work.

'Then she dies,' he replied quietly.

I looked down at her. Her life – maybe only twenty years of it – was running out over her hands, down her shirt and into the floorboards. Collecting with all the other blood that had been spilled in this room.

36

We headed down the track, towards the second building. It was an old slate farmhouse with an extension
on the back. At the front was a veranda, like the one
in the Polaroid of Alex, and a wooden sign, nailed to
the inside of the railings. It said LAZARUS. Beyond,
grass dropped away to the sea, heather scattered across
it, spreading in all directions. Either side, more fields
ran like squares on a quilt. A few had been dug up.
Spades, pickaxes and garden forks had been left on
the hard ground.

A hush settled across the farm as we approached.
The only sound came from a set of wind chimes,
swinging gently in the breeze coming off the water,
and, at the side of the house, the grinding sound of
metal against metal as a weathervane turned in the
wind. As the wind died down, I looked up to the top
of the roof and saw what the weathervane was: an
angel.

I stepped up on to the veranda and looked in
through the front window. Alex had been in there
once to have his picture taken. Frozen for a moment
in time. Framed by the window, the wooden railings
of the veranda and the blue of the sea and sky. The
picture must have been taken right back at the start,

when he'd first arrived on the farm. Before the programme. Before whatever came after.

Myzwik pushed me along the veranda.

'Open the door and go inside,' he said.

I tried the door. Like Bethany, Lazarus opened into a kitchen. It was small, dark, with all three windows covered in black plastic sheeting. Two doors led from the kitchen. One was closed. The other was open, and I could see into a stark living room with a table in the centre and a single chair pushed underneath. On the walls of the kitchen were picture frames and shelves full of food. Above the cooker was a newspaper cutting. BOY, 10, FOUND FLOATING IN THE THAMES.

The same one I'd seen in the flat in Brixton.

Myzwik flicked the lights on and closed the door. He grabbed my shoulder, pressed his gun into my spine and sat me in a chair at the kitchen table. Behind me I heard him open and close a drawer. The tear of duct tape. He started to wrap it around my chest and legs, securing me to the chair. When he was finished, he threw the duct tape on to the table and stood in front of me. Looked down at me. Touched a finger to one of the bruises on my face. As I jolted away from him, avoiding him, he grabbed my face and moved in.

'You're going to *die*,' he whispered.

I wriggled free from his grip and stared at him. He held my gaze for a moment, then turned away, removing his mobile phone. He flipped it open and speed-dialled a number.

'Yeah, it's me. He's here.'

He killed the call.

He looked at me. 'You're not here to hurt people, David, is that right? You're here to – what? – *liberate*?'

I didn't reply.

He shook his head. 'You believed you were doing something good. On some kind of crusade. But all you were doing was pissing in the wind.'

'You know that's not true.'

'Do I?'

'If I was pissing in the wind, two of your friends wouldn't have driven me to the middle of a forest to execute me.'

His eyes narrowed. Then he moved around to the other side of the table and his expression changed. Softened. I realized why: he could say what he wanted now, because when I left the farm, it would be in a body bag.

'I don't think we ever really clicked, Alex and I. A lot of us here tried to help him, but you've got to meet in the middle. He didn't want to do that.'

'So, where is he?'

Myzwik shrugged. 'Not here.'

He pulled out a chair and sat down.

'I'm sure his mother painted a beautiful picture for you. But Alex is a killer. He made mistakes.' He glanced at the newspaper cutting on the wall, and back at me. 'When he had nowhere else to turn, we were there for him. Just like we've been there for everybody else in this place.'

I turned away from him. Said nothing.

Dismissing him.

'What does that look mean?'

He leaned towards me.

'*Huh?*'

'You don't care about anyone.'

'We do.'

'By giving them more drugs?'

'*Yes.*'

'By taking out their *teeth*?'

He shoved the table towards me. It juddered against the lino, sticking. Rocking back and forth.

'Don't sit there and judge what you don't understand!' he screamed. 'You don't know the programme, you piece of shit! We give them a *chance*!'

I didn't reply.

He came around the table, teeth gritted, hand reaching for my hair. I turned in the chair and ducked beneath his grasp – but the binds stopped me from moving any further. He clamped a hand around my throat and pushed me back so I was looking up at him. He was out of breath. Rage boiling. But as we stared at each other his eyes narrowed again, and he saw everything clearly. He saw I'd got to him.

He let go of me.

'You're clever, David.'

'If I was clever, I would have put a bullet in your head before you murdered a teenaged girl in cold blood.'

'You mean Sarah?' He shook his head. '*You* murdered her by turning up here.'

'I didn't pull the trigger.'

He didn't answer, and walked back around to the other side of the table.

'There's a cause greater than her,' he said.

'She was one of your own.'

'She was your bargaining chip. You'd use her against us until you got what you wanted. Without her, you had nothing.'

I stared at him. 'So, you just do what your boss says?'

'What?'

'Whoever phoned you before you killed Sarah. He just gives you the orders and you do what he tells you. Even if it means killing an innocent girl?'

He didn't reply.

'Don't you value life?'

He shot a look at me. 'I value it greatly,' he said. 'I value it more than you can possibly imagine.'

He leaned over and removed a wallet from the pocket of his trousers. Inside the wallet was a driver's licence. He held it up to me. There was a photograph of him on it.

'I'm sure you've already read about me. I served ten years for stabbing an old man with a piece of glass. You know why?'

'You were a drug addict.'

'Right. I needed saving. That's what redemption is. Digging up a bad seed and planting a good one in its place.'

'And you've redeemed yourself?'

'Yes.'

'Your idea of redemption is different from mine.'

'Not so different, David,' he said, smiling. 'You're also a killer.'

Click.

A noise from behind me. The door opening. Myzwik looked over my shoulder. Suddenly, his expression changed completely: everything fell away, all control.

He was scared.

In front of me, in one of the picture frames, I saw a reflection. A shape standing close to my shoulder. A silhouette. I couldn't see his face. Couldn't see whether he was looking at me, or looking at Myzwik. But I could smell something.

A smell like decay.

I glanced at Myzwik. His eyes flicked between me and the man behind me, and then he edged away slightly, clearing his throat, as if he couldn't stand the smell. He slid away, along the kitchen counter, back towards the corner of the room.

When I looked at the picture frame again, I saw why.

In the reflection was Legion, his mask half-hidden in darkness, a needle in his hands. And before I had a chance to do anything, he came at me and plunged the needle into my neck.

Everything went black.

37

When I came round, I was sitting in the middle of a disused industrial fridge. There were no windows, and it was lit by the dull glow from a single strip light above me. Meat hooks hung from a long metal tube to my left. There were two doors, both of them closed: one seemed to be the entrance, dotted brown and orange with rust; the second was some sort of side door, painted the same cream colour as the walls. Speckles of blood ran across its surface.

I was sitting in an old wooden chair, but they hadn't tied me to it. My shoeless feet were flat to the floor, exactly parallel to one another, my arms flat to the sides of the seat. My fingers had been spread out, equally spaced, and my wedding ring had been removed and placed on the top of my hand. They'd taken off my shirt and trousers. All I had on were my boxer shorts.

And I couldn't move.

My head could turn from side to side – but the rest of me was paralysed. I couldn't shift a single muscle. Couldn't even wriggle a finger. I knew what I wanted to do, *begged* my body to do it, but nothing happened. I was dead from the neck down.

I yelled out. A huge, guttural noise, fed by anger,

which echoed around the fridge. When it faded out, I yelled for a second time, louder and longer.

The noise died again.

'*What have you done to me?*'

Nothing. The only sound was the dripping.

I swallowed.

Inside I could feel everything. The saliva sliding down my throat. The pounding of my heart against my ribs. A sharp, acidic burn, like fire in my lungs. The freezer was cold but I could feel a bead of sweat pop from a pore on my forehead and run down my face. Past my eyes, my nose, my mouth and down towards my neck. As soon as it passed the middle of my throat, the sensation disappeared. On the surface of my skin, from the neck down, there was no feeling at all. I was dead. It was like my organs and muscles were no longer connected to my blood vessels and nerves.

Clunk.

The entrance door started opening. A slow, grinding rumble as it forced its way out from the door frame. A man filled the doorway. Not Legion. Another. He was massive: probably six foot four and eighteen stone. His blond hair was closely cropped, and he was dressed head to toe in black. He watched me for a moment. Tilted his head slightly. Seemed vaguely amused by what he was seeing. And then he stepped forward and brought his arms out from behind his back. There was something in his hands. At first I thought it was a belt. Then I realized it was something worse: a multi-thonged whip, twelve tassles dangling from the end. It looked like a medieval scourge.

'What the hell have you done to me?'

The man didn't reply. Just stepped further inside the freezer and pushed the door shut behind him. It made another immense wheeze. He walked over to the side door next to the meat hooks and opened it. Beyond, it was dark. He looked back at me once, and disappeared inside.

'*What the hell have you done to me?*' I shouted after him. Silence.

I looked down at myself again, tried desperately to move my fingers, my hands, my legs. All I got in return was the *sensation* of it happening. My wedding ring remained perched on top of my hand. Perfectly still.

The man stepped back out of the darkness. He was still carrying the scourge, but in his other hand he held a chair. He walked over to me, placed the seat down opposite, so our feet were almost touching, and sat and watched me.

'My name is Andrew,' he said eventually.

'What have you done to me?'

'It's good to finally meet you, David.'

'What have you don–'

'In a lot of ways I admire you,' he cut in, holding a finger up for me to be quiet. 'A *lot* of ways. My organization has managed to protect itself against people like you. On the rare occasions outsiders have got close to us before, we've thrown them off the scent. But not you, David. You're *special*. Until you came along, no one ever found out about what we have here. We made some mistakes, I suppose. But I think we underestimated you too.'

I glanced at the scourge, then back at him. He hadn't taken his eyes away from me. Hadn't even blinked.

'Everyone here has made mistakes, some bigger than others, but we give people a chance to start again. In exchange, we require certain things. We require them to give themselves up to the programme. *Completely*.'

He paused, studied me.

'And we require secrecy.'

He stopped again, this time for longer. Breathing in and out. Just staring at me, as if trying to decide whether I was capable of understanding.

'Are you listening to me? We've worked too hard on this. Gone too far. This isn't going to unravel because some no-note kid is lost in the ether.'

He meant Alex.

We looked at each other, his eyes deep and powerful. Staring each other out. Eventually he blinked and turned his gaze away, down to the wedding ring on top of my hand.

'What you've never understood, David, is that our old lives don't exist any more. We don't have a space we can fit back into. We remove ourselves from society and we don't go back. If you took one of these kids out of the programme because you thought you were saving them –' he looked at me again '– where do you think they'd go?'

I glanced around the fridge. 'Somewhere better than here.'

He studied me, as if waiting for me to correct myself. Then, when I refused to turn away from him, refused to say anything else, he started nodding his head.

'Better than here,' he repeated quietly.

Suddenly – just a blur of movement – he thrashed the scourge against my left leg. The tassles wrapped around my thigh. Circling it. Clinging to it. As they dropped away again, I looked down. A series of thin red marks were carved across my skin, tiny pricks of blood emerging inside them.

But I felt nothing.

'It must be nice not feeling any pain,' he said, looking down at my leg, then at the rest of my body. 'Can you imagine going the rest of your life without pain?'

I felt a twitch in one of my toes. An odd sensation, like the nerve endings had finally fired up.

He tilted his head again, a half-smile on his face.

'Is the feeling coming back?'

I glanced at him.

'It will do. First your toes, then your feet, then your legs. You'll start to feel normal again as it passes through your groin, up into your abdomen . . .' He paused. Leaned forward. Pressed a finger against my chest, just below the ribcage. 'It's when it gets to here that you'll wish you were dead.'

'What the fuck have you done?'

He smiled. He'd clearly got the reaction he wanted.

'We've drugged you, David. Well, actually, *technically*, we've partially paralysed you. Don't worry, it won't last for ever. But I should probably warn you that side effects can include sweating, salivation, rashes and vomiting. You shouldn't suffer cardiac arrest . . . but, as with everything, you can never be sure.'

He pulled one of the thongs out from the scourge, and held it up to me. My blood was on it. Other blood too: darker, drier, stained on the leather. He studied it, turned it. There was more. The scourge was awash in it.

'You know, I think some of this blood is Alex's.'

He smiled again, a flash of darkness in his face for the first time.

'The only way you can change someone is by removing temptation from their life,' he continued, his expression softening – that same unblinking look. 'The kids we bring here, especially the addicts, if we dried them out and sent them back, the temptation would still be there.'

I got a feeling in my toes again, stronger this time. A shooting sensation.

He leaned into me.

'We promise them shelter. Food. Support. A family. But most of all, we help them *forget*. Forget about their addiction. Forget about their past. Do you honestly think *any* of them want to remember what they've done? What they've been through? One of the girls here stabbed a man in the chest after he raped her. Do you think she wants to remember what it feels like to have him forcing himself inside her?'

I didn't reply. There was sensation at the top of my feet now. It lasted longer, like it was drifting across the surface of the skin.

'So, we help them trade one life for another.'

He was still leaning in to me, his head at an angle.

'Did you know that ketamine is the closest you'll ever get to dying without your heart actually stopping? Users call it the 'k-hole'. We mix it with a little dimethyl-tryptamine . . . and call it a resurrection.'

'You're crazy.'

'When we resurrect them,' he continued, ignoring me, 'some of the people on our programme find they come out of their bodies. Some see their lives played back at them. Some see bright lights in the darkness. It's a symbolic rebirth. A resurrection into a new existence. A way to separate what's been done in the past with what's to come in the future.'

'You're fucking crazy.'

He laughed, and ran his fingers through the thongs. 'No, David. The only crazy thing is that you think you're doing good by stopping us.'

38

Andrew stared at me, his fingers running through the scourge. I looked back, conscious of the fact that they were trying to make me feel weak. They'd paralysed me. They'd taken my clothes. But they weren't going to watch me crumble. His head tilted back again – a quirk of his – and then he broke out into a smile, as if he'd guessed what I was thinking.

'I've spent a long time building this place, David. I've spent a long time getting the right people into position to help me. Surely you understand the need for me to protect what is important.' He glanced at the wedding band on the top of my hand. 'You'd protect what was important to you, wouldn't you?'

'The right people?'

He nodded.

'Like that fucking *freak* in the mask?'

He didn't move. Didn't reply.

'What's right about him?'

'He does what is necessary to secure our survival. We had problems at the beginning. He helped us with those problems. In return, we helped him.'

'Was he helping you when he came for me in my home?'

More sensation in my feet. Both of them now.

'He was ensuring–'

'He's not helping anybody. *You're* not helping anybody.'

'We're taking away their pain.'

'You're erasing their *memories.*'

'What memories do you think a heroin addict has, *David?*' he said, his voice raised for the first time. 'What about the girl we have here whose father molested her for eleven years?'

'This isn't right.'

He grunted. 'How would you know what's *right?*'

'You're forcing them.'

'We ease their pain.'

'You're forcing *drugs* into them!'

'We're helping them build a new life!' he shouted back. 'We give them food and shelter. We give them company. They start again. They *live* again.'

Now I could feel the nerves igniting in my ankles and the balls of my feet. I looked down and saw my toes wriggling. Twitching. Moving.

When I looked up he was watching me.

'You're pushing it out of your system impressively fast,' he said.

My ankles shifted position on the floor.

'You're a fighter, David. I like that.'

'You've lost control here.'

He laughed. 'Oh, no. We're in total control.'

'You've lost control!' I said again, forcing the anger up through my throat. I gritted my teeth and willed myself to move. Just an inch. Anything at all.

All I felt was one of my calf muscles twitch.

'Where's Alex?'

He laughed. 'Don't you know when to give up?'

'*Where is he?*'

He flicked the scourge again, the thongs brushing his leg.

'Alex was different. He came to me just over a year ago after a long time in the wilderness. I didn't go out and find him. He was given to me.' A pause. 'He was different.'

Another twitch – this time in my knee.

'Different?'

'When I first started the farm, I suppose I expected every kid I took in to respond to what we were doing. They had problems. We were offering them a way out. And for a while it all worked beautifully. The first two became wonderful, clean-living people. People I could *use*. I got Zack off drugs, and he became a recruiter for me. Then I gave Jade her dignity back after years of abuse and she contributed to our operations down in London.'

He leaned back in his chair. It creaked under his weight.

'But then things got more difficult. Zack found this heroin addict down in Bristol. She'd been beaten by her dealer and raped by her pimp. He found her in an alleyway in the middle of winter, left for dead. So we started her on a detox programme.'

He paused, breathed out.

'But then one night she told me she didn't want to be here any more. I told her she had made her choice and now she had to stick to it.' His body sank a little. 'So, she pulled out a pair of scissors – and stabbed one of my people in the chest.'

I looked up at him.

'I hit her,' he said, stamping a foot on the ground. 'And then I hit her again and again and again. And when I finished, she wasn't moving any more.'

He stopped, glanced at me.

'She pleaded with us to help her, so we brought her here with the promise of a new life. And she repaid us, repaid *me*, by murdering one of my best friends.'

Regret passed across his eyes.

'But I had an epiphany after that. A watershed moment. When others fought us like she did, threw everything we offered them back in our faces, I realized we had to deal with them. We'd taken them out of society, given them a roof over their head. We'd made sacrifices for them. So, they'd make a sacrifice for us. They'd become martyrs.'

'That's why you brought in Legion.'

'Yes,' he said matter-of-factly, and got to his feet. 'We'd been in the army together. He had some unique skills. You see how a man values life when you're on a battlefield, David. You see how quickly he is prepared to turn life into death. Most soldiers, most *people*, don't want to have to kill. They have a line that they don't ever want to cross.' I followed him as he moved around to my side, the scourge dangling from his hand. 'But, for him, there *was* no line.'

'I thought this was a mission from God?'

'It is.'

'You ever read the Ten Commandments?'

He smiled. 'I was protecting the project.'

'You brought in a *murdering psychopath.*'

'You will never understand, David. You've never had a cause to fight for.' He looked briefly at the wedding band. 'Other than the memory of your dead wife. And what sort of cause is that?'

He smiled again as he saw the anger burning in me, and then disappeared behind me, out of sight.

'So, he just killed the ones that didn't work out?' I said.

Andrew didn't reply.

And then it came to me.

'Oh, *shit* – you used their *bodies* . . .'

'Yes,' he replied from behind me. 'We used the bodies of the ones that didn't respond to the programme. We have people in useful places; a net cast wider than you can possibly imagine. In the hospital system. In the police. Do you know how to remove evidence from a police database, David? I think you'd be surprised at how easy it is.'

I heard him move again.

'You don't have to work your way up the tree. You can get someone trained in HOLMES in a very short space of time and from there . . . well, it's amazing what you can do just by sitting at someone else's computer and using their login details.'

'You're framing people.'

He reappeared on my other side, looking down at

me. There was a frown on his face, as if he couldn't comprehend my simplicity.

'It's a bigger win. Our men and women on the inside, they've experienced redemption. They're like Zack and Jade were. Once broken, now repaired. They give others that same chance by protecting what we have.'

The first pang of something flickered inside my body, close to my groin. A dull ache. The sensation was moving through my body like an oil spill.

He smiled and pressed a finger against my forehead.

'Feel something?'

I wriggled my head, and his finger fell away.

I closed my eyes. Tried to use the darkness to re-focus myself. When I reopened them, he was staring at me, the smile still there.

'Whose body did you use for Alex?'

He shrugged. 'Does it matter?'

'It matters to the people who love him.'

He watched me for a moment. 'You don't know anything, David. Most of their families don't care if they're dead or alive.'

'You think Mary cares whether Alex is alive?'

'She does now she's seen him.'

'She did anyway!'

He paused for a moment.

'Like I said, I didn't have a choice with Alex. My hand was forced.'

Then I lost my train of thought. The dull ache came again, but this time it was stronger. It flared in my groin. In my lower back.

I sucked in some air.

'This thing is out of control,' I said.

The sound of my voice amused him. He leaned in a little closer to me, stooping slightly, looking up at me. 'Oooooh, ouch,' he mocked quietly. 'Does it hurt?'

My mouth was filling with saliva. And I was sweating. Trails of it were coming off my hairline and running down my face. Deep inside – in my stomach, at the bottom of my throat – vomit bubbled, burning in the middle of my breastplate. Worse was the feeling emerging from the base of my back, in my groin, crawling up my spine. As every nerve end started to fire, my back tightened, the skin stretching across my muscles. The pain was focused there. Whatever they'd done to me was in my back.

Andrew stood again, staring down at me with a mixture of amusement and disgust in his face. Picking up the chair, he moved back towards the door and disappeared inside. He slammed it shut behind him – and I could feel the vibrations pass across the floor. Pain suddenly burst its way out from my back and into the centre of my chest.

'*Fuck!*'

I yelled out again.

It felt like someone was squeezing the life out of my heart. When I tried to shift my weight from one side to another, it was torture. My whole body spasmed. And, finally, my wedding ring fell, pinging against the floor of the fridge and rolling away.

The door opened again, and Andrew emerged from

the darkness without the chair. The scourge was hanging from his belt now. Clasped in his hands was a long mirror. There were marks all over it – greasy drag marks, as if fingers had clawed across the glass.

He stood in front of me, the mirror turned away, and pulled the scourge from his belt. He held it up by its handle, so the tassles dropped down in front of me.

'After I left the army, I got into some trouble,' he said. 'I couldn't find work. I missed the routine the military had brought to my life. The discipline. So, I resorted to stealing, and I hurt some people. And after that, I deservedly went to prison.'

He glanced behind me, and then back.

'But after I got out, I found God. I *really* found Him. Eventually, I even managed to get to the Via Dolorosa in Jerusalem. I saw the path Jesus walked on his way to the crucifixion. You gain an appreciation of what he had to endure when you visit those places.' He paused. Dropped the scourge to his side. 'And afterwards, you look at people differently. You look at yourself differently. You realize, if people could experience even a *little* of what he had to go through, they might have a greater appreciation of what they've been given in this life.'

I couldn't think of anything but the pain now. Couldn't force up any more anger. Couldn't concentrate on his face. It felt like the skin was slipping away from my back. I lifted a hand, shaky like an old man, and touched my back. There was blood on my fingers.

'Legion brought an idea to me one day. At first I

thought it was a little . . . medieval. But then when I considered it some more I realized the kids we took in were *exactly* the sort of people I was thinking about when I visited Israel. Like me, they never appreciated what they'd been given in their first lives. The opportunity. But if they could get a taste of what Jesus went through, if they could carry around with them a *reminder* of that, maybe they'd appreciate life more the second time round.'

And then he turned the mirror.

I looked into the reflection.

Legion was standing in a double doorway behind me, dressed in black, like Andrew, but with a white butcher's apron on.

I swallowed. Coughed. Hacked up saliva.

When I looked in the mirror again, Legion was a step closer, his mask up on the top of his head. He was the same man who had come up to me in the pub in Cornwall, except now he looked more manic. More frantic. As if on the cusp of something exciting. Something he had been desperate to do for a long time.

He glanced at Andrew and back to me and smiled, his tongue breaking through between a flat, lipless mouth.

His tongue.

I could see it now. Dark, almost crimson. Forked. His arms twitched and his legs spasmed, as if electricity was pumping through him.

'Wait,' I said quietly.

And then he stepped aside and I saw what was behind him.

Through the double doors was a small room, probably fifteen foot square, with very high ceilings. It was another fridge, but the walls were painted black. In the centre of the room, under a spotlight, almost touching the ceiling, was a huge wooden crucifix made from railway sleepers. At each end of the horizontal sleeper were handcuffs. Midway down the vertical sleeper was a footrest.

Legion stepped in closer again and grabbed the back of my chair, pouncing on it like the closing jaws of a bear trap. Then, slowly, he started to turn me around. The chair scraped across the floor, the legs catching, until I was side on to the mirror.

I turned my head and looked at my reflection.

'What the fuck have you done to me?'

My back had been whipped with the scourge while I was knocked out, leaving thin slivers of pink skin, running in lines across my back, from the base of my neck to three-quarters of the way down my spine. The rest was just flesh.

'He seems worried,' Legion said, smiling.

Andrew nodded. 'We all get like that at the end.'

Then Legion reached for the mask on top of his head and pulled it down over his face. And – as I desperately tried to move, tried to will myself to fight back – I felt a needle enter my neck again.

39

I felt the pain before anything else. From my neck, all the way down through my chest, into my groin and the top of my thighs. It felt like I'd been dropped into boiling hot water. My skin was on fire. Every movement of my chest, every expansion of my lungs, made it worse.

In the darkness, I could hear someone moving around. Footsteps, barely audible. And a squeak, rhythmic and soft, like the wheels of a trolley.

I opened my eyes.

My head was forward, against my chest. Gravity had forced it there. When I tried to straighten, to look around, agonizing prickles spread across my neck and back.

I breathed in.

I was handcuffed to the cross, five feet off the floor. The ceiling in the room was about three times as high. The soles of my feet were flat to the footrest and my arms outstretched either side of me. I was still only dressed in boxer shorts.

The room was cold. I wriggled the fingers on both hands, trying to get my circulation going. But the movement of the tendons sent a ripple all the way up my arms and into my shoulders. I sucked in as much air as I could for a second time, and closed my eyes.

Darkness. Solitude.

Then the squeak came again.

I opened my eyes. To my left, a metal trolley – the type used in operating theatres – moved into view. Legion's fingers were wrapped around the handle. On top, in individual metal plates, a scalpel and a hammer sat next to two pencil-sized nails. Next to that was a third nail: bigger, thicker, longer – like a rusting iron tube. It must have come from the sleeper itself.

As the trolley came to a stop, he spent a moment making minuscule adjustments to the position of the instruments on the plates, before slowly turning his head towards me. A long drawn-out movement, his eyes never blinking inside the mask.

He disappeared from view again. I tried raising my head, forcing back the pain, and could see the double doors into the next room, where I'd been sitting before. But now the doors were closed.

I looked left.

There was an aluminium stepladder leaning against the wall. Legion came back into view, picked up the stepladder and looked up at me. His eyes moved again, back and forth across my body, his tongue making a scratching sound against the inside of the mask. And then he placed the ladder underneath my left arm.

'Why are you doing this?' I said, looking down at him.

He didn't respond. Instead, he picked up the scalpel and climbed to the second step of the ladder. As he leaned towards me, the mask stopping about a foot from my face, his odour started to fill the air, pouring off his body. Suddenly, he seemed more threatening. I looked down at the scalpel and back up to his eyes. The more dangerous a man, the more difficult it was for him to suppress the darkness in him. His smell was like an animal scent: a warning not to come close unless you were looking to get hurt.

'Why are you doi—'

Lightning fast, he swiped the scalpel across my hip. I cried out, automatically trying to reach for the wound. My arm, tightly handcuffed, locked into place on the sleeper.

Legion descended the ladder again, his eyes dancing with enjoyment now. When he got down, he tossed the scalpel on to the trolley and looked up. Watched me for a moment. Enjoyed the sight of my face wincing. The pain started to spread out from the cut, across my skin, under it, into my muscles and bones.

He scooped up the hammer and the thinner nails, leaving the third, larger one on the tray. Then he started to climb the ladder again.

'It's amazing how much punishment the human body can take,' he said, his voice short and sharp. More clipped than I remembered, like his mouth was full of glass. 'The lengths it will go to in order to survive.'

At the top of the ladder, he glanced at me, lowering his head slightly. I imagined, behind the plastic, he was smiling. Enjoying this. Feeding off my pain. And I imagined his face – in that moment – wasn't all that different to the one on the mask.

'Stop,' I said.

He ignored me, selected one of the nails and pressed the point against my index finger. It was razor sharp, immediately piercing the skin.

'They tell me you're right-handed,' he said.

'Stop.'

'So, we'll have some fun with the left first.'

'*Stop*.'

He smashed the hammer against the head of the nail. I felt it carve through my finger, out through the fingernail, and split the sleeper beneath – then, seconds later, I felt the pain. Immense waves of it, crackling down my arms and into my hand like a lightning strike. I yelled out, the noise bouncing off the walls and coming back at me.

'The hand's a *very* complex piece of anatomy,' Legion continued, his voice even and serious, talking over my cries of pain. He placed the tip of the second nail against my middle finger. 'Twenty-seven bones, including eight in the wrist alone. Muscles, tendons, ligaments, cartilage, veins, arteries, nerves . . . You've got to make sure you don't hit anything important.'

My hand started twitching, like a dying animal left in the road. He watched it for a moment. Tilted his head. Studied me, like I was on the other side of the glass in a zoo.

Then he hammered the nail through the second finger.

I screamed out.

'We're going to kill you, David,' he said.

I screamed again, even longer and louder, trying to

317

force some of the pain out through my throat and drown out the sound of his voice. But he just waited for me to quieten. And once I did, he reached into the front pocket of his apron and brought out a syringe.

'But first you're going to feel . . .'

He raised the needle.

'. . . what it's like to be resurrected.'

I died quickly.

All sound was swallowed up. Light turned to darkness. Then the darkness changed and suddenly I was looking down at myself. My near-naked body frozen on the cross. The handcuffs on my wrists. Legion watching me from below. I could see everything: the top of my head, the nails, the scourge marks on my back. I still felt conscious. I could still feel the wood of the cross against the back of my arms, and my inner voice telling me, over and over, that I wasn't dead yet.

But then something shifted.

A feeling washed over me, like the little control I'd had left was slipping away. And – as that went – scenes from my life began to play out. In the forest with my dad. Sitting beside his bed when he'd died. Meeting Derryn for the first time. The day I asked her to marry me. The day we got told we couldn't have kids. The day she told me to find the first missing girl.

'*It's perfect for you, David.*'

Her voice again. And after her voice, a different kind of darkness: devouring everything, consuming it, until all that was left were the echoes of voices I once loved.

And beyond that, waves crashing on top of one another.

Like the sound of the sea.

Family

There were four in a group, digging flowerbeds in the earth outside Bethany. Across from them, a man and a woman watched. He was forgetting so much now – dates, faces, conversations he'd vowed never to lose – but he remembered their names. The man was Stephen, the first person he'd met when he arrived on the farm. And the woman was Maggie. He didn't remember much about her. He wasn't sure he had ever spoken to her. But he knew her face. In the darkness at the back of his mind, where he stored what he was determined they wouldn't take, he had a clear memory of her, leaning over him, clamping his mouth open and taking his teeth.

It was early spring. The earth was wet. He scooped up a pile of soil and tossed it to his side. Further down, he could see Rose, the girl who had been punished, like him, by being taken to the room with the rings.

He'd got to know her quite well. They'd spent three days in that room together until she'd been taken away. She would talk to him a little, tell him things – as much as she could remember, anyway. And then she was moved on to the next part of the programme. She looked better now – less grey, more colour – but she also barely seemed to remember him. Sometimes he would pass her and he could see her big, bright eyes linger on him, her brain firing as she tried to remember where she'd seen him, or what they had talked about. But most times, she just looked right through him, as if he were a ghost passing across the fields of the farm.

He pounded the shovel down into the ground and felt it reverberate up the handle. The fingers of his hands throbbed for a moment, and then the pain faded into a dull ache. He turned his left hand over. At the fingertips, where once he'd traced creases and lifelines, were patches of smooth, white skin. Wounds. Half an inch across and vaguely circular in shape. When he turned his hand over, he could see the same wound, replicated beneath the veneer of the fingernail. Except, while the nail had grown back, the space around the wound hadn't fully – and never would. It dipped, like a groove; a bloodless, colourless patch of skin.

The last stage of the programme.

The programme destroyed and rebuilt them, ready for their next life. A new life free from the memories of addiction, and rape, and violence. But free, as well, from the memories of anything else they'd once done.

Any places they'd been. Any people they'd loved. By the time the programme was over, they had no recollection of their first life. And no past.

Except he did – and always would.

He slid a hand into his pocket and touched the top of the Polaroid. He didn't need to take it out. He knew what it looked like. Every inch of it. And he knew what he was going to do with it if he ever got the chance. He'd fought the programme all the way through. And the memories he'd managed to cling on to, in his pocket and in his head, they would never get to find.

He pulls up to the kerb and kills the engine. There's a crack in the windscreen, from left to right. In the corner, over the steering wheel, he can see blood. A lot of blood.

He gets out and locks the doors.

At the front of the car the grille is broken, one of the headlights has smashed and there's blood across the bonnet. Splashed like paint. Running across and down, covering the badge and the lights, the bumper and the registration plate. He turns and looks up the path to the house.

Through the window, he can see his dad.

He moves quickly up the path, on to the porch and opens the front door. The house smells of fried food. In the kitchen he can see his dad, standing over a frying pan, moving the handle. His dad doesn't notice him at first, then – as he turns – he jumps.

'Oh, you frightened me,' his dad says. He looks him up and down. 'What's the matter?'

'I did it, Dad.'

'Did what?'

'Al.'

'What about him?'

'I took care of him.'

His dad smiles. 'You talked to him?'

'No. No. I mean I took care of him. Like we said.'

His dad frowns. 'What are you talking about?'

'We can keep the money.'

'What?'

'The money,' he says, a little more desperate now. 'We can keep it. We can do what we want with it. Al's gone, Dad. I took care of him. He's gone.'

'What do you mean, gone?'

'You know.'

'No, I don't know. What do you mean, gone?'

'Gone,' he says quietly. 'Dead.'

His dad's face drops. 'You killed him?'

'Yes.'

'Wha– why?'

He frowns. 'The money.'

'The money?'

'Remember we talked about it. About keeping it.'

'You killed him for the money?'

'For us.'

'Don't bring me into this.'

'Dad . . .'

'Don't you dare bring me into this.'

'But you wanted to keep the money. To take care of Al.'

'You offered to talk to him, not kill him.'

'Dad, I thought that's what you wanted.'

'I wanted you to talk to him, to reason with him.'

'But you told me—'

'I told you to talk to him.'

'You told me to kill him.'

'What? Are you out of your mind?'

'You told me to do it.'

'What the hell were you thinking?'

'I was the one who said I didn't want him dead.'

'What the fuck were you thinking?'

'You wanted him dead, Dad. I did this because you wanted it done. I did this for you. And now you're trying to deny you ever said it.'

'I never told you to murder him.'

'You di—'

'No! Just shut up for a minute and think about what you've done. Have you any idea what you've done? You shouldn't even be here. You should be running for the bloody hills.'

'What?'

'Where's Al?'

'You want me to run?'

'Where's Al?'

'In the car park.'

'At the strip club?'

'You want me to run away?'

'At the strip club?'

'Yes.'

'You just left him there?'

'Of course I left him there.'

'Bloody hell. What have you done?'

'You want me to run?'

'What do you suggest?'

He looks at his dad, then backs away, out of the kitchen and into the living room.

'You're just going to turn your back on me.'

'Find a place to stay.'

'That's it?'

'Lay low for a while.'

'Lay low?'

'Let it blow ov—'

'Why should I lay low? You're as much a part of this as me. You talked about wanting him dead. You talked about taking the money. Why do you think I did this? I did this to save you and Mum. I did this to save our family.'

'What you did was wrong.'

'You're turning your back on me.'

'What do you expect?'

'What do I expect? I expect your protection.'

'You killed someone.'

He still has the car keys in his hands. He feels for them, runs a finger along the ignition key, feels the grooves against his skin. Now he only has the car.

'I won't come back.'

'Let it blow over.'

'No, Dad. If I go, I don't come back.'

His dad looks at him.

'That's it?'

'What do you expect me to say, son?'

He turns and heads for the front door. Then he remembers something. He looks back over his shoulder at his dad, standing in the doorway to the kitchen.

'Al told me something tonight.'

'You need to go.'

'Were you ever going to tell me?'

'What?'

'Were you ever going to tell me?'

'Tell you what?'

'About the brother I never knew I had.'

They stay like that for a while: Malcolm staring into space, his eyes glistening in the light from the kitchen; and Alex opposite him, a tear rolling down his face.

Then, finally, Alex turns and leaves.

PART FIVE

40

When I came round, Legion was to my right. He was standing on top of the ladder, holding the bigger nail level with my right hand.

And there was a noise.

He was staring off, behind me, to another set of doors. I heard them open inwards, and the noise became louder.

It was an alarm.

'What's that?' Legion said.

'The Red Room alarm,' a voice replied.

It was Andrew.

'Why's it going off?'

Silence. No reply.

Legion didn't move. He was still poised, the nail pressing against my palm, the hammer in his other hand, ready to strike.

'*Why?*' he said again.

'We must have a break-in.'

Legion glanced at me, then back at Andrew. Anger flared in his eyes.

'I'm finishing this.'

'Later,' Andrew replied.

'No. We don't let him go again.'

'*Later*,' Andrew said again. 'Someone's set the alarm

off, and it's not one of us. We sweep the compound and *then* you finish.'

'Who would break into the Red Room?'

Legion stared at Andrew and then – briefly – flicked a look at me. *They think I'm working with someone. They think, whoever it is has set off the alarm.*

'Let's go.' Andrew again.

Legion moved the nail away from my hand and leaned into me again, the mask brushing against my cheek.

'This just makes it worse for you,' he whispered.

He climbed down the ladder, dropped the nail and hammer on to the trolley and disappeared from sight. The doors slammed shut. The alarm was muffled now. Outside I heard voices – arguing – and after that there was nothing.

Just the alarm.

I moved my right hand. The handcuffs were locked tightly around my wrist. I could feel the metal binds and imagined they'd rubbed a couple of layers of skin away. I tried to concentrate on that, tried to imagine how the skin might look – speckled red, like a graze, maybe some purple bruising – because the pain in my back, in the fingers on my left hand, in my neck, in the top of my legs, was immense. It raged, like thunderous, violent tidal waves.

I closed my eyes again.

Blackness and silence. Then it felt like I was turning around and suddenly, in front of me, was a door.

There was light on the other side. It was startlingly bright: burning through the keyhole, the cracks in the wood, a knot about halfway up that had two pinprick-sized holes in it. I moved up to the door, looked down at the handle and felt myself reach out for it. I couldn't see my arms, didn't reach for it with my fingers, but could *feel* my hands on it. Could feel I was turning the handle.

Then I stopped.

In the space behind me, I felt someone move in close. A presence. And with it came a distant sound. A sound I recognized. I let go of the door handle and realized the sound was waves turning over, crashing on the shore.

The sound I heard the first night I ever met Derryn.

I felt the presence nod at me. Telling me I was right.

Is Derryn waiting for me beyond the door?

No reply.

I want to see my wife.

I felt the presence drift away.

Please, let me see my wi—

'David?'

I opened my eyes. Below me a man was looking up: scruffy, his skin smeared with filth. He looked home-less: stained, mismatched clothes; the hood up on his jacket; an unkempt beard that consumed his face. I wasn't sure whether he was real or not. I was drifting in and out of consciousness so fast and so often, I was finding it hard to tell the two apart.

He took a step closer.

Something flickered in me, the smallest fire of recog-nition. Then it was gone again. But as he took another step closer to the ladder, I clawed at the memory and it came to me. The man who had broken into my car. The man I'd lost outside Angel's. The man I'd seen outside my house. I knew him. Knew him all along.

'Alex . . .'

He looked past me to the doors, and then climbed up the steps to my right hand. Glancing at me, he unzipped his coat and took out some bolt cutters. He opened them up, placed them on the chain between the handcuffs, and cut through.

Snap.

Alex caught my arm as it dropped, but the movement still unbalanced me. I wobbled on the footrest, the cross vibrating as I leaned forward, but he pressed a hand flat to my stomach and steadied me. Slowly, he guided my arm down to my side.

He moved down the stepladder, picked it up and placed it under the left arm of the sleeper. He came back up the steps.

'I'm going to take the nails out,' he said. His voice was soft, almost soothing. A complete contrast to the way he looked. 'It's going to hurt. But I need you to keep quiet. If you scream, if you make a noise, they will hear – even above the alarm.'

He perched the bolt cutters on top of the sleeper, and slowly wrapped a hand around the end of the nail in my index finger. He glanced at me once.

Then he yanked it out.

The pain was colossal – like having my whole arm pulled from its socket. Every inch of the nail, every groove, every fleck of rust, bit, tore and ripped at my flesh as it came back out. When I looked at him, he held the nail up to me, as if trying to motivate some sort of response. Anger maybe – or revenge.

I looked at him, my vision blurring.

And then I blacked out again.

David.

David.

I came round to find him looking at me, both nails in the palm of his hand. He swapped to the bolt cutters, and placed a hand around my lower arm. He snapped through the handcuffs, his hand still pinning my arm to the cross. He placed a second hand under my wrist and slowly guided it back to my side. I wobbled a second time, the strength fading from my legs, and this time he let me fall forward, on to his shoulder.

At the bottom of the steps, Alex laid me on my stomach and started picking at the locks on the handcuffs. Inside a minute he was done. 'John Cary taught me how to do that,' he said quietly, unfastening them. Then, through the corner of my eye, I could see his attention switching to my back, his fingers tracing the scourge marks.

'I need you to sit up.'

I shook my head. *I'm not getting up.*

'I need you to sit up, David. If you don't want to die here tonight, I need you to sit up so I can cover these marks.'

I shook my head again.

'*Yes,*' he said, forcefully, and rolled me over on to my back.

I cried out.

He pulled me up, so I was in a seated position, and took off his coat. He laid it on the floor next to him, and started to pull out something from the inside pocket. Long. Clear. I dropped my head forward and closed my eyes. *Where's the door?* I searched for it, but couldn't see it. Couldn't feel anyone behind me any more. Couldn't feel anything but pain.

'Right,' Alex said.

He was on his haunches in front of me, a long stretch of cling film doubled up in his hands. He started wrapping it around my body, so tight it felt like he was crushing my chest cavity. He circled me, securing the cling film in place under my arms, all the way down to my beltline. After circling me a fourth time, he stopped.

'This'll hurt when you take it off again,' he said, 'but the cling film will kill some of the pain for now.'

He gently took my hand in his, looked at the wounds, then started wrapping cling film around both of the fingers individually. Round and round, until everything was covered from the tips down to the top of the palm.

I looked at him. 'Why?'

'Why what?'

'Why come here?'

He hauled me to my feet.

'Because someone has to pay.'

And then the alarm stopped.

41

Immediately outside the crucifixion room was a long, thin, partially lit corridor. It looked like a military compound or a bomb shelter. There were no windows, just an arrow on the wall pointing to the left, underneath the words SURFACE. We were underground.

Alex carried me along, my arm slumped around his shoulder, my feet barely working. He'd been right: the pain in my back had been contained by the cling film, at least above the surface of the skin. Beneath, it felt like razor blades were running through my veins.

Naked lightbulbs dangled on cords above us, and every so often we passed other doors. Most were closed, but a couple were open. I glanced in at one of the rooms. It was small, empty apart from a pair of bunk beds facing one another.

The corridor got darker the further along we went. It was damp, with a musty, enclosed smell to it. Rust ran in strips next to the joins in the walls. Alex stopped about halfway down and listened. Above us there were voices – muffled, echoing slightly. It was hard to make out words, hard even to tell whether the voices were male or female. I started to drift away again as we stopped moving, set loose in the darkness. Then Alex pulled me back by forcing me to move forward.

Eventually we reached a set of doors, and pushed through them. On the other side was a triangular-shaped anteroom with two further doors. The one on the left had a glass window in it and was marked MEDICAL. Inside I could make out whitewashed walls, a dentist's chair, a panel of switches and plugs above the headboard of a bed, an oxygen tank, and a trolley like the one Legion had used, this one full of scalpels, chisels, scissors and clamps. The adjacent door, on the right, wasn't marked, but also had a glass window – it was mostly dark, except for one strip light, dull and creamy in the blackness beyond.

Alex pushed through the right-hand door. On the other side there was very little lighting – only the strip light I'd glimpsed, and two identical ones further down, spaced about ten metres apart. They gently buzzed above us as we walked. The corridor was shorter, with two doors on either side, and a further one, standing open, at the end. Steps led up from the open door, a block of light at the top.

Suddenly, silhouettes started forming in the light.

Alex yanked me forward and through the first door on the right. Inside, it was similar to the room I'd seen before: two sets of bunk beds and a table. He closed the door and switched on the light. On the back of the door hung two green training tops with hoods, and two pairs of green tracksuit trousers. On the floor were two pairs of slippers.

'Put these on,' he said quietly, and pressed a finger to his lips as the voices passed the door. He glanced at his watch, and sat me on one of the bunk beds, handing me the training top. 'You'll need it. It's freezing outside.'

I looked at him. He was incredibly focused, decisive, so different from the person I had imagined. Perhaps being on the run for so long changed you like that.

He looked at my left hand.

'Do you want me to put it on for you?'

I shook my head and took the top. When I raised my arms, the scourge marks burnt, as if alcohol had been poured into the wounds. I fed my arms through the sleeves and pulled it down over my body. Above the line of the cling film, where some of the cuts were still open – deep, dark tears of flesh – I could feel the training top stick.

He put on the second one and grabbed both pairs of trousers off the hook. I looked down at my boxer shorts. At my legs. The scourge mark on my thigh was starting to bruise.

'These are standard issue,' he said, then quietened again as more voices passed the door. When they were gone he turned back to me. He looked at his watch. 'The alarm will go off again in sixty seconds. Once it does, we make a break for it. Understood?'

I nodded.

He pulled on the pair of tracksuit trousers and watched as I did the same – slow, tentative movements, like an old man. When I was done, he pushed the slippers across the floor. The lining was soft, like fur, and it felt good against my skin. I still had the cuts and bruises on my toes, on the arches of my feet, where I'd run for my life in the forest.

He opened the door a fraction and looked through. Opened it a little further and flicked a look both ways. He glanced once more at his watch.

'Five seconds,' he said.

Then the alarm burst into life. This time it sounded different: a long drawn-out wail rather than the short, staccato beeps of the first one.

'Okay,' he said, grabbing my wrist. 'Let's go.'

We moved out into the corridor and towards the stairs. As we did, he flipped the hood of the training top up over my head, and pulled up his own too. At the bottom of the first step, I looked up. In the block of light, shapes began to form: others, dressed like us, coming down towards us. Three of them. They all glanced at us as we passed, their eyes firing as they tried to recall who we were and what part of the farm they might have seen us in before. I looked back over my shoulder and saw one of them, a girl, stop on the steps. She was following Alex as we headed up.

'Alex–'

'Just keep moving.'

'She *knows* you.'

'She recognizes me.'

'That's what I said.'

'No,' he replied. 'It's two different things. She recognizes me, but she doesn't know me any more.'

At the top of the stairs, in hazy grey light, I could see

the side of Bethany: the A-shape of the roof, the bathroom window under it, flowerbeds beneath that. There were people next to the flowerbeds, also dressed like us. They were digging – ten, maybe twelve of them. I could hear the sea, could see the fields of heather running all the way down to the beach.

'Are we in Lazarus?' I asked.

Alex was behind me, further back in the shadows.

'Yes,' he said. 'Part of it, anyway. The house is new. This underground part isn't. This used to be a training facility for the army in the fifties. They built the farmhouse on top.'

I glanced at the people digging.

'What are they doing?'

'Turning over the soil.'

'Why aren't they following the others down here?'

'I don't know. But we haven't got time to find out.' He stood next to me and glanced at his watch. 'Okay. The first alarm was because someone broke the locks on the Red Room.'

'The Red Room?'

'Where they keep all the memories.' He turned to me. 'That's where all your stuff is: your gun, your wallet, the bullet, the photos of your wife. Your wedding ring. I broke the locks on it before I came down here for you. That was the diversion.'

'And this alarm?'

'This is the compound alarm. It goes off if the door to Calvary is left open for more than five minutes.'

'What's Calvary?'

'Calvary was where Jesus was crucified,' he said. 'But in this place, it's the crucifixion room.'

The Calvary Project. What they'd called the dummy corporation that all their money was fed through. Now it made sense.

He looked at the diggers, a few of them glancing towards us. An army of faces in their late teens and early twenties.

'Follow me,' he said.

We angled left, out of the darkness and into the light. It was freezing cold, snow still on the ground. It must have been late afternoon – in the distance, the sun was starting to drop in the sky, melting away behind patches of thick white cloud.

The mouth of the compound was built into the extension on the side of Lazarus. We moved past a blacked-out window. Then a second. Finally we reached a red door at the back of the house. Next to it was a small car port. It curved around to the side of the farmhouse and joined up with the main track back up towards Bethany. Parked underneath were a Shogun and a Ford Ranger.

Alex had split the lock to the Red Room with a chisel. It was hanging out of the side of the door, and the door was ajar, moving slightly in the breeze. Inside was a small storage room, probably ten foot square, with floor-to-ceiling shelving on three sides and dull red walls. On the shelves were long rows of shoeboxes, stacked one after the other, covering almost all the space. Countless surnames were scribbled on their fronts. Some I recognized – Myzwik, O'Connell, Towne – but most I didn't. I took Alex's down and looked inside.

'There's nothing in there,' he said.

'How come?'

'I had nothing when I came back.'

'Came back? Came back from where?'

He glanced out through a small gap in the door, and back at me. 'I'll tell you, but not now. We haven't got time. Get your things.'

I looked for my belongings. Further along the middle shelf I saw a box with 'Mitchell' on it. I leaned in a little closer. Underneath the surname was a Christian name: Simon. Simon Mitchell. *Alex's friend.* The one Cary said had also disappeared, never to be seen again.

'Is that your friend Simon?'

He nodded.

'He came here too?'

A noise outside. Someone at the Shogun.

I pushed the door closed, leaving only a sliver of a gap. Through it, I could see Myzwik reaching on to the back seat of the car for something. He pulled out a jacket and pushed the door closed. When he turned around, his eyes passed the door.

And zeroed in on us.

He'd seen movement inside, through the gap.

His eyes narrowed. He took a couple of steps forward. I looked around the storage room for something to arm myself with, and saw Alex doing the same. But there was nothing except shoeboxes.

Then I remembered my gun.

I searched for my box, glancing back over my shoulder to see Myzwik about six feet from the door. He was unarmed, but his hands were balled into fists at his side. I scanned the rows of boxes, one after another, trying to spot my name among them all.

Quicker.

He was five feet away now; I could hear snow crunch under his feet.

Quicker.

Alex glanced at me – the first glint of fear in his eyes – and back out at Myzwik.

Quicker. Quicker.

Then I saw it, off to my left, high up on one of the top shelves. I went to reach up, and my whole back felt like it was tearing open. I sucked air in through my teeth, wanting to cry out in agony. Instead, I brought the box down and flipped the lid. Inside was my life. The car keys. My wallet. My photos of Derryn. The wedding ring I thought I'd lost for ever when I'd watched it roll away, across the floor of the fridge. Next to that was the bullet.

And next to that was the gun.

I grabbed the Beretta, placed the box on the floor, and stepped back behind the door next to Alex. It opened fractionally by itself. Between the door and the frame, I could see Myzwik reaching out for the handle. I flipped the safety on the gun – and it made the tiniest of clicks.

Enough to stop him dead.

He was on the other side of the door now, only a

strip of his back visible through the gap in the frame. I couldn't see the rest of him. What he was doing. Where he was looking.

We stayed like that for a long time. And then he started opening the door again, inch by inch, more daylight leaking in, covering the shelves, the shoe-boxes, the floor. I looked down. The sun was behind him, low in the sky, and his shadow was long across the floor of the storage room. It got smaller as he stepped further in.

Then he was inside.

Immediately he saw me, spinning round to face us. I levelled the gun at his head. He started and stepped back, hitting one of the shelves. A shoebox tumbled over his shoulder and scattered across the floor. Photographs. A necklace. A letter. Someone's forgotten life spilling across the room.

Myzwik looked at me. At the gun.

At Alex.

'You shouldn't have come back.'

We were two feet apart. I jabbed the barrel of the gun forward, smashing Myzwik square in the nose. Blood burst out, down over his lips and chin. As he bent forward, clutching at his face, I turned the gun around and swung it into the side of his face. He fell backwards to the floor with a thump.

The pain numbed me for a moment. When I finally shook it off, I looked up. Alex's eyes were lingering on Myzwik – uncertain, as if a flood of memories were passing through him. And then he turned and peered through the door, up the rutted track, towards where the group were digging. A couple of them were still looking in our direction, trying to see what was going on.

He opened his mouth to speak to me when the alarm stopped.

As silence descended across the farm, it became eerily quiet. Only the sound of shovels against the ground could be heard; the *ching* of metal meeting earth.

Alex knelt down and started going through Myzwik's pockets.

'What are you doing?'

'Trying to find a key,' he said.

'Key?'

He didn't reply, just kept searching. Eventually, though, he stood and looked at me – his face etched with unease – and then up to the group again.

'We have to join them,' Alex said.

'What?'

'There's no instructor up there with them.'

'So what? I'm fifteen years older than anyone else up there. They're going to know I'm not part of the programme. What's to stop one of them finding someone in charge and raising the alarm?'

'They won't,' he replied, his eyes still fixed on the group. 'They're too deep into the programme to remember if we're part of the farm or not. They won't care about the age thing either.' Finally, he looked at me. 'When you've got no memory, you can't be sure about anything.'

'How much time have we got?'

'Andrew will be securing the compound, room by room, making sure everything's as it should be. He'll get to Calvary last, which means we've got –' he looked at his watch '– about a minute before he and his attack dog discover you're not nailed to that cross any more. Which gives us about two minutes before they get to the surface again.'

'I cut a hole in the fence – we can go back out that way.'

'The electricity's on.'

'Electricity?'

'In the fencing.'

I looked at the fencing that ran in a gentle curve from the top entrance, all the way down the hill, dissecting a field of heather before hitting the beach. When the wind dropped away, and the sea quietened, I could hear the gentle buzz of a current.

'When the alarm goes off, the electricity comes on, and stays on for thirty minutes,' Alex said. 'You can only switch it off from inside the compound, but we're not going back in there. So the little hole you crawled through to get in here? That's no longer an option. The only other way to get out is to find one of the master keys and use it to unlock the main gate. That isn't electrified. But I haven't got one of those. Only the instructors have them. So, we join the group and wait for one of the instructors to come back. Once they do, we spring him and take the key.' He glanced at his watch again. 'Are you following me?'

I nodded. My body ached so badly I wasn't sure which part hurt the most.

'Good,' he said.

I pocketed everything from the box, slid the gun in at the front of my trousers and then followed him out. But after only a short distance, I started to fall behind. Alex jammed a fist around my arm, yanking me forward. Something twinged in my chest, forcing me to suck in air. I felt pain snake around to my side, where Legion had sliced it open.

'This could take a while,' I said.

'We need to be quick,' he replied, glancing back at the mouth of the compound. He was staring at something. I looked back and could see the CCTV camera attached to the roof of Lazarus panning in our direction.

The ground beneath our feet was uneven. Snow and stones everywhere. I could feel every bump and piece of gravel through the soles of the slippers, the pain rippling across my skin. Alex tried to quicken the pace by dragging me up the hill. Every time I looked up and expected to see the group getting closer, it was like they were being pushed further away.

'Is this all they do all day?'

'No. Some work locally too.'

'The locals are in on this?'

'No. Only the ones that used to work here. When someone like you breaches security, or gets too close, Andrew swaps everyone around. There'll be new people working out of Angel's now, and someone else managing the flat. The people down in London will be in Bristol; the people in Bristol will be up here – on the farm or in the villages somewhere. The project owns a couple of shops along the coast. Every time you open up a hole, they will close it.'

I looked up towards the group digging in front of us.

'What do they do in the villages?'

'The same as they do here. Digging, planting, fetching, carrying, maybe standing behind a counter and serving. Menial tasks. *Nothing* tasks. Andrew argues it's a purer, untarnished existence. But the truth is, by the time they've finished with you here, you're not good for much else.'

A few of the faces were visible beneath the hoods, staring down the hill towards us. They looked normal, even healthy, until you watched their eyes, darting between us, desperately trying to fit memories together like broken pieces of a jigsaw puzzle.

We finally reached them and a couple more looked up: a teenaged girl, a man in his mid-twenties, a girl of about the same age. In front of them, cracks and fissures in the frozen earth were gradually opening up. Their hands, wrapped around the shovels, were red with cold.

There were four shovels propped against the wall behind the group. Alex and I both grabbed one and pretended to dig, using our hoods to disguise our faces, but with a clear sight of the compound. A couple of the group still watched us, especially Alex, but then, as we started to dig, they gradually turned their attention back to their work.

'I'm not going to be able to fight them for much longer,' I said. My body was on fire: every muscle, every bone. 'I will slow you up.'

'We both leave.'

I looked at him. 'You make a break for it.'

'And go where?'

'Run.'

'There's nowhere for me to go, David.'

Then, from the mouth of the compound, they came.

42

There were two of them. One I recognized immediately as Andrew; the other was smaller, maybe female, and had the hood up on her top. As soon as they emerged from the darkness of the compound, they were looking right to left, their eyes adjusting to the dusk. They knew we were on the farm somewhere – it was just a question of where.

They both looked up towards us and studied the group. The slow, rhythmic digging; the sound of the shovels; the wind blowing in from the mountains and the sea. *What if they did a head count before we joined the group?* I looked at Alex briefly. He shot a glance back, as if he knew what I was thinking.

Andrew headed towards the front of Lazarus. The woman turned and started making her way towards us. Alex and I turned away slightly, and started digging properly.

It took her about sixty seconds to get from the mouth of the compound. She was wearing heavy-duty boots, the steel toecaps scuffing against the gravel and the snow on the ground. Apart from Andrew, the instructors dressed like the people they were supposed to be saving – hooded tops, tracksuit trousers – only in blue instead of green. With my back half-turned I couldn't make out her face clearly, and as she got closer to the group I turned away from her a little more so she was side-on to me.

I dug the shovel into the earth, and flicked another look at her as she moved level with the group. She was looking off somewhere else. When I jammed the shovel down again, into the ground, I felt the wounds throb in my chest, and my back, and my hand. I stopped momentarily, breathed in, then continued digging.

A minute passed.

When I glanced again at her, she'd moved around, closer to Bethany. She was bent over, watching one of the women brushing away some of the earth at her feet. Then the instructor moved again, finally disappearing from my line of sight.

I flicked a glance at Alex.

He was at the opposite angle to me, almost facing the other way. I could see his eyes following the woman as she moved behind me.

We continued digging.

Thirty seconds later I saw Alex glance up at the woman again, then sideways at me.

A brief nod.

It was time.

I gripped the handle of the shovel, my knuckles whitening, and waited for a second nod from Alex. We hadn't agreed anything, hadn't made any sort of plan. But I knew the first nod was the primer, the indication that I needed to get ready.

The second would be the trigger.

From my left, the woman reappeared, her eyes fixed on a girl digging next to me. She stopped about six feet from me. A sudden gust of wind swept up the hill, lifting the hood from her face. Then it fell away.

Evelyn.

Through the corner of her eye she must have seen me staring at her. She turned and faced me, her eyes narrowing. Then she realized who it was beneath the hood. For a second she must have thought she could reason with me. Play on our history, on the fact we'd once got on; laughed together; even been drawn to each other in some way. But then she remembered how she'd held a gun to my head and let them take me out to the woods to be buried.

'I'm sorry, Evelyn,' I said.

She started to call out for help.

I swung the shovel at her, dirt spitting off as it arced, and caught her in the side of the head. The impact reverberated along the handle, into my hands. She stumbled sideways. Fell to her knees, and then her stomach, one side of her face puncturing the earth as she hit the ground.

And then she was quiet.

The rest of the group looked up.

Alex glanced between me and the others, and back down towards the farm. No sign of anybody else. He dropped his shovel to the floor and moved across to Evelyn, who was drifting in and out of consciousness. He went through her pockets. Eventually he found a keyring in her trousers and removed it. On the ring were two keys: a brass Yale key, and a silver one with a blue head. Alex selected the blue one and held it up to me.

Then his eyes fixed on something behind me.

His whole face collapsed, the colour draining out of it. Suddenly, he looked terrified.

I turned and followed his gaze.

In the middle of the group, surrounded by men and women, Legion stood staring at us. He was wearing the same clothes as we were, his hood up, the mask still on. In his hand was a submachine gun. It looked like a Heckler & Koch MP7. Black and compact. Short barrel. I glanced at the gun, and back up at him. His eyes were fixed on Alex now. He had been among us the whole time.

He flipped back his hood.

'Alex,' he said, almost a whisper.

Despite the wind, the sea, the sounds drifting through the late afternoon light, it was difficult to hear anything but his voice. Sharp, almost scratchy, like a needle cutting across an old record.

Alex held up both his hands.

'We have something to finish, David,' Legion said, not looking at me – just staring along the ridge of the gun he was now pointing at Alex.

'No,' I said, anger in my voice. I reached into my trousers and brought out the Beretta. A twinge in my chest and back. 'We're finished.'

This time he looked at me. Body perfectly still. Head swivelling. Eyes dark and focused. For a second, it was like looking at a ventriloquist's dummy – as if his head shared none of the muscle, bone and sinew of the rest of him.

Legion glanced at my gun.

'We will finish what we started, *cockroach*,' he said, every word, every syllable, cutting across the ground between us. 'Put the gun down or I slice Alex in two.'

'Don't put the gun down, David,' Alex said.

I glanced at Alex, then back at Legion. He was still looking at me, standing completely still, even as a gust of wind blew across the group.

'Put the gun down,' he said again.

'They can't kill me, David.'

I glanced at Alex.

'Put the gun down,' Legion said for a third time.

'Don't, David – they can't kill m–'

In a flash of movement, Legion jabbed the barrel of the gun forward, right into the centre of Alex's forehead. Alex's head lurched backwards. He was instantly unconscious, even as he stood. He toppled over and hit the ground like a sack of cement. No grace, no arms out, no reactions at all.

Legion turned to me, and dropped the gun to his side. He didn't see me as a threat. He took a step towards me, pushing a couple of the group aside. One of the girls fell to the floor. A couple of the others turned and looked towards the sea, to the ground; too petrified to even turn in the direction of the killer standing among them.

'Stop,' I said.

He took another step forward.

'I'll shoot you.'

'No, you won't.'

'You better believe I will.'

'No.'

The good things are worth fighting for.

Her voice, suddenly, unexpectedly.

Legion noticed something in my face – a flicker of a memory – and finally did stop. I could feel sweat on the tips of my fingers, feel the adrenalin, hear my heart pumping in my ears. I glanced down at the gun again, and back up at the man in front of me.

Take this chance, David.

I fired once. It hit Legion in the shoulder. He staggered back against one of the others in the group. Somewhere behind me, one of the women screamed. A shovel clanged against the earth. Legion lurched away from the group, clutching his wound.

I pulled myself out of the moment and headed for Bethany, leaving Alex on the ground, face down. Maybe dying. Maybe dead. I moved quickly around the edge of the house and towards the back door.

Snow crunched behind me.

The devil was coming.

I kicked open the back door, immediately realizing I'd led myself into a trap. Half-inside the kitchen, I turned back and saw his silhouette pass across the windows.

It was too late to go back.

Swivelling, I headed through to the living room – dark now, as daylight began to fade – and towards the staircase. I glanced back. From the semi-darkness of the kitchen he came: the horns on the mask; the eyes moving inside the holes; the mouth wide and leering.

I ran for the stairs, landing awkwardly when I reached them. Pain tore across my chest as I scrambled up on all fours, the first shots piercing the wall behind me. I could hear the old brickwork spitting out dust and debris, could hear the *ping* of a ricochet. I heard him move across the living room, broken tiles beneath his feet. I launched myself on to the landing and a shower of bullets followed me up, popping in the walls, bouncing off the stonework, lodging in the wooden floor.

I fired back three times, then made for Room A. As I moved, he followed. I could hear him pad up the stairs. The occasional creak but nothing more. He was quick. Lean. Streamlined.

He fired as he got to the top. Beyond the noise, I thought I could hear him whisper something, then the words were swallowed up as more bullets followed me into the room. The smell of rotting damp hit me.

I looked around.

The chimney flue, running from the fireplace downstairs, was angled enough to provide cover from the door. I dropped behind it. Flowers of light erupted from the landing. Bullets hit the door frame and walls. Wood splintered. Plaster spilled. Legion kept firing into the bedroom: the flue disintegrated beside me, floorboards cracked and broke, bullets ricocheted. One bullet missed my leg by an inch as I rolled to my side.

The window closest to me fractured and blew out. Glass landed on the floor and snow from the roof swept in. I clutched the gun with both hands. One of Legion's feet hit a floorboard at the door to the room. A creak. I waited for him to move closer, but, instead, heard the clicking of his gun.

He was out of bullets.

The silence was like a shockwave.

I leaned out, as quickly as I could, and loosed off six shots. One didn't even get beyond the room, hitting the door itself. One headed straight across the landing to the wall at the top of the stairs. The others lodged in the walls on the landing – every one a wasted bullet. Legion had already taken cover to the left of the doorway.

I stayed like that, leaning out towards the doorway, waiting for him to appear again. But he had second-guessed me. All I could hear was my breathing.

'C-c-c-c-c-cockroach,' he whispered.

The sound of something snapping into place.

Reloading.

There was a long pause, the silence hanging in the air.

And then I coughed.

Legion came in at me, firing quickly. I ducked back for cover, shielding my face from the dust and the glass. Bullets fizzed past me. One tore through the floorboards about two inches from my hand. Another made contact with my slipper, taking part of the toe off.

I knew I had to fire back, knew I had to attempt to repel him. If I didn't, he would get closer and closer until he was near enough to put me down. I gripped the gun, lay my arm across my chest and emptied the rest of the clip.

The first three shots missed, going so wide of the mark he didn't even stop shooting. The fourth got closer, briefly interrupting the noise from his gun.

Then the fifth hit something.

I heard footsteps – barely audible – retreating from the room.

I looked down at the gun, unsure whether he was really hit or whether this was all part of the game. The pain was becoming unbearable. Huge chunks of air escaped from my chest. Glass was embedded in my skin. I didn't want to move.

I held the Beretta up in front of me and removed the magazine with a shaky right hand. I'd fired all fifteen bullets.

I waited for a moment. Breathed.

My teeth throbbed. My eyes were watering. I listened for Legion, for any sign of movement. All I could hear was the wind.

'It doesn't have to be like this,' I said.

Nothing. No reply. No sound of movement.

I looked down into my lap. The gun felt heavy now. My whole body felt heavy. As if it had been turned inside out. It felt like Legion held all the cards, even if I'd somehow managed to hit him. He would wait. He was a soldier. He was trained to use silence and time to his advantage.

I swallowed and felt the saliva slide down my throat,

moving towards the centre of my chest, where it blew up like an explosion. Pain scattered across my chest and back.

'It doesn't have to be like this,' I said again.

Silence.

I reached into my pocket and quietly removed everything I'd taken from the shoebox: my wallet, my car keys, my photographs of Derryn, my wedding ring. And the bullet. A fine mist settled on the metal casing as the chill of the evening slithered its way in through the broken windows.

The bullet.

Sliding out the empty clip, I slotted the bullet into it and pushed the clip back into the Beretta.

43

Slowly, I edged out from the chimney flue. Held the gun up in front of my face. Slid along the floor on my knees. A shiver passed through me. Ahead of me, on the landing, I could see zigzags of snow, compacted, fallen from the soles of his shoes. I moved along the floorboards, churned up by the gunfire.

As I closed in on the doorway, I tried to angle the gun towards the sliver of wall that joined the two bed-rooms. Legion had hidden there while he was reloading – but he wasn't there now. I looked right to the bath-room, then left to the top of the stairs. Shadows were everywhere, but I couldn't make him out. That meant there was only one place he could be.

Next door. The room with the rings.

I kept close to the wall as I approached the door. Held the Beretta as straight as I could. My hands turned red as I squeezed the handle. The muscles in my arms tightened, the veins in my wrists prominent through the skin. An image flashed in my head of Legion sitting in the corner of the room, opening fire as I tried to get in the first shot. I hesitated. Stopped short of the door.

Then, suddenly, I could smell him.

There was no aftershave overpowering his stench now. All I could smell was decay, as if death were crawling across the floor of the house towards me. I'd been right. It was like an animal scent, trailing him. A warning system. It was telling me not to come any closer. Except I had to if I was ever going to leave the farm alive.

I peered around the door a fraction, my eyes darting from one corner to the next. I thought I could see him, half-covered by darkness, directly across from me.

Then it felt like I got hit by a train.

I hadn't seen Andrew coming. Hadn't even thought about it. But the impact sent me flying, my knees leaving the floor, the gun dropping from my grasp. I looked up to see him clutching a table leg. I went for the gun – an automatic reaction, even though it was too far away – but he hit me again, low in the ribs.

I screamed out.

Instinct kicked in: I tried to gain some purchase on the floorboards, tried to crawl away so I could gain some distance, but my fingers slipped and he hit me again, in the ankles. I yelled out in pain as a paralysing tremor hummed up my leg. Then a third blow: in the small of my back, and this time I could feel my skin break beneath the cling film.

He stopped. Looked down at me. His black clothes made him seem bigger in the semi-darkness. More powerful. As he stepped into what little light there was left, in his face I could see regret. Maybe even a little mercy.

'I understand,' he said, gently, and dropped to his haunches beside me. 'I understand how you feel. How desperate you must be to get her back.'

I jabbed a leg at his kneecap. It missed, but unbalanced him, one of his hands planting on the floor behind, trying to prevent him falling on to his backside. I looked across the landing for the Beretta. It was slightly to my left, about six feet in front of me.

Hauling myself on to all fours, I started towards it.

But Andrew was on his feet again. He took one step in my direction and smashed the table leg into the same spot as before: the small of my back, right where one of the wounds had opened up.

I yelled out and collapsed on to my stomach.

There was silence for a moment. He was watching me, seeing if I was going to try to make a move again. When I didn't, through the corner of my eye, I saw him drop down for a second time, but further away, so I couldn't make contact.

'After I got out of prison,' he said, turning the table leg in his hands, 'my parole officer found me a job teaching kids how to play football at a youth club. He knew the people who ran it. The first evening I turned up there, the guy in charge pulled me aside and said, "I know you've got a record. You're just a favour for a friend, so if you mess up *once*, even if it's forgetting to tell me we're out of orange squash, you're finished." I got twenty pounds cash in hand, and was claiming every week as well. When Sunday came round, I had nothing. The temptation to steal, the temptation to claw it back, whoever I hurt, was immense.'

I looked across the landing, to the Beretta.

'Go for the gun, and I will put my foot through the back of your head.'

I glanced at him.

'Just give me an excuse, David. I can't wait to see what your face looks like as it leaks through the floorboards.'

I closed my eyes. Tried to memorize the layout of the building. Tried to recall anything I could use as a makeshift weapon.

He started talking again.

'Prison was tough,' he continued, and I opened my eyes and watched him. 'So, I didn't want to go back. And, anyway, about five months after I started there, everything changed. I got talking to the mum of one of the boys. He'd had leukaemia, but it was in remission. And the way she spoke about him, about the love she had for him, it just absolutely stopped me dead. When I found out she was on her own, I asked her out – even before I knew her name. She was the one who first took me to church. She was how I found my faith.'

He stood. Looked down at me.

'Charlotte,' he said.

There was a long pause as he stared at me.

'We'd been seeing each other for about two years when her son's leukaemia came back. I'd already moved in with them by then and had a job. Everything in my life was perfect. But when Charlotte found out the disease had come back, something just turned off in her, as if she knew this time it wasn't going until it took her boy with it.'

Something moved in his eyes.

'I came home three months after he passed away and she was lying beneath the surface of the water in the bath. She'd overdosed on sleeping pills.'

He gripped the table leg harder, both hands wriggling to get a better grip.

'That was when I came up with the idea for this place. A place to help people start again. To leave behind the memories, everything they wish they could forget. I went to the bank and they turned me down on the spot. But eventually, a few months later, someone cared enough to help me out.'

I shook my head.

'What's that supposed to mean?' he said.

I turned my head, pain shooting down the centre of my back.

'You're not helping *anyone*.'

He paused. Watched me.

Then, suddenly, he moved, hitting out at me with the table leg. It caught me in the chin.

'*Fuck!*'

My head hit the floor, blood in my mouth, on my lips, across my face. White spots flashed in front of my eyes. I was disorientated, unable to make anything out.

'You of all people should understand what I'm trying to do!' he screamed from behind me, his voice trembling with rage.

I looked for him, but my vision was still blurred. One doorway became the next. He'd moved back. Briefly faded into the night.

'This place is *built* for people like you!'

Then he emerged from the darkness and leaned into me.

'And it's not going to stop now.'

His face shifted back into focus.

'*You're* not going to stop me, David.'

He raised the table leg above his head. His grip tightened, his teeth clenched. I curled up into a ball, protecting myself.

But the final blow never came.

A dull thud sounded.

Andrew staggered sideways, clutching his head.

At the top of the stairs behind him was Alex. He turned and punched a piece of the table up into Andrew's guts. The air hissed out of him. He doubled over, clutching his stomach.

Alex struck again.

This time he pounded the chunk of wood into the base of Andrew's spine. The tall man stumbled forward and fell to the floor, his legs giving way under him like a deer shot down in a hunt. A fourth and fifth blow came, a chunk of wood splintering this time, breaking at the sheer force of the blow. It spun off into the bathroom and landed among the glass.

Alex briefly glanced at me, and then kicked Andrew in the face. More blood, spraying out over the wall behind him; over the carpet. Then he kicked him again. And again. And again. Gradually, Andrew's eyes glazed over and all that came after were sounds without reaction: skin splitting; bones breaking. No grunts.

No groans. No breathing. Just a *slapping* sound, like raw meat being tenderized.

'Alex,' I said.

He stopped, panting heavily, and looked around towards me, across to the room with the rings, to my gun, and to the blood on my clothes.

He came across and helped me up, lacing his arms through mine. My balance was affected. My body felt like it might fall apart. He guided me back towards Room A. I went straight for the gun, grasping it as tightly as I could. Once we were inside, hidden by the darkness, I brought his head towards me.

'Legion,' I whispered, pointing towards the wall that divided the two bedrooms. I could see in his face he got it immediately. Dread rose to the surface.

Click.

We both turned, looking towards Andrew. But the noise had come from the room with the rings.

Click.

Click.

'Oh, shit,' Alex said. 'He's coming.'

44

Alex turned to me. 'You need to use me,' he whispered, glancing towards the door. 'You need to pretend you will kill me.'

'*What?*'

He stood up. I grabbed hold of his arm and pulled him back down.

'What the hell are you doing?'

He looked at me. 'They can't kill me.'

'They can.'

'They can't.'

'They can kill you, Alex.'

'Grab hold of me and follow me out on to the landing,' he said.

'*What?* Are you fucking *crazy?*'

'Do it,' he said, and looked me square in the eyes. 'Put a gun to my head and walk me through. When you see him, threaten to kill me.'

'You must be out of your fucking mind.'

'No,' he replied. 'Trust me.'

I looked at him.

'Please, David. *Trust* me.'

He got to his feet so his back was to me. I looked up at him, waiting for him to turn around. Waiting to see the fear in his eyes. But he didn't look down. He stood and stared into the darkness like a soldier about to clear the trenches and head over the top.

'*Do* it,' he said.

'He will kill you, Alex.'

'He *won't*,' he said, fiercely this time.

He remained still, looking out on to the landing. I stood and inched in close to him so Legion wouldn't have a clear shot at me. Then we began to move forward. The floorboards creaked beneath our feet. Alex's shoes kicked up splintered wood and shattered pieces of glass. We stepped out on to the landing, briefly sliding in Andrew's blood. And then we turned right and edged into the room with the rings, little by little, every footstep feeling heavier.

Further and further into the lair.

'I'll kill him,' I said, staring into the darkness. All around us was the night, hanging from the walls and the windows like blankets. I looked from corner to corner, pressing the gun into the back of Alex's head. 'If it's him or me, I swear I'll kill him.'

A half-step towards the centre of the room.

'I swear.'

There was no reply. No movement.

'Are you listening to me?'

I glanced left and right.

'I'll kill him, I promise you.'

My eyes adjusted a little more. Shapes started to emerge from the corner of the room. An uneven floorboard. The hole in the wall with the message *help me*. The rings. The water running down the brickwork.

'Do you want that?'

More shapes.

'Answer me.'

We shuffled further forward.

'*Answer me.*'

Click.

A gun cocked behind me and, before we had a chance to turn, I felt it at the back of my neck. The end of the barrel pushed in against the top of my spine.

Legion had tricked us. He'd moved to the shadows on the stairs while Alex and I had been forming a plan in the next room.

'*Cockroach,*' he said quietly.

'I'll kill him.'

He pushed the gun in harder.

'You're not a killer, cockroach.'

'Put your gun down,' I said, pushing back against his gun's muzzle.

'No.'

'Put it down.'

The same tone, the same control: 'No.'

'Put your gun down *now.*'

In the blink of an eye his head was at my ear. I could feel the mask brush against the side of my face. His smell. His hot breath passing through the holes in the plastic.

'*No,*' he said again.

'I've got a gun against his head,' I said slowly. 'Do you want to take that chance?'

He moved his head back and pushed the gun in against me.

'You're a fucking cockroach, you know that?'

'Put it down.'

'You belong in the dirt.'

'Put the fucking gun *down*.'

The gun pressed harder against the back of my head, digging in against the curve of my skull. It felt like he was weighing up his options.

'You've got three seconds,' I said.

The gun didn't move.

'One.'

Nothing.

'Two.'

I cocked the Beretta.

'Thr—'

With one last push of the barrel, I heard glass crunch beneath his feet as he stepped back, the gun going with him.

I swivelled, so hard Alex almost stumbled, and looked across at Legion. He was standing in the doorway. The gun was at his side, a second one – what looked like a SIG Sauer P250 – in his belt. His sleeves were rolled up, the tattoos creeping out from underneath. His eyes were fixed on me, peering through the eyeholes. Blinking slowly. His tongue came through the mouth slit, and moved along it, making a cutting sound on the plastic. There was some blood close to his right shoulder, but he hardly seemed to notice.

'Put it down,' I said, nodding at the submachine gun.

He didn't move.

'I'll put a bullet through his face, I promise you that.'

He looked at me, at Alex, then back to me. Maybe he didn't believe I would kill Alex. If you're a killer, you wear it – like a cut that doesn't heal. He could see I didn't wear it. But maybe he'd heard about what I'd done to their people before. So he knew, if I had to, I could kill. If it came to that, it would be them before me.

'You want me to start counting again, you fucking freak?'

His eyes narrowed inside the mask. Then his hand opened and the submachine gun dropped to the floor. Glass scattered as it turned over and came to rest.

'Now the other one,' I said, my eyes snapping to his belt.

He paused, then placed a hand on top of the SIG. His fingers slid down the side, like insect legs, one moving in against the trigger, the others in around the grip. Wriggling. Long, grey stalks; dirt and blood under the nails. I shifted the Beretta sideways, from Alex's neck across his shoulder. I aimed at Legion's head. His eyes flicked down to the gun and back up to me, and he slid the SIG out from his trousers, held it out in front of him and dropped it to the floor. It hit the ground with a *clunk*.

'I can *taste* your fear, *cockroach*.'

I nodded, as if I barely heard him. But every word out of his mouth was like the end of a knife blade. He lived off any flicker of fear. Even with both guns on the floor, he was still dangerous.

'Kick the guns over here.'

I expected to have to repeat myself but he did it straight away. That instantly worried me. Everything else had been a struggle. Now he was sending his weapons across to me, out of reach, without even pausing for thought.

'Put your hands behind your head.'

He snorted, and instead moved his hands up to his mask and slowly lifted it away from his face. I felt Alex shift a little in front of me. The devil tossed his mask away. He blinked, his eyes fixed on me, and ran a hand across the top of his shaved head. And then he smiled, his mouth widening, his tongue pushing through his lips. Running across them. Tasting them.

'I'm gonna *eat* you.'

'Put your hands behind your head.'

He smiled again. But he did what I asked, sliding his hands behind his head. Too easy again. Something was up. I'd forgotten something. Missed something. What had I missed?

'Turn around,' I said.

Legion picked up on something in my voice. Another smile broke out on his face. 'What's the matter, *cockroach*?'

'Turn around.'

'You scared?'

'*Turn around.*'

His eyes widened, like huge holes in his head, sucking in the darkness from the room. I felt myself losing control.

371

'You *sssssssssscared*?' he said quietly, menacingly.

'Shut up and turn arou—'

He swung then, a sudden bloom of movement, pulling a knife out from somewhere behind his back. The handle was small, but the blade was long, slightly curved, glinting even in the gloom. He brought the knife out in front of him, a blur that moved from his waist, and slashed across Alex's chest. Alex stumbled backwards, knocking me off balance.

Legion lunged forward again, further this time, flipping the knife and jabbing the butt into Alex's temple. Alex staggered sideways, his legs giving way. I could see a long, thin, shallow tear in his clothes. There was no blood, but it had torn though his top like paper.

He moved in a third and final time and punched the knife's handle into the side of Alex's head again. Alex lost his footing completely and tumbled to his left – pulling me down with him. At first, as everything shattered around me, I couldn't understand why he'd done it. Why he'd grabbed me too. Then, as he crashed to the floor and rolled over on top of me, I could see what he was doing. He was protecting me. Legion couldn't go through him.

He came towards us, the knife out in front of him. I was still too close to Alex for him to get careless, so he stabbed the blade into the floor next to my ear. Trying to force a reaction movement from me, away from Alex. But I couldn't move. I was trapped beneath Alex. He rammed a foot into Alex's face and the back of Alex's head hit my nose – a force like a hammer blow. White light flashed in my eyes. Blurring. Soundless blurring. Blood splashed on to my skin, into my mouth and eyes. Then as noise returned, Legion was rolling Alex off me, on to the floor. Alex was dazed. I looked for the Beretta, and found it: out of reach.

I could see Legion again, bent over, dragging Alex across the room. Legion's hooded top was hoisted up across his back. Criss-crossing between his shoulder blades was a leather strap. A knife sheath was perched three-quarters of the way up his spine, empty now.

When he was done, he turned back to face me, eyes flashing. He flipped the knife, the blade now an extension of his palm, and came across the room at me.

I got on to all fours and looked for the nearest gun. It was Legion's SIG, about five feet to my left. I threw myself towards it as he jumped on my back, his knee cracking against the base of my spine, just below the scourge marks. I hit the floor face first. We slid across the floorboards, glass scattering. Out of the corner of my eye, I could see a tattooed arm pinning me down by the neck. The other raising the knife above his head.

The final act.

Suddenly, the power faded from his arms.

I inched my face further around and could see Legion looking over his shoulder. Alex was standing behind him, with a gun to the back of his head. Legion smiled, glanced at me, and released some of the pressure on my neck.

'What are you doing?'

'Let him go,' Alex said, sounding dazed.

'What are you doing, *cockroach*?'

One side of my face was flat to the floor. I could feel shards of glass embedded in my cheek. As I tried to lift myself up and shake them off, Legion looked down at me and pushed his knee harder against my spine. His fingers wriggled at my neck.

He looked back over his shoulder at Alex.

'Are you *listening*, Alex?'

My eyes darted across the room. I had a narrow field of vision, but I could see the SIG about a foot away, level with my face. When Legion had launched himself into my back, he'd pushed us both across the floor towards it.

'You should have been dead a long time ago,' he said to Alex.

I moved my hand an inch away from my body. Waited for any reaction. When none came, I moved it another inch.

'I should have made you suffer.'

I carried on moving my arm in an arc, sweeping through the debris. Sooner or later, I expected the movement of my body to register, but Legion had become consumed by his venom for Alex. For the first time, he was starting to lose some control.

'I should have sliced you open.'

Closer to the gun. Inch by inch.

'That's what you deserved.'

My fingers touched the SIG. I could feel the rough texture of the grip.

'That's what you've always deserved.'

I pulled the gun towards me. Worked my palm around the grip and my finger around the trigger. The SIG was in against my hand now. I could feel everything. The curve of the trigger, the weight of its casing. The finality of it.

'You deserved to be *tortured*,' Legion said, almost spitting the words back across his shoulder at Alex. 'You're a *cockroach*, just like this . . .'

He looked down at me.

His fingers wriggled at my neck.

I raised the gun off the ground. Bent my arm back and forced the SIG in against his stomach.

And I fired.

He fell off me, his grip releasing instantly. I rolled over and saw his hand clutching a space just under the ribcage. Blood was spilling out over his fingers. He brought the knife up, swung it at me, but the power had gone from his arms. The effort pulled his body backwards. He hit the nearest wall and slid down, the knife falling from his hand.

Dead.

I looked up at Alex. He nodded and threw the gun to the floor. He was retching; choking on the fear and adrenalin.

I dropped the SIG next to me. Slowly got to my feet. My Beretta was midway between where I was lying and Legion's body. I went over and picked it up, then pulled out the clip.

One bullet still inside.

The one I always kept on me.

I moved across the room and used the barrel to prod the devil's body. He shifted a little; a dead weight. The wound under his ribcage was small, but there was a lot of blood. It was spilling out on to his clothes and running down on to the floor. I reached over to him and lifted up his top. Underneath, he was wearing a thin black padded vest. Sleeveless. It looked thermal. Maybe military. There were a series of zip pockets on its front.

Inside one of the pockets I found three photographs.

One was a long lens shot of me standing outside Mary's house, talking to her on the porch. The second was me talking to Jade outside Angel's. The third was the photo of Derryn and me that he had stolen from my bedroom the night he had come for me. My face had been circled in red pen, over and over and over until the photograph had started to tear.

Behind me Alex moved. He was leaving the room and heading for the landing, clutching his face and limping slightly. He disappeared out of sight. After a while, I thought I could hear him crying.

I turned back. Saw Legion had shifted slightly.

And his eyes were open.

An arm came up, clamping on to my throat, closing around my windpipe. His fingers burrowed in against the skin, trying to dig deeper and deeper into my flesh. I froze. Couldn't move. Stared down at him as air stopped passing to my head – a feeling so cold, so final, it was like drowning in an icy lake.

Pull yourself out.

I found the trigger of the Beretta.

Pushed the gun in against the first piece of skin I could find.

Take this chance, David.

I fired.

The bullet blew through his throat.

He slumped sideways, his eyes darkening even more, like the gates of hell had opened up for him. Then the devil was still.

45

Before daylight started to break, I brought the Shogun up the track to Bethany. Alex and I carried Legion out, and dumped his body in the back of the car. We stood there for a moment, staring in at him. Even as death claimed his body, his eyes still looked out at us. As powerful as when they blinked and moved behind the mask.

Next, we got Andrew. He was bigger, more difficult. We carried him, his body broken, the bones shifting and moving inside his skin. When we got to the Shogun, we dropped him into the back, and then Alex rolled him on top of Legion as best he could. When I asked him why, he said it was so that he no longer had to look at the eyes of the devil.

After that, we rounded up the people we could find – all the drug addicts and victims of abuse that had come to the farm with the promise of a better life – and led them to the living room in Lazarus.

There were twenty-two of them in all. Every one the same: healthy, but virtual amnesiacs, a few of them at the beginning of the programme and still strung out on whatever drugs they were being forced to take. They watched us as we sat them down, one by one, their expressions fixed, a few of them looking like their will had gone; as if they were dying from the inside out. As Alex and I made hot drinks and passed seats and blankets through, I started to wonder how they would ever be able to start to live again.

Myzwik was still lying on the floor of the Red Room. There was blood matted to his hair. It had congealed beneath him, where the back of his head had hit an uneven patch of concrete. When I rolled him over, I could see a hole about the size of a peach at the base of his skull. A piece of concrete, not set straight like the rest of the floor, had pierced the back of his head when he'd landed. As I moved out of the Red Room, out into the bitter cold, I realized I was now a killer four times over.

And not a single one I regretted.

The other instructors – Evelyn included – were gone. The property was deserted, and if we drove to the next village – where the tendrils of the organization spread – they wouldn't be there either. None of them would be back. They were running now; perhaps understanding some of the desperation those on the farm felt as their lives crashed around them.

Finally, as the sun started coming up on a new day, we drove the Shogun along the coast to a cove. Majestic cliffs rose out of the sea for three hundred feet. Waves crashed on the shore below, their sound swallowed up by the wind. We'd found a couple of concrete blocks in Lazarus' yard. At the edge of the cliff, we tied the blocks to Legion and Andrew – and then pushed both bodies off the side. They turned in the air as they dropped, and quickly disappeared in the spray. When we saw them again, they were fading into the depths of the sea, sinking further and further under. Legion sunk last, as if clinging on to his existence even after life had left his body.

Eventually, darkness consumed them both.

Back at the house, we told the group everything would be all right. They eyed us with suspicion. They'd been tied to rings in rooms that smelt of death, terrified by a killer who watched them from the dark, and nailed to a crucifix. Their memories might have gone, but they weren't stupid. They knew this new existence wasn't the one Michael, Zack, Jade and all the others had promised them.

Finally, when we were done, we left the farm through the main gates and headed to my car. Alex drove while I sat forward in my seat, careful not to put any pressure on my back.

Ten minutes down the road, we stopped at a payphone and put in an anonymous call to the police.

46

We stopped at a service station outside Manchester. The temperature readout inside the building said it was minus three. We sat at a table by one of the windows, looking out at a children's play park, both of us nursing coffees. The fingers of my left hand were still wrapped in cling film. As the adrenalin wore off, I was starting to feel more: the dull ache of bones locking up, nerves over-compensating, the burn of torn flesh in and around the wounds.

In the glass, I could see people staring at us. One of us bruised almost beyond recognition, the other looking like he'd spent every day of the last six years living on the streets. I could see my injuries too – my face, my fingers – and wondered how I would explain it all when I went to a hospital. *If* I went to a hospital. After that, we headed out to the car, cranked up the heaters and disappeared back on to the motorway.

Snow started falling about twenty minutes later, coming out of the pale afternoon sky. I turned to Alex. He was driving, a fresh coffee steaming in the car's cup holder.

'How did you know about me?' I asked him.

He glanced at me, then back out to the road in front of us.

'I broke into Mum and Dad's home and found your name and address,' he said. 'That's what I'd become. A fugitive. I wanted Mum to see me that day. I let her follow me so she would believe enough, and then I prayed she would go to someone. I used to watch her when she came into London. Follow her from the train to her work, hope that one day she might stop somewhere and ask for help. And eventually she did. She came to see you. I didn't know anything about you, couldn't find you in the Yellow Pages, couldn't find your number in the telephone book. That was why I went back to Mum and Dad's place. To find out who you were.'

'How did you get out of the farm in the first place?'

His hands shifted on the wheel.

'One night – it was about nine months after Mat persuaded me to go to that place – I heard a voice I recognized passing in the corridor outside my room. When I went to the door, I looked out – and it was Simon.'

'Your friend Simon?'

He nodded. 'I couldn't believe it was him.'

'But it was.'

'Yes,' he said. 'It was. They treated him . . . I'd never seen them treat anyone like that. They'd put him on a leash and were pulling him around like an animal. So, I followed them, expecting to be stopped, but I got to the end of the corridor and no one came after me. I passed beneath their CCTV cameras and no one tried to stop me. It was like the whole place had been abandoned. Normally you couldn't breathe without someone hearing you, but I managed to walk out of the complex, and up on to the surface.'

'Did you find Simon?'

'No. I was too far behind him . . .' He trailed off, glanced at me. 'And I guess I forgot about him as soon as I got to the surface.'

'Why?'

'Because the entrance had been left open.'

'The main gate?'

He nodded. 'It was open enough to allow me to escape. My body was telling me to make a break for it, but my brain was holding me back. They never left it open – ever.'

'Was it some kind of trap?'

'That was my first thought. But, after a couple of minutes of standing there, I started walking towards the gate.'

'And that was it – you just went through?'

'No. When I got to the top . . . Andrew was there.'

'Just waiting for you?'

'Just there. In the shadows. I was about four feet from the gate, close enough to run for it if he tried to come for me – but he didn't. He just stood there.'

I looked at him. 'And did what?'

'And did nothing. He just stayed like that. And then, when I finally made a move towards the other side, he said, "Bringing you here was a mistake. We never wanted you, Alex. None of us. I'm sick of fighting you; of not being able to give you the drugs I need to. If you really were a part of this programme, we would have sacrificed you already. But you're not – *never will be* – and I'm willing to take whatever consequences come my way now. I don't want to see your face any more.""'

'That's what he said?'

Alex nodded. 'It still felt like a trap, but when I stepped through the gate, on to the road, I realized it wasn't. I looked back and watched him push the gate shut behind me. Then he said, "If things get bad, if you try to do anything to us, bring anyone here, we will get to you. And when we get to you, we won't care what kind of protection you have – we will kill you." And then he headed back to the farm.'

'What did he mean by "protection"?'

He shrugged. 'They can't kill me.'

'Why?'

'I don't know.'

We drove for a little while without speaking, both of us thinking about the night Alex had escaped. My mind was racing, trying to put things together. Something didn't add up.

'Did they say anything else to you?'

'No. I just ran. I didn't look back. I hitched a lift to the first station I could find, and then got on the train down to London. I hid in the toilets all the way. I sat there, too scared to go out in case they'd tricked me. I couldn't tell people what they'd done, in case they followed through on their promise to kill me. That's why

I had to get you to go to that place. I had to get *someone* to stop it. Every day since I left, I've been cowering in the shadows with my back to the wall, terrified they would find me. I was sick of feeling frightened.'

I looked at him. 'It's strange . . .'

'What?'

'You never seemed frightened today.'

He nodded. 'I suppose a part of me expected to die. They told me never to come back, but that's what I did. When you think you might not live to see another day, it gives you some focus. And I just needed to make sure you got out.'

'What about Al?'

He looked at me. 'You know about him?'

I nodded.

'I've had a lot of time to think about what I did,' he said. 'I spent a lot of months being scared about dying. And then I spent the last few weeks wondering what they would do to me if I came back here. After what I did to Al, maybe I would have deserved to die today. But I couldn't die before I did something about the farm. I know what happened today doesn't make up for what I've done . . . but it's the only thing I could do.'

'So, why did you kill him?'

'I did it for Dad,' he said. 'Dad and Al, they went way back. Dad used to work for a bank in the City, then Al offered him a job doing the books at his stores. We got a new TV, a new kitchen, went on a nice holiday to the south of France. But then it started to go wrong.

Everything Mum and I thought we owned, Dad knew differently. Because Al really owned it all. He'd loaned Dad money for just about everything, told us we never had to pay it back because we were like family to him. Then one night he flipped. Dad came home and told me Al wanted to take back what was his. Everything we'd ever got from him, he wanted repaid. There was no way we could do it. If we gave him back all that was his, we would have had nothing.'

'Why did he suddenly turn like that?'

'I don't know, but it just got worse and worse. Dad invited Al round to the house when Mum was out, to try and talk him round. They went down into the basement, and Al absolutely lost his head. He punched Dad. When Mum asked, we told her he'd had a fall while we were out at the lake, fishing. Dad couldn't bring himself to tell Mum, couldn't bring himself to tell her everything he had bought for her, the life he had created for her, was about to fall apart. That our home and everything in it would be gone.'

Alex looked out of the window.

'This went on for a few months – and then Dad came up with an idea. We'd pay Al back with his own money. Dad could fiddle Al's books quite easily. Al had three stores, each making a lot of cash. That was when we first got talking about the five hundred grand.'

'Five hundred grand?'

'The money we would take from him. After that, we realized the only person who could stop us was Al himself. Because eventually he would find out. If we stopped Al, we got to keep the money.'

'Your dad helped come up with the plan to kill him?'

'We just got swept along by it, corrupted by the idea . . .' He seemed to fade a little then. 'In the end, I did it. But, that night, I never set out to. The closer we got to the idea, the less certain I became, until eventually I said to Dad it might be better for me to go and talk to Al. Dad didn't want that. By then, he was very sure of the path we needed to take, but the thought of . . . the thought of what we were going to do to Al, it scared me shitless.'

We passed under a set of signs. Eighty miles to London.

'So, I went to meet him at that strip club in Harrow. He was drunk by the time I got there, sitting next to the stage, letting these strippers rub their tits in his face. He wasn't in a fit state to talk. He wasn't in a fit state to do anything. Every time I tried to reason with him, he turned his back on me and told me I didn't know what I was talking about. I tried to give him a chance, tried to let him *give* me a chance, but in the end I lost it with him. I told him to stay the hell away from my family. I told him if he ever came near us again, I would kill him.'

He stopped. We both knew what came next.

'I told him I would kill him,' Alex said gently, 'and that's what I ended up doing. Mum had the car that night. She was out with friends. I guess I could have got the train, but I just wanted to get in and get out again. I didn't want to spend time with Al, I just wanted to do what was necessary. So I hired a car at a place close to Mum and Dad's. It was a Hertz but the manager there was this old guy. I showed him my ID, but lied on the form, so nothing could be traced back to me. The guy looked at the form after I was done, but didn't even twig the name and address were different. I guess, deep down, I knew there would be trouble that night.'

He paused for a moment.

'Anyway, I came out of the bar and headed back to the car and he came after me. He was so drunk he couldn't stand up, let alone walk in a straight line. But he charged over to me and started pointing at me. Telling me what a piece of shit my dad was. There were a couple of people standing outside the bar. As soon as they went in, I hit him. He was so drunk he didn't see it coming. When he was on the floor . . . I broke his nose with the heel of my shoe.'

The lights from the motorway flashed in his eyes. He was caught somewhere, silent for a moment. Then he turned back to me.

'When he finally got up, he was a mess, could hardly speak properly. But he looked straight at me and said, "You just made a big fucking mistake, Alex. I was trying to help you. I was trying to help your mum. You came down here for your dad, right? Your *fantastic* dad. Well, why don't you go and ask him about his dirty little secret in Wembley?"'

'What did he mean by that?'

Something glistened in his eyes.

'I got in the car and tried to calm myself. Then he started again. He was spitting blood all over the bonnet, telling me to go fuck myself, telling me he'd make a special journey to watch Dad being kicked out on to the streets. And then, before he went to walk away, he looked at me and said, "Go and ask your dad about your brother."'

'Your *brother*?'

He nodded. There were tears on his face now.

'I put my foot to the floor, and went straight through him. He hit the middle of the car, just flew off to the side. And I left him there. When I looked in the mirror, he was lying in a puddle. And he was still. Absolutely still.'

47

'Where did you go?' I asked. It was dark, almost nine o'clock, and we were ten miles from my house, stuck in traffic on the edge of London.

'France,' he replied. 'After I left home, I took my bank card, withdrew the maximum amount of money they would let me take in one day, and headed down to Dover. I dumped the car in long-term parking, then found a trawler willing to take me across the Channel. I didn't have my passport, so I paid them whatever it took. Just to keep them quiet.'

'What did you do in France?'

'Worked some crappy jobs, cleaning toilets, waiting tables at cafés. I just tried to keep my head down. I didn't spend more than three months in each job, just in case the police were on to me.'

'So, what brought you back?'

'I got homesick. I ended up hating everything about my life there. The jobs were terrible, the places I lived in were worse. I spent five years doing that, and every day ground me down a little more. So I found a boat that would take me back, and went and saw Michael.'

'You knew him from before?'

'Yeah,' Alex said. 'He used to be a friend. A good one. Back when I lived with Mum and Dad, he worked at our local church. Called himself Mat back then. Michael Anthony Tilton. Then he went travelling. When he got back, he took that job in east London, and I noticed small changes in him – like, he never talked about his family any more, and he got uncomfortable when I still called him Mat. Andrew was changing him too, I suppose, just not with the drugs and the torture and the fear. I went and visited him at the church a few times before I disappeared. The last time was just before I killed Al.'

'That was when you bought the birthday card in the box?'

He nodded.

'Why did you go to Michael after you came back?'

'I thought he would know what to do. I thought I could trust him. I couldn't go to Mum, because of Dad. I couldn't go to John, because of his job. Kath wouldn't have understood. None of them would have. I thought Mat might. So, he made a few calls and arranged for me to be driven up to the farm. They were fine for a few hours. Took my picture, talked to me, told me everything would be okay. But do you know what they did after that?'

I shook my head.

'They knocked me out. I turned my back on them once, and they knocked me out. And then . . . Then they tried to take my memory away. I could feel my body pleading for the drugs, but I had some fight in me. I managed to cling on to something. And so, even in the darkest times, I could see the outline of the people I loved. Could hear things Mum had said to me. See places I'd been with Kath. I used that as strength, to help me get out of there.'

'Do you know how they faked your death?'

He nodded. 'They used Simon.'

'*Simon* was supposed to be you?'

'Yes.'

'Why?'

'We had the same blood type. I remember that from when Simon and I used to give blood at uni. That made it easier to disguise the fact it wasn't me in that car. And I think maybe Andrew and the others on the farm . . . they liked the symmetry of it.'

'What do you mean?'

'I mean, one friend making the ultimate sacrifice for the other.'

Based on what I'd found at the farm, I imagined Alex was right.

'Simon had been on the farm for a few months. They'd fed him drugs – but he'd fought them. He fought back against the programme. He pushed down the terror he felt at everything that was going on, and he pushed back at them. But in the end he pushed back too hard. One night, when one of the women came in with his meal, he launched himself at her. He beat her so badly she lay there until morning in a pool of her own blood.'

'How do you know all this?'

'There was a girl with me in the room with the rings. Rose. She was drying out when they put me in there. She wouldn't speak at night, because of Legion. She knew, at night, he watched us. But, in the day, before she started to disappear into the programme, she would talk a little and tell me things she had heard. And Simon was one of the things she heard . . .'

Darkness. And then light. Hands grab at him and pull him out of the boot of the car. Cool air bristles against his skin as he's dropped on to a patch of grass. A foot comes down and pins him to the ground. He can feel wet mud against one side of his face and the last weak rays of evening sunlight against the other. Fields and a dirt road stretch out in front of him, and an old Toyota is parked further down, rope attached to its underside.

'So, they killed him in that car crash.'

'Yes. When I saw him, when I watched them take him away on that leash, it was the day after he beat that woman. I could smell the petrol on him right from the other end of the corridor. It was only afterwards, when I found out I was supposed to be dead, that I realized why – and what they did to him.'

'They used your teeth.'

Alex left one hand on the wheel and peeled back his lips with the other. He placed a finger and a thumb on his two front teeth. And pulled. The teeth came away.

They were all false.

'One of the women on the farm used to be a dentist. They put my teeth into Simon's mouth, plied him with so much alcohol he could hardly stand, and doused him with petrol. Then they led him out of that farm on a leash, and drove him nine hours down to Bristol, so it looked like I'd been close to home the whole time. Simon was supposed to be me.'

Through the windscreen of the Toyota he can see a car close in front. Maybe only three or four feet away. The two vehicles are attached by a length of rope.

Everything in the car smells of petrol: the dashboard, the seats, his clothes. He glances at the speedo. They're still accelerating. Sixty. Seventy. Eighty. He tries to move, but can't. He looks down. His arms and body are paralysed.

Suddenly, there are headlights up ahead.

And something pings.

There's the brief, grinding sound of metal against metal, like a clasp being released. Brakes squeal. Then the car in front veers left, the rope trailing behind it, swinging across the road.

A horn blares.

Simon desperately tries to jab at the brakes, the insides of the Toyota swimming in the light from the lorry. But his feet don't move. Not an inch.

And then there is only darkness.

Alex pulled into a parking bay at a train station about a mile from my house. I gave him enough money to get a ticket, and some more so he could get wherever he needed to go. He climbed out of the car and shook my right hand.

For the first time I glimpsed the wounds in his fingers.

'It's ten o'clock, Alex,' I said.

'I know.'

'Why don't you just stay at mine?'

'I'm still on the run,' he said. 'I think the less time you spend with me, and the less you know about where I'm going, the better it is for you.'

He got ready to go, but then turned back. He ducked his head inside the car again, and stared at me for a moment.

'Do you know what the last thing you hear is?'

I looked at him. 'Last thing before what?'

'Before dying.'

I knew. I'd heard it myself when I'd been bound to the cross.

'The last thing you hear is the sea,' Alex said, and nodded as if he knew I understood. 'Waves crashing. Sand washing away. Seagulls squawking. Dogs running around on the beach. If that's the last sound I hear in this life, it won't matter to me. Because I like that sound. You know why?'

I shook my head.

'It reminds me of sitting on the sand, in a cove in Carcondrock, with the person I loved.'

After that, he turned around and disappeared into the crowds.

48

I didn't want to go home, so I stayed the night in a motel across the street from the train station. The woman booking me in glanced up a couple of times at the dried cuts around my cheeks, at the streaks of purple and black on the side of my head, but didn't say anything. As I limped to my room, I could see her reflected in a thin strip of glass by the elevators. She was looking again. My body was exhausted, and a dull ache coursed through my system, but the cling film had helped to quell some of the pain, even if the injuries to my face were more difficult to hide.

The room was small and plain, but it was clean. I set the holdall on the bed and sat down on the edge of the mattress for a while, breathing in and out, trying to relax. But the more I relaxed, the worse I started to feel; as the adrenalin ebbed away, it took the numbness with it. I got up again and went to the bathroom. Alex had stopped outside a pharmacy before we got to the train station so I could pick up some medical supplies. The smell of the bandages, of the antiseptic cream, of peeling away the plasters, suddenly reminded me of Derryn's years as a nurse. Then a memory formed: of her attending to my face three weeks after she'd come to join me in South Africa. I'd fallen into some masonry in a desperate run from a Soweto shootout.

'It's a Steri-Strip today,' she'd said, placing the transparent plaster over a cut close to my eye. 'I don't want it to be a coffin tomorrow.'

My eyes fell to my newly bandaged fingers, and – finally – to my body. Cling film was still wrapped around it, blood pooling at the sides, crawling around from my back in thick, maroon tendrils. I couldn't see the lacerations themselves; wasn't sure I ever wanted to. One thing I did know, though, was that I didn't have the courage to start removing the cling film.

Not yet.

Once I was cleaned up, I went back to the bed, dropped on to my stomach and faced the door. And twelve, restless hours later, I woke again.

49

It was 13 December, eleven days after she'd first come to me, when I headed to Mary's for the final time. It was late afternoon by the time I got there. I drove, but with difficulty, sitting forward the whole way. My back was still stiff from sleep, and I could feel the cling film loosening. By the time I got out of the car, pain was crackling along my spine.

I slowly moved up the path and on to the porch. Snow had collected in thick mounds at the front. Christmas lights winked in the windows of the house. Mary answered after a couple of knocks, lit by the fading dusk sky.

'David.'

'Hello, Mary.'

'Come in,' she said, backing away from the door.

She looked at me, at the cuts and bruises I'd patched up. I inched past her, my body aching.

'Your face . . .' she said.

'It looks worse than it is,' I lied.

'What happened?'

'I got into a fight.'

'With who?'

I looked at her, but didn't reply. She nodded, as if she understood that I didn't want to talk about it. At least not yet.

'Let me fix you something to drink,' she said.

She disappeared into the kitchen. I made my way to the windows at the back of the living room. They looked out over the garden. The snow was perfect. No footprints. No bird tracks. No fallen leaves. It was like no one had ever been out there.

Mary came through with two cups of coffee, and we sat on the sofas.

'Where's Malcolm?'

'Upstairs,' she said.

'How is he?'

She paused. 'Not good.'

On the table in front of her I placed the envelope she had given to me with the rest of her money in it. She looked down at it, studied it, but didn't reach for it. Instead, her eyes flicked back to me.

'You don't need any more?'

'No, Mary,' I said. 'We're finished now.'

There was little emotion in her face. I wondered whether she'd already talked herself into believing it had all been a mistake.

'Finished?' she said.

'He was in Scotland.'

'Alex?'

'Alex.'

She took a moment, her mouth opening a little. All the doubt, all the times she'd told herself she must have been seeing things, fell away. Her eyes started to fill with tears.

'What was he doing in Scotland?'

'I don't know,' I lied.

'Is he still there?'

'I'm not sure.'

'Have you spoken to him?'

'No,' I lied again, and when I could bring myself to look at her, I suddenly wasn't sure this was the right path, despite Alex having asked me to play it this way. 'I think he wants to see you, but I think he's also confused.'

'He can come back home,' she pleaded.

No, he can't. I looked at her, a single tear breaking free.

'Why doesn't he come *home?*'

I didn't answer. It had to be like this. Alex had to decide when the time was right. He had to find his own way back in. They all had to find a way back into a world that had forgotten they existed. A world that had given them nothing the first time. It would be easier for Alex in many ways, despite the baggage he carried with him. He had something to grasp on to, memories he'd never let go. For some of the others, what awaited them was simply a blank. No memories of their first lives. No life to fit back into. Perhaps no chance at starting again.

'After he left home, he went to France,' I said, hoping that would be something. 'That's where he went before he came back.'

'Why did he go there?'

I looked at her and thought of Al, of Malcolm, of the way he had shut Alex out. Kept secrets from him. From the family. I guessed his brother was also unknown to Mary. It was up to Alex to bring that to her, not me.

'Why did he go there, David?' she asked again.

'I don't know,' I said, but couldn't look at her when I said it.

She broke down and started crying into the sleeve of her cardigan, using her arm to cover her face. Eventually, she calmed a little and I looked at her. She was staring into space. I saw what I might do to her with these lies, but I'd given Alex my word.

Briefly, I thought of another lie; a way to comfort her. It was a lie about the friend of mine who just decided one day that he needed to break away – even if it was just for a short time – to clear his head and decide what he wanted. But I didn't feed her that one. The deeper I dug, the further away from safety I got. And I didn't want to get caught out. Not like the people on the farm, making mistakes that cost them their most precious, most necessary commodity. Secrecy.

50

Mary led me to the basement and we talked in there for a while, like we had before. The wind had found a way in somewhere, making a sound like a child blowing into a bottle. The place was still a mess. The cardboard boxes were still stacked high like pillars, wood and metal still strewn across the floor. There were books in one corner, stacked twenty or thirty high. A lawnmower. More cardboard boxes. Some old walking sticks, different colours and weights, probably all Malcolm's.

Mary was quiet. I knew she was fighting back tears. It felt wrong to leave, so I offered to sit with her for a while. The last time anyone had sat down and really talked to her was probably before Malcolm got ill. Since then she'd had to fight every demon herself.

'What did Alex do in France?' she asked.

'Just worked some jobs there.'

'Good jobs?'

I smiled. 'He'd probably say not.'

She nodded. Rubbed her palms together. Her hands were small, the nails bitten. To her side was a cup of coffee. She reached down to it and placed her fingers over the top, as if trying to warm herself up.

'How can he still be alive?'

I knew she'd ask. I just didn't want to answer.

'I don't know,' I said. 'All I know is that he misses you, and he will phone you. He's just spent a long time on the outside, and now he has to make the step back inside.'

'What do you mean?'

Above us, floorboards creaked. Malcolm was shuffling across the living room.

I looked back at her. 'I mean, he needs time.'

Mary glanced around the basement, her eyes locking on the photograph albums in the opposite corner.

She raised her head to the ceiling, then turned back to me.

'The AD has been really bad these past few weeks.'

'How do you mean?'

'He can't retain anything. Not even things he used to repeat before. When I bath him, he looks at me and I can see he has no memory of me at all.'

'I'm sorry,' I said quietly.

'I know I can't do anything about it. But it hurts.' She looked again at the ceiling. 'I'd better go and check he's all right.'

I nodded. 'And I'd better go.'

We walked up the basement stairs, into the kitchen and through to the living room. Malcolm Towne was sitting in front of the television, the colours blinking in his face. He looked tired and old. He didn't turn to face us. When Mary went to him, and put a hand on his shoulder, he glanced up at her. His eyes drifted across to me. Total confusion. Behind those eyes, there were conversations with Alex that would never come out, and Mary would never know. I felt sorry for them – for both of them.

'Are you okay, Malc?' she said.

He didn't reply – just gazed at her. His mouth was slightly open, a blob of saliva on his lips. Mary spotted it and immediately wiped it away with her sleeve. He didn't even move. He glanced at me again and I smiled at him, but nothing registered.

'Would you like a sweet?' Mary asked him.

The minute detail in his face had become important to her. When a part of his mouth twitched, she took that as a yes. She went to the drawer and got out a bag of sweets. Took one out and unwrapped it.

'Here we are,' she said, slipping it into his mouth.

'Aren't you worried about him choking on it?'

'No.' She shook her head. 'He seems to be all right with these.'

She held the bag of sweets against her, and watched him suck on it. His lips smacked a little, the only part of him moving with any kind of normality. I could see what she meant about his illness – it had definitely got worse since the last time. After a while, he slowly turned back to the television.

'Would you like a sweet, David?'

She held out the bag to me. I took one.

'They're Malcolm's favourites,' she said, following me towards the front door. 'It's about the only way he'll interact with me these days.'

We walked on to the porch and down the driveway

towards my car. I could see her hanging on the back of that last sentence. Staring into the face of what had become of the man she loved, and wondering how it might have been different without his illness.

As I flipped the locks on the car, a fierce winter wind ripped up the road. Distantly, something registered – a noise I recognized – and I looked back at the house.

Mary was standing behind me.

'What's the matter?' she said.

I listened.

'David?'

I shook my head. 'Guess it's nothing.'

I got into the car and pulled the door shut, buzzing down the window. As Mary stepped in towards the car, I unwrapped the sweet and popped it into my mouth.

'Thank you for all your help, David,' she said.

'It *will* come together, Mary.'

'Okay.'

'You will get the closure you need,' I said. 'You were right. Right to come to me, right to force me to believe you. But something like this . . . it's more complicated than a simple missing persons case. There's no file, no proper line of enquiry. Your son has been places and seen things that he needs to process himself before he can come back to you. I don't know everything, but what I do know is that a lot of those things need to come from him.' I put my hand on hers briefly. 'He'll be back, Mary. Just give him time.'

Wind roared up the road again and pressed in at the car windows, so hard they creaked. Mary stepped sideways, pushed by the wind, her hand sliding out from beneath mine.

And then that noise again.

I looked past Mary to the house. Hanging baskets swayed in the wind. The front door swung on its hinges. Leaves swirled around.

'What's the matter, David?' she asked again.

'Uh, nothing, I gue . . .'

Then I saw it.

On top of the house, almost a silhouette in the evening light. A weathervane. The wind buffeted it, spinning it around. And then, as the wind died down again, the weathervane gently started squeaking, as if a part of it had come loose. Metal against metal. A noise I'd heard before.

On the farm.

The weathervane was an angel.

'Where did you get that?' I asked her, pointing at it. She looked back at the house. As she did, a second reaction hit me, even more powerful than the first.

My mouth.

'. . . colm bought it from a shop before he got Alz . . .'

I lost what she was saying. Suddenly it was like I'd been smashed across the face with a baseball bat. *At the tip of my ear, I could feel someone's breath, warm and saccharine like the smell of boiled sweets.* The night down in Bristol, before they'd taken me out to the woods to kill me. The man with the saccharine breath.

His tone had altered, but I'd recognized his voice.

It hadn't been Andrew.

It was Malcolm.

I opened the door and headed up the path. Behind me, I could hear Mary saying my name. I turned to her and held up a hand.

'Wait there,' I said.

I left her like that and moved back inside. The heat of the house hit me. I could see Malcolm had changed positions. He had his back to me.

'I knew there was something off about you.'

He almost fell off the sofa. When he saw who it was, surprised at the sound of my voice, he held up a hand, made a noise. A grunt. Fear darted across his eyes.

'Don't hurt me.'

'I saw it that first time I came round.'

'Don't hurt me,' he said again.

'Is this all an act?'

He shifted position on the sofa, moving back to where he'd been before. He looked me up and down. His eyes darted backwards and forwards. Left to right. He was trying to see whether there was anything nearby he could use to protect himself with. There wasn't. He moved further across the sofa.

'Don't hurt me,' he said a third time.

His voice trembled. Frightened.

'Is this all an *act*?'

'Where's Mary?'

'You want Mary?'

He remembered her.

'Where is she?'

I took a step closer. 'You know her now?'

'Mary!' he yelled, looking beyond me.

'Malcolm,' I said again. 'Are you listening to me?'

'Where's Ma—'

'I know about you.'

He was up on his feet now, over on the other side of the sofa. In front of the window that looked out over the garden. He glanced over my shoulder again.

'Mary!'

'You wanted me dead.'

'Mary!' he screamed again.

'You tried to kill me.'

Tears filled his eyes.

'Do you *remember*?'

'David?'

I turned. Mary was in the doorway, her face white.

'David, what the hell are you doing?'

Her eyes darted from me to Malcolm, then back again.

'Wait there, Mary.'

'*David!*'

'Wait *there*.' I turned back to Malcolm. 'How did you do it?'

'Take whatever you want,' he said.

'Are you listening to me?'

'Take it!'

'You know I'm not here for that.'

'There's money in the kitchen!'

I paused. 'You remember where Mary keeps the money now?'

He realized what he had said even before he'd finished the sentence. I could see him wince, like the air had been punched out of him. His shield cracked a little.

'Malcolm?' Mary said, a small voice from behind me.

He glanced at his wife as the crack started fragmenting, the shield disintegrating, piece by piece. After a few seconds, his body relaxed. Straightened. He smiled and held out his hands.

'You got me, David,' he said.

This time his voice was different.

The same one I'd heard in Bristol.

'Malcolm?'

Mary again, even weaker this time. I looked back over my shoulder. Her eyes were fixed on her husband, tears running down her face. When I turned back, Malcolm was staring at me, his face, his physicality, changing in front of my eyes. He seemed to broaden, to fill out, nothing of him sagging any more. He ran a hand through his black hair, the grey flecks passing between his fingers, and then the fading shell of a dying man was gone completely.

'You're him,' I said. 'You're the one Jade talked about. You're the reason they couldn't kill Alex. That's how you were on to me from the beginning.'

He shrugged, glanced at Mary. Back to me.

'The first time you came here, I spoke to Andrew and told him it might come to this. That was why he sent that . . . freak down to visit you in Cornwall. We wanted to see what kind of a man you were. When

Legion told us about the photo you had of Alex, I knew we might have to fight you. We were protecting a secret, and part of the secret was with you. By the time you made it down to Bristol, to the house we had down there, I thought decisive action was needed. I needed to sort things out myself.'

I ran a hand across my face, across the bruises put there by him.

'How did you get to Bristol without Mary knowing?'

'Mary's a nurse, David. She works shifts. The people she gets in here to look after me . . .' A pause. A smile. 'They're fucking monkeys. Useless. That night I came to see you . . . I drugged them.' He brushed himself down, like he was blowing dust away from an old book cover. 'I wanted to see first hand what we were dealing with.'

I looked at him.

'How did you become involved?'

'*Involved?*' he said, smirking. 'I didn't become *involved*, David. I ran the fucking thing.'

'The farm?'

'*Everything.* Where do you think Al's money went?'

'You took the five hundred grand?'

'I took more than that.'

'How much?'

'It doesn't matter now. It's untraceable. The money's been through the system and back out again. Al threatened us, threatened all of us. I took what was mine.'

'It wasn't yours.'

'Don't take the moral high ground, David. You have blood on your hands, remember. More than me.'

'I doubt that.'

'Whatever helps you sleep at night. Buying a farm and a bar and renting a flat with some stolen money – that's not the same as murder, David. It's not the same at all.'

'You murdered Al.'

'*What?*'

Mary's voice from behind me.

'No, I didn't,' he said.

'Malc?'

He glanced at her, then back at me.

'It was *your* idea,' I said to him. 'You wanted to do it. But you didn't have the balls. You pushed Alex into doing what you wanted then turned your back on him when he cried out for help.'

'I never asked him to do anything.'

'You put the seed of an idea in his head, hoped and prayed he would do it, even *told* him to do it when he started having doubts – and then turned your back on him when he did *exactly* what you wanted. Have you any idea what you did to him?'

'Malcolm?'

Mary again, her voice barely audible. I glanced back at her. Tears were streaming down her cheeks, her face white and fixed, almost frozen by the shock. She swayed a little and placed a hand on the wall. I turned back to Malcolm – his eyes hadn't left me.

He shook his head. 'You amuse me, David. You've

no idea what it's like to raise a child. No idea. I loved Alex, *loved* him, but he was reckless. What he did was stupid. Talking about it and doing it are two entirely different things. He offered to talk to Al, not to drive a car through him. When he came to me, he came expecting me to believe in what he had done. But what he had done was wrong. I told him to go somewhere and lay low. It ripped the heart out of me, but it was the best way to protect him.'

'It was the best way to protect yourself.'

'I was protecting our *son*.'

'You sent Alex to the farm. You weren't protecting him.'

'He turns up on Michael's doorstep after five years – it wasn't going to be long before he started leaving a trail. I wanted him away from the places that could hurt him.'

'You tried to erase his memory.'

'You've got it all wrong, David. I protected myself at the beginning. I had to. When the police came calling I was very focused. When Alex's car turned up in Dover they came here and asked some questions about Al, but by then I'd decided to use this disease as cover, which made it difficult for them. Mary answered most of their questions. She could handle that. They were generic questions. I could tell they didn't have a clue where to start. But it wasn't them I was worried about. They were the front line. If it got any further, they would bring out their best soldiers. That was what I was really worried about. But, as it turned out, we never heard from the police again. And by that stage – unfortunately – I had chosen to take this route. And I've had to stick to it.'

'And this is it now – one big lie?'

He didn't reply. But I could see the answer in his face. This wasn't it. *It* was going to be Mary waking up one day and finding he was gone.

'No one wanted him on the farm,' Malcolm said. 'No one. Andrew fought against me, so did Legion, even Michael didn't know if it was a good idea. *Michael*. This was a boy I'd known since he attended the church down the road. A boy who watched his brother get stabbed to death dealing ecstasy. A boy who tried to get away, go travelling, but came back because he had nothing here and nothing out there. His parents were dead. And I *took him in*, told him about what we were doing and what a difference he could make to our cause. I changed his life. Turned it around. And when I asked for *one thing*, he fought me on it.'

'Michael has some humanity, whatever his flaws,' I said. 'He could see what you were doing to Alex. To all of them.'

'Malcolm?' Mary said from behind us again.

He didn't acknowledge her. 'You don't understand.'

'You knew what they would do to him.'

'I knew because they told me,' he said. 'After he left, I thought about Alex every day for five years. I thought he was *dead*. Then when he came back, when he went to see Michael, I knew the next stage of his life might be even harder for us than the last. Because

I had to learn to know my son again through other people. Through Michael and Andrew and the others on the farm. And Alex had to forget in order to get on with the process of living. It was painful, but I helped him. I gave him a way out. But he couldn't know the farm was mine. He couldn't know I knew about him. It would have been too difficult for him.'

'You mean it would have been too difficult for you.'

'I never forced him to meet with Al. I told him Al might listen to him. I told him Al liked him. He *did* like him. But I never believed Alex would do what he did. I've thought about it often since he left, and after he came back. Thinking is what I've got instead of a voice. I've wondered whether I would sacrifice what I have now for a moment again with Alex. If I had the time over again, I'm always thinking what choice I might make.'

'Why would there even *be* a choice?'

'Al would have ruined our lives. If he had got his way, we'd be living on the street somewhere, looking in the gutters for dinner. You think he would have had second thoughts? He wouldn't. So, what Alex did changed our lives. Because our lives carried on. If he hadn't done that, we all would have been dead, dying in some fucking dump somewhere. There's a choice, David, believe me.'

He sat down on the edge of the sofa.

'Eight years ago – it was 29 May – I was working for the bank, and a man came to me and asked me for a loan. When I enquired what it was for, he said he wanted to set up a rehabilitation clinic for kids with problems. A safehouse. A place they could come and start again. I didn't know how the hell he would ever repay the loan. When I asked him how he was going to make money from it, he didn't know. Didn't have a clue. He just wanted to do it because of something that had happened in his life. He had no plan, and a criminal record. So, of course I turned him down. It would have been financial suicide even if he hadn't been a convicted felon, and if I'd given it to him I would have got the sack.'

'Andrew.'

He nodded. 'Then I began to feel very strongly about the idea.'

'Alex's brother.'

For the first time he glanced at Mary. A brief look. Then back at me. 'I watched someone else I loved dearly die on the streets with a needle in his arm, and I wasn't going to stand by and watch other kids do the same.'

'The boy in the photograph.' I thought of the kid kicking a ball around in the picture Jade had showed me the night she'd died. She'd talked about the boy's father. *I think, in some ways, he's even worse.* 'The boy is yours.'

Malcolm nodded.

Mary made little noise. That surprised me, but I didn't turn around to look at her. Malcolm was in full flow now, feeding off the fact he could finally say what he'd stored up.

'He wasn't Mary's son?'

'What do you think?'

'So, whose son was he?'

'A girl I met through the bank,' he said. 'At the end, she was just a junkie, selling herself to fund her habit. But the boy was wonderful. I tried to see him as often as I could. That was why I took the job with Al. The office was in Harrow. Robert lived in Wembley.' He paused. 'But then Al found out about him.'

'About the boy?'

'He saw me taking Robert to school one day.'

'That was why he flipped?'

'When he found out who Robert was, he wanted me to tell Mary. I refused. He said he'd tell her himself. So I threatened him, told him I'd kill him if he said anything. He said, if I didn't tell her, he'd take back everything that was his. I don't think he believed I would kill him. So, it became a stand-off. Mary hated Al – but, in the end, all Al was doing was trying to help her.'

'But Mary never found out.'

'No. It had been going on for two months, Al threatening to tell her. I tried to close off all other avenues, like paying Robert's mother to keep her trap shut. But she ended up using the money to buy smack. One day when I went round there, I found a needle mark in his arm. He was *ten years old*. If I'd known that was going to happen, I would have killed her and brought him back here. I would have done that. In the end, she was just a hooker. No one would have missed her. But, a couple of days later, she called me on the phone and told me he'd been found in the Thames. He'd overdosed. A *ten-year-old boy*.'

I remembered the newspaper cuttings, in the flat and on the farm. BOY, 10, FOUND FLOATING IN THE THAMES. *This is the reason we do it.*

'Al didn't have anything on me then, not once the boy was dead, but all I felt was anger. All I wanted was to hit out at someone. I suggested to Alex we take his money. That was the first step. But that wasn't enough. It didn't quell anything. So I started thinking about killing Al, thought a lot about it. Then Alex really *did* kill him. When it happened, it suddenly seemed so huge. But after Alex had gone, I started to feel it again, eating away at me. I couldn't suppress it. Couldn't suppress the hatred I felt for Al, even after he was dead. And the hatred I felt for her.'

'The boy's mother?'

He nodded.

'I'd taken a lot of my contacts from the bank with me when I went to work for Al. Sneaked them out, just in case I ever started up my own business. One of the numbers was Andrew's. I called him after Al died, told him I wanted to help him with his plan. It was the right thing to do after what happened to Robert. And we grew close, got on well. But all the time, the anger just burned in me. I think if she'd shown any kind of remorse, I would have let her live. But she didn't. She seemed pleased to be free of the responsibility.'

'So you killed her?'

'About a year after we bought the farm, I just exploded.

Couldn't contain the anger any more. So I asked Andrew whether he knew anyone. He said he did, a guy he was in the army with, and that was when he sent Legion out to see her. Some things you regret. I don't regret that.'

'What about the other kids you killed? Do you regret them?'

'We tried to save them.'

'You murdered them.'

'No one died who didn't deserve it.'

'Did Simon deserve it?'

'Simon,' he said, disgust in his face.

'Did he deserve it?'

'Simon became a problem.'

'Because he refused to give up his memories?'

'*No!* Because he almost beat one of our instructors to death! I never wanted the violence. I only wanted Legion's help for that one thing. She killed that boy. She deserved it. But things happened up there, and I started to realize it was the only way we could protect ourselves. What we built and what we worked for *had* to be protected. And, in the end, we protected what I cared about most. We protected Alex. What we did to Simon protected Alex.'

'But you *murdered* Simon.'

'We gave him a chance, but he threw it back in our faces. Some of these kids were so fucking *ungrateful*. When they fought back, what the hell were we supposed to do with them? They couldn't go back. We couldn't put them back on the streets. They would have talked to people and we would have been found out and everything we built would have come tumbling down. They gave us no choice.'

'So you killed them.'

'There were challenges.'

'So you *killed* them.'

'There were unexpected challenges. And when one of our instructors, one of Andrew's friends, was killed right back at the start, we realized that, in order to continue our work, we'd always have to make a sacrifice. In an ideal world, every kid we took to the farm would understand the magnitude of what we were doing for them. But some gave us nothing in return but their bile.'

'What did you expect? You *kidnapped* them.'

'Kidnapped them?' He smirked again. 'Hardly. We invited them, we didn't force them to come to the farm. We've never had a kid turn us down. They took the opportunity they were given because they knew it was a good one.'

'What about Alex?'

He paused for a moment. 'Andrew and the others, they made mistakes. Terrible mistakes. Alex wasn't like the other kids we tried to help. He wasn't wheeled in on a trolley with a needle in his arm. They were treating him differently, how he was *meant* to be treated. Not the same drugs. Not the same programme. But then that freak didn't like it, and eventually neither did Andrew. They put Alex on the programme when he shouldn't have been anywhere near it. They put him on it because they didn't think he deserved special

419

treatment. He was my fucking *son*! He deserved special treatment! And when he didn't respond how they wanted, when he fought back, they put him on that fucking cross! All I'd done for them, all the money I'd put in, and that's how they repaid me.'

He paused, his eyes moving left and right. Thinking.

'Andrew used to call me when Mary was out and I listened to his reports about Alex, about what they were doing to him, and I *knew* it would go wrong. Putting him on the programme just because he spoke to them in the wrong tone of voice? That was a massive misjudgement. But I was powerless to intervene. I knew Alex would fight the drugs, I knew he'd fight the containment. Alex was a fighter.'

He looked at me; thought he saw something in my face.

'I don't give a fuck what you think,' he said.

'You protected your son by sending him to a place where they'd make him forget about you like you pretended to forget about him. That wasn't for his sake. You sent him there to protect *yourself*. All of this has been about you.'

I paused, thought I had him.

But I was wrong.

The smallest of smiles wormed its way across Malcolm's face, and – very gently – I felt a gun barrel press against the back of my neck. I turned my head an inch to the left. In the window, I could see a reflection. Michael. There was strapping around his thigh where I'd shot him. Mary had been pulled in to him, her fingers wrapped around his arm, her mouth covered by his hand. It was the reason she'd gone quiet.

'I told you to walk the other way,' Michael said. 'I tried to help you. All I want is to go back to helping those in need.'

'You fucked with the wrong people, David,' Malcolm said, coming around the sofa. 'The minute I found out Mary was going to you, I knew it would end in bloodshed.'

I glanced around me. Nothing to pick up. No weapons.

'You don't give up secrets worth protecting,' he said. He moved up close to me. Nose to nose. 'Not without a fight, anyway. You've injured us, killed us and called in the police – but good will always triumph over evil.'

I spat the sweet into his face.

He backed away, wiping his chin with the back of his hand.

'I'm going to enjoy this,' he said.

Behind me, Mary tried to scream, as if she could see what was coming next – and I felt the gun move a fraction across the back of my head as Michael tried to contain her.

I ducked below the barrel of the gun, dropped my shoulder and made a dash for the kitchen. Michael fired. A bullet fizzed off right, hitting the top of the wall on the far side of the room. The sound was devastatingly loud, ringing in my ears, even as I made for the basement. Behind me, over my shoulder, I could see Michael pushing Mary away. She made a break for it, scrambling across the carpet on her knees and diving for cover behind a sofa.

Malcolm and Michael headed after me.

I took the basement stairs so quickly I almost fell down. The lights were off. I headed for the place Mary and I had been sitting before, and sank back into the darkness.

It was black.

Above me I could hear movement, but not much. The occasional creak. A short whisper. I tried to force my eyes to adjust quicker to the darkness, but it was like trying to force yourself to hear something that wasn't there. Darkness became shapes. Shapes became movement. I shifted right, my back against the wall, trying to give myself a clearer view of the stairs.

Then the lights came on.

For a moment I was completely disabled, as if I'd been hit in the face with a concrete block. Then, as the white light started to dim, shapes formed again, blurs becoming edges, and I could see them coming down the stairs, Malcolm taking two at a time, Michael limping more slowly behind him.

Malcolm had the gun out in front of him.

I looked around me. About six feet further to my right were the electrics. Next to that, propped against the wall, were the walking sticks I'd seen earlier. They were thin and breakable. Except for one. It was thick, maybe three inches wide, with a hard ball for a handle.

There was a cardboard box close to it, probably four feet deep, with a second box, smaller, on top. I edged to my right, half-crouching, using the cardboard boxes close to me for cover. Briefly, as I passed from one to another, they spotted me. A second shot rang out, hitting the roof close to where I'd been. Plaster fell to the floor like snow.

I got to the electrics box and flipped the front. Rust had eaten into the casing, but the wires looked new. There were a series of switches across the top and a main red lever to the left. I reached down and gripped the walking stick, turning it over so I was holding it at the tip and not by the handle. Then I flipped the red lever.

Everything went black again.

In the darkness, sound became important. I heard shuffling. Frustration. Readjustment. One of them said something quietly, but not quietly enough. It sounded like Malcolm.

I ducked left again, back towards the place I'd been before. In the stillness, I could feel little stabbing pains right inside the cuts on my back, travelling through the torn flesh and up to the surface of the skin. And as my brain registered that, it remembered the pain in the fingers of my left hand too, moving down from the remains of my nails to my knuckles and wrists. A shiver passed through me.

As my eyes adjusted to the gloom, I could see one of them, edging towards me without knowing it. Michael. He was nervous, moving tentatively, way out of his depth. The strapping around his leg looked like an amateur job. They hadn't taken it outside the organization. Someone within it, probably someone with some medical knowledge, had removed the bullet.

I gripped the walking stick as tightly as I could and slid down on to my haunches, using the wall for support. The darkness was as thick as oil. He looked ahead of him, slightly off to my left, where some of the gardening equipment was stacked, then back in the direction he had come. He was still too far away, even with his back turned.

Within seconds, something else caught my eye. On the other side of the electrics box, I could see Malcolm. He was coming around one of the cardboard box pillars, half-covered. The gun was out in front of him. It was difficult to define him, but I could see some of his face and a circle of light in his eyes.

His eyes. *He can see you.*

I used the wall as a springboard and went for Michael, just as he was turning to face me. A third shot hit the space I'd left, ripping through cardboard and into the garden tools. They clattered to the floor behind me.

I swung the stick into Michael's knees, and he collapsed on all fours. As his fingers grabbed hold of a piece of wood nearby, I thumped the fat end of the stick into the base of his spine. He howled in pain, and went down on his stomach, flat to the floor, his hand clutching the area I'd hit. His eyelids fluttered and both of his legs twitched.

He was quiet.

I peered around the box, back to where Malcolm had been. He was gone. Only darkness now. If he was gone, he was coming back towards the middle of the room.

Back behind me.

As I turned he was on to me. A huge hand clamped on to my face, trying to cover my mouth, trying to force me away from him so he could get a clear shot. I could see the gun, could see him trying to jab it towards me, but I managed to knock him off balance, punching the stick into his gut. He stumbled, landing against one of the boxes, the cardboard pillar toppling to the floor.

I shoulder-charged him, lifting him off his feet, and pushed him down to the ground. The gun spun off, out of his grasp, turning circles across the floor.

But then my body locked.

Suddenly, the pain in my back erupted. Something ruptured in the cuts, and I could feel flesh tear and blood run, my vision blurring as if a nailbomb had gone off in my head. I stumbled sideways, reaching out for whatever was nearest.

It was Malcolm.

He was in front of me now, on his feet, pushing boxes aside so I couldn't get at them for support. I stumbled further towards him, and he threw a punch that hit me square in the face. I went down hard, on to my hip, and cried out as the impact sent a tremor through my back.

He came at me a second time, turning me over. This time, something – maybe adrenalin, or instinct – helped me block his punch with an arm. I jabbed my right hand into his throat. He wheezed, a sound like air leaving a valve, and stumbled back towards what little light there was, coming from upstairs.

I looked around me. The gun was within reach. Four or five feet.

But then he came at me again, kicking me in the side of the head. I wheeled around, cracking my cheek on something hard. The walking stick fell out of my grasp. Then he hit me again. Hard. Right in the ear. A ringing sound passed through my skull. The room span for a moment, coming back into focus in time to see him land a third punch. He'd tried to get me in the throat, the same place I'd got him, but instead hit my collarbone.

But the blow to the head had paralysed me.

My body was broken. Everything they'd done to me had finally caught up. They'd shut me down. Relentlessly burnt away my strength until all that was left were ashes.

Malcolm stood unsteadily and looked down at me.

'I was prepared to give you a second chance, David,' he said breathlessly. 'Do you remember that? We told you not to get involved.'

He wiped some blood away from his nose.

'But I can't help you a third time.'

He stepped over me and went for the gun. I tried to get up, but I didn't have the strength. Every wound that had been carved into my body over the last few days started to come back to life, snapping away at me, scratching at me, swallowing whatever fight I had left.

I coughed, blood spilling out over my lips, and opened my hands and lay there. Waiting to be shot.

Waiting for the darkness to take me down like it had taken Legion. The water of my existence covering me until everything went quiet.

Then, in my hand, I felt something.

I turned my head and, to my side, about four feet away, I saw Mary. She was huddled in the corner, partially lit by the light from upstairs. She'd crept down into the basement. Tears were running down her face, her eyes following Malcolm. She was down behind one of the boxes to the left of where he'd been.

She glanced at Malcolm again, back at me, then away.

I heard Malcolm pick up the gun.

When I looked again, back to Mary, I could see what she'd put in my hand. The walking stick. Somewhere in her eyes I could see a small spark of hope. As if, whatever came next, had to be better than this.

Slowly, painfully, I forced myself up.

Malcolm was looking down at the gun, checking it was primed.

I caught him across the back of the head with the stick. The impact sounded soft and hollow. He went down as if every muscle in his body had immediately stopped working. I hit him again when he crashed to the floor, the ball of hard wood at the end of the stick slapping in against his stomach. The third time no sound came from him.

Mary continued crying from the same position.

Distantly I could hear sirens.

I collapsed to the floor and looked at Mary. My

head crashed. My body was powering down. I was on the verge of blacking out.

'Are you okay, David?' she said, wiping tears from her face.

Slowly, I reached into my pocket and removed my phone.

'I need you . . .' I coughed, could taste blood in my mouth. 'I need you to call someone. Her name is Liz.' I coughed a second time. 'Tell her I'm in trouble.'

And then I finally drifted away.

51

The most difficult thing was getting back. When the police turned up at the farm, the kids were taken into a temporary shelter where the authorities probably thought their suffering would end. A group of stolen lives they'd brought back into the cold light of day.

But Malcolm and Michael knew differently.

The majority of the kids had come to rely so heavily on what the farm brought to them, they were no longer prepared for the outside world; a world that had damaged them irreparably the first time round. The Calvary Project had ensured the people they were supposed to be redeeming would never be fully prepared for the return. They had been robbed of their identities. They had been robbed of their memories. They were taken back to their families, but to families who thought they were dead. On both sides it was like starting again; like having a stranger inside your home.

Alex was different because Alex remembered most of his past. He just wanted to keep it buried. There was an irony to that – after all, keeping secrets buried was what life on the farm was about. He could have lived out the rest of his days there and never heard Al's name mentioned again. But Alex could see the sacrifice he'd have to make – relinquishing control to a group who had forgotten the reason they existed in the first place – and he wasn't prepared to turn into the person they wanted him to become. Once he broke away he took with him the one memory he would have given his life to remove. And he knew the moment he came up above the surface, Al would be back. But despite that, despite everything, it was worth it.

I spoke to Mary about two weeks after the police led us away from the house. By the time she called, I was a fortnight into recovery. They'd cut a hole in the cling film, and given me an injection in my back so I wouldn't feel them cut away the rest. By the time they were finished, I had sixty-two stitches in my back, three in my foot, and a doctor telling me I might never recover all the feeling in my two injured fingers.

Mary cried the entire time we were on the phone. She'd lost her son, and now she had lost her husband as well – the man she'd spent years caring for. Every day she'd been by his side because every day she feared it might be his last. I didn't tell her I knew how it felt. Derryn would always be a part of me, her face so clear in the darkness, her voice so clear in my head. For Mary, Malcolm would only be a reflection obscured by ripples. A convicted drug dealer and kidnapper, eventually charged with manslaughter, who she knew nothing about.

I looked at Malcolm as the police led him out, and, in his eyes, saw the trade. I wouldn't mention the girl who'd had his child, Simon and all the others who had died under his watch, and neither he nor Michael would mention my part in the deaths of Jason, Zack, Andrew, Myzwik or Legion. It was a better trade for them. Malcolm had so much blood on his hands, it would never wash out. And while I remained silent, his son remained hidden, and that also worked in his favour – even if his son was lost to him for ever.

Liz sat with me during the interviews, mostly in silence, as it became obvious early on that the police weren't going to charge me with anything. They could see my injuries. They could see what sort of people they were dealing with. More difficult, though, than lying to the detectives, was lying to her. I think, deep down, she knew I wasn't being honest with her, but she never said anything. A part of me liked her even more for that.

The farm and Angel's stayed Malcolm's. The deeds were in his name. No one could touch them. The last time Mary ever visited him in prison, he told her he'd use the money to start again on his own when he got out. She never went to see him after that.

Michael wasn't so lucky. He only got two years after striking a deal with the police, but he had no money to come back to and no reason to come out. He was the man people had trusted. The man they confided in. Now he was nothing to anyone, just a topic of discussion on Sunday mornings. Malcolm had gone down, and taken Michael with him, and while Michael would be getting out of prison first, he'd return to nothing. No job. No house. No life.

*

About two months later, something good happened. As the first spring sunlight broke through the trees, Mary got a phone call at the hospital. She was on the ward at the time. The caller was told he could phone back or he could wait. He decided to wait. When Mary finished her rounds, she took the call. It was Alex. He wanted her to come and meet him in France.

Sometimes the good things were worth fighting for.

I drove back to Carcondrock about a month after Malcolm and Michael had tried to kill me. I buried the box full of photographs, because it seemed like the right thing to do. I called Kathy to tell her Alex was alive, and then Cary, but couldn't tell either of them more than that, for all the reasons I couldn't tell Mary. Every day, Alex nudged a little closer to the light, carrying the weight of what his father had done, and what he himself had done to Al. When he got there, he could tell all his friends himself – and he could finally explain to Kathy face to face why he left, and why she was never a mistake.

When I filled in the hole, after burying the box, there wasn't enough sand. The top of the hole sank in, making it look disturbed. I didn't want to leave it like that, but there was a kind of resonance to it. Because each of those memories – every photograph in that box – had been disturbed a little as well.

Finally, on my way home, I stopped at the cemetery. But this time there were no birds in the trees. No birds flying to freedom. I like to think it was because they had already flown. Everything in that cemetery, all the sorrow it contained, had escaped to the skies.

And Derryn had gone with it.

When I got home that night, the house felt different. I couldn't explain it, wasn't even sure I was meant to. But it felt more welcoming, as if something had changed. I didn't put the TV on, like I always did when I got home. I forgot about it. And by the time I became conscious of the fact that I hadn't, I was in the shower in the bathroom wiping soap from my eyes. Afterwards, I felt a strange compulsion to be close to Derryn's things, and sat on the edge of the bed, running my fingers down the spines of her books.

The next time I really became lucid, clear about what I was doing, it was three o'clock in the morning, and I was staring up at the ceiling. For the first time in a long time, I'd gone back to the bedroom and fallen asleep in our bed. And the sound I was hearing, on the boundaries of sleep, wasn't the sound of the television as it always was.

It was the sound of something else.

My thoughts were of Derryn, looking across at me from her rocking chair the first time I ever considered helping someone. Everything about her was so clear to me. I had a feeling wash over me, the feeling that this was the end of one stage of my life and the beginning of another. And then I heard that same sound again.

I don't know how much time went by, but what started out as an abstract noise quickly consumed me, then pulled me away with it. And as I fell away into the darkness of sleep, the darkness I wasn't scared of, the darkness that took me down below the surface, all I could hear was the sea.

Acknowledgements

There are a great many people who have helped with the writing of this book.

My agent Camilla Bolton has been a constant source of guidance and encouragement, and is always armed to the teeth with incredible ideas and suggestions. Plus, she pretends to laugh at my jokes, and never fails to answer an email (even the really boring ones, of which there are many). Maddie Buston and everyone else at Darley Anderson also deserve a special mention for all their hard work and support, and for getting behind me from day one.

A big thank you to my editor Stefanie Bierwerth, who took a chance on a book by a first-time author and whose eye for a story helped to massively improve the novel when it arrived on her desk. She was also kind enough to give me a say in other areas of publication when she really didn't have to. I also want to say a huge thanks to the fantastic team at Penguin, who have worked so tirelessly on my behalf.

The 'Just Switch It On And Let Him Talk' award goes to Bruce Bennett, whose fascinating tales of police life provided more hours of Dictaphone tape than I could ever hope to use (or want to transcribe). Any errors are entirely of my own making.

For their faith, support and prayers: my mum and dad, whose belief never wavered and who I have so much to thank for; my little sis Lucy; and my extended family, both in the UK and in South Africa. And lastly, the two girls in my life: Erin, who I love more than anything in the world – even football. And my partner-in-crime, Sharlé, who had to put her evenings and weekends on hold for two years, but who has been there since before the book was even an idea, and who is, quite simply, the best.

Find out more about the next David Raker thriller *at www.timweaverbooks.com*

TIM WEAVER

NEVER COMING BACK

A secret that will change lives forever.

It was supposed to be the start of a big night out. But when Emily Kane arrives at her sister Carrie's house, she finds the front door unlocked and no one inside. Dinner's cooking, the TV's on. Carrie, her husband and their two daughters are gone.

When the police draw a blank, Emily turns to investigator David Raker. He's made a career out of finding missing persons. He knows how they think. But it's clear someone doesn't want this family found.

As he gets closer to the truth, Raker begins to unravel a sinister cover-up, spanning decades and costing countless lives. And worse, in trying to find the missing family, he might just have made himself the next target . . .

'I couldn't put it down' *The Sun*

'Weaver's books get better each time – tense, complex, sometimes horrific, written with flair as well as care' *Guardian*

'Weaver has delivered another cracking crime thriller' *Daily Mail*

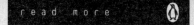

TIM WEAVER

THE DEAD TRACKS

'I've worked murders for fifteen years, and you can just feel when a place is bad. You get a sense for it. And those woods . . . something's seriously wrong with them . . .'

Seventeen-year-old Megan Carver was an unlikely runaway. A straight-A student from a happy home, she studied hard and rarely got into trouble. Six months on, she's never been found.

Missing persons investigator David Raker knows what it's like to grieve. He knows the shadowy world of the lost too. So, when he's hired by Megan's parents to find out what happened, he recognises their pain – but knows that the darkest secrets can be buried deep.

And Megan's secrets could cost him his life.

Because as Raker investigates her disappearance, he realises everything is a lie. People close to her are dead. Others are too terrified to talk. And soon the conspiracy of silence leads Raker towards a forest on the edge of the city. A place with a horrifying history – which was once the hunting ground for a brutal, twisted serial killer.

A place known as the Dead Tracks . . .

'I couldn't put it down' *Sun*

'Weaver has delivered another cracking crime thriller' *Daily Mail*

He just wanted a decent book to read ...

Not too much to ask, is it? It was in 1935 when Allen Lane, Managing Director of Bodley Head Publishers, stood on a platform at Exeter railway station looking for something good to read on his journey back to London. His choice was limited to popular magazines and poor-quality paperbacks – the same choice faced every day by the vast majority of readers, few of whom could afford hardbacks. Lane's disappointment and subsequent anger at the range of books generally available led him to found a company – and change the world.

'We believed in the existence in this country of a vast reading public for intelligent books at a low price, and staked everything on it'
Sir Allen Lane, 1902–1970, founder of Penguin Books

The quality paperback had arrived – and not just in bookshops. Lane was adamant that his Penguins should appear in chain stores and tobacconists, and should cost no more than a packet of cigarettes.

Reading habits (and cigarette prices) have changed since 1935, but Penguin still believes in publishing the best books for everybody to enjoy. We still believe that good design costs no more than bad design, and we still believe that quality books published passionately and responsibly make the world a better place.

So wherever you see the little bird – whether it's on a piece of prize-winning literary fiction or a celebrity autobiography, political tour de force or historical masterpiece, a serial-killer thriller, reference book, world classic or a piece of pure escapism – you can bet that it represents the very best that the genre has to offer.

Whatever you like to read – trust Penguin.